IRISH SECRETS

Skin Deep

and

Irish Rose

Sign of Seven Trilogy
Blood Brothers • The Hollow • The Pagan Stone

Bride Quartet
Vision in White • Bed of Roses • Savor the Moment • Happy Ever After

The Inn Boonsboro Trilogy
The Next Always • The Last Boyfriend • The Perfect Hope

The Cousins O'Dwyer Trilogy
Dark Witch • Shadow Spell • Blood Magick

The Guardians Trilogy
Stars of Fortune • Bay of Sighs • Island of Glass

The Chronicles of The One
Year One • Of Blood and Bone • The Rise of Magicks

The Dragon Heart Legacy
The Awakening • The Becoming • The Choice

The Lost Bride Trilogy
Inheritance

EBOOKS BY NORA ROBERTS

Cordina's Royal Family
Affaire Royale • Command Performance • The Playboy Prince • Cordina's Crown Jewel

The Donovan Legacy
Captivated • Entranced • Charmed • Enchanted

The O'Hurleys
The Last Honest Woman • Dance to the Piper • Skin Deep • Without a Trace

Night Tales
Night Shift • Night Shadow • Nightshade • Night Smoke • Night Shield

The MacGregors
The Winning Hand • The Perfect Neighbor • All the Possibilities • One Man's Art • Tempting Fate • Playing the Odds • The MacGregor Brides • The MacGregor Grooms • Rebellion/In from the Cold • For Now, Forever

The Calhouns
Suzanna's Surrender • Megan's Mate • Courting Catherine • A Man for Amanda • For the Love of Lilah

Irish Legacy
Irish Rose • Irish Rebel • Irish Thoroughbred

Jack's Stories
Best Laid Plans • Loving Jack • Lawless

Summer Love • Boundary Lines • Dual Image • First Impressions • The Law Is a Lady • Local Hero • This Magic Moment • The Name of the Game • Partners • Temptation • The Welcoming • Opposites Attract • Time Was • Times Change • Gabriel's Angel • Holiday Wishes • The Heart's Victory • The Right Path • Rules of the Game • Search for Love • Blithe Images • From This Day • Song of the West • Island of Flowers • Her Mother's Keeper • Untamed • Sullivan's Woman • Less of a Stranger • Reflections • Dance of Dreams • Storm Warning • Once More with Feeling • Endings and Beginnings • A Matter of Choice • Summer Desserts • Lessons Learned • One Summer • The Art of Deception • Second Nature • Treasures Lost, Treasures Found • A Will and A Way • Risky Business

NORA ROBERTS & J. D. ROBB

Remember When

J. D. ROBB

Naked in Death • Glory in Death • Immortal in Death • Rapture in Death • Ceremony in Death • Vengeance in Death • Holiday in Death • Conspiracy in Death • Loyalty in Death

Dead of Night
(with Mary Blayney, Ruth Ryan Langan, and Mary Kay McComas)

Three in Death

Suite 606
(with Mary Blayney, Ruth Ryan Langan, and Mary Kay McComas)

In Death

The Lost
(with Patricia Gaffney, Ruth Ryan Langan, and Mary Blayney)

The Other Side
(with Mary Blayney, Patricia Gaffney, Ruth Ryan Langan,
and Mary Kay McComas)

Time of Death

The Unquiet
(with Mary Blayney, Patricia Gaffney, Ruth Ryan Langan,
and Mary Kay McComas)

Mirror, Mirror
(with Mary Blayney, Elaine Fox, Mary Kay McComas, and
R. C. Ryan)

Down the Rabbit Hole
(with Mary Blayney, Elaine Fox, Mary Kay McComas, and
R. C. Ryan)

ALSO AVAILABLE . . .

The Official Nora Roberts Companion
(edited by Denise Little and Laura Hayden)

IRISH SECRETS

Skin Deep

and

Irish Rose

TWO NOVELS IN ONE

NORA ROBERTS

St. Martin's Paperbacks

Published in the United States by St. Martin's Paperbacks, an imprint of St. Martin's Publishing Group.

IRISH SECRETS: SKIN DEEP copyright © 1988 by Nora Roberts and IRISH ROSE copyright © 1992 by Nora Roberts.

All rights reserved.

For information, address St. Martin's Publishing Group, 120 Broadway, New York, NY 10271.

www.stmartins.com

ISBN: 978-1-250-33387-2

Our books may be purchased in bulk for promotional, educational, or business use. Please contact your local bookseller or the Macmillan Corporate and Premium Sales Department at 1-800-221-7945, ext. 5442, or by email at MacmillanSpecialMarkets@macmillan.com.

Printed in the United States of America

St. Martin's Paperbacks edition / March 2024

10 9 8 7 6 5 4 3 2 1

Skin Deep

To my sisters,
Mary Anne, Carol, Bobbi, Carolyn, Maxine,
Reba, Barbara and Joyce, all of whom I've been
lucky enough to inherit through marriage.

PROLOGUE

I don't know what we're going to do with that girl."

"Now, Molly." With his eye on the mirror, Frank O'Hurley added a touch of pancake makeup to his chin to make certain his face didn't shine onstage. "You worry too much."

"Worry?" As she twisted to pull the zipper up the back of her dress, Molly remained at the dressing room door so that she could watch the corridor backstage. "Frank, we have four children and I love every one of them. But Chantel's middle name is trouble."

"You're too hard on the girl."

"Because you're not hard enough."

Frank chuckled, then turned around to scoop his wife into his arms. More than twenty years of marriage hadn't dulled his feelings for her a whit. She was still his Molly, pretty and bright, even though she was the mother of his twenty-year-old son and his three teenage daughters. "Molly, my love, Chantel's a beautiful young girl."

"And she knows it." Molly peeked over Frank's shoulder at the backstage door, willing it to open. Where was that girl? They had fifteen minutes before they were due onstage, and Chantel had yet to make an appearance.

When she had given birth to her three daughters, each within minutes of the next, she hadn't known that the first one would give her more to worry about than the other two combined.

"It's her looks that are going to get her in trouble," Molly muttered. "When a girl looks like Chantel, boys are bound to come sniffing around."

"She can handle the boys."

"Maybe that worries me, too. She handles them too well." How could she expect a man as simple and kind-hearted as her Frank to understand the complexities of women? Instead, she fell back on an old standard. "She's only sixteen, Frank."

"And how old were you when you and I—?"

"That was different," Molly said, but she was forced to laugh at the grin Frank sent her. "Well, it was." She straightened his tie, then brushed powder from his lapels as she spoke. "She might not have the good fortune to meet a man like you."

Cupping his hands under her elbows, he held her still. "What kind of man is that?"

With her hands on his shoulders, she looked at his face. It was thin and already lined, but the eyes were the eyes of the smooth-talking boy she'd lost her head over. Though he'd never quite come up with that moon on a silver platter that he'd once promised her, they were partners in every sense of the word. For better or worse—through thick and thin. There had been a lot of thin. She'd spent more than half of her life with the man, Molly thought, and he could still charm her.

"A dear one," she told him, and brought her lips to his. At the sound of the back door closing, Molly pulled away.

"Now don't jump on her, Molly," Frank began as he caught his wife's arm. "You know it'll just put her back up, and she's here now."

Grumbling, Molly drew away as Chantel danced down the corridor. She was wearing a vivid red sweater and snug black slacks that showed off her blooming young shape. The brisk fall air had whipped color into her cheeks, highlighting already elegant bones. Her eyes were a deep, deep blue and held a breezy, self-satisfied expression.

"Chantel."

With her natural flair for drama and timing, Chantel paused outside the door of the dressing room she shared with her sisters. "Mom." Her lips turned up at the corners, and the smile spread farther when she saw her father wink at her over Molly's shoulder. She knew she could always count on Pop. "I know I'm a little late, but I'll be ready. I had the most wonderful time." Excitement added spark to beauty. "Michael let me drive his car."

"That fancy little red number—?" Frank began. Then he coughed into his hand as Molly leveled him with a look.

"Chantel, you've only had your license a few weeks." How she hated to lecture, Molly thought as she wound herself up for it. She knew what it was to be sixteen, and because of that, she knew there was no way around what she had to do. "Your father and I don't think you're ready to drive unless one of us is with you. And in any case," she continued before Chantel could get out her first protest, "it isn't smart to get behind the wheel of someone else's car."

"We were on the back roads." Chantel came over and kissed her mother on both cheeks. "Don't worry so much. I have to have some fun or I'll just shrivel up."

Molly recognized the ploy too well, and she stood firm. "Chantel, you're too young to go off in some boy's car."

"Michael's not a boy. He's twenty-one."

"That only makes my point."

"He's a creep," Trace announced calmly as he came into the corridor. He only lifted a brow when Chantel turned on him, eyes flashing. "And if I find out he's touched you, I'll rip his face off."

"It's none of your business," Chantel told him. It was one thing to be lectured by her mother, quite another to hear it from her brother. "I'm sixteen, not six, and I'm sick and tired of being hovered over."

"Too bad." He took her chin in his hand, holding it steady when she tried to jerk away. He had a rougher, masculine version of Chantel's beauty. Looking at them, Frank felt pride swell in him until he thought he was going to burst. They were the fire-eaters of the family, more like their mother than him. He loved them with all his heart.

"All right now, all right." Playing peacemaker, he stepped up. "We'll get into all this business later. Right now, Chantel has to change. Ten minutes, princess," he murmured. "Don't dawdle. Come on, Molly, let's go warm up the crowd."

Molly sent Chantel a quiet look that warned her the business wasn't over, then softened and touched her daughter's cheek. "We've a right to worry about you, you know."

"Maybe." Chantel's chin was still high. "But you don't need to. I can take care of myself."

"I'm afraid you can." With a little sigh, she walked with her husband down toward the small stage where they would earn their living for the rest of the week.

Far from mollified, Chantel put her hand on the knob of the door behind her before she faced her brother. "I decide who touches me, Trace. Remember that."

"Just make sure your friend with the fancy car behaves himself. Unless you'd like both his arms broken."

"Oh, go to hell."

"Probably will," he said easily. Then he tugged her hair. "I'll be clearing a path for you, little sister."

Because she wanted to laugh, Chantel yanked open the door, then shut it in his face.

Maddy glanced over as she buttoned the back of Abby's costume. "So, you decided to show up."

"Don't you start." Moving quickly, Chantel pulled a dress that matched her sisters' off an iron bar that spanned the width of the room.

"Wouldn't dream of it. Sounded interesting out in the hall, though."

"I wish they'd stop fussing over me." Chantel tossed the dress down, then peeled off her sweater. The skin below was pale and smooth, the curves already soft and feminine.

"Look at it this way," Maddy said as she finished Abby's

buttons. "They're so busy fussing at you, they hardly ever pick on Abby and me."

"You owe me." Chantel slipped out of her slacks with brisk movements and stood in bra and panties.

"Mom really was worried," Abby interjected. Since her own makeup and hair were finished, she arranged the tubes and pots that would set Chantel's face for the stage.

Feeling a little pang of guilt, Chantel plopped down in front of the mirror the three of them shared. "She didn't have to be. I was fine. I had fun."

"Did he really let you drive his car?" Interested, Maddy picked up a brush to fix Chantel's hair.

"Yeah. It felt . . . I don't know, it felt important." She glanced around the cramped, windowless room with its concrete floor and dingy walls. "I'm not always going to be in a dump like this, you know."

"Now you sound like Pop." With a smile, Abby handed her a makeup sponge.

"Well, I'm not." With years of experience already behind her, Chantel added the color to her face in quick strokes. "One day I'm going to have a dressing room three times this big. All white, with carpet so thick you'll sink up to your ankles."

"I'd rather have color," Maddy said, dreaming herself for a moment. "Lots and lots of color."

"White," Chantel repeated firmly. Then she stood to put on her dress. "And it's going to have a star on the door. I'm going to ride in a limo and have a sports car that makes Michael's look like a toy." Her eyes darkened as she pulled on the dress, which had been mended too many times to count. "And a house with acres of gardens and a big stone pool."

Because dreams were part of their heritage, Abby elaborated as she did up Chantel's buttons. "When you walk into a restaurant, the maître d' will recognize you and give you the best table and a bottle of champagne on the house."

"You'll be gracious to photographers," Maddy went on, handing Chantel her earrings. "And never refuse an autograph."

"Naturally." Enjoying herself, Chantel clipped the glass stones at her ears, thinking of diamonds. "There'll be two enormous suites in the house for each of my sisters. We'll sit up at night and eat caviar."

"Make it pizza," Maddy instructed, resting an elbow on her shoulder.

"Pizza *and* caviar," Abby put in, then stood on the other side.

With a laugh, Chantel slipped her arms around her sisters' waists. They were a unit now, just as they had been in the womb. "We're going to go places. We're going to be somebody."

"We already are." Abby tilted her head to look at Chantel. "The O'Hurley Triplets."

Chantel looked at the reflection the mirror tossed back. "And nobody's ever going to forget it."

CHAPTER 1

The house was big and cool and white. In the early morning hours, a breeze came through the terrace doors Chantel had left unlatched, bringing in the scents of the garden. Across the lawn, hidden from the main house by trees, was a gazebo, painted white, with wisteria climbing up the trellises. Sometimes, when the wind was right, Chantel could catch the perfume from her bedroom window.

On the east side of the lawn was an elaborate marble fountain. It was quiet now. She rarely had it turned on when she was alone. Near it was the pool, an octagonal stone affair skirted by a wide patio and flanked by another, smaller, white house. There was a tennis court beyond a grove of trees, but it had been weeks since she'd had the time or the inclination to pick up a racket.

Surrounding the estate was a stone fence, twice as tall as a man, that alternately gave her a sense of security or the feeling of being hemmed in. Still, inside the house, with its lofty ceilings and cool white walls, she often forgot about the fence and the security system and the electronic gate; it was the price she paid for the fame she had always wanted.

The servants' quarters were in the west wing, on the first floor. No one stirred there now. It was barely dawn, and she was alone. There were times Chantel preferred it that way.

As she bundled her hair under a hat, she didn't bother to check the results in the three-foot mirror in her dressing room. The long shirt and flat-heeled shoes she wore were chosen for comfort, not for elegance. The face that had broken men's hearts and stirred women's envy was left untouched by cosmetics. Chantel protected it by pulling down the brim of her hat and slipping on enormous sunglasses. As she picked up the bag that held everything she thought she would need for the day, the intercom beside the door buzzed.

She checked her watch. Five forty-five. Then she pushed the button. "Right on time."

"Good morning, Miss O'Hurley."

"Good morning, Robert. I'll be right down." After flipping the switch that released the front gate, Chantel started down the wide double staircase that led to the main floor. The mahogany rail felt like satin under her fingers as she trailed them down. Overhead, a chandelier hung, its prisms quiet in the dim light. The marble floor shone like glass. The house was a suitable showcase for the star she had worked to become. Chantel had yet to take any of it for granted. It was a dream that had rolled from, then into other dreams, and it took time and effort and skill to maintain. But then she'd been working all her life and felt entitled to the benefits she had begun to reap.

As she walked to the front door, the phone began to ring.

Damn it, had they changed the call on her? Because she was up and the servants weren't, Chantel crossed the hall to the library and lifted the receiver. "Hello." Automatically she picked up a pen and prepared to make a note.

"I wish I could see you right now." The familiar whisper had her palms going damp, and the pen slipped out of her hand and fell soundlessly on the fresh blotter. "Why did you change your number? You're not afraid of me, are you? You mustn't be afraid of me, Chantel. I won't hurt you. I just want to touch you. Just touch you. Are you getting dressed? Are you—"

With a cry of despair, Chantel slammed down the receiver.

The sound of her breathing in the big, empty house seemed to echo back to her. It was starting again.

Minutes later, her driver noticed only that she didn't give him the easy, flirtatious smile she usually greeted him with before she climbed into the back of the limo. Once inside, Chantel tipped her head back, closed her eyes and willed herself to calm. She had to face the camera in a few hours and give it her best. That was her job. That was her life. Nothing could be allowed to interfere with that, not even the fear from a whisper over the phone or an anonymous letter.

By the time the limo passed through the studio gates, Chantel had herself under control again. She should be safe here, shouldn't she? Here she could pour herself into the work that still fascinated her. Inside the dozens of big domed buildings, magic happened, and she was part of it. Even the ugliness was just pretend. Murder, mayhem and passion could all be simulated. Fantasyland, her sister Maddy called it, and that was true enough. But, Chantel thought with a smile, you had to work your tail off to make the fantasy real.

She was sitting in makeup at six thirty and having her hair fussed over and styled by seven. They were in the first week of shooting, and everything seemed fresh and new. Chantel read over her lines while the stylist arranged her hair into the flowing silver blond mane her character would wear that day.

"Such incredible bulk," the stylist murmured as she aimed the hand-held dryer. "I know women who would sell their blue chip stocks for hair as thick as this. And the color!" She bent down to eye level to look in the mirror at the results of her work. "Even I have a hard time believing it's natural."

"My grandmother on my father's side." Chantel turned her head a bit to check her left profile. "I'm supposed to be twenty in this scene, Margo. Am I going to pull it off?"

With a laugh, the stringy redhead stood back. "That's the least of your worries. It's a shame they're going to dump rain all over this." She gave Chantel's hair a final fluff.

"You're telling me." Chantel stood when the bib was removed. "Thanks, Margo." Before she'd taken two steps, her assistant was at her elbow. Chantel had hired him because he was young and eager, and had no ambitions to be an actor. "Are you going to crack the whip, Larry?"

Larry Washington flushed and stuttered, as he always did during his first five minutes around Chantel. He was short and well built, fresh out of college, and had a mind that soaked up details. His biggest ambition at the moment was to own a Mercedes. "Oh, you know I'd never do that, Miss O'Hurley."

Chantel patted his shoulder, making his blood pressure soar. "Somebody has to. Larry, I'd appreciate it if you'd scout up the assistant director and tell him I'm in my trailer. I'm going to hide out there until they're ready to rehearse." Her costar came into view carrying a cigarette and what Chantel accurately gauged to be a filthy hangover.

"Would you like me to bring you some coffee, Miss O'Hurley?" As he asked, Larry shifted to distance himself. Everyone with brains had quickly figured out that it was best to avoid Sean Carter when he was dealing with the morning after.

"Yes, thanks." Chantel nodded to a few members of the crew as they tightened up the works on the first set, a train station complete with tracks, passenger cars and a depot. She'd say her desperate goodbyes to her lover there. She could only hope he'd gotten his headache under control by then.

Larry kept pace with her as she crossed the set, walking under lights and around cables. "I wanted to remind you about your interview this afternoon. The reporter from *Star Gaze* is due here at twelve thirty. Dean from publicity said he'd sit in with you if you wanted."

"No, that's all right. I can handle a reporter. See if you can get some fresh fruit, sandwiches, coffee. No, make that iced tea. I'll do the interview in my dressing room."

"All right, Miss O'Hurley." Earnestly he began to note it down in his book. "Is there anything else?"

She paused at the door of her dressing room. "How long have you been working for me now, Larry?"

"Ah, just over three months, Miss O'Hurley."

"I think you should start to call me Chantel." She smiled, then closed the door on his astonished pleasure.

The trailer had been recently redecorated for her taste and comfort. With the script still in her hand, Chantel walked through the sitting room and into the small dressing area beyond. Knowing her time was limited, she didn't waste it. After stripping out of her own clothes, she changed into the jeans and sweater she would wear for the first scene.

She was to be twenty, a struggling art student on the down slide of her first affair. Chantel glanced at the script again. It was good, solid. The part she'd gotten would give her an opportunity to express a range of feeling that would stretch her creative talents. It was a challenge, and all she had to do was take advantage of it. And she would. Chantel promised herself she would.

When she had read *Strangers,* she'd cast herself in the part of Hailey, the young artist betrayed by one man, haunted by another; a woman who ultimately finds success and loses love. Chantel understood Hailey. She understood betrayal. And, she thought as she glanced around the elegant little room again, she understood success and the price that had to be paid for it.

Though she knew her lines cold, she kept the script with her as she went back to the sitting room. With luck she would have time for one quick cup of coffee before they ran through the scene. When she was working on a film, Chantel found it easy to live off coffee, a quick, light lunch and more coffee. The part fed her. There was rarely time for shopping, a dip in the pool or a massage at the club until a film was wrapped. Those were rewards for a job well done.

She started to sit, but a vase of vivid red roses caught her eye. From one of the studio heads, she thought as she walked over to pick up the card. When she opened it, the script slid out of her hand and onto the floor.

I'm watching you always. Always.

At the knock on her door, she jerked back, stumbling against the counter. The scent of the roses at her back spread, heady and sweet. With a hand to her throat, she stared at the door with the first real fear she'd ever experienced.

"Miss O'Hurley . . . Chantel, it's Larry. I have your coffee."

With a breathless sob, she ran across the room and jerked open the door. "Larry—"

"It's black the way you— What's wrong?"

"I—I just—" She cut herself off. Control, she thought desperately. You lose everything if you lose control. "Larry, do you know anything about these flowers?" She gestured back but couldn't look at them.

"The roses. Oh, one of the caterers found them while she was setting up breakfast. Since they had your name on them, I went ahead and put them in here. I know how much you like roses."

"Get rid of them."

"But—"

"Please." She stepped out of the dressing room. People. She wanted lots of people around her. "Just get rid of them, Larry."

"Sure." He stared at her back as she walked toward the set. "Right away."

Four aspirin and three cups of coffee had brought Sean Carter back to life. It was time to work, and nothing could be allowed to interfere with that—not a hangover, not a few frightening words printed on a card. Chantel had worked hard to project an image of glamour and style. She'd worked just as hard not to develop a reputation as a temperamental actress. She was ready when called and always knew her lines. If a scene took ten hours to shoot, then it took ten hours. She reminded herself of all of this as she approached Sean and their director.

"How come you always look as though you stepped out of the pages of a fashion magazine?" Sean grumbled, but Chantel observed that makeup had dealt with the shadows under his eyes. His skin was tanned and shaved smooth. His thick, mahogany-colored hair was styled casually, falling across his brow. He looked young, healthy and handsome, the dream lover for an idealistic girl.

Chantel lifted a hand and let it rest on his cheek. "Because, darling, I did."

"What a woman." Because the aspirin had made him feel human again, Sean grabbed Chantel and leaned her back in a dramatic dip. "Let me ask you this, Rothschild," he said, calling to the director while his lips hovered inches from Chantel's. "How could a man in his right mind leave a woman like this?"

"It hasn't been established that you—or Brad," Mary Rothschild corrected, referring to the role, "is in his right mind."

"And you're such a cad," Chantel reminded Sean.

Pleased to remember it, Sean brought her up again. "I haven't played a real cad in about five years. I don't think I've properly thanked the writer yet."

"You can do it later today," Rothschild told him. "He's over there."

Chantel glanced over to the tall, rangy man who stood, chain-smoking nervously, on the edge of the set. She'd met him a handful of times in meetings and during preproduction. As she recalled, he had said little that hadn't dealt directly with his book or his characters. She sent him a vaguely friendly smile before turning back to the director.

As Rothschild outlined the scene, Chantel pushed everything else out of her mind. All that would be left was the heartbreak and hope her character felt as her lover slipped away. Mechanically, their minds on angles and continuity, she and Sean went over their brief but poignant love scene.

"I think I should touch your face like this." Chantel reached up to rest her palm on his cheek and looked pleadingly into his eyes.

"Then I'll take your wrist." Sean wrapped his fingers around it, then turned her palm to his lips.

"I'll wait for you and so forth." Chantel skipped over the lines as one of the crew dropped a barn door into place with a clatter. She gave a small, broken sigh and pressed her cheek to his. "Then I'll start to bring my arms up."

"Let's try this." Sean took her shoulders, held her for a moment while they stared at each other, then placed two nibbling kisses on either side of her mouth.

"Oh, Brad, please don't go . . . Then I kiss you until your teeth rattle."

Sean grinned. "I'm looking forward to it."

"Let's run through it." Rothschild held up a hand. Women directors were still the exception to the rule. She couldn't afford to give herself, or anyone else, an inch. "I want a lot of steam when you get to the kiss," she told both of them. "Keep the tears coming, Chantel. Remember, deep in your heart you know he's not coming back."

"I really am a cad," Sean said pleasantly.

"Places." Extras scrambled to their marks. A few members of the camera crew broke off making plans for a poker game. "Quiet on the set." Rothschild moved over, too, until she had the best angle for Chantel's entrance. "Action."

Chantel dashed out on the platform, looking around frantically while groups of people milled around her. It all showed on her face, the desperation, the last flames of hope, the dream that wasn't ready to die. There would be a thunderstorm brewing, thanks to special effects. Lightning flashing, thunder rolling. Then she spotted Brad. She called out his name, pushing her way through the crowd until she was with him.

They rehearsed the scene three times before Rothschild was satisfied enough to roll film. Chantel's makeup and hair were freshened. When the clapper came down, she was ready.

Throughout the morning they perfected the first part of the scene, her search, the impatience and rush of the crowd, her meeting with Brad. Take after take she repeated the same moves, the same words, at times with the camera no more than a foot away.

On the sixth take, Rothschild finally gave the signal for the rain. The sprinklers sent down a drizzle that misted over her as she stood facing Brad. Her eyes filled and her voice trembled as she begged him not to leave. Wet and cold, they continued to go over what would be five minutes on the screen until lunch break.

In her dressing room, Chantel stripped out of Hailey's clothes and handed them to the wardrobe mistress so that they could be dried. Her hair would be styled again, then soaked again, before she could call it a day.

The roses were gone, but she thought she could still smell them. When Larry came to the door to tell her that the reporter had arrived, she asked him to give her five minutes, then send him along.

She'd put it off too long, she told herself as she picked up the phone. It wasn't going to stop, and she'd reached the point where she could no longer ignore it.

"The Burns Agency."

"I need to speak to Matt."

"I'm sorry, Mr. Burns is in a meeting. May I—"

"This is Chantel O'Hurley. I have to speak to Matt now."

"Of course, Miss O'Hurley."

Chantel couldn't resist a slight smirk at how quickly the receptionist had changed her tune. Searching a drawer for the pack of cigarettes she kept for emergencies, she waited for Matt to come on the line.

"Chantel, what's up?"

"I need to see you. Tonight."

"Well, sweetheart, I'm kind of tied up. Why don't we make it tomorrow?"

"Tonight." Some of the panic fought its way through. Chantel lighted the cigarette and drew deeply. "It's important. I need help." She let the smoke out in a slow stream. "I really need your help, Matt."

Because he'd never heard fear in her voice before, he didn't question her. "I'll come by, what . . . eight?"

"Yes, yes, that's fine. I appreciate it."

"Can you tell me what it's about?"

"I can't. Not over the phone, not now." She was calm again, just knowing she was about to take a step seemed to help.

"Whatever you say. I'll be there tonight."

"Thanks." She hung up the phone just as the knock came at her door. Chantel carefully stubbed out her cigarette, tossed her still-damp hair back and ushered the reporter in with a gracious smile.

* * *

Why in the hell didn't you tell me about this before?" Matt Burns paced around Chantel's spacious living room with an unfamiliar feeling of helplessness. In twelve years he'd scrambled his way up from mail clerk to assistant to top theatrical agent. He hadn't gotten there by not knowing what to do in any given situation. Now, he had a hornet's nest on his hands, and he wasn't sure which way to toss it. "Damn it, Chantel, how long has this been going on?"

"The first phone call came about six weeks ago." Chantel sat on a low oyster-colored sofa and nursed a glass of mineral water. Like Matt, she didn't like the feeling of helplessness. She disliked having to ask someone else to do something about a problem of hers even more. "Look, Matt, the first couple of calls, the first couple of letters, seemed harmless." Ice clinked in her glass as she set it down, then picked it up again. "With my face plastered all over magazines and all over the screen, obviously I'll attract attention. Not all of it's healthy. I figured if I ignored it, it would stop."

"But it didn't."

"No." She looked down at her glass, remembering the words printed on the card. *I'm watching you always. Always.* "No, it got worse." She shrugged, trying to pretend to herself, and to him, that it wasn't as bad as it sounded. "I had my number changed, and for a while it worked."

"You should have told me."

"You're my agent, not my mother."

"I'm your friend," he reminded her.

"I know." She held out a hand. Real friendships were few and far between in the world she'd chosen. "That's why I called you before I went off the deep end. I'm not a hysterical woman."

He laughed, then released her hand to pour himself another drink. "Anything but."

"When those roses— Well, I knew I had to do something, but I didn't know what."

"The *what* is to call the police."

"Absolutely not." She lifted a finger when he started to object. "Matt, I imagine you can write the scenario as easily as I can. We call the police, then the press gets hold of it. Headline: Chantel O'Hurley Haunted by Twisted Admirer. Whispered Phone Calls. Desperate Love Letters." She pulled a hand through her hair. "We might be able to laugh that off, even use it to a point, but it wouldn't be long before a few more unbalanced personalities decided to write me some fan letters. Or camp out at the front gate. I don't think I can handle more than one at a time."

"What if he's violent?"

"Don't you think I've thought of that?" She plucked one of his French cigarettes from his pocket and waited for him to light it.

"You need protection."

"Maybe I do." She took a quick, hurried drag. "Maybe I'm just about ready to admit that, but I'm in the middle of a film. You bring cops on the set and people wouldn't stop talking."

"Since when has gossip worried you?"

"Never." She managed an easy smile. "Except when it's about something really personal. My, ah . . . extraordinary love affairs and hedonistic life-style are one thing. My life, as it really is, is quite another. No police, Matt, at least not yet. I need another alternative."

He took the cigarette from her and inhaled thoughtfully. Chantel's first job on the screen had been negotiated by him. He'd seen her through everything from shampoo commercials to feature films, and it was rare, very rare, for her to ask for help with something personal. In all the years he had known her, even Matt had seldom gotten beneath the image of the woman they had both manufactured.

"I think I have one. Trust me?"

"Haven't I always?"

"Sit tight. I'm going to make a call."

Chantel settled back and closed her eyes when Matt left the room. Maybe she was overreacting. Maybe she was being foolishly jumpy about a fan who'd taken admiration just a few steps too far.

I'm watching you . . . watching you. . . .

No. Unable to sit, Chantel sprang up to pace around the room. She enjoyed being watched—on the screen. She could accept being photographed whenever she swept in or out of a club, whenever she attended a party or a premiere. But this was . . . frightening, she admitted. As if someone were just outside the windows, looking in. The thought made her glance nervously over her shoulder. Of course there was no one there. She had the electronic gate, the walls, the security. But she couldn't stay locked in her house twenty-four hours a day.

She stopped by the antique mirror above the white marble fireplace. There was the face she was familiar with, the face critics had called devastating, incomparable, even heartlessly beautiful. A lucky accident, she sometimes thought, the combination of pearly skin, Nordic blue eyes and ice-sharp cheekbones. She'd done nothing to earn the face, the classic oval shape of it, the full, lush mouth or the thick mane of angel blond hair. She'd been born with that, but she'd worked for the rest. And worked hard.

She'd been performing since she could walk, traveling endlessly around the country with her family, in clubs and regional theater. She'd paid her dues long before she had come to Hollywood at nineteen, not starry-eyed but determined. In the years that had passed, she had won roles and lost them, had hawked shampoo and sold gallons of perfume in unapologetically sexy, often silly commercials. When her first break had come, she'd been ready, more than ready, to play the soulless man-eater who stayed on screen less than twenty minutes. She'd stolen that movie from a pair of veterans and had gone on to star in one of her own. There'd been no looking back.

That first break had brought her the stardom she had always craved. And had, indirectly, nearly destroyed her life.

Yet, she'd survived, Chantel reminded herself as she faced her own reflection. She hadn't allowed what had happened all those years ago to ruin her. She refused to allow what was happening now to ruin her, either.

"He's coming right over."

She turned away from the mirror as Matt strode into the room again. "What?"

"I said he's coming right over. Let me fix you a real drink."

"No, I have to be on the set at six thirty. Who's coming right over?"

"Quinn Doran. He might just be the answer, and since we go back a ways, I was able to . . . persuade him to think about it."

Chantel stuck her hands in the pockets of her white satin loungers. "Who is Quinn Doran?"

"He's sort of a private investigator."

"Sort of?"

"He runs a security business . . . corporate, small business, whatever. At one time he worked in some sort of covert operation. Might have been for our government, but I couldn't swear to it."

"Sounds fascinating, but I don't think I want a spy, Matt. A three-hundred-pound wrestler might be more appealing."

"And obvious," he reminded her. "You could hire yourself a couple of bruisers for bodyguards, sweetheart, but what you want here is brains—and discretion. That's Quinn." He finished off his drink and contemplated having another. "He doesn't do much of the legwork himself now. He has plenty of operatives or whatever they're called to handle that. Keeps himself available as a troubleshooter. But in this case I want you to have the best."

"And that's Quinn," Chantel mimicked, dropping onto the arm of the sofa. "What's he supposed to do?"

"I don't have any idea. That's why I called him. He's a moody bastard," he said reminiscently. "Not too, well . . . polished, but I'd trust him with my life."

"Or, in this case, mine."

Matt's expression changed immediately. "Chantel, if you're really that worried—"

"No, no." With a wave of her hand, she brushed off his concern. "I have the feeling that this Quinn Doran of yours is likely to listen to what I have to say, roll his eyes and give me a lecture on how to handle the obscene phone caller. I don't like him already."

"You're just nervous." Matt patted her knee as he crossed to the bar. "You're allowed to be nervous, Chantel."

"No, I'm not." She smiled, determined to lighten her own mood. "Nerves don't fit the image. It's an image you helped me mold."

"You didn't need any help with that." With a smile for her, he turned back and studied the flow of white satin that suited her so well. "You were born with the talent. I just helped you expand it."

She tilted her head and gave him a long, luxurious smile. "How'd we do?"

"I'll say this, no one looking at you today would think that you'd once mended your panty hose."

She laughed and slid down on the sofa. "You're so good for me, Matt."

"I've been telling you that for years. There's the bell. I'll get it."

Chantel picked up her warming mineral water and swirled it. If Matt thought Quinn Doran was an answer, she'd have to take his word for it. But it galled her, it galled her right down to the ground, to tell her personal problems to a stranger.

Then the stranger walked in.

If she had had to cast someone in the roll of a spy, a private investigator or an alley fighter, her choice would have been Quinn Doran. He filled the archway to her living room, inches taller than Matt, inches broader in the shoulders, yet with a wiry leanness that made her think he could move fast and move well. The quick flutter of feminine approval she accepted as natural even before she looked at his face. Then she thought it unnatural.

He wasn't leading-man handsome, but he had tough go-to-hell looks that would make any woman's pulse uneven. Dark, thick hair curled over his ears and trailed over the collar of a denim work shirt. His skin was tanned and taut over strong facial bones, and the pale shade of his eyes seemed almost startlingly cool. His lashes were too long, too thick for a man, but they were anything but feminine. There was nothing about him that wasn't totally masculine. When he walked, he walked with the soft, measured stride of a man who knew how to stalk. His mouth turned up slightly as he crossed to her, but Chantel didn't see humor or appreciation in his eyes. She saw, recognized and stiffened against derision.

"So this is the ice palace," he said in a surprisingly beautiful voice. "And the queen."

CHAPTER 2

He'd seen her before, of course. On the screen she looked larger than life, indomitable, untouchable. The face, almost mystically perfect, could rule a man's fantasies. A facade. Quinn understood facades, how they could be formed, altered or hacked away as circumstances demanded. He wondered, as with a casual glance he took in everything about her, how much substance there was beneath that silk-and-satin exterior.

Matt had known Quinn too long to be disturbed by his cavalier attitude. "Chantel, Quinn Doran."

Satin slid over satin as she crossed her legs. With a lazy kind of grace, she offered her hand. "Charming," she murmured, stiffening as his fingers curled firmly over hers. He didn't shake her hand, nor did he bring it to his lips in the casual European gesture she suddenly felt he was capable of. He just held it while his pale green eyes held hers. Her skin was like the satin she wore, smooth, fragrant and coolly feminine. His was hard, unyielding and darkened by the sun. They froze for a moment, her on the sofa, him on his feet, with their hands still locked. Chantel had been in combat with men before, and only once had she lost. She understood that the glove had been tossed down, and she accepted the challenge.

"Is it still vodka rocks?" Matt asked Quinn as he turned to the bar.

"Yeah." With a slight inclination of his head, Quinn indicated that he knew the game was on. He relaxed his fingers slowly to let her hand slide from his. "Matt tells me you have a problem."

"Apparently I do." Chantel plucked a cigarette from a porcelain holder on the table, then lifted a brow. When Quinn drew a lighter out of his pocket and flicked it on, she smiled and leaned a bit closer. "I'm afraid I don't know if you're the man to deal with it"—her gaze lifted and held his before she leaned back again—"Mr. Doran."

"I'm inclined to agree with you . . . Miss O'Hurley." For the second time their gazes locked, and something not entirely pleasant hummed between them. "But since I'm here, why don't you tell me about it?" Quinn accepted the glass from Matt, then shot him a look before he could speak. "Why don't we let Miss O'Hurley fill me in, since it's her problem?"

As an agent, Matt knew when to negotiate and when to back off. "Fine, I'll just fill my mouth with a few of these canapés." He sat, leaving them to each other.

"I've been getting some annoying phone calls." She said it casually, but the tension showed briefly in the way her fingers curled and uncurled. Quinn was used to picking up on small details. At the moment he noticed that her hands were quite small and narrow, with long fingers, the rounded tips painted with clear lacquer. The fingers themselves were never quite still.

"Phone calls?"

"And letters." She moved her shoulders and the satin whispered quietly. "It started about six weeks ago."

"Obscene phone calls?"

Chantel lifted her chin, unable to resist the urge to look down her small, straight nose. "I suppose that would depend on your definition of obscene. Yours might be quite different than mine."

Humor touched his eyes and made them strangely appealing. She wondered fleetingly how many women had stepped into his lion's den and been devoured. "I'm sure it is. Go on."

"At first—at first you could say I was almost amused. It seemed harmless enough, though annoying. Then . . ." She moistened her lips and brought the cigarette to them. "Then he became a bit bolder, more explicit. It made me uneasy."

"You should change your number."

"I've done that. The phone calls stopped for about a week. They started again today."

As he leaned back, Quinn sampled the vodka. Like her, it was a quality brand. "You recognize the voice?"

"No, he whispers."

"You could change your number again." The ice clinked in his glass as he shrugged. "Or have the police put a tap on it."

"I'm tired of changing my number." With quick impatience, she stubbed out the cigarette. "And I don't want the police. I prefer to keep this discreet. Matt seems to think you're the answer to that."

Quinn drank again. The room was done in different shades of white, but it wasn't virginal. The very absence of color, with her at the center, was outrageously alluring. He was sure she knew it. In every one of her films she had acted the role of a woman who deliberately played on a man's needs, his weaknesses, his most private dreams. Quinn could drum up little sympathy for a woman who deliberately projected an image designed to arouse men, then complained about a few harmless phone calls.

"Miss O'Hurley, you're probably aware that men who make these kind of calls don't do anything but talk. I'd suggest you change your number again, then have one of your servants answer the phone for a while, until he gets tired of it."

"Quinn." Matt swirled his own drink. He had a habit of keeping in motion when under pressure, his hands, his feet. Now, he cleared his throat and tried to settle. "That's not much help."

"She can hire a bodyguard if it makes her feel better. Her security here could certainly be tightened."

"Maybe I need barbed wire, vicious guard dogs," Chantel interjected, and rose.

"That's the price you pay," Quinn told her coolly, "for being what you are."

"What I am?" Her eyes, already a vivid, searing blue, sharpened. "Oh, I see. I parade myself on the screen, I don't dress in burlap and wear a veil over my face, therefore, I asked for what I got. And I deserve it."

Her cool beauty was compelling, but her passionate outburst was like seeing fire in ice. Quinn ignored the tightening in his gut and shrugged. "That's close enough."

"Thank you for your time," she said, and turned away. Before she could stop herself, she was whirling back. "Why don't you take a walk into the twentieth century? Just because a woman is attractive and doesn't disguise the fact doesn't mean she deserves to be abused—verbally, physically or emotionally."

"I don't believe I said an attractive woman, or any woman, deserves abuse," Quinn commented.

His careless tone only stoked the fires. "Just because I'm an actress and sexuality is part of my craft doesn't mean I'm fair game for any man who wants a piece of me. If I play the part of a murderer, it doesn't mean I should go on trial."

"You appeal to a man's most primitive fantasies, Miss O'Hurley, and you do it in Technicolor. There's bound to be a little backwash."

"So I should just take my medicine," she murmured. "You're an idiot. You're the kind of man who wears his brain below his belt. The kind who thinks if a woman agrees to have dinner with him she should pay for it with a romp between the sheets. Well, I can pay for my own dinner, Mr. Doran, and I can handle my own problems. I'm sure you can find the door."

"Chantel," Matt began, but she turned on him like a cat. "I'll just have a few more canapés," he muttered.

"Miss O'Hurley."

"What?" Chantel spun around to face her tall, aging majordomo, then drew in a long, cleansing breath. "Yes, Marsh, what is it?"

It was the tone that had Quinn narrowing his eyes. There was an underlying straightforward quality to it that ignored any domestic caste system and spoke human to human. Though nerves had her body strung tight, she smiled at the old man.

"These were just delivered for you."

"Thank you." Chantel crossed the room to him and took the vase of daylilies. "I won't need you any more tonight, Marsh."

"Very good, Miss."

Stepping behind Quinn, she went to a table by the windows. "Why don't you show your friend out, Matt? I don't think—"

She had the card in her hands and was staring at it. Her fingers trembled momentarily before she crushed the paper. Before she could drop it on the floor, Quinn had her wrist and was slowly drawing the mangled note from her. What he read made his stomach tighten, this time in disgust.

"No more than I deserve?" Chantel's voice was cold, almost detached, but her eyes, when Quinn looked into them, were terrified. He slipped the paper into his pocket as he took her arm.

"Why don't you sit down?"

"Was it another one?" Matt started toward them, but Quinn motioned to the bar.

"Get her a brandy."

"I don't want a drink. I don't want to sit down. I want you to go." When she started to pull her arm away, Quinn merely tightened his hold and led her to the sofa. "How often do you get one of these?"

"Nearly every day." She picked up a cigarette, then put it back.

"All of them as . . . direct?"

"No." She took the brandy and sipped at it, hating to admit she needed it. "That started a couple of weeks ago."

"What did you do with the notes?"

"I tossed out the first few. Then, when the tone started to change, I was going to burn them." The brandy warmed her but did nothing to settle her. "I kept them. I'm not sure why. I suppose I thought I should have them if things got out of hand."

"Call your servant back in. I want to ask him some questions. And go get the other letters."

His orders did what the brandy hadn't. Chantel felt her spine straighten. "It's none of your concern, Mr. Doran. We've already settled that."

"This just unsettled it." He drew the paper out of his pocket and watched her slight but definite recoil.

"I don't want your help."

"I didn't say I'd give it yet." He let that hang as they continued to stare at each other. "The letters? Unless you've got a better idea what to do about all this."

At that moment, at that one shimmering moment, she despised him. She could have hidden it. She was skilled enough. She didn't bother. Before she could speak, Matt laid a hand on her shoulder. His fingers moved as restlessly as hers.

"Please, Chantel. Think before you say anything."

She kept her eyes on Quinn's. "I wouldn't want to say what I'm thinking." When his lips curved again, she gritted her teeth. "Or perhaps I would."

"Chantel." Matt gave her shoulder a light squeeze. "I don't like ultimatums, but if we can't deal with Quinn, I'm going to call the police. No," he continued when her head shot back, "I mean it. You're a smart woman. Be practical."

She hated being backed into a corner. Quinn could see it. She was a woman who insisted on having the choice and the control in her own hands. It was something he could admire, even respect. Maybe, just maybe, there was more to Chantel O'Hurley than met the eye.

"All right, we'll do it your way. For now." She rose, at once regal and strong. "Don't badger Marsh." She met Quinn's eyes levelly. "He's old and getting frail. I don't want him upset."

"I haven't kicked a dog all day," Quinn told her.

"Only small children and kittens," she murmured, then swept from the room.

"Quite a woman, your client."

"She's all of that," Matt agreed. "And she's scared right down to her toes. She doesn't scare easily."

"I bet she doesn't." Quinn took out a cigarette and tapped it idly against the pack. He was forced to admit that he had thought she was simply dramatizing. The few sentences printed on the card had changed his mind. They were just short of vile. For Quinn, the line of demarcation between right and wrong was flexible, but the card fell well on the wrong side. Still, before he decided just how much he wanted to be involved, there were a few things he had to know.

He glanced back at Matt, watching him pace. "Just how close are the two of you?"

"We have a solid, mutually advantageous arrangement." Matt gave Quinn a sober smile. "And she doesn't sleep with me."

"You're slipping."

"She knows what she wants and what she doesn't want. She wanted an agent. But I do care about her." He cast a worried look at the doorway. "She's already gone through enough."

"Enough of what?"

With a shake of his head, Matt sat again. "Another story, and nothing to do with this. Are you going to be able to help her?"

Quinn drew slowly on his cigarette. "I don't know."

"Excuse me." Marsh stood in the doorway, still dressed in his black suit and starched collar. "Miss O'Hurley said you wanted to speak with me."

"I wondered if you could tell me about the person who delivered the flowers." Quinn gestured toward them and watched the old man squint. Nearsighted, he thought.

"They were delivered by a young man, eighteen, perhaps twenty. He rang from the gate and explained that he had a delivery for Miss O'Hurley."

"Was he wearing a uniform?"

Marsh's brows knit as he concentrated. "I don't believe so. I can't say for certain."

"Did you happen to see his car?"

"No, sir. I took the flowers at the back door."

"Would you recognize him if you saw him again?"

"Perhaps. I think I might."

"Thank you, Marsh."

Marsh hesitated. Then, remembering his position, he bowed stiffly. "Very good, sir."

As he walked back into the hallway, Quinn heard Chantel stop him for a brief, murmured conversation. Her voice, he noticed, was soothing from a distance, quiet and easy. Up close, its smoky quality could twine around a man's nerve endings and make him want. She came back in, carrying a small pack of letters.

"I'm sure you'll find it fascinating reading," she said as she tossed them into Quinn's lap. "My guess is it's close to the technique you use to court women."

She'd regained her spirit, Quinn decided as he ignored her and opened the first envelope. The address on it, like the text inside, was printed in small block letters. The paper was dime-store quality. He could work for weeks and never trace it.

The first few notes he read were fawning in their admiration and subtly suggestive. And well written, Quinn added silently. The work of an educated person. As he went on, the prose and syntax remained good but the content deteriorated. Even a man who had seen and done what he had felt instant distaste. The writer went into graphic and pitiless detail, outlining his fantasies, his needs and his intentions. The last few letters added veiled hints that the writer was close by. Watching. Waiting.

When he'd finished, Quinn stacked the letters in a neat pile. "You sure you don't want the cops in on this?"

Chantel had seated herself across from him, and now she folded her hands in her lap. She didn't like him, she told herself. She didn't like the way he looked, the way he moved. She didn't like the fact that his voice was almost poetic, so very different from his lived-in face. So why, if all this was true, did she feel as though she wanted, even needed, his help? She kept her eyes on his. Sometimes you made bargains with the devil.

"No, I don't want the police. I don't want publicity on this. What I want is for this man to be found and stopped."

Quinn rose and poured himself another drink. Both the glasses and ice bucket were Rosenthal. He appreciated elegant things, just as he appreciated the cruder things in life. Beer from a bottle or wine from a crystal glass, it hardly mattered, as long as your thirst was quenched. He appreciated beauty, but he wasn't duped by it. An outer shell meant nothing. He'd shed plenty of his own when the occasion had called for it.

Chantel O'Hurley had beauty, had elegance. If he took the job, by the very nature of it he was bound to discover how much was shell, how much was substance. That was what had him hesitating. He understood just how dangerous knowledge of another person could be—to all involved.

He could control the attraction he felt for her looks, as long as he chose to. His mood on that could change from day to day. What he wouldn't control, had never been able to control, was his curiosity as to what lay beneath the skin.

Swallowing his vodka, he turned back around. She was sitting back in her chair, and one would have thought from looking at her that she was relaxed, even aloof. The fingers on her left hand moved, just a little, curling together, spreading apart, as if she had managed to center her nerves only there. He shrugged and matched his mood to hers.

"Five hundred a day, plus expenses."

She lifted a brow. It was the only movement she made. With it, she conveyed a range of feeling—amusement, consideration and dislike. What it didn't show was the surge of relief that passed through her.

"That's a princely sum, Mr. Doran."

"You'll get your money's worth."

"That's something I insist on." Leaning back, she steepled her fingers under her chin. Her wrists were slender, and her hands were as delicate as her face. A diamond flashed on her right hand, then became as white and cool as the rest of her. "Just what do I get for five hundred a day plus expenses?"

His lips curved just before he brought the glass to them. "You get me, Miss O'Hurley."

She smiled a little. Sparring helped. She was back in control again, and the fear was ebbing. "Interesting." The look she sent him was designed to pin a man to the wall and make him beg. Quinn felt the punch and acknowledged the power. "What do I do with you?"

"You've got it backward." He walked to her then, stopping by her chair to lean close. She caught a hint of scent, not cologne, not soap or powder, but raw and completely comfortable masculinity. Though she didn't retreat from it, she braced herself, recognizing her own attraction.

"Just what do I have backward, Mr. Doran?"

She looked like a painting, one he thought he'd seen in the Louvre a lifetime ago. "It's what I do with you. Five hundred a day, angel, and your trust. That's my price. You pay it, and you get twenty-four-hour protection, starting with one of my men posted as a guard at that gate of yours."

"If I already have the gate, why do I need a guard?"

"Did it ever occur to you that a gate doesn't do a hell of a lot of good if you're going to open it up to anyone who asks?"

"What didn't occur to me was that I'd have to lock myself in."

"Get used to it, because whoever's sending you flowers doesn't have a clean bill of health."

Panic came and went in her eyes. He gave her points for how quickly she mastered it. "I'm aware of that."

"I need your schedule. Starting tomorrow, one of my men goes with you every time you stick your pretty nose out the door."

"No." The O'Hurley stubbornness came through as she rose

to face him. "For five hundred a day I want you, Doran. You're the one Matt trusts, and you're the one I'm paying for."

They stood close, very close. He could smell the scent that seemed to seep through her pores, neither quiet nor subtle. The perfection of her face could take a man's breath away. Her hair swept back from it in a glorious cascade, like an angel's. If a man touched it, would he find heaven or be cast from the clouds? When it came to that, Quinn wouldn't worry about the consequences.

"You might regret it," he murmured, then smiled slowly.

So she might. Chantel already knew that, but pride wouldn't let her back down. "I pay for you, Mr. Doran. That's the deal."

"You're the boss." He lifted his drink to her. "Two of my men will come by in the morning to wire the phone."

"I don't want—"

"I don't take the job if you tie my hands." His easy smile was gone as quickly as it had formed. "We tap the phone, maybe he says something to give himself away, maybe we get lucky and trace it. Just think of us as doctors." He smiled at her again, enjoying himself. "If you want to say something intimate to one of your . . . friends, don't worry. We've heard it all and more."

Temper had always been the most difficult of her emotions to master. It surged up and was fought back down before she spoke again. "I'm quite sure you have. What else?"

"I'll take the letters with me. It's doubtful we'll be able to trace the paper, but we'll give it a shot. Now, is there anyone you know who you think could be doing this?"

"No." The answer came immediately and with complete confidence. He decided to run a check on everyone close to her.

"Dump anyone in the last few months that may be carrying a torch for you?"

"Thousands."

"Cute." He drew a pad and the stub of a pencil out of his pocket. "I need the names of who you've slept with. We'll go back three months."

"Go to hell," she said sweetly, then started to sit. He caught her by the wrist.

"Look, I'm not going to play games with you. I'm not personally interested in how many men you've had in your bed. This is business."

"That's right." She tossed her head back. "My business."

Her skin was warmer than it looked. That was something he filed away to think about later. "One of them might just have gone off the deep end. Maybe you slept with him a couple times, and it gave him delusions of grandeur. Think about it. This all started six weeks ago, so who were you with before that?"

"No one."

Annoyance covered his face as he tightened his hold. "Give me a break, angel. I haven't got all night."

"I said no one." She yanked her arm away. For a moment she wished she could rattle off a dozen names, two dozen names, just to see him sweat. "Believe whatever you like."

"I tell you what I don't believe, and that's that you spend your evenings alone, darning socks."

"I don't jump into bed with every man who passes within five feet of me." In a calculated move, she dropped her gaze down as if measuring the distance between them.

"It looks like about ten inches to me," he murmured.

"Sorry to disappoint you, but I have to be interested first, and I haven't been. Besides, I've been working, and it tends to take up a great deal of my time." Unconsciously she rubbed at her wrist, where his fingers had pressed. "Satisfied?"

"Come on, Quinn, ease off." Feeling trapped in the middle, Matt moved over and put an arm around Chantel's shoulders. "She's had it rough enough."

"It's not my job to hold her hand." Quinn scooped up the letters, annoyed by the twinge of self-disgust he felt. "I'll be back tomorrow. What time do you get up?"

"Five fifteen." She couldn't resist a smirk when he only

stared at her. "I leave for the studio at five forty-five. That's a.m., Mr. Doran. Can you handle it?"

"You just write the check. Fifteen hundred in advance."

"You'll have it. Good night, Mr. Doran. It's been unusual."

"Do yourself a favor and don't answer your phone any more tonight." With that, he nodded to Matt and strode out. Chantel waited for the sound of the door closing behind him. She went to the coffee table and drew out another cigarette.

"Your friend's a bastard, Matt."

"Always has been," he agreed. "But he's the best."

CHAPTER 3

Chantel had thought she wouldn't sleep. The house had seemed so enormous around her, and so enormously quiet. But she had climbed into bed with a vision of Quinn Doran hovering in her mind. Just the thought of him made her furious, insulted her intelligence, nipped at her ego. And made her feel safe.

She slept only six hours, but she slept deeply.

Music woke her, pouring from the wall unit beside the bed. She rolled over, surrounded by pillows, covered with ivory linen sheets and nothing else.

The bed had been one of the first luxuries she had indulged herself with, almost before she could afford it. It was huge and old, with a carved cherry wood headboard that had made her think of princesses waking up from a hundred years of sleep. Growing up, she had invariably slept in hotel beds, and she'd decided that a sinfully beautiful bed was something she deserved to indulge herself with when she signed her first film contract. A small part in a full-length feature had been enough to pin her hopes on. Years later, when she awoke in the antique four-poster, it still gave her the same satisfaction.

She thought back to the time when she had still lived in the small apartment in L.A. The bed had taken up the entire room, and she had had to crawl over it to reach the doorway. Her two sisters had visited once, and the three of them had stretched across it and talked and giggled for hours.

She wished they could be with her now. The feeling of safety would be more tangible.

She'd nearly told Maddy about the letters and calls when she'd gone to New York a few weeks before. Part of her had wanted to, needed to, but Maddy had been so preoccupied. She'd been entitled, Chantel reminded herself as she sat up and stretched. Her play had been nearly ready to open, and her heart had been wrapped up in the man who was backing it. All for a good cause, Chantel thought with a smile. The play was a smash, and Maddy was planning her wedding.

He'd better be good to her, Chantel thought as the old protective instinct rose up in her. She had had to watch one sister go through a miserable marriage. She couldn't bear it if Maddy was hurt as well.

Maddy would be fine, she reassured herself. Just as Abby was fine. They had both found the right man at the right time. So she had one sister planning a wedding and the other preparing for the birth of her third child. She couldn't spoil all that by dumping her problems on them now. Besides, she was the eldest triplet, if only by a matter of minutes. To Chantel, that meant that she had the responsibility to be the strongest. They would be there for her, of course, just as she would be there for them. But she was the oldest.

They'd come so far. Chantel sat in the middle of the lush bed and looked around a room that was larger than the whole of her first apartment in California. Why was it she felt as though she still had so far to go?

Now wasn't the time for philosophizing. After turning up the volume on the radio, she climbed out of bed and prepared to face another day on the set.

*   *   *

Quinn wasn't accustomed to rising before dawn. It was much more his style to see the night through and find his bed at sunrise rather than climbing out of it at that hour. Not that he didn't appreciate an L.A. sunrise. It was simply more to his taste to watch the sky take on color after a night of celebration—in bed or out.

He drove across town under a pink and mauve sky, casting an occasional look of mild contempt at a jogger. Designer sweat suits weren't his style. If he wanted to tone up, he went to the gym. And not one of those pastel-walled spas where they piped in classical music, a real gym. You didn't see cute leotards there, and the sweat ran as free and healthy as the four-letter words. A man's world—and no one drank carrot juice frappés. A woman like Chantel O'Hurley wouldn't poke her million-dollar nose through the front door.

Quinn shifted in his seat and scowled at nothing in particular. He couldn't remember the last time a woman had made him uncomfortable. Chantel's looks were designed to make a man squirm—and ache. The hell of it was she knew it and, Quinn was certain, enjoyed it.

He couldn't let that be a problem. She was paying him to do a job. The only thing he could be concerned about from this point on was her security. The check she would give him entitled her to the best, and he *was* the best. Besides, he didn't care for the content of the letters she'd shown him.

Not that Quinn was a supporter of the women's movement. To his way of thinking, men and women were different. End of story. If a woman walking by a construction site was insulted because she got a few whistles or invitations, he figured she should walk someplace else. After all, that was just good clean fun. There'd been nothing clean, or fun, in the letters, though. And Chantel hadn't looked insulted, either. If he knew anything, Quinn knew what genuine fear looked like.

Sooner or later he would find out who had written the letters. That would take patience. In the meantime, he'd give Chantel the round-the-clock protection she was paying for. Remembering her face, Quinn acknowledged that would take willpower. He had it, he thought with a shrug as he pulled up

to the iron gates. Besides, chances were that she'd look like a
hag at this hour of the morning.

He reached out the window and leaned on the buzzer.

"Yes?"

The frown moved into his eyes. Even in one word, Chantel's voice was easily recognizable. He hadn't expected her to
answer the intercom herself. "Doran," he said curtly.

"You're prompt."

"You get what you pay for."

There was no answer, but the gates slowly swung open.
Quinn cruised through them, then stopped to make certain they
shut behind him.

In the daylight, he got a better look at the lay of the land.
Anyone determined enough could find his way over the wall.
He and a partner had once scaled a sheer cliff in Afghanistan
with nothing more than rope and nerve.

The trees that flowered over the lawn sent up a sweet scent.
And would provide more-than-adequate cover for an intruder.
He was going to have to get a good look at the alarm system in
the house, though he knew anything that could be put in could
be deactivated.

Quinn pulled up just beyond the steps, then got out to lean
on the hood of his car. You couldn't hear any traffic from
here. Just the sound of birds. He took out a cigarette. A glance
around showed him a few floodlights, maybe a dozen ground
lights, obviously placed more for aesthetic purposes than for
added security. After a look at his watch, Quinn decided to
walk around the house and check a few things out for himself.

Perhaps out of spite, Chantel decided to let Quinn cool his
heels outside while she dallied in her dressing room. Under
other circumstances she might have invited him in for a quick
cup of coffee before the limo arrived. She wasn't feeling gracious. Instead, she took her time, bundling her hair back from
her face, checking the contents of her bag, then writing a few
instructions for her maid. When the buzzer from the gate rang
again, she spoke to her driver, then gathered up her script.

She turned toward the bedroom and walked into Quinn. He watched initial shock turn to anger.

"What the hell are you doing in here?"

"Just checked out your security system." He leaned against the doorway and noted, with a quick twinge, that regardless of the hour she looked fantastic. "It's pitiful. A Boy Scout with two merit badges could get past it."

Chantel settled the strap of her bag on her shoulder and promised herself she would pay Matt back if it was the last thing she ever did. "When it was installed, I was assured it was the best on the market."

"Supermarket, maybe. I'll have my men beef it up."

She'd been born practical, and the years had done nothing to change that. "How much?"

"Don't know for sure until they're into it. Three to five, I'd say."

"Thousand?"

"Sure. Like I said, you—"

"Get what you pay for," she murmured, walking around him. "All right, Mr. Doran, you go right ahead." As she spoke, she moved to her nightstand. "But the next time you decide to check out the system, I wouldn't advise you sneaking into my bedroom." When she turned, she had a pearl-handled .22 in her hand. "I tend to be nervous."

Quinn regarded the gun with a raised brow. He'd been on the wrong end of one plenty of times before. "Know how to use one of those, angel?"

"You just pull this little trigger here." She smiled. "Of course, my aim's terrible. I'd point at your leg and end up shooting you right through the brain."

"There's only one rule about guns," he began, then scowled over her shoulder. When Chantel turned to look, he was on her. With a move too quick to judge, he had the gun in his hand and her beneath him on the bed. "The rule is, don't point one unless you intend to use it."

She didn't squirm beneath him, but lay still, letting the heat of fury and dislike pour out. With a casual gesture he flipped open the pistol's chamber.

"It's not loaded."

"Of course it's not. I wouldn't keep a loaded gun in the house."

"A gun's not a souvenir." He closed it again before he looked down at her. Her face was untouched by makeup, and it was as beautiful as it was furious. Despite himself, Quinn found the combination very much to his liking. Her body was small and strong beneath his, not as cushioned and feminine as he'd expected. But her scent was there, as it had been the night before, outrageously feminine.

"Nice bed," he murmured, unable to resist the urge to sweep his gaze down to her mouth. He thought, but couldn't be sure, that her heartbeat increased.

"Your approval means everything to me, Mr. Doran. Now, if you don't mind, I have to get to work."

How many other men had pinned her between their bodies and this wide, firm mattress? How many other men had felt this wild, edgy flare of desire? Both thoughts ran through his head before he could stop them. Because they did, he rolled aside and yanked her to her feet. But she was still close.

"Maybe we'll keep this business," he told her quietly. "And maybe we won't."

Though her pulse was racing, Chantel wasn't dishonest enough to blame it on temper. Desire was something she understood, even if she had rarely felt it for a man. It was also something that could be controlled. Instinct warned her that it was vital to do that now, and to continue to do so when it applied to Quinn.

"You tempt me to put bullets in that gun, Mr. Doran."

"It wouldn't hurt." Quinn dropped it back in her bedside drawer. "And make it Quinn, angel. After all, we've been to bed together." Taking her arm, he escorted her downstairs and outside.

"Good morning, Robert." Chantel smiled at her driver as he

opened the back door of the limo. "Mr. Doran will be accompanying me to the studio for a few days."

"Very good, Miss O'Hurley."

Quinn didn't miss the wistful look the driver sent him before they were closed in behind smoked glass. "How does it feel to infatuate the male of the species?"

Chantel settled back. "He's just a boy."

"Does that make a difference?"

Behind her dark glasses, Chantel shut her eyes. "Oh, I forgot. I'm one of those heartless women who tease and flaunt, then toss men aside after I've drained them, like empty pop bottles."

Amused, Quinn stretched out his long legs. "That pretty much covers it."

"You have a remarkable disdain for women, Mr. Doran."

"No, you're wrong. Women happen to be one of my favorite pastimes."

"Past—" Chantel caught herself before she sputtered. She drew her glasses completely off, wishing she could see if he was baiting her or speaking the simple truth. Wanting to believe the worst of him, she went with the latter. "You're a classic chauvinist, Mr. Doran. I'd thought your species nearly extinct."

"We're a hardy breed, angel." He pushed a button and watched the compact bar rotate toward him. Quinn considered mixing a Bloody Mary but settled for straight orange juice.

Replacing her glasses, Chantel decided against beating her head against a brick wall. "I prefer not to introduce you as my bodyguard. I can do without that sort of speculation."

"Fine. How do you want to handle it?"

"They'll just assume you're my lover." Coolly she took the glass of juice from him and sipped. "I'm accustomed to that sort of speculation."

"I bet. It's your game. Play it any way you want."

She handed him back the glass. "I intend to. And what will you do?"

"My job." As they passed through the studio gates, he drained the glass. "You just smile pretty at the cameras, angel, and don't worry about it."

She found that her jaw was tensed so tightly it hurt. Acting on impulse, Chantel turned to him and curled her fingers into his shirt. "Oh, Quinn, it's just that I'm so frightened. I'm so very frightened. Not knowing from one minute to the next if I'm safe." Her voice broke as she leaned closer. "I can't tell you what it means to me just to know you'll be there. Protecting me. I'm defenseless, vulnerable. And you're so . . . strong."

She was close, so close he could see her eyes flutter shut behind the tinted glasses. Her body trembled lightly as she leaned into him. Desire flared, along with a need to comfort and protect. She was soft, pliant and helpless. As he drew her nearer, her scent tangled around his senses until his head throbbed with it. "You don't have to worry," he murmured. "I'm going to take care of you."

"Quinn." Her head tilted up until her lips were only a whisper away from his. When she felt him tense, she jerked back and pressed something into his hand. "Your check," she said carelessly, then stepped out of the limo.

Quinn sat for a full ten seconds and wondered why he'd never entertained thoughts of strangling a woman before. When he stepped out beside her, he curled his fingers around her arm. "You're good. Very, very good."

"Yes, I am." She gave him a slow, easy smile. "And I get much better."

As Chantel went through her morning routine of makeup and hairstyling, Quinn simply observed. There were a dozen people Chantel came in contact with during the first hour alone. There were other actors, technicians and a parade of assistants. He'd want a list, and he was beginning to realize just how extensive it would be. Whoever was hounding her obviously knew her routine. That made the people she worked with his priority.

"Miss—ah, Chantel." Larry stopped by her side with a cup of fresh coffee.

"Oh, thanks. You read my mind."

He preened a bit, pleased. "I knew the hair was going to take longer this morning." He watched as the stylist patiently threaded pearls through the already complicated arrangement. "You're going to be just beautiful for the ballroom scene."

"A far cry from yesterday." She sipped the coffee. "If they'd watered me one more time, I'd have melted."

"Miss Rothschild said the dailies were great. I checked."

"Thanks." She caught sight of Quinn's reflection in the mirror and decided that moment was as good a time as any. "Larry, this is Quinn Doran, a friend of mine." Only years of training kept her from choking on the word as she held a hand over her shoulder for Quinn's. "Larry's my right hand. And often my left as well. Quinn's going to watch the filming for a few days."

"Oh, well . . ." Larry cleared his throat. "That's nice."

Quinn saw that the young man thought it was anything but. Another conquest, he thought. But he couldn't afford to feel sympathy, only suspicion.

"I'll keep out of the way," Quinn promised, making the most of it by rubbing his thumb over Chantel's knuckles. "I just want to see Chantel at work."

"Isn't that sweet?" Chantel said with a brilliant smile. "Quinn's between jobs at the moment and has time on his hands. Now don't be sensitive, darling." She gave his hand a pat before drawing hers away. "We all understand how difficult the job market is, especially for botanists." Satisfied, Chantel rose. "I have to get into costume."

"They've scheduled publicity shots this morning," Larry told her after an uncertain glance at Quinn. "As soon as you're ready, you're supposed to go to the ballroom set."

"Fine."

"I'll go with you, darling." Quinn slipped an arm around

her shoulders and squeezed, just a few degrees too hard. "You might need some help with buttons and snaps"

"Ease up, Doran," she muttered as they walked away. "I'm wearing a strapless dress for this scene, and I can't afford the bruises."

"You tempt me to put them where they won't show. A botanist?"

"I've always been attracted to the sensitive, introspective type."

"Like Larry?"

"He's my assistant. Leave him alone."

"Don't tell me how to do my job."

"He's a nice boy; he came with excellent references and—"

"How long ago?"

Annoyed, Chantel yanked open the door of her trailer. "About three months."

When the door shut at his back, Quinn drew out a notebook. "Let's have his full name."

"Larry Washington. But I don't see—"

"You don't have to. What about the makeup guy?"

"George? Don't be absurd, he's old enough to be my grandfather."

Quinn merely shifted his gaze until it met hers. "The name, angel. There's no age limit on a disturbed mind."

She muttered it, then swept back into the private dressing alcove. "I don't like the way you work, Doran."

"I'll notify the complaint department." Lowering to the arm of a chair, he took a quick, interested look around her dressing room. Like her home, it was meticulously decorated in white on white. "While we're at it, give me the names of the rest of the men you deal with on the set."

There was a brief, pregnant pause. "All of them?"

"That's right."

"That's impossible," she told him. "I couldn't possibly remember everyone. Oh, most by sight and by first name, but not everything about everyone."

"Then find out."

"I have a job to do. I can't—"

"So do I. Get me the names."

Chantel yanked up the zipper at her back and scowled at the wall that separated them. "I'll see if Larry can get me a list."

"No, you won't. I don't want to rouse anyone's suspicions."

"All right, all right." For a moment she was convinced the cure was more trouble than the problem. Then she remembered the contents of the last note. Like it or not, she needed Quinn. "The assistant director's name is Amos Leery. The cinematographer's Chuck Powers. And damn it, they didn't walk into town yesterday. They've been in the business for years. They have families."

"What difference does that make? An obsession's an obsession." When she walked back into the room, Quinn was still sitting, scribbling in his notebook.

"What about the director?"

"The director's a woman." Chantel slipped off her watch and laid it aside. "I think we can rule her out."

"What about the—" He made the mistake of looking up as he spoke. The words stopped because his thought processes simply disintegrated. She was wearing red, a hot, vibrant red that seemed to lick at her skin. The dress scooped low and snug at her breasts, then followed the lines of her body. The skirt hung straight, hitched up on one side nearly to the hip, where it was secured by a circlet of glittering stones. His mouth went suddenly and completely dry.

Chantel saw the look, recognized it. Normally it would have made her smile, either with pleasure or in automatic response. Now she found she couldn't, because her heart was thudding too hard. He rose slowly and she stepped back. It wouldn't occur to her until much later that it was the first time in her life she had retreated from a man.

"I'll have to give you the rest later," she said quickly. "They'll be waiting for me on set."

"What are you supposed to be in that?" He didn't take another step toward her. Self-preservation held him back.

Chantel moistened her lips. "A woman out for revenge."

He looked at her again, gradually, up, then down, then up again until their eyes met. "I'd say you get it."

Making a conscious effort, she drew in a breath, then let it out again. Play the role, she told herself. It was always possible to play the role. "Like it?" Deliberately she turned in a slow circle, revealing the daring plunge at the back.

"It's a bit much for seven thirty in the morning."

"Think so?" She smiled, more comfortable now. "Wait until you see the hardware that goes with it. Cartier's lending us a necklace and earrings. Two hundred and fifty thousand dollars worth of all that glitters. We'll have two armed guards and a very nervous jeweler here shortly."

"Why not use paste? It shines, too."

"Because the real thing makes for better publicity. Coming?"

He stopped her at the door with just a fingertip on her bare shoulder. Each of them felt the jolt. "One question. You wear anything under that?"

She managed another smile only because her hand was already on the knob. "This is Hollywood, Mr. Doran. We leave little details like that up to your imagination." She stepped out, hoping the constriction in her chest would ease before the first take.

* * *

By noon, Quinn had been forced to revise his opinion of Chantel at least in one area. She wasn't the pampered, temperamental prima donna he had expected. She worked like a horse—a Thoroughbred, perhaps, but she went through her paces time and time again without complaint.

She'd been gracious to the photographers even when the session had run on for ninety minutes. She hadn't snapped at the makeup artist, as one of her costars had, when it had been time for yet another retouch. The temperature on the set was sizzling, thanks to the lights, but she didn't wilt. Between takes she sipped from an ever-present glass of mineral water, unable to sit, because wardrobe had fussed about creases in her costume.

Two armed guards kept their eyes trained on her, and on the quarter million in jewels she wore. They suited her, Quinn was forced to admit—the thick gold band encrusted with diamonds and rubies that circled her neck, the symphony of diamonds and hot red stones that dripped from her ears. She wore them with the ease of a woman who knew she deserved them.

Quinn stayed well off the set and wondered how the actors could take the sheer monotony of repetition.

"Incredible, isn't it?"

Quinn turned his head and glanced at the tall, graying man beside him. "What's that?"

"How it takes them hours and hours to film a two-minute scene." He pulled out a thin black cigarette and lighted it from the butt of another. "I don't know why I come. It makes me nervous, but I can't stay away while they dissect my brainchild."

Quinn lifted a brow. "No, I suppose not."

He drew in smoke deeply before he smiled. "I'm not mad—or perhaps I am. I wrote the screenplay. Rather, I wrote what it appears this will loosely resemble." He offered a well-kept, rather thin hand. "James Brewster."

"Quinn Doran."

"Yes, I know. You're Miss O'Hurley's friend." He smiled again with a negligent shrug. "Word travels fast in small towns. She's quite brilliant, isn't she?"

"I don't know much about it."

"Oh, I assure you, she is. There was really no one else who could be Hailey. Cold, vindictive, clawing, and at the same time vulnerable and desperate for love. One of the few things

I don't worry about as far as this little extravaganza goes is Chantel's interpretation of Hailey."

"She seems to know what she's doing."

"More, she feels what she's doing." Brewster took another quick puff as the crew set up for the next take. "It gives me enormous pleasure just to watch her."

Quinn slipped his hands into his pockets and mentally added Brewster to his growing list of men to check out. "She's an extraordinarily beautiful woman."

"That goes without saying. But then, to use a cliché, that's only skin deep. It's what's inside Chantel O'Hurley that fascinates."

Quinn's eyes narrowed fractionally. "And what's that?"

"I would say, Mr. Doran, that every man would have to discover that for himself."

The director called for quiet, and Brewster lapsed into a nervous silence. Quinn contemplated his own considerations.

She did seem to feel the part. The key scene called for her to confront her lover three years after he had left her, alone and abandoned. Even after a half dozen takes, her eyes would frost over on cue, her voice would take on just the necessary hint of venom. On a dance floor crowded with people, she set out to seduce and humiliate. Chantel did both with such apparent ease that Quinn felt she must enjoy it.

Even to him, a man who'd learned how to look beyond illusions, it seemed that she was only aware of the man in whose arms she danced. There might not have been any cameras, any technicians, any dollies or lifts.

It went on for hours, but Quinn was patient. It interested him to see that whenever a break lasted longer than five minutes her assistant appeared at her elbow with a fresh glass of mineral water. More than once the assistant director came over to take her hand and murmur to her. The makeup artist retouched her face time and again, as though it were a rare canvas.

It was after seven before they wrapped. They had taken an

hour for lunch, and apart from that, Quinn calculated, she had been on her feet for fourteen hours. All in all, he decided, he'd rather spend eight hours digging ditches.

"Ever think of another line of work?" Quinn asked her as they closed themselves in her trailer again.

"Oh, no." Chantel eased out of her shoes and felt her arches cramp instantly. "I love the glamour."

"Where was it?"

The smile came automatically. "You catch on fast. If she'd called for one more take, just one more, I was going to ask you to shoot her in the knee. Get the zipper for me, will you? My arms are like rubber."

"That's because you had them wrapped around Carter for most of the day."

"Just one of the perks of the job." She arched her back as Quinn brought the zipper down below her hips.

"He's okay, if you like the smooth poster-boy type"

She looked over her shoulder with a half smile. "I adore them."

"Ever think it might be Carter who's sending you flowers?"

She stiffened a bit, then walked into the dressing area. "He's too busy trying to untangle himself from his third wife. Besides, I've known him for years."

"People change or do the unexpected. And you spend several hours a day in a clinch with him."

"That's work."

"Nice work if you can get it. In any case, you shouldn't trust anyone."

"Except you."

"That's right. Brewster seemed pretty taken with you, too."

"Brewster? The writer?" Really amused, Chantel walked back in, still buttoning her blouse. "James is much more interested in his characters than the people who play them. And he's been happily married for twenty-odd years. Don't you ever read the gossip columns?"

"Never miss them." He stopped in the act of reaching for a cigarette when she sat abruptly and grabbed her foot. "Problem?"

"It's always after you take those damn things off that you're in agony." She winced, swore and kneaded. "I can tell you, it was a man who invented the high heel—the same one who invented the bra."

"It's you women who wear the things," he pointed out, but knelt down and took her foot in his hand. "Got you in the arch?"

"Yes, but—" Her protest died on her lips as he began to press. With a long, sincere sigh, she leaned back. "Yes, that's wonderful. You've missed your calling. You could make a fortune as a masseur."

"You should see what I could do for the rest of you."

She opened one eye. "We'll just stick with the feet, thanks. If I were a few inches taller, or Sean a few inches shorter, I could have gotten away with flats for most of the shots."

"I'll tell you this, his love scenes with you seemed pretty sincere."

"They're supposed to." Bone-tired, she opened both eyes. "Look, we're professionals. It looked that way because we played it that way, not because either one of us has any physical interest in the other."

"It looked like interest from my angle. Especially when he put his hand on your—"

"Try another tune, Doran."

"I think you're about to tell me how to do my job again."

"I'd like you to do your job," she shot back, "instead of harping on a man just because he's good at his work."

"Just checking him out, angel."

"I don't want my friends and associates spied on."

"If you want someone who's afraid to step on toes, you hired the wrong man."

"I've come to that conclusion several times myself." She couldn't have said why her temper was building so quickly, but his hands moving slowly up and down the arch of her foot were doing things they shouldn't to her system. She wanted him out and gone. "Why don't you take a walk, Doran?" She jerked her foot away. "You're just not my style." Rising, she stepped around him. "You can keep the change."

"Fine." He was as angry as she, and just as baffled as to the cause. He only knew that for one quick moment he'd felt something for her, something soft and easy. It was gone now, erased as if it had never been. In its place was the anger, and a need, just as strong, that demanded physical release. "I might as well take a bonus while I'm at it."

He grabbed her. She'd known he wouldn't be gentle. His hand tangled in her hair as his mouth came down on hers. She'd known he would show little finesse. What she hadn't known, or hadn't admitted, was that she could respond so completely.

No man held her when she didn't choose to be held. No man took from her what she didn't willingly offer. Yet he *was* holding her, and she found nothing within herself to make him stop. His face was rough against her, and his fingers dug into her skin as he held her close. Defending herself should have been simple, even automatic, yet she didn't struggle in his arms. Her knees trembled, but she didn't even feel it. Everything was bound up in the sensation of his mouth on hers and the explosion of the taste of him. Delectable. Her lips parted and invited him in.

He rarely worried about consequences and even less frequently questioned his instincts. When he had felt the need to touch her, to take her this way, he had done so. He was already paying for it. She was more than he had imagined she could be. Softer, smoother, warmer. It wasn't an image he held in his arms but a passionate, hot-blooded woman. Even as he discovered and explored the flavor and texture of her lips, he understood that he needed more. That was the trap, and he'd fallen right into it.

He drew her away because he wanted to see her face after she had tasted him. Her eyes opened slowly, so dark, so very blue that for an instant he was more vulnerable to her than either of them could have guessed. He felt the need shift to an ache, and the ache to uncertainty, before he pulled himself back.

"It's been an interesting day, angel." And one he was afraid he wouldn't easily forget. "Why don't you tell Matt to find you somebody else?"

It had been a long time since she had felt rejection. It hurt more than she remembered. Training and pride had her straightening and kept her voice icy cool. "If you've finished your show of male dominance, you can go." The image was back, even before her pulse had started to level. "If I hear of someone who needs a bodyguard for their poodle, I'll give them your card."

Chantel turned away when the phone rang. She picked up the receiver, then looked over her shoulder until she saw Quinn open the door. With a toss of her head, she brought it back to her ear. "Yes, hello."

The voice was too familiar now, and a degree more frightening. "I've waited all day to talk to you. You're so beautiful, so exciting. All day I've been imagining how we would—"

"Why don't you stop?" Control snapped as she shouted into the phone. "Why don't you just leave me alone?" Before she could slam the receiver down, Quinn snatched it out of her hand.

"Don't be angry." The edgy desperation in the voice had him tensing. "I love you. I can make you happy, happier than you've ever been."

"Miss O'Hurley's happier without you," Quinn said calmly. "You really should stop bothering her."

There was a long silence, and Quinn heard the breathing on the other end of the phone grow heavier. "She doesn't need you. She needs me. She needs me," the voice repeated before the connection was broken. Quietly Quinn replaced the receiver. Chantel's back was to him, but after a moment she turned around.

He could see that she'd worked hard, even in those few moments, to regain her composure. But her skin was as white as the room around them. "I thought you'd gone."

"So did I." He made it a policy never to apologize for his actions. It was not that he didn't believe he could be wrong, just that apologies tended to weaken his position. In this case, he decided to come as close as possible without crossing the line. "Look, we don't have to like each other much to get this job done, and I don't like to leave things before they're finished. Why don't we just forget about what happened before?"

She didn't care for compromises any more than Quinn did for apologies. But she cared less for the thought of going on alone. To satisfy both her needs and her pride, she gave him a bland smile. "Did something happen before?"

He acknowledged the gibe with a slight nod. "Not a thing. Let's get out of here."

CHAPTER 4

Chantel had long ago acknowledged that one couldn't have both privacy and fame. In order to achieve and maintain the second, the first almost invariably had to be sacrificed. If she went out for a quiet dinner with a friend, she would read about it the next day. If she danced with another celebrity, there would be pictures and speculation before the music stopped. According to the press, her life was full of men, full of wild, sizzling romance and blistering affairs. She accepted that. She was also shrewd enough to know that if she were rude or belligerent to the paparazzi, both her reputation and her photographs would be unflattering. So she was willing, within reason, to court them and present a glamorous and unflappable image to the public.

But the tap on her phone and the guard at her gate were entirely different. They weren't part of the creamy silk-and-diamonds mystique she'd chosen to develop. If she had the choice . . . Every time that thought ran through her head, Chantel gritted her teeth and reminded herself that she didn't.

She should be grateful. It was difficult to acknowledge that fact, but she knew she should be. Since the phone call in her dressing room there had been nothing—no letters, no flowers, no whispering voice. She told herself she should be relieved. Instead, she felt as though she were waiting for the other shoe to drop.

During the week her work kept her too busy to think. She could, for a few hours a day, plunge herself into Hailey's character and her problems. As long as the film was rolling and the pressure was on, it was difficult to think of her own personal crises. Work had gotten her through other rough periods. She counted on its doing the same for her now.

But it was Saturday and the film was going smoothly, so she had no call. Normally she treasured mornings when she could lounge in bed for a few extra hours, indulging in the things that were reported to be part of her everyday life.

By seven she was awake. Disgusted, she ordered herself back to sleep. At seven fifteen she was staring at the ceiling and thinking a great deal too much for her own peace of mind. Beautiful, glamorous women were supposed to sleep until noon, then pamper themselves with massages and facials. She'd have believed that herself if she hadn't been in the game so long.

Tossing the covers aside, she went into the office that adjoined her dressing room. Of all the rooms in her home, this one, and only this one, showed the other side of her. The furnishings, though sophisticated, were simple and functional; the material for the curtains might have been imported from Paris, but the space as a whole was imbued with a sense of organization and practicality. Her desk had been purchased for its usefulness as well as its appearance. And she did use it. She also used the computer that rested on it.

It was true that she had an agent and personal manager, a team of publicists and an assistant, but Chantel believed in keeping a handle on her own life, her own business. She knew what stocks she owned and the gross she received from the pictures she'd made. Copies of her contracts were meticulously filed. Chantel didn't simply sign them, she read them.

She went directly to her desk and, ignoring her thick appointment book and the pile of phone messages left by her maid, picked up a fat stack of papers. There were three scripts she hadn't so much as glanced at. The filming on *Strangers* wouldn't last forever. The sooner she started thinking about her next project, the less idle time she'd have.

Chantel got back into bed, propped the first script on her knees and told herself she would wait until eight o'clock for coffee. It only took half that time for her to discover that the first script was hopeless. The story itself had a few things going for it, but most of them were scenes with her naked, wrapped in one passionate embrace after another. She wasn't a prude, but neither was she willing to use her body as a selling point for a mediocre script. In any case, she was tired of playing the vamp or the victim. She tossed the script aside and picked up another. It caught her from the first page.

A comedy. At last someone had sent her an intelligent story that didn't rely exclusively on her sexuality to sell it. Not only was the dialogue sharp, the plot had twist after twist and made her chuckle out loud. The jokes were as much physical as verbal and would, she knew, exhaust her. Her character would make a fool of herself on-screen time after time. She'd end up with her face in the mud. And Chantel would love it.

Bless you, Matt. Halfway through the script, Chantel hugged it to her breast. He knew she wanted to do something at odds with the image they had both carefully created over the last six years. It would be a risk. Would people pay to see her face with mud on it? Chantel was willing to bet they would.

Happier than she'd been in weeks, Chantel pushed the intercom button and ordered breakfast brought up. She wasn't budging until she finished the last page. And when she did, she was going to call Matt. If she had to go to a casting call for this one, she would. If she had to read for the part, she'd read for it. She'd take a cut in salary if need be, but this was going to be hers.

Chantel snuggled back against the pillows, brought up her knees and turned the next page.

When the knock came at her door, she was totally absorbed.

She answered absently, then began to chuckle as the character, *her* character, punched her way out of another crisis.

"Must be pretty funny stuff," Quinn commented.

Chantel's head whipped around. The amusement in her eyes turned instantly to annoyance. It was too bad, she thought, that he had to look so damn good. "A pity I didn't load that gun."

"You wouldn't shoot a man who's bringing you breakfast in bed." He moved across the room, set the tray on her lap, then made himself comfortable on the bed beside her. He wore a T-shirt and faded jeans, and didn't seem to mind that his sneakers were on her hand-sewn spread. "What are you reading?" he asked, then stretched out his legs and crossed his arms behind his head.

"The stock market reports."

"Yeah, I always get a kick out of them, too." The pillows carried her scent, sexy, exotic and alluring. She was a bit rumpled from sleep, her hair tumbling around her shoulders and down her back. Even in the strong morning light he couldn't find a single flaw on her face. There were two skinny straps over her shoulders and a very little bit of lace low at her breasts. He remembered what he shouldn't have—what it felt like to hold her against him and kiss her until his mind went dim. He plucked a piece of toast off the tray and reached for the jelly.

"Help yourself," she muttered, fighting the urge to inch away.

"Thanks." He leaned over the tray as he spread on a healthy portion of jelly. When his breath whispered warm over her bare shoulder, she stiffened and reminded herself how much she disliked him. "Like I said before, this is a great bed."

"When I get the bill for laundering the spread, I'll deduct it from your fee." Determined not to show any reaction, Chantel reached for the pot of coffee and poured a cup. "What can I do for you, Doran?"

He nibbled on the toast and just looked at her. The smile bloomed slowly, very slowly.

"Don't embarrass yourself," she told him, and sipped the coffee while it was too hot. When it scalded her tongue, she decided she didn't simply dislike him. She detested him.

"Ask a silly question," he began, then proceeded to pour himself a cup of coffee.

"Look, I'm busy, so if—"

"Yeah, I can see that."

"I happen to be reading some scripts."

"Any good?"

Chantel drew a deep breath. Some men were more thick-headed than others, she reminded herself. Perhaps if she humored him a little . . . "As a matter of fact, yes. I want to finish this one this morning, so if we've business to discuss—"

"You going to chew up another man in this one?"

Patience, Chantel told herself. It was compassionate to show patience to an idiot. "No. As it happens, this is a comedy."

"A comedy?" He let out one quick laugh before he drank. "You?"

Her eyes narrowed. "Don't push your luck, Doran."

"Come on, angel. Yours isn't the kind of face that a man pushes a pie into."

"It's mud."

"What?"

"In this case, my face gets pushed in mud."

He chose a piece of melon from her bowl. "That I'd have to see."

"I'm counting on several million people having your attitude." With a natural flair, she whipped the napkin from its ring and passed it to him. "You are, after all, the common man, aren't you?"

"As common as they come," he said easily.

"Now, why don't you tell me why you're here this morning with your feet on my bed and your hands in my breakfast."

"Just part of the service. Great coffee."

"I'll give your compliments to the chef. Now, why don't you get to the point?"

"Aren't you going to eat?"

"Doran."

"Okay." He took a small folder out of the side basket of the tray and opened it. "I have a couple of preliminary reports. Thought you'd be interested."

"Reports on what?"

"Larry Washington, Amos Leery, James Brewster. Also have a bit on the makeup guy and your driver."

"My driver? You're investigating Robert?" Her appetite gone, Chantel pushed herself farther up in bed. Quinn saw dark rose silk beneath the lace and wondered how far down it went. "That's the most ridiculous thing I've ever heard."

"Angel, don't you ever read mysteries? The one you least suspect is always the one who done it."

"I'm not paying you to play Sam Spade, and I'm damned if I can see paying you to run investigations on people like Robert and George."

After brief consideration, Quinn decided on a strawberry. "Have you ever noticed how your Robert looks at you?"

The lace rose up, then settled again with her breathing. Deliberately Chantel tilted her head. "Darling, *all* men look at me like that."

He gave her a long stare before he sipped his coffee again. Even he had problems separating her act from reality. "Since I have to start somewhere, I'm starting with the men closest to you."

"The next thing you'll tell me is you're investigating Matt." When he said nothing, she looked at him again. "You must be joking. Matt's—"

"A man," Quinn finished for her. "You just said that was all it takes."

Furious, Chantel picked up the tray, then dumped it in his lap. Coffee sloshed over the rims of the cups. "Look, let's just stop this right now. I'm not going to have people I care about spied on and embarrassed. Matt's the closest friend I have, and I was under the impression he was your friend, too."

"This is business."

"Let's say our business is concluded. The calls have stopped and so have the letters."

"For a whole forty-eight hours."

"That's enough for me. I'll pay your fee through today, and we'll—" She broke off, the words sticking in her throat as the phone beside the bed began to ring. Without realizing it, Chantel found her hand in Quinn's, her fingers locked tight.

"They'll pick it up downstairs," he murmured. "Don't panic. If it's him, just keep calm. Try to get him to talk, to stay on the line as long as possible. We need time to run a trace." When the intercom buzzed, she jumped. "Pull yourself together, Chantel. You can handle it."

Working at keeping her breathing steady, Chantel spoke into the intercom. "Yes?"

"There's a man on the line, Miss O'Hurley. He won't give his name, but he says it's important. Shall I tell him you're unavailable?"

"Yes, I—" Quinn's hand curled around her wrist. "No, no, I'll take it. Thank you."

"Take it slow," Quinn told her. "Just let him talk."

Her fingers were stiff and cold as she picked up the receiver. "Hello." Quinn only had to look at her face to know she was hearing the familiar whisper.

"Don't lose it," he said quietly, keeping her free hand in his. "Just keep him on the line. Stay calm and answer him."

"Thank you," she managed, despite the block in her throat. "Yes, yes, I've gotten all your letters. No, I'm not angry." She closed her eyes and tried to pretend that the things he was saying didn't make her skin crawl. "I wish you'd tell me who you are. If you'd—" Caught between frustration and relief, she brought the receiver away from her ear. "He hung up."

"Damn." After setting the tray on the floor beside the bed, Quinn leaned over her and punched a few buttons on the phone. "It's Quinn." He swore again. "Yeah, just keep on it. Right. Not enough time," he told Chantel as he hung up the phone again. "Did he say anything that rang a bell, anything that makes you think of someone you know?"

"No." She trembled once before she regained control. "No one I know has a mind like that."

"Drink some coffee." He poured more into her cup, then handed it to her. She drank to ease the tightness in her throat.

"Quinn." She had to swallow again. "He said—he said he had a surprise for me, a big surprise." When she turned her head to look at him, her eyes were huge and dark. "He said it wouldn't be much longer."

"Let me worry about him." He'd always had a soft spot for the defenseless. It had gotten him into trouble before—in South America, in Afghanistan, and in countless other places. Even though he knew it might be dangerous in a more personal way, he slipped an arm around her shoulders and brought her close. "That's what you're paying me for, angel."

"He's going to get to me." She said it with such flat finality that he tightened his hold. "I can feel it."

"He'll have a hard time doing that with me in the way. Listen, I've got two men patrolling the grounds, two others monitoring the phones."

"It doesn't seem to help." She closed her eyes and for a moment let herself lean on him. "Maybe it's because I can't see them."

"You can see me, can't you?"

"Yeah." And she could feel him, could feel the hard, working muscles of his arm and shoulder, the not-so-smooth skin of his face.

"Want to see more of me?"

Cautious, Chantel lifted her face to look into his. There was humor there, but—she was sure she was mistaken—it looked as though there were genuine concern, as well. "I beg your pardon?"

"I like the way you do that. Angel, you could cut a man off at the knees without lifting a finger."

"It's a talent of mine. Explain, Doran."

"Why don't I move in for a while? Now don't let your ego get the best of you," he warned as she started to stiffen. "You've got plenty of rooms in this place, and though I am developing a real fondness for your bed, I can make do with another. What do you say, angel? Want a housemate?"

She frowned at him, hating to admit how much safer she would feel with him around all the time. The house was certainly big enough to keep them out of each other's way, though privacy would go out of the window. The real problem would be remembering just how he'd made her feel during that one sizzling kiss. If he were around twenty-four hours a day, remembering might not be enough.

"Maybe I should buy that vicious dog," Chantel muttered.

"Your choice."

That was true. It was. And she knew exactly how to handle it—and him. "Go ahead and get your duffel bag, Doran. We'll find a corner for you to sleep in." Sitting up, she flipped through the script again. She felt better; she couldn't deny it. The icy fist in her stomach had loosened. "How much extra is this going to cost me?"

"Meals—and I want more than a bowl of fruit in the morning—use of the facilities and, since this is going to play hell with my social life, another two hundred a day."

"Two hundred?" Chantel gave a quick, unladylike snort. "I can't imagine your social life's worth more than fifty. Isn't that the going rate in the massage parlors?"

"What do you know about massage parlors?"

She slanted him a look. "Just what I see in the movies, darling."

"How about a hands-on demonstration?" He lifted a finger

and slid a strap from her shoulder. Instead of replacing it, Chantel simply studied the script.

"No, thanks. I doubt if there's anything you could teach me."

"I was thinking more the other way around." When he nudged the other strap aside, Chantel lifted her gaze to his. He was baiting her, and she wasn't ready to nibble.

"Try me when I've got a few weeks to spare, Doran. With you, I'm afraid we'd have to start from scratch."

"I'm a fast learner." He slid his hand up her shoulder until his thumb brushed her jaw.

She grabbed his wrist before she could stop herself, but her voice remained steady. "Watch your step."

"If you watch your step, you miss too much."

He'd wanted to touch her again, to feel her skin smooth and warm under his hands. He'd wanted to see her eyes darken, partly from anger, partly from temptation, when he did. She looked ready to rake his face, but the bite of her nails wouldn't stop him from sampling the fire she held so well banked inside her. The fire she let flame so explosively on screen.

When her free hand came up, he grabbed it. She held one of his, he held one of hers. As far as Quinn was concerned, they were even. He thought it was pride that kept her from struggling, pride and the confidence that she could bring him to his knees whenever she chose. He wasn't as certain as he wanted to be that she couldn't.

He was just about to let her go when her chin lifted and her eyes dared him. He'd always been a sucker for a dare.

With his eyes open and on hers, he lowered his mouth. But he didn't kiss her. Chantel felt the impact, both surprised and aroused, when he caught her bottom lip between his teeth. The chilly nonresponse she'd been determined to give him began to heat.

She could have stopped him. Her brother, Trace, had taught her and her sisters how to defend themselves from overamorous members of the male sex. Chantel was aware that she could take Quinn by surprise and have him bent over double and gasping for air with one quick jerk of her knee. She lay still, hypnotized by the green eyes that watched her.

She wasn't supposed to have these kinds of feelings, this kind of hunger. She had blocked them out years before, when her emotions had made a fool of her. She wasn't supposed to have this slow, curling sensation in her stomach. Her bones weren't supposed to liquify at a touch. She'd done love scene after love scene—choreographed, blocked out, shot and reshot for the camera—and had felt nothing that hadn't been programmed into her character. She knew just how little the most passionate embrace could mean to the two people involved.

This light, nibbling sensation on her lip should have done nothing but annoy her. But she lay still, trapped by an urgent desire to absorb the rushing range of feeling it brought to her.

Impossible. It had to be impossible, but he felt innocence shimmering around her. If it was an act, she was more skilled than she had a right to be. If it wasn't—but he couldn't think. She did something to his mind that she shouldn't be permitted to do. She pushed her way into it and filled it until he was ready to forget everything but her.

Desire. Desire was something easily quenched and easily forgotten. It would pay to remember that. Any man was bound to want her. But he wasn't sure any man would be able to forget her. There was too much power in her, the power to make a man hunger, to make him ache, to make him weak. Quinn couldn't afford to lose his hold. With her lips warm and soft under his, he reminded himself that he had two priorities. One was to keep her safe. The other was to look out for himself.

When he felt himself sinking, he pulled back. The ground was too unsteady here. For once he would indeed watch his step. "You pack a punch, angel."

Steady, she told herself, struggling to find a foothold. It meant nothing to him, nothing more than the eternal war of wills men and women fought. He hadn't gone soft inside or felt the need to be loved, the need to believe that maybe, just maybe, this was right. She wouldn't give him the satisfaction of knowing she had.

"Next time it'll flatten you."

"You might be right," he muttered, and shifted away. "Your skin's a little pale." He skimmed his gaze over her bare shoulders and cursed himself for the twist of need he felt. "Get dressed and meet me out by the pool. I'll bring you up to date on what we have so far." He rolled from the bed and, taking the file with him, left her alone.

He needed some air, fast.

*   *   *

Quinn cut through the water of the pool like an eel, smooth, fast and quiet. When Chantel came onto the patio, she stood in the sunlight and watched him. She hadn't been wrong about the feel of his muscles. She could see them now, rippling with each stroke of his arm, bunching with each kick of his leg. He'd chosen brief black trunks from the stack she kept in the pool house for guests. They fit low and snug over his hips.

Still, she imagined he'd picked them for comfort rather than impact. As far as she could tell, Quinn Doran considered himself too irresistible to think about such things. She chose a chair by an umbrellaed table and waited for him to surface.

The physical exertion helped. Quinn realized he'd pushed himself closer to the limit with her than he'd intended. He still wasn't sure why he'd made a move toward her when he knew she was the kind of woman a smart man kept his distance from. He'd always been smart. That was the way you survived. But he'd also always had a habit of giving in to temptation. That was the way you lived. Though his life had never been dull, Chantel O'Hurley was his biggest temptation so far.

By the time he'd crossed the length of the pool and back thirty times, most of the tension had drained. Under other circumstances he would have used a punching bag to relieve it, but he was willing to make use of whatever was available.

Tossing wet hair from his face, he stood in the shallow end, water lapping at his thighs. And he saw her.

Tipped back in the chair, her face shaded by a big, white umbrella, she was the epitome of cool, gut-wrenching beauty. She'd pulled her hair up and back so that her face was unframed. It needed no framing. The sleek, severe style only accented that fact. The snug top she wore was cut deep at the shoulders and cinched into the waistband of cropped shorts that showed off long, long legs. His gaze lingered on those legs as he hauled himself out of the pool.

"You've got a hell of a foundation, angel."

"So I'm told." Reaching beside her, she picked up a towel. "I see you're finding your way around all right." She tossed the towel to him, but he did no more than sling it around his neck. The sunlight shimmered on the drops of water on his bronzed skin.

"Nice pool."

"I like it."

"Then you should use it more. Swimming's a great way to keep in shape."

"I'll worry about my shape, Doran." Temper was licking its way to the surface. Chantel coated it with sarcasm. "Is this going to take long? I want to get my nails done this afternoon."

"We'll fit it in."

"We?" She couldn't prevent a smile as he sat across from her. "Somehow I can't picture you in a chi-chi little place like Nail It Down."

"I've been in worse." He shifted the chair slightly, placing himself in full sunlight. "Anything else on your agenda today?"

"Oh, maybe a little window-shopping on Rodeo Drive," she said on the spur of the moment, just to make things tougher. "Lunch at Ma Maison, I think, or perhaps the Bistro." She rested her chin on the back of her hand. "It's been *days* since

I've seen anyone. You do have something appropriate to wear, don't you?"

"I'll get by. Then there's that charity dinner tonight."

Her smile faded. "How did you know about that?"

"It's my job to know." Though he didn't need them Quinn flipped through his notes. "My secretary contacted Sean Carter and explained you had another escort."

"Then she can contact him again. Sean and I arranged to go together to help promote the film."

"Are you willing to get into a dark limo with a man who might be—"

"It's not Sean." After cutting him off, Chantel reached for the pack of cigarettes Quinn had tossed on the table.

"We'll just play this my way." Quinn picked up his lighter and flicked it on. "I'll take you to your little party, and if you like, you can cuddle with Sean for the cameras. What about tomorrow?"

Chantel gave him a poisonous look. "You tell me."

Quinn patiently flipped open his file. "You've got a reporter and photographer from *Lifestyles* coming at one to do a story on you and the house. That's all I've got."

She dropped the cigarette in an ashtray and let it smolder. "Because that's all there is. I have some personal things to attend to here at home, then I go to bed early because Monday's a working day."

"Matt said you were practical." Quinn flipped the page over. "Larry Washington."

"Get on with it," she told him. "You won't be happy until you do."

"The kid looks clean enough on the surface. Graduated UCLA last year with a degree in business management. Seems he always had a thing for the theater, but preferred the setups and backstage stuff to the acting."

"Which is exactly why I hired him."

"Apparently he had a pretty heavy thing going with a coed

until about six months ago. A very attractive blue-eyed blonde. She dumped him."

He didn't have to spell out the implications. "A lot of women have blue eyes, and a lot of college romances break up."

"Amos Leery," he continued, ignoring her. "Did you know his first wife divorced him because he couldn't keep his hands off other women?"

"Yes, I know. And it was fifteen years ago, so—"

"Old habits die hard. George McLintoch."

"That's pitiful, Doran. Even for you."

"He's been a makeup artist for thirty-three years. Has five grandchildren and another due in the fall. Since his wife died a couple of years ago, he's had a few problems with the bottle."

"That's enough." She rose and paced to the edge of the pool. The water was calm and crystal clear. So had her life been only a few weeks before. "That's really enough. I'm not going to sit here and listen to you dissect the personal problems of people I work with." She looked back over her shoulder. "You're in a filthy business."

"That's right." Not by a flicker did he reveal his feelings on the subject. "James Brewster. Seems like a pretty stable family life. Married twenty-one years, one son studying law in the east. Interesting that he's been in analysis for over ten years."

"Everyone in this town's in analysis."

"You're not."

"I will be if I keep you around."

He smiled briefly, then turned the page. "Your driver, Robert, is an interesting character. Young Robert DeFranco has himself a string of ladies."

"Just your kind of man."

"Can't help but admire his stamina. Matt Burns."

She turned all the way around then. This time he saw not anger but revulsion. It ripped at something inside him. "How could you?" She said it quietly and painfully. "He's your friend."

"This is my job."

"It's your job to spy into the personal lives of people you're supposed to care about?"

He kept his eyes on hers. "I can't afford to care about anyone but my clients when they're paying me. That's the service."

"Then keep this part of it to yourself. Whatever you dug up about Matt, I don't want to know."

He wouldn't allow her to make him regret what he'd done. He'd done worse, much worse. He wondered how she'd look at him if she knew. "Chantel, you're going to have to consider all the possibilities."

"No, *you* are. And at this point you're getting seven hundred a day to do it. It's your job to find whoever's hounding me and to keep me safe while you're doing it."

"This is the way I do it."

"Fine. Since it is, all I want to see from you is the bill."

She started to storm back into the house, but he blocked her path. "Grow up." Taking her by the shoulders, he held her still. She was hurting, he realized, really hurting for the people she cared for. He had to convince her that she couldn't afford to. "Anyone at all could be making those calls. Maybe it's someone you've never even met, but my instincts tell me different. He knows you, lady." He gave her a quick shake to accentuate his point. "And he wants you real bad. Until we find him, you're going to do just like I say."

That morning's call was still too fresh in her mind. If a compromise had to be made, she'd make it. But she wouldn't like it. "I'll do what you say, Doran, to a point. I'll have my phone tapped, I'll have the damn guards at the gate and you in my house, but I won't listen to this garbage."

"In other words, you'll make a good showing, but you don't want the details."

"You got it."

He dropped his hands. "I thought you had more guts than that."

She opened her mouth to yell, then shut it again because he was right. She just didn't have the stomach for it. "Dry off, Doran."

She turned on her heel and walked away. As he stood watching her, Quinn decided his instincts were as reliable as ever. When push came to shove, she wouldn't crumble.

CHAPTER 5

When they got through the weekend without chewing any pieces off each other, Chantel decided they might make it. It hadn't pleased her to go to dinner with him and pretend, in front of three hundred other people, that she enjoyed being with him. Chantel had told herself to look at it as a job—a particularly difficult and unappealing job. Then Quinn had thrown her a curve. He'd been charming.

Surprisingly, black tie suited him. Though it didn't quite disguise his rough edges, it made them all the more appealing. He would never be suave or smooth or glossy. For some reason, Chantel found she was pleased to know that. He might wear a silk tie and the trappings of sophistication, but you knew—at least if you were a woman you knew—that a barbarian lay underneath.

Before the evening was over, he had drunk champagne with this year's top box-office draw and had danced with a three-time-Oscar-winning actress. The seventy-year-old veteran had patted Chantel on the knee and told her that her taste in men was improving. Though that had been difficult to swallow, not once during the evening had Quinn given Chantel the opportunity to smirk at him.

On Sunday he left her to herself. When the reporters came and she gave them an interview and a tour of her home, it was as if he weren't even there. She knew he was around, somewhere, but he didn't infringe on her privacy. She was free to get back to her reading, to indulge in a long, soothing whirlpool bath and to catch up on correspondence and a few niggling business matters. By the time they left the house on Monday morning, Chantel was almost ready to revise her opinion of him.

She felt rested and eager for work. The night before, she had finished the script she'd begun on Saturday morning and was more enthusiastic than ever. She'd woken Matt out of a sound sleep to tell him to go after the part. It might have been shy of 6:00 a.m., but Chantel felt wonderful.

She glanced over at Quinn beside her, legs stretched out, eyes closed behind tinted glasses. From the look of him, he hadn't shaved since Saturday. It seemed unfair that the slightly dissipated aura suited him so.

"Rough night?"

He opened one eye. Then, finding it too much effort, he closed it again. "Poker game."

"You played poker last night? I didn't know you'd gone out."

"In the kitchen," he muttered, wondering how soon he could get his hands on another cup of coffee.

"My kitchen?" Chantel frowned, a little annoyed that she hadn't been asked to play. "With whom?"

"Gardener."

"Rafael? He hardly speaks English."

"Don't have to, to know a full house beats a straight."

"I see." A smile tugged at her lips. "So you and Rafael played poker in the kitchen, got drunk and told lies."

"And Marsh."

"And Marsh what?" She stopped in the act of reaching for a glass. "Marsh played cards? *My* Marsh?"

"Tall guy, not much hair."

"Really, Quinn, he's nearly eighty and quite creaky. I'm surprised even you would take advantage of him."

"Took me for eighty-three dollars. Canny old son of a—"

"Serves you right," she said with satisfaction. "Sitting down in my kitchen, swilling beer and smoking cigars and bragging about women when I'm paying for your time."

"You were asleep."

"I hardly think that matters. You're being paid to watch out for me, not play five-card stud."

"Five-card draw, jacks or better. And I was watching out for you."

"Really?" She brought a glass of juice to her lips. "That's odd. I didn't see hide nor hair of you yesterday."

"I was around. You enjoy your whirlpool?"

"I beg your pardon?"

"You spent damn near an hour in that tub." He took the glass from her and drained it. Maybe it would wash the cotton out of his mouth. "Funny, I figured a woman like you would have two dozen bathing suits. Guess you couldn't find one."

"You were watching me."

He handed the glass back to her, then settled back again. "That's what you're paying me for."

Indignation rippled through her as she slammed the glass back in its holder. "I'm not paying you to be a Peeping Tom. Get your prurient kicks on your own time."

"My time is your time, angel. I saw nearly that much of you when I plunked down ten bucks to see *Thin Ice*. Besides, if I'd been out for kicks, I'd have joined you."

"I'd have drowned you," she tossed back, but he only smiled and shut his eyes again.

His head was pounding like a jackhammer. He'd gotten less sleep before, but that had usually been of his own choosing. The poker game had been his way of distracting himself from the knowledge that she was sleeping upstairs, his way of trying to forget the way she'd looked stretched out in the foaming water of the spa that afternoon.

He hadn't, as he wanted her to believe, watched her. He'd seen her go into the pool house. Then, when she hadn't come out, he'd gone to check on her. She'd been lounging in the big tub, Rachmaninoff wafting from the overhead speakers. Her hair had been left down and floated in the frothing water. And her body . . . her body had been long and slender and pale. He could still feel the impact, like a sledgehammer straight to the solar plexus.

He hadn't stayed to tease and taunt, but had left as quietly as he'd come. There had been a fear, a definite fear that if she'd opened her eyes and looked at him he'd have crawled.

Thoughts of her haunted him day and night. He knew he should be able to prevent it. Nothing and no one was permitted to have power over him. But he was beginning to understand how a woman could become an obsession by simply existing. He was beginning to understand how a man could become overwhelmed by his own fantasies.

It made him worry about himself, but it made him worry more about her. If another man had become obsessed with her, and that other man had crossed certain lines, to what lengths might he go to have her? The letters and calls were gradually becoming more urgent. When would he stop them and try something more desperate?

As frightened as she was, Quinn didn't believe Chantel had any conception of just how far that kind of madness could push a man. The longer he was around her, the more he realized just how far that was.

* * *

They would shoot on the back lot that day. Another camera crew was already in New York filming exteriors. Chantel was looking forward to the time when she and other members of the crew would fly east for the handful of scenes to be shot on location. It would give her a chance to see her sister Maddy and, with any luck, catch her play on Broadway.

The thought of it brought back her earlier cheerful mood. It lasted even through an hour's delay while technicians worked out a few bugs.

"Looks like New England," Quinn commented as he glanced around the open-air set.

"Massachusetts, to be exact," Chantel told him, nibbling on a sticky bun. "Ever been there?"

"I was born in Vermont."

"I was born on a train." Chantel broke off another piece of her bun and laughed. "Well, nearly. My parents were on their way to a gig when my mother went into labor. They stopped off long enough to have my sisters and me."

"Your sisters *and* you?"

"That's right. I'm the oldest of triplets."

"There are three of you. Good God."

"There's only one of me, Doran." She popped a piece of the bun in his mouth, enjoying the fresh air and sunshine. "We're triplets, but each of us manages to be her own person. Abby's raising horses and kids in Virginia, and Maddy's currently wowing them on Broadway."

"You don't look like the family type."

"Really." She felt too good to be offended. "I also have a brother. I can't tell you what he does, because no one's quite sure. I lean toward professional gigolo or international jewel thief. You'd get along beautifully with him." She watched one of the prop men pick up a boulder and move it a few feet. "Amazing, isn't it?"

Quinn studied the trees. They looked real, just like the ones back home, until you saw the wood base they sat on. "Anything real around here?"

"Not a great deal. Give them a few hours and they could make this a jungle in Kenya." Stretching her back, she toyed with the ice in her cup. She was used to waiting. "We were going to shoot this on location, but there were some problems."

"There's a lot of wait around in this business."

"It's not for the restless. I've gone back to my trailer and sat for hours to be called back for a five-minute scene. Other days you put in fourteen hours nonstop."

"Why?"

"Why what?"

"Why do you do it?"

"Because it's what I've always wanted to do." It was a stock answer. Why she felt obliged to elaborate on it, she didn't know. "When I was little and I sat in a theater and saw what could happen, I knew I had to be a part of it."

"So you always wanted to be an actress."

She tossed her hair back and smiled. "I've always been an actress. I wanted to be a star."

"Looks like you got what you wanted."

"Looks like," she murmured, shaking off a hint of depression. "What about you? Did you always want to be a— whatever it is you are?"

"I wanted to be a juvenile delinquent and was doing a pretty good job of it."

"Sounds fascinating." She wanted to know more. To be honest, she wanted to know everything about him, but she'd take care how she asked. "Why aren't you serving ten to twenty in San Quentin?"

"I got drafted." He grinned, but she sensed the joke was very much his own.

"The army builds men."

"Something like that. Anyway, I learned to do what I was good at, make a profit and stay out of jail."

"And what are you good at?" He turned his head, just enough that she could see the amusement and the challenge in his eyes. "Forget I asked. Let's try something else. How long were you in the army?"

"I didn't say I was in the army." He offered her a cigarette, then lighted it himself when she shook her head.

"You said you were drafted."

"I was. Drafted and government trained. Want some more coffee?"

"No. How long were you in?"

"Too long."

"Is that where you learned not to give a direct answer?"

"Yeah." He smiled at her again. Then, before either of them realized his intention, he reached out to touch her hair. "You look like a kid."

Her heart shouldn't have been hammering, but it was. It was only a touch, after all, only a few words and a long look in a pretend world teeming with people. "That's the idea," she managed after a moment. "I'm twenty in this scene, innocent, eager, naive . . . and about to be deflowered."

"Here?"

"No, actually, just over there." She pointed to a small clearing in the forest the crew had created. "Brad the cad seduces me, promising me his everlasting devotion. He taps the passion that so far I've only given to my painting, then exploits it."

Quinn clucked his tongue. "With all these people watching."

"I love an audience."

"And you got mad because I watched you in the tub."

"You—"

"They're ready for you, Chantel."

After giving her assistant a nod, Chantel stood up, then carefully brushed off the seat of her pants. "Get yourself a good seat, Doran," she suggested. "You might learn something."

Taking her advice, Quinn watched her run through the scene several times on low power. From his angle, it seemed a lukewarm stock scene—a gullible woman, a clever man in a pretty springtime setting. Plastic, he thought, pure plastic, down to the leaves on the trees. Quinn kept his eyes on George as the makeup artist retouched Chantel's face to keep that dewy, never-been-touched look intact. One of the prop men handed her back her sketchpad and pencil.

"Places. Quiet on the set." The hubbub died away, to be replaced by silence. "Speed. Roll film." The clapper came down for take one. "Action."

It began the same way, with Chantel sitting on a rock sketching. Sean made his entrance and stood watching her for a moment. When Chantel glanced up and saw him, Quinn felt his mouth go dry. Everything a man could want was in that look. Love, trust, desire. If a man had a woman look at him that way, he could win wars and scale mountains.

He'd never wanted to be loved. Love tied you down, made you responsible to someone other than yourself. It took as much as or more than it gave. That was what he'd thought, that was what he'd been certain of, until he'd seen the look come into Chantel's eyes.

A movie, he reminded himself when he realized he'd missed five minutes of shooting. They were already doing a second take. The look in her eyes was as much an illusion as the forest they were in. And it hadn't been aimed at him, in any case. It was a movie, she was an actress, and it was all part of the script.

The first time Sean Carter touched her, Quinn felt his jaw lock tight. Fortunately for him, the director cut the scene.

When they continued, Quinn told himself he was under control. He told himself that he was only there because he was paid to be. She meant nothing to him personally. She was a case. It didn't matter to him how many men she made love with, on or off camera.

Then he watched her touch her lips softly, hesitantly, to Sean's, and he thought of murder.

It was only a scene in a movie, with fake rocks, fake trees and fake emotions. But it seemed so real, so honest. There were dozens of people around him with machines to run the lights, the mikes. Even as Sean gathered Chantel closer, a camera edged in on them.

But she trembled. Damn it, he saw her quiver as Sean pulled the band from her hair and let it tumble free. Her voice shook when she told him she loved him, she wanted him, she wasn't afraid. Quinn found his hands werc balled into fists in his pockets.

Her eyes shut as Sean rained kisses all over her face. She looked so young, so vulnerable, so ready to be loved. Quinn didn't notice the camera come in close. He only saw Sean unbuttoning her blouse, and her eyes, wide and blue, locked on her lover's. Hesitantly she unbuttoned his shirt. Color washed her cheeks as she drew the shirt aside and pressed her cheek to his chest. They lowered to the grass.

"Cut."

Quinn came back to reality with a thud. He watched Chantel sit up, then say something to Sean that made him laugh. She was wearing a brief strapless bra that would stay below camera range and a pair of baggy jeans. Larry draped her discarded blouse over her shoulder, and she gave him an absent smile.

"Let's take it again. Chantel, after you take off his shirt, I want you to lift your head." Mary Rothschild hunkered down as Chantel rebuttoned her blouse. "I want a kiss there, a good long one, before you two go down on the grass."

Sometime during the fifth take, Quinn found his objectivity. He searched the faces of those looking on. If there was an uncomfortable stirring in his stomach, he could ignore it now. His job was to find out who might be watching Chantel, not clinically, not approvingly as she completed the scene, but someone who might be eaten alive with jealousy. Or fantasizing. It wasn't going to do either one of them any good if it was him.

Quinn took out another cigarette and watched the faces around him. He had reports coming in on everyone from the cinematographer to the prop man. Gut instinct told him that whoever was sending her letters was someone she knew, someone she might speak to casually every day.

Quinn wanted to find him, and he wanted to find him quickly. Before he developed an obsession of his own.

The assistant director put his arm around Chantel's shoulders and, with his head bent close to her ear, led her off the set. Before they reached the trailer that was Chantel's dressing room, Quinn was in front of them.

"Going somewhere?"

Chantel shot him a narrow look but hung on to her temper. "As a matter of fact, I was going to get out of the sun for a while. Amos was giving me the rest of today's schedule. You'll have to forgive Quinn, Amos. He's a bit . . . possessive."

"Hard to blame him." Good-natured and a bit tubby around the middle, Amos patted her shoulder. "You were terrific, Chantel, just terrific. We'll call when we need you for the close-ups and reaction shots. You should have about a half hour."

"Thanks, Amos." She waited until he was out of earshot before she turned on Quinn. "Don't do that."

"Do what?"

"All you needed was a knife between your teeth," she muttered, jerking open the door of the trailer. "I told you Amos was harmless. He—"

"Has a habit of touching women. One of those women is my client."

Chantel chose a diet drink from the small refrigerator and collapsed with it onto the sofa. "If I didn't want him to touch me, I assure you, he wouldn't. This isn't the first time I've worked with Amos, and unless you insist on acting like an idiot, it won't be the last."

Quinn opened the refrigerator and, to his satisfaction, found a beer. "Look, angel, I can't narrow down the list of suspects to suit your requirements. It's time you stopped pretending that the person you're so afraid of isn't someone you know."

"I'm not pretending," she began.

"You are." He chugged back some of the beer before he sat beside her. "And you're not pretending with half as much style as you were out there rolling on the grass a few minutes ago."

"That's work. This is my life."

"Exactly." He took her chin in a way that made her eyes flash. "I'm supposed to take care of it. If it makes you feel better, I've just about eliminated Carter."

"Sean?" She felt a quick surge of relief, then one of caution. "Why?"

"Simple enough reasoning." He took another sip of beer and

kept her hanging. "Seems to me that if a man was obsessed with a woman— We'll agree that we're dealing with an obsession?"

"Yes, damn it." She snatched the bottle out of his hand. "What are you getting at?"

"Just that if I were going over the edge about a woman, I wouldn't be able to stand up, dust myself off and turn aside after I'd spent a good part of the day tangled half-naked with her."

"Is that so?" Chantel handed him back his beer. "I'll be sure to keep that in mind." Relaxed again, Chantel leaned back against the pillows and stretched out her legs. "So, what did you think of the scene?"

"It ought to fog up a few bifocals."

"Oh, come on, Quinn." She held up her drink and watched moisture bead the sides of the bottle. "It wasn't just a matter of sex, you know. It was a betrayal of innocence and trust. What happened to Hailey in that New England wood will affect the rest of her life. A quick tumble on the pine cones doesn't do that."

"But a quick tumble on the pine cones sells tickets."

"This is television. We're after ratings. Damn it, Quinn, I put a lot into that scene. It's the turning point of Hailey's life. If it doesn't mean more than—"

"You were good," he cut in, and had her staring at him.

"Well." She set her drink down. "Mind repeating that?"

"I said you were good. I don't hand out the awards, angel."

She brought her knees up and dropped her chin onto them. With the thin slash of sunlight coming through the curtains, she still looked young and innocent. "How good?"

"How do you manage to feed that ego when you're alone?"

"I've never denied the size of my ego. How good?"

"Good enough to make me want to give Carter a black eye."

"Really?" Delighted, she caught her bottom lip between her teeth. She'd play it light. It wouldn't do to let him know just how much it meant to her to hear him praise her work. "Before or after the cameras were rolling?"

"Before, during and after." Unexpectedly he reached over and took the front of her shirt in his hand. "And don't push your luck, angel. I've got a habit of taking what looks good to me."

"You've such class, Doran." She uncurled his fingers from her blouse. "Such low class."

"Just keep that in mind. You know, angel, you gave me a twinge or two when I watched you and Carter paw each other."

"We weren't—"

"Give it any name you want. But good as you are, I didn't spend all my time watching you. I looked around and saw a few interesting things."

"Such as?"

"Brewster smoked a half a pack of cigarettes while you and Carter were . . . working."

"He's a nervous man. I've seen writers do worse when their script's being filmed."

"Leery practically fell in your lap trying to get a closer look."

"It's his job to look."

"And your assistant nearly swallowed his tongue when Carter took your shirt off."

"Just stop it." Springing up, she paced to one of the windows. They would call her soon. She wouldn't be any good if she let what Quinn was saying get her all churned up. "As far as I'm concerned, you're giving your own gutter-height views to everyone on set."

"That brings up another thought." He settled back and waited for her to look around at him. "Matt's yet to show up on the set. Strange. Aren't you his top client?"

She stared at him for a long moment. "You're determined to leave me without anyone, anyone at all."

"That's right." He ignored the quick, bitter taste in his throat. "For the moment, you trust me and only me."

"They'll be calling me soon. I'm going to go lie down." Without looking at him again, she walked to the back of the trailer and through a doorway.

Quinn had a sudden fierce urge to throw the bottle against

the wall. Just to hear it shatter. She had no business making him feel guilty. He was looking out for her. That was what he was paid for. And it was easier all around if she was suspicious. If that meant she shed a few tears, it couldn't be helped. He wasn't worried about it. He didn't give a damn.

Swearing, he slammed the bottle down on the table beside him. Lecturing himself all the way, he strode through the trailer to the bedroom. "Look, Chantel—"

She was sitting at the foot of the bed, staring down at an envelope in her hands. He smelled the dark, sweet scent of wild roses before he saw them on the dresser.

"I can't open it," she murmured. When she looked up at him, something twisted in his stomach. It wasn't just her pallor. It wasn't just the fear he could see in the way her fingers shook. It was the complete and utter despair in her eyes. "I just can't take any more."

"You don't have to." With a compassion he thought had been erased in him years before, he sat beside her and gathered her close. "That's what I'm here for." He slipped the envelope out of her numb fingers. "I don't want you to open any more of the letters. If they come, you give them to me."

"I don't want to know what it says." She shut her eyes and hated herself for it. "Just rip it up."

"Don't worry about it." He stuffed the letter into his back pocket as he pressed a kiss to the top of her head. He had questions to ask, a lot of questions as to who might have gone into her dressing room that day. "Part of the deal is that you trust me. Just let me take care of things."

The head resting against his shoulder shook once in quick denial. "You can't take care of the way this makes me feel. I always wanted to be someone. I always wanted to feel important. Is that why this is happening?" With a dry sob, she pulled away from him. "Maybe you were right. Maybe I asked for this."

"Stop it." He took her hard by the shoulders and prayed she'd control the tears he could see were threatening. "I was out of line. You're beautiful, you're talented, and you've made use of it. That doesn't mean you're to blame for someone's sickness."

"But it's me that he wants," she said quietly. "And I'm afraid."

"I'm not going to let anything happen to you."

She let out a deep breath as her hand wrapped around his. "Sign that in blood?"

He smiled and ran a fingertip down her cheek. "Whose?"

Needing the contact, she rested her cheek against his for a moment. The gesture left him shaken. "Thanks."

"Sure."

"Look, I know I haven't been making this easy for you." She drew back again. As he'd hoped, the tears hadn't fallen. "I haven't wanted to."

"Trouble is my business. Besides, I like your style."

"While we're being nice to each other, I guess I'll say I like yours, too."

"A red-letter day," he murmured, and brought her hand to his lips.

It was a mistake. They both realized it the instant the contact was made. Over their joined fingers, their gazes met and held. She thought she could feel the tension jump from his palm to hers. This wasn't a matter of temptation, or of anger, or of passion flaring quickly, but of need. She needed to feel his arms around her again, holding her tight. She needed to feel his lips on hers, warm, hard, demanding. Everything else would fade, she knew, if only they came together now.

Their hands were still joined, but she didn't protest as his fingers tightened painfully on hers. What was he thinking? It suddenly seemed imperative that she understand, that she see, what he felt in his mind, in his heart. Did he want her, could he possibly want her as badly this moment as she wanted him . . . ?

No other woman had ever made him ache like this. Not just from wanting. No other woman had ever made his blood swim. Not just from looking. He thought it would be possible to sit there through eternity and just look at that face. Was it only her beauty? Could it possibly be that he was twisted around inside because of a flawless facade?

Or was it something else, something that seemed to glow from within? There was something elusive, almost secretive, that showed in her eyes only if you looked quickly and carefully enough. He thought he saw it now. Then all he could think of was how much he wanted her.

With his free hand he reached up to trail his fingers through her hair. Spun gold, like an angel's. That's what it made him think of. But she was flesh and blood. Not a fantasy, a woman. He leaned closer, then watched her lashes flutter down.

The knock on the trailer door had her shooting up like an arrow out of a bow. She put both hands to her face but shook her head when Quinn reached for her.

"No, it's all right. That's just my call to go on the set."

"Sit down. I'll tell them you're not feeling well."

"No." She dropped her hands to her sides. "No, this isn't going to interfere with my work." The fingers of her left hand balled into a fist, but he could see she was working to regain control. "I can't let that happen." Turning her head, she stared at the roses on the table. "I won't let it."

He wanted to overrule her but knew this was the one thing he'd admired about her from the first. She was strong, strong enough to fight back. "Okay. You want a few more minutes?"

"Yeah, maybe." She walked to the window and drew the curtains aside to let in more sun. It was frightening, much too frightening to think about darkness. At night she was alone with her thoughts and her imagination. The sun was out, she reminded herself, sighing deeply. She had work to do.

"Would you mind letting them know I'll be out in a minute?"

"I'll take care of it." He hesitated, wanting to go to her, knowing it would be a mistake for both of them. "I'll be right outside, Chantel. Don't come out until you're ready."

"I'll be fine."

She waited until she heard him walk away before she

dropped her forehead onto the glass. Weeping would be such a relief. Weeping, screaming, just letting go, would ease the hammerlock her nerves had on her system. But she couldn't let go, any more than she could allow herself to get churned up like this. There were hours more to put in that day. She needed her wits, and her stamina.

She'd make it, Chantel promised herself. Drawing a deep breath, she turned from the window. The flowers were gone. She stared at the table with a foolish sense of relief. He'd taken them away. She hadn't even had to ask.

What kind of a man was he? Rude and rough one moment, tender the next. Why couldn't he be easy to understand and easy to dismiss? With a shake of her head, she started down to the front of the trailer. He was impossible to understand. And he stirred things in her. He was anything but the kind of man a woman could be comfortable with. And she felt so safe knowing he was close by.

If she hadn't known herself so well, been so certain of her own control, she would almost have believed she was falling in love with him.

CHAPTER 6

It was anything but a quiet, restful week, though Chantel spent a good chunk of it in bed. The bed was big and plush and ornate—and it was on the set, on soundstage D. The major scene to be shot was her wedding night—Hailey's wedding night—not to the man she loved but to the man she wanted to love.

The props included an ice bucket with champagne, a full-length sable draped over a chair and a table laden with roses that had to be spritzed constantly to keep them fresh under the lights. Don Sterling, a relative unknown, had been chosen to play the man she would marry. He'd been selected mainly because of looks and chemistry. Though his final reading with Chantel had been excellent, his nerves had him blowing the scene a half-dozen times during the morning.

Locked in his arms, Chantel felt him tighten up. Before he could do so himself, she flubbed the scene, hoping to take some of the pressure off him.

"Sorry." She gave a delicate shrug. "Can we take five, Mary? I'm getting stale."

"Make it ten," Rothschild ordered, then turned to consult with her assistant.

"How about a cup of coffee?" Chantel accepted the robe she was handed and slipped into it as she smiled at Don.

"Only if I can drown myself in it."

"Let's try drinking it first." She signaled to Larry, then found two seats in a relatively quiet corner. When she saw Quinn start to approach, she shook her head and leaned closer to Don. "It's a tough scene."

"It shouldn't be." He ran a hand through a mass of thick dark hair.

"Look, the order they're shooting this miniseries in, we've only had a couple of scenes together so far. The first thing you know, we're married and on our honeymoon." She took the coffee from Larry. "I don't know about you, but I think it's easier to jump into bed with someone if you have more than a passing acquaintance."

He held the coffee in both hands and managed a chuckle. "I'm supposed to be an actor."

"Me, too."

"You could run through this scene with your eyes closed." He sipped the coffee, then, with a sound of disgust, set it aside. "I'll be honest. You intimidate the hell out of me." When she only lifted a brow, he let out a long breath and looked away. "When my agent called and told me I had this part and that I'd be playing opposite you, I almost went into a coma."

"That makes it tough to work up any passion." She put a hand on his. "Look, your reading with me was great. No one else even came close."

"The bit in Hailey's art studio." He picked up his coffee with a rueful look. "Not a bed in sight."

"The first love scene I ever played was opposite Scott Baron. Hollywood legend—the world's sexiest man. I had to kiss him, and my teeth were chattering, I was so scared. He took me aside, bought me a tuna-fish sandwich and told me stories, half of which were certainly lies. Then he told me something true. He said all actors are children and all children like to play games. If we didn't play the game well, we'd have to grow up and get real jobs."

The tension she'd spotted around his mouth had already relaxed. "Did it work?"

"It was either that or the tuna fish, but we went back on the set and played the game."

"You stole that movie from him."

She smiled. "I've heard it said." She continued to smile as she sipped coffee. "Don't think I'm going to let you steal this one from me."

"You blew that last line on purpose."

She could become a prima donna with little more than a tilt of her head. "I don't know what you're talking about."

"You have a reputation for being cold and driven," he mused. "I never expected you to be, well, nice."

"Don't let it get around." Rising, she offered him a hand. "Let's get this honeymoon off the ground."

The scene went like clockwork. Quinn didn't know what Chantel had said during her brief huddle with her costar, but it had done the trick. For himself, he was learning not to tense up when Chantel was in someone else's arms. It was difficult to work up any resentment when so much technology went into setting the scene. The lights had to be adjusted to simulate candlelight. Chantel and Don lay in the bed, he stripped to the waist, she in a thigh-length chemise. The camera was nearly on top of them. The director knelt on the bed and went over the moves. On cue, Chantel and Don turned to each other as if they were the only two people on earth.

It was so easy for her, Quinn reflected, to fabricate passion. When he watched her like this, he wondered if she had any real feelings at all. Her emotions were turned off and on as direction indicated. Like an exquisitely crafted puppet, he thought, beautifully formed on the outside, hollow within.

Yet he'd held her himself. He'd felt passion shimmer in her. The feelings, needs, uncertainties had been there for him to touch. Had that been just part of her act as well? It shouldn't matter to him, he reminded himself as he lighted a cigarette. He couldn't let it matter. She was an assignment and nothing more. If she stirred feelings in him, as she did with uncanny regularity, he would just have to take a step back. Involvement with a woman like Chantel O'Hurley was suicide for a man who didn't have himself under complete control.

But when he looked at her, his mouth went dry.

Just desire, he told himself. Or, more accurately, lust. There was no denying that wanting her was as easy, as natural, as drawing breath. But it hadn't been desire or lust he had felt when he'd held her in his arms moments ago.

So he had some compassion left in him. Quinn found a chair, then discovered he was too wired to sit. He'd have been pretty low if he hadn't felt sympathy or been able to offer comfort to a frightened and vulnerable woman.

But it hadn't been sympathy, it had been rage. He recognized it even now, that hot, bubbling fury at the thought of his woman being threatened. His woman. That was the problem. The longer he was with her, the easier it became to think of her as his.

Take a step back from that, Doran, he ordered himself. And make it fast. If he didn't pull himself together soon, he was going to be in over his head. A man could only hold his breath for so long.

He crushed out his cigarette and wished the interminable day would end.

There had been two more letters that week, letters he hadn't shown her. The tone had shifted from pleading to near whimpering. It worried Quinn more than the subtle menace the earlier letters had contained. The author was about to break. When he did, Quinn was certain it would be like a geyser, fast and violent. Because his own patience was thin, he hoped it would be soon. It would give him some outlet for the fury building inside him.

"That's a wrap, people. Don't have too much fun over the weekend. We want you alive and coherent on Monday."

Still in her chemise, Chantel sat on the edge of the bed and held an earnest conversation with Don. Jealousy. Where it had come from and why, Quinn couldn't begin to answer. Quinn had always been a live-and-let-live sort of person. If a woman, even a woman he was involved with, decided to look to another man, that was her prerogative. No strings, no pain, no complications. He'd managed very well that way for years. He'd never experienced this sharp twist in the gut over a woman before. He felt it now, and he didn't like it, or himself. Unable to stop himself, he walked over and drew Chantel to her feet.

"Playtime's over," he said, and pulled her with him.

"Let go of me," she told him under her breath as he walked toward her trailer. Larry started forward with her robe, saw the look on Quinn's face and backed away.

"Just shut up."

"Doran, this is my place of business, but if you keep it up, I'm going to create the biggest, juiciest scene even your twisted brain can imagine. You'll read about it in the paper for weeks."

"Go ahead."

She set her teeth. "Just what is your problem?"

"You're my problem, lady. For a woman who should be watching her step, you were awfully chummy with that kid."

"Kid? Don? For God's sake, he's an associate, and he's not a kid. He's two years older than I am."

"You were steaming up his contact lenses."

"Don't you get tired of playing the same tune?" She jerked her arm free and pulled open her dressing room door herself. "If you've been doing your job, you already have a report on Don Sterling, and you know he's practically engaged to a woman he's been involved with for two years."

"And the woman in question is three thousand miles away in New York."

"I know that." As she pushed her hair out of her face, the chemise shifted, whispering silkily over her skin. "He was just telling me that he's going to catch the red-eye to the East Coast so that he can spend the weekend with her. He's in love, Doran, though I realize you might not understand the term."

"A man could be in love with another woman and still want you."

She slammed the trailer door and leaned back against it.

"What would you know about love? What would you know about any genuine emotion?"

"You want emotion?" He slapped his palms on the door at either side of her head. Though her eyes widened in shock, she stood firm. "You want a taste of the kind of emotion you push out of a man? The real thing, angel, not something out of the pages of a script. Think you can take it?"

Her heart was beating in her throat. It was crazy to actually *want* to be dragged against him, to be plundered, drained and weakened. She could see nothing but raw fury in his eyes, but somehow she relished it. If it was all he could feel for her, it was almost enough. She'd be willing to settle, and that scared the hell out of her.

"Just leave me alone," she whispered.

"You're smart to be scared of me."

"I'm not scared of you."

He leaned a little closer. "You're trembling."

"I'm furious." She pressed her damp palms against the door.

"Maybe you are. And maybe that's because you're not quite sure of what happens next. It's not written out for you, is it, Chantel? Not so easy to turn the switch off and on."

"Get out of my way."

"Not just yet. I want to know what you feel." His body pressed lightly against hers. "I want to know *if* you feel."

She was losing ground, and what she had left was shaky. If he touched her now, really touched her, she was afraid she would lose everything. How could she tell him what she felt, when what she felt was against all the rules? She wanted to be held, protected, cherished, loved. If she told him that, he'd only smile and take what he wanted. She'd been left empty before, and it would never, ever happen to her again.

Chantel lifted her chin and waited until his lips hovered an inch from hers. "You're no better than the man I hired you to protect me from."

He stepped back as if she'd slapped him. The stunned look

on his face made her want to reach out to him. Instead, she pressed back against the door and waited for his next move.

"Get some clothes on," he told her, and turned aside. As she walked away, he reached into the refrigerator for a beer. She was right. Quinn twisted off the top and took two long swallows. He'd wanted to frighten, to weaken, then take her there, on his terms. If he could have proven to himself that what happened between them was cold and calculated, he might have believed she meant nothing to him.

He'd wanted to hurt her. She was threatening his peace of mind, and he'd needed to strike back. He would have used sex to purge himself and to repay her for the restless nights. The wave of self-disgust was as unfamiliar and as unpalatable as the surge of jealousy he'd felt earlier.

He'd told himself to take a step back, yet he'd taken a leap forward and had landed in the mire. He'd done things and seen things in his life that would have left others pale and speechless. Yet, for the first time in his life, he felt truly soiled.

When he heard her coming back, he tossed the bottle into the trash. She wore rose-colored linen slacks and a jacket with a muted floral design. She looked cool, composed and nothing like the restless, questing character she'd played all day.

Without a word she walked by him and put her hand on the knob. Before she could open the door, Quinn placed his hand over hers. He cursed himself when she stiffened and sent him a cool, disinterested look.

"You're entitled to take a few shots," he said mildly. "I won't even duck."

For a moment she said nothing. Then, as the anger dissipated, she sighed. She was tired, drained from the constant play and replay of emotion. "I'll take a rain check."

As she twisted the knob, he tightened his hand on hers. "Chantel . . ."

"What?"

He wanted to apologize. It wasn't his style, but he wanted

badly to tell her he was sorry. The need was there, but the words wouldn't come. "Nothing. Let's go."

They rode home in silence while guilt ate at him. It would fade, he assured himself. It was just one more of the odd emotions she drew out of him. She looked exhausted now, though he remembered she'd looked fine—in fact, she'd looked wonderful—before he'd . . .

Damn it, he couldn't waste his time worrying about things like that. He had a job to do, and if he'd stepped out of line, it wouldn't happen again. Case closed. He'd see her into the house, make certain the doors were locked and the alarm on. Then he'd relax. He needed to go over the report from his field man, though he was already aware they'd turned up nothing on the stationery. They needed a mistake. So far, no matter how mentally unstable Chantel's admirer was, he'd been smart.

Quinn sat back as the limo cruised through the gates, wishing he could say the same thing about himself.

He preferred to act on impulse. As he stepped out of the car, he didn't hesitate or think twice. Taking Chantel by the hand, he began to lead her around the side of the house.

"What are you doing?"

"It's Friday night and I'm sick of being cooped up in that house. We're going out to eat." He stopped by his car and nodded to one of the men who patrolled the grounds.

"Did it ever occur to you that I might not feel like going out?"

"Where I go, you go." He opened the door and started to nudge her inside.

"Doran, I've put in sixty hours this week and I'm tired. I don't want to go to a restaurant and be stared at."

"Who said anything about a restaurant? Just get in, angel. You don't want to embarrass yourself in front of my man over there."

"I'm not hungry."

"I am." He gave her a quick shove, then shut the door behind her.

"Has anyone ever mentioned that you're totally lacking in manners or any of the other social graces?"

"Constantly."

He gunned the motor and sent the car barreling down the drive. Chantel reached for her seat belt. "If you wreck this heap with me in it, the producers are going to have your head on a platter." For a moment she wondered if it wouldn't be worth it.

"Nervous?"

"You don't make me nervous, Doran, you simply annoy me."

"Everyone's got to be good at something." He turned the radio dial, and loud, throbbing rock poured out. Chantel closed her eyes and pretended to ignore him.

When the car came to a halt, she didn't move. Determined to show nothing but indifference, she sat still as the silence grew. Outside the car she heard the bump and grind of weekend traffic heating up. She had no idea where they were and told herself she didn't care. Quinn's door opened and closed, and she still didn't move. But she did open her eyes.

She saw him stride up to the little fast-food joint and fought back a chuckle. She would not be amused. At home she could have had a nice glass of wine and a crisp salad with her cook's special herb dressing. God knew what Quinn was carrying back to the car in the white bag. She simply wouldn't eat, she told herself. She'd let him get whatever he had in his system out, but she wouldn't eat.

Closing her eyes again, she tried not to react as aromas, really wonderful aromas, filled the car. He glanced over, smiled, then started the car again.

Again she didn't know where he was heading, but the road began to wind and the sounds of traffic faded. She very nearly dozed off as her system absorbed the quiet sunset drive. She hadn't realized how much she'd needed to get away, from work, from her house, maybe from herself. It was going to be hard not to be grateful to him. But Chantel told herself she would manage.

When the car stopped again, she refused to move. Curiosity

gnawed at her, but she kept her eyes firmly shut. Saying nothing, Quinn reached for the bag, rattling it so that the scent seeped through the car. Then he stepped out and closed the door behind him.

Chantel's stomach contracted, reminding her that the plate of fruit and cheese she'd had for lunch wasn't enough. The least he could do was force her to eat something, the way he'd forced her to do other things she hadn't wanted to. But no, she thought as her temper began to rise, he would just go off and gobble up whatever was in that bag and let her starve.

Opening her eyes, Chantel pushed open her door. As she let it slam behind her, the noise seemed to echo forever. Astonished, she looked around her.

They were farther up in the hills than she had ever gone before. Below, miles below, L.A. stretched forever, glistening just a bit as lights winked on. She could see the separate levels of color in the sky as the sun went down. Deep blue led to paler blue, and paler blue to mauve and rose and pink, all glistening with gold. The first star blinked to life overhead and waited patiently for others to join it. The breeze whistled through the brush, but the city she knew so well seemed encased in glass, it was so quiet.

"Pretty impressive, isn't it?"

She turned and saw Quinn leaning against a giant *H*. The Hollywood sign, she realized, and nearly laughed. She'd seen it so often it no longer registered. From the hills it looked white, invulnerable and perhaps immortal. Up close, like the town it heralded, it was mostly illusion. It was big and bold, certainly, but a little grimy, a little shaky. Graffiti was etched in clumps near the base.

"It could use a fresh coat of paint," she murmured.

"No, it's more honest this way." He kicked aside a beer can. "Teenagers come up here to hang out—and make out."

She tilted her head. "And you?"

"Oh, I just like the view." He climbed over a few rocks effortlessly and planted himself on the base of an *L*. "And the quiet. If you're lucky, you can come up here and not hear a thing, except for a coyote now and again."

"Coyote?" She glanced over her shoulder.

"That's right." Not bothering to hide a grin, he dug in the bag. "Want a taco?"

"A taco? You dragged me all the way up here to eat tacos?"

"Got some beer."

"Lovely."

"It's getting warm. You'd better drink up."

"I don't want anything."

"Suit yourself." He unwrapped a taco and bit into it. "Got some fries, too," he said with a full mouth. "A little greasy, maybe, but they're not cold yet."

"I don't know how I can resist." She turned away from him to look down at the city again. As fate would have it, the breeze carried the spicy scents to her. Her mouth watered. Chantel scowled down at the lights and wished Quinn Doran to hell.

"I guess a woman like you turns her nose up if it isn't champagne and caviar."

Spinning around, Chantel stood with the city and the sunset at her back. Quinn felt his heart turn over in his chest. She'd never looked more beautiful. "You know nothing about me, nothing at all." Her voice had an edge to it now, a dull, gritty edge that had his eyes narrowing. "I spent nearly the first twenty years of my life shuffling from town to town, eating in greasy spoons or over a hot plate in a motel room. Sometimes, if we were lucky and the gig was good, we got to wolf down a meal in the hotel kitchen. If we weren't so lucky, there were always hard-boiled eggs and coffee. Don't you sit there in your smug little world and toss stones at me, Doran. You don't know what I am, or who I am. All you know is what I've made myself."

Slowly he set the beer on the rock behind him. "Well, well," he said quietly. "I wouldn't read any of that in your official bio, would I?"

She could only stare. What was it about him that made her

lose control? Why had she been compelled to yank herself out and expose her roots to him?

"I want to go back."

"No, you don't." His voice wasn't curt now, but gentle. It was that gentleness that chipped away her defenses. "There's no one here but me, Chantel. Why don't we just sit up here and look down at the rest of the world for a while?"

Before she'd thought it through, she'd taken a step toward him. When he rose and held out a hand to help her up, she reached for it without hesitation. Hesitation came the moment his palm met hers. She remembered the feel of it, the strength of it, and her gaze lifted and locked with his. They stood there a moment with the sky darkening around them. Then he hauled her up.

"I'm sorry." The apology surprised him as much as it did her.

"For what?" She started to draw her hand from his, but he reached up to brush back her hair.

"For what happened before. I don't know why, but something about you makes me edgy."

She kept her eyes level with his. "Then we're even."

The wind tossed the hair back from his face. In every situation, he knew, there came a time for honesty. Perhaps this was such a time. "Chantel, I want you. I'm having a hell of a time dealing with that."

Other men had wanted her, other men had told her so in more beautiful ways. But the words had never made it difficult for her to breathe. "I could fire you."

"It wouldn't matter."

"No, I don't suppose it would." She looked away, surprised at how strong a longing could be. "Quinn, I can't go to bed with you."

"I figured you'd feel that way."

"Quinn." She took his hand again as he started to step away. "I don't know what you think my reasons are, but I guarantee you, you're wrong."

"Not your style," he said, picking up his beer again. "Not your league."

Chantel snatched the bottle from him and heaved it. Spray spewed against the rocks before the glass shattered. "Don't tell me what I think. *Don't* tell me what I feel."

"Then you tell me." He grabbed her and pulled her against him.

"I don't have to tell you *anything*. I don't have to explain myself to you. Damn you, I just want some peace. I just want a few hours where the pressure's off. I don't know if I can take being squeezed at all sides for much longer."

"Okay, okay." His hold gentled immediately. As he murmured, his hand stroked up and down her back. "You're right. I didn't bring you up here to fight with you, but you make me edgy."

"Let's just go back."

"No, sit down. Please," he added, brushing his lips over her hair. "Let's see if we can stay here for an hour together and not pick on each other. Have a taco."

He smiled at her as he pulled her down to sit. Chantel took one look at the bag and gave up.

"I'm starving."

"Yeah, I figured as much." He handed her a wad of paper napkins. For the next few minutes they ate in companionable silence. "Was your childhood rough?"

Chantel stopped in the act of opening a little packet of salt for the fries. "Oh, no, I didn't mean that. It was just different. My parents are entertainers. They've been a song-and-dance team for over thirty years. The six of us trouped around the country, and some of the places we played were dives. But my family . . ." She smiled, absently accepting a beer. "They're wonderful. Trace did some routines, but he was best on the piano. It always used to frustrate me that no matter how hard I tried I couldn't play better than he did."

"Sibling rivalry."

"Sure. Life would be pretty dull without it. Trace and I were always so much alike that we couldn't stay off each other's backs for very long. There was never much of that between my

sisters and me. We were just too much a part of each other."
She sipped the beer straight from the bottle and looked down
at the city below. "We still are. God, sometimes it's so hard to
be away from them. When we were little, we made all these
plans for keeping the act together forever." She remembered
them with a little pang of regret. "Then we grew up."

"What kind of an act?"

Laughing, she licked salt from her fingers. "You never heard
of the O'Hurley Triplets?"

"Sorry."

"You'd probably be sorrier if you had heard of us. Three-part
harmony, show tunes and popular music, a few old standards
thrown in."

"You sing?"

"Doran, I don't just *sing*, I'm terrific."

"You never sing in your movies."

She shrugged a shoulder. "It hasn't come up. Matt keeps saying we should give the public a surprise one of these days and
get a guest spot where I can do a few numbers and dance,
maybe, too. Yes," she added when he slanted a look at her, "I
can dance—my father would have died of shame otherwise."

"Why don't you do it?"

"The time just hasn't been right. Besides, I've been concen-
trating on what I'm best at."

He balled up the empty bag and set it beside his feet. "What's
that?"

She gave him a quick, mocking look. "Playing roles."

Instead of smiling back, he tucked her hair behind her ear.
"My guess is you're not playing one now."

She turned her head quickly and looked out. The sky was
nearly dark, but there was only a smattering of stars. "You can't
be sure. I'm not sure myself half the time."

"I think you're sure."

When she turned her head back, his mouth was close. Close
and tempting. "Don't. I told you I can't—" But his lips brushed
over hers, light as a whisper, and stopped her cold.

"Do you know how I felt when you were lying on that bed with Sterling today?"

"No. I don't want to know. I've told you, it's my job."

She was already half-seduced; he could hear it in her voice. There was a thrill of anticipation along his skin as he thought of taking her beyond the next step. "I wasn't sure if I wanted to put my hands around his throat or yours, but I did know I wanted you to look at me the way you were looking at him."

"It's just a part. I'm supposed to—"

"There aren't any cameras here, Chantel. Just you and me. And that's what I think you're afraid of. No one's here to tell you what you're supposed to be feeling. No one's going to yell 'cut' before things go just a little too far."

"I don't need anyone to tell me what to feel. I don't need anyone," she repeated, and tugged his mouth back to hers.

She wanted it. She wanted to experience the wild flood of sensation he could bring her. No one else. She could tell him there'd been no one else who had touched her just this way, but he'd never believe her. The image, her image, was all but carved in stone, and she'd polished it herself. What she was inside belonged to her. She was determined that no one would ever share that part of her again.

But she could have this, the heat, the need, the desperation. She could take this, and she could give it back to him as long as she promised herself she wouldn't give him too much. As long as she didn't give him everything.

The sky darkened above them, and the wind whistled through the brush.

She was pulling something from him, drawing something out of him. He couldn't seem to stop her. His hands weren't steady as they reached up to tangle in her hair. His mind was swimming in a mist of his needs, but the needs weren't as simple as he'd told himself they had to be. Desire could make you ache, but it shouldn't be allowed to slice you open.

He wanted to take her there, there in the rocks and dirt. He wanted to treat her like porcelain, delicately and with intense care.

His body was coiled tight, ready to explode. God, he had to touch her, even if it was only once. In one smooth stroke he brought his hand along her leg, over her hip, until he found and cupped her breast. She was small, incredibly fragile, and as soft as water. Compelled, he flicked open the two buttons on her jacket to feast on the warm flesh inside.

It had been so long, so long since she had allowed herself to be touched, since she'd felt the need for intimacy. She wanted his hands on her, his lips on her, his body hard and demanding against hers. The hell with where they were, who they were. The hell with the price she would surely pay for allowing herself to love him.

In an act of surrender that left him shaken, she brought her arms around him and buried her face against his throat.

"Chantel . . ." He started to tilt her face up, longing, for reasons he couldn't be sure of, to see what was in her eyes. Then he heard it, a rustling in the brush that came once, then twice, and had him tensing.

"What? What is it?" She had heard it, too, and she dug her fingers into his arm. "An animal?"

"Yeah, probably." But he didn't think so. His nerves were humming as he drew her aside.

"Where are you going?"

"To take a look. Just stay here."

"Quinn—" She was already standing.

"Just sit tight. It's probably just a rabbit."

It was no rabbit. She heard it in his voice. He wasn't nearly the actor she was. Fear made her want to cringe away. Pride had her matching him step for step. "I'm going with you."

"Chantel, sit down."

"No." She held his arm and scrambled over the rocks.

Resigned, Quinn helped her regain her balance. "All right, then, be careful. You get any scratches on that skin and I'll get blamed for it."

"Damn right."

Because the light had faded, he went to his car and found a flashlight. "Why don't you just sit—"

"No."

Swearing under his breath, he took her by the arm again. He walked slowly toward the brush, casually angling his body to shield hers. "Lot of game up here," he began, but his muscles were coiled and ready. He moved softly, quietly pushing brush aside as Chantel hung on to his hand.

"I remember, coyote."

"Yeah." He crouched down when he spotted prints in the soft dirt. The beam of his light swept over them, then held.

Chantel pressed her lips together. "I guess coyote don't wear shoes."

"None that I've seen." He hated hearing that hint of fear in her voice. "Look, it was probably just a kid."

"No. You don't believe that and neither do I." She stared down at the scuffed prints. The brush where they were wasn't more than five yards from where they'd been sitting a moment before. "Someone was watching us, and I think we both know why. God." She pressed her fingers to her eyes. "He was here. He was right here, just watching. Why doesn't he stop? Why doesn't he—"

"Get a hold of yourself." Quinn took her by the shoulders and shook. She took a deep breath, then nearly screamed when the sound of an engine starting echoed back to them.

"He followed me." She stopped trembling. Her body felt too numb even for that. "How many other times has he been there, watching me?"

"I don't know." Frustrated, Quinn stared out at the darkening road. Even if he dared leave her there alone, he'd never catch up with the other car now. "Just remember, he's watching us now. I'm not going to let him get to you."

"For how long?" she said quietly, then turned away. "I want to go back."

CHAPTER 7

"I t just doesn't seem like we're getting anywhere." Chantel poured herself a brandy, then freshened Matt's glass.

"I'm sorry, Chantel. I'd have sworn if anyone could dig up an answer it would be Quinn."

"I'm not blaming him." Cupping her brandy in both hands, she walked to the window. The sun was setting. It reminded her of another dusk. With the snifter at her lips, she watched night fall.

"You've changed your tune from the first time we talked about him."

More than you know, she thought, but shrugged her shoulders. "I can't claim he's not doing everything he can, that's all."

"Then maybe I have to," Matt returned, hating to hear the tired resignation in her voice. "He hasn't come up with anything solid. What about the letters?"

"The stationery the letters were written on could have come from any of dozens of dollar or drugstores in the L.A. area. There's no way for him to trace it."

"But the flowers." Restless, Matt walked to the white baby grand, then back to the fireplace, his cigarette trailing expensive smoke behind him. "There has to be a way to trace where they were bought."

"Apparently not. Most of the time they just appear in my

dressing room or somewhere on the set. So far no one's seen who delivers them."

"Florists keep records."

"If you pay cash and pick up the flowers yourself, there wouldn't be any reason to ask for ID." She pressed her fingers to the back of her neck, pressed and released, fruitlessly working at a knot of tension.

"Someone might remember who—"

"Quinn tells me his men have done a sweep of the florists in the area. There's nothing."

"The phone calls."

"They haven't been able to get a trace."

"Damn it." If something—or someone—existed, Matt felt there must be a way to find him. "Chantel, maybe you should reconsider the police."

She turned back. With him, she could allow the weariness to show. "Matt, do you really think they could do more than Quinn's done?"

"I don't know." The quiet desperation in her eyes was difficult to face. He scowled down at his brandy. "I just don't know." Setting down his drink, he crossed to her. "I was sure this thing would be tied up in a matter of days."

"It's not as simple as that. It seems he's clever, or cautious at any rate."

"Are you sure you've told Quinn everything you know?"

"What I don't tell him, he finds out." Nerves had her swirling the brandy around and around in her glass but not drinking. "He's running investigations on everyone I know."

"Well, that—"

"Including you."

He stopped to stare at her. With a grimace, he stuck his hands in his pockets and nervously pulled out his lighter. "He's thorough, anyway."

"I don't like it, Matt." For the first time, real emotion came into her voice, into her eyes. "I feel . . . I don't know, sleazy when I think of him poking into the keyholes of people's lives, and on my account."

Not quite comfortable, Matt slipped an arm around her shoulder. "Look, baby, if rattling a few skeletons in my closet helps get to the bottom of this thing, then it's worth it." He was silent a moment, then cleared his throat. "So, what did he find out?"

"About you?"

"That's a good place to start."

"I don't know." Letting out a long breath, she leaned her head on his shoulder. The sun had disappeared completely, leaving only a hint of color streaking the clouds. "I told him I didn't want to know, Matt. He started to give me reports on people like Larry and James Brewster, and I hated it." She could still remember his cool disapproval of her cowardice. Chantel gritted her teeth against the memory. "We agreed that I'd take the precautions he'd outlined, and that he'd keep what information he had to himself."

With one hand Matt flicked on the silver monogrammed lighter he'd been toying with. "That's burying your head in the sand, Chantel."

"I don't care."

"Listen, there's no one, certainly no one who's made it past twenty, who hasn't done something they're ashamed of, something they'd prefer to keep covered." He shifted but made himself speak matter-of-factly. "Quinn's got a right to investigate, and because of who he is, nothing he finds out will go any further."

"Thanks for the vote of confidence." Quinn paused in the doorway and studied them. Matt still had his arm around her. Chantel's head rested on his shoulder as the dim light through the window behind them settled over her hair. She looked comfortable with him, Quinn realized with a twinge of resentment. She looked as though she'd be content to snuggle up against him and sit for hours.

"I'm the one who recommended you," Matt said easily. "I'd hate to say I'd made a mistake."

"You didn't." Quinn crossed to the bar to pour himself a double shot of brandy. "How've you been, Matt? I thought we'd be seeing more of you."

"I've been tied up."

Sensing the restraint between them, Chantel took a step forward. "Just stop it," she told Quinn. "Don't start on him."

"You're telling me how to do my job again, angel."

"I'm not going to allow you to use your third degree on my friends."

Quinn tossed back his brandy. "Too bad I left my rubber hose upstairs."

"Why don't we sit down?" Matt put a hand on Chantel's shoulder. "I appreciate it, babe, but it isn't necessary." His gaze locked with Quinn's. "I guess when I told Chantel to hire you, I should have figured you'd dig it up."

Quinn met the look, but there was nothing to show his feelings. "Yeah, you should have."

"Dig what up?" she demanded.

Quinn lifted his glass in a half salute. "Maybe you'd like to tell her yourself."

"Yes, I would. Sit down, Chantel." When she only looked at him, Matt squeezed her shoulder. "Please, sit down."

She felt the now-familiar churning in her stomach as she chose a chair. "All right, I'm sitting."

"A few years back, almost ten now, I ran into some financial problems." He retrieved his brandy and took a deep swallow.

"Matt, you don't have to tell me about this."

"Yes, I do." He looked back at Quinn. "I want you to hear it from me." He held up a hand before she could protest again. "Just hear me out. When I'm finished, maybe I won't feel as though the blade's about to fall on my neck."

"All right," she said evenly, but her left hand moved restlessly on the arm of her chair.

"Gambling," he said with a hint of fear in his voice.

"Matt, that's absurd." She nearly laughed. "You won't even play gin for matchsticks."

"That's now. This was then. I couldn't keep away from the horses." With a self-mocking smile, he looked back at her. "It's a fever, and mine ran pretty hot until I'd dropped more than I could afford. I was desperate. I'd borrowed money from a certain group of people—the kind who break small bones in your body if they don't get their weekly payment."

"Oh, Matt."

"I needed ten thousand I didn't have. I forged a check. A client's check." He closed his eyes before he took another swallow. Chantel sat in silence. "Of course, it didn't take long for it to come to light. My client didn't want the publicity, so he didn't press charges. I mortgaged my soul, then hocked the rest to pay him back. You could call it a turning point in my life." This time he laughed, but there was no humor in it. "My career was on the line, so I took a good hard look at myself. Because what I saw left me pretty shaken, I checked into an organization for obsessive gamblers. It's been nearly eight years since I've been to the track. Even though gambling nearly ruined my life, I have to fight the urge every day to place just one bet." He set down his glass and looked at her. "If you want another agent, I'll understand."

She rose slowly and walked to him. Without a word, she put her arms around him and gathered him close. Over his shoulder she sent Quinn a long, neutral look. "I don't want another agent. You know I insist on the best."

With a muffled laugh, he pressed a kiss to her brow. "You're a special lady."

"Someone's always telling me that."

He gripped her fingers hard, and she felt how damp his palms were. "I wouldn't let you down, Chantel."

"I know."

He kissed her again before he drew away. "I've got to get going. You'll call if there's anything I can do?"

"Of course."

He turned to Quinn. For a moment the men studied each other across the room. If there was regret on either side, they didn't show it. "Take care of her."

"I intend to."

With a brief nod, Matt let himself out.

Chantel turned on Quinn immediately. "How could you? How could you humiliate him that way?"

"It was necessary." But necessary or not, it left a foul taste in his mouth. Quinn poured another brandy, knowing that taste wouldn't be so easily washed away.

"Necessary? Why? What does a gambling debt nearly ten years ago have to do with what's happening to me now?"

"If a man can develop one obsession, he can develop another."

"That's ridiculous."

"No, that's a fact."

A quiver ran through her, not of fear but of anger. "Matt Burns has never attempted to be anything to me other than my agent and my friend. And he's had abundant opportunity."

"Would you have let him?"

Chantel took a cigarette, then flicked the table lighter three times before she managed to get it to flame. "What does that have to do with it?"

He came closer, curling his hand firmly around her arm. "Would you?"

"No." Tossing her head, she blew out smoke. "No."

"And he knows it." When she jerked her arm away, he watched her pace the room. "You're good with scenarios. Try this one. The man works with you for years, he watches you soar straight to the top. He's helped you, layer by layer, to build that illusion of cool, ice-hard sexuality. Maybe he wants what he helped to create."

A shiver ran down her spine, but her eyes were calm and level when she turned to him. "It doesn't play, Doran."

"It plays as well as anything else."

"No, it doesn't." The fear was back. She fought hard to keep it from showing. "Why wouldn't a man I know, a man I'm close to, just approach me openly?"

"Because he's a man you know, a man you're close to," Quinn countered. "He knows he doesn't have a chance with you on that level."

Impatient, she stubbed the cigarette out. "How would he know if he's never asked?"

Quinn put a hand to her cheek to stop her nervous pacing. "Don't you think a man knows when a woman's interested?" Running a thumb down her jaw, he brought her an inch closer. It was there, as it had been from the first, humming between them. She felt it, damn it, he knew she felt it, even though she refused to show that she did. "Don't you think he can look at a woman, see the way she looks at him, and know if they're going to be lovers?"

She put a hand to his wrist and carefully drew his away. Her skin felt as though it would stay warm for hours. "I'm tired," she told him. "I'm going to bed."

When he was alone, the brandy tempted him. Because it seemed too easy a way out, he turned his back on it. He went outside to walk the grounds.

* * *

Chantel was finding sleep harder and harder to come by. In the late hours she would toss and turn, then fall into a light doze, only to awake again, nervous and groggy, to toss and turn some more. Several times she had been tempted to give in and get a prescription for sleeping pills. Each time she remembered her promise never to tranquilize herself against pressure, personal or professional.

She thought of Matt, of the self-disgust and apology in his voice as he'd told her something she had no business knowing.

She thought of Quinn, firm and unyielding but offering Matt the chance to explain for himself.

Oddly enough, she thought of her brother and an argument they'd had when she'd been a teenager. Trace had threatened to knock some boy's block off if he got too familiar with her. Chantel remembered being furious at him for interfering and telling everyone she could handle things.

Why wasn't she in control now?

She always had been. Even Trace had known then she hadn't needed him to stand up for her. Perhaps because she'd been one of three in the womb, she'd been born ready to handle her own problems. She'd faced tragedy, personal loss and disillusionment but had always managed to fight her way back. She wasn't fighting now, and she should be. It had never been necessary for her to look to a man for protection, and yet . . .

Then she thought of Quinn again and his promise to protect her. She wanted to believe him. When he was there, right beside her, she did.

But it was the middle of the night, and her brain was hazy. She only wanted to sleep. The sheets twisted around her as she turned again and finally drifted off.

When the phone rang, she groped for it. Half dreaming, she thought it was her mother calling to scold her for being late for rehearsal. "Yes," she mumbled into the receiver. "Yes, I'm coming."

"I can't sleep. I can't sleep for thinking of you."

The whisper had a low, desperate edge to it that shocked Chantel fully awake.

"You have to stop this."

"But I can't. I've tried, but I can't. Don't you know what you do to me? Every time I see you, every time I'm near you, I—"

"No!" she shouted into the phone. Then, to her disgust, she began to weep. "Please leave me alone. Please. I don't want to hear any more."

But she could hear him as she turned her face into the pillow. She could hear him still as she fumbled to hang up the phone. Even when she had the receiver cradled, she could hear his voice echoing in her head. Chantel curled into a ball and let the tears come.

* * *

Quinn was staring out his window when the phone rang. Cursing, he dashed across the room, hoping to get to it before it awakened Chantel. But the whispering had already started. For a moment he thought he recognized something—a speech pattern, accent, or turn of phrase. He tried to focus on it, block out the words themselves and Chantel's terror. Then his mouth tightened to a grim line as he heard Chantel plead, then begin to cry. He heard her hang up, then heard a man sobbing before the connection was broken.

After slamming down the receiver, Quinn plunged his hands into his pockets, his fingers balling into fists. He'd lost something, maybe something vital because his concentration and his objectivity had been broken when she'd begun to cry.

The woman was making him soft. He couldn't allow it. Wouldn't allow it. He had to leave her alone. She'd *want* to be alone, he told himself. She wouldn't like to have him see her now that she'd lost control. A woman like Chantel would shed her tears in private. Even if she looked for consolation, the last person she'd want it from was him. Struggling against an overpowering sense of rage and helplessness, he stalked back to the window.

She'd sounded so frightened.

He couldn't leave her alone now. Not now, he thought as he pounded his clenched hand lightly against the windowsill. She might want to be alone, but she needed to be with him. He only hoped he could figure out what to do once he was with her.

There were a few slashes of moonlight coming through her windows. They turned everything to silver. He came in quietly, hoping she'd fallen asleep again and that he could just check on her, maybe sit with her awhile without her being aware of it. If she knew how badly he wanted to be with her, protect her—damn it, cherish her—wouldn't that give her all the more reason to push him aside?

He'd never had to use caution with a woman before. Because, he was forced to admit, no woman had really mattered until her. And she mattered too much.

She wasn't asleep. Quinn could hear her muffled weeping as he crossed to the bed. He stopped where he was, terrified by the small, helpless sound. He knew how a grenade sounded when it exploded in the dirt and sent shrapnel hurtling through the air. He'd heard the horrific noise of gunfire and the unspeakable sound of a bullet striking flesh. Those were things he'd faced with more confidence than he faced Chantel's quiet sobbing now.

If she had been angry, he could have played on it. If she had merely been frightened, he could have insulted her out of it. But she was weeping.

Soundlessly he went to the side of the bed and crouched down. Wishing he knew the right words but knowing he didn't, he laid a hand on her hair. At his touch she sprang up, screaming.

"It's me. It's only me." He took both her hands and squeezed. "Relax. No one's going to hurt you."

"Quinn." Her hand went limp in his, then tensed again as she fought for control. "You startled me."

"Sorry." The moonlight was strong enough that he could see her face, and the tears damp on her cheeks. "You okay?"

"Yes." Her chest was hurtfully tight, her throat raw from unshed tears. "Yes, I'm fine. I guess you heard the phone."

"I heard it." He dropped her hands because he was afraid he'd break her fingers. "Why don't I get you something? Water." He stuck his hands in his pockets again. "Something."

"No. I don't need anything." She brought the heels of her

hands over her face to dry her tears. "I couldn't keep him talking. I just couldn't do it."

"It's all right."

"No, it's not." Bringing her knees up, she dropped her head on them. "It's my problem, and as long as I keep running from it, it's not going away. Everything you've said so far has been true, everything you've done has been right, and I haven't been holding up my end."

"Nobody's blaming you, Chantel." He started to reach out for her again, to touch her creamy shoulders, which were slumped in despair. Catching himself, Quinn clenched his hand. "You should try to get some sleep."

"Yeah."

He strained against his own helplessness. Where had he gotten the stupid idea that she needed him? He didn't know the way to comfort and soothe. He didn't have the pretty words that would relax her and help her sleep again. He had nothing but a rage boiling inside him and a fierce desire to keep her safe. Neither of those would help her now.

"Look, I can get you something. Go downstairs and make, I don't know, some tea."

With her face still pressed against her knees, she squeezed her eyes tight. "No, thanks. I'll be fine."

"Damn it, I want to do something." The explosion ripped out of him before he could stop it. "I can't stand seeing you like this. Let me get you some aspirin or sit in the chair until you can get to sleep. Something. You can't ask me to just leave you alone."

"Hold me." The words came out in a sob as she lifted her head. "Could you just hold me a minute?"

He sat beside her and, gathering her close, pressed her head to his shoulder. "Sure. As long as you want. Go ahead and let go, angel."

She didn't have the strength to stop it, and she no longer wanted to. With his arms strong around her, she let the full force of the tears come. Quinn cradled her close and murmured things he hoped would help, things he wasn't even certain she heard. When she began to quiet, he stroked the hair back from her face and said nothing at all.

"Quinn?"

"Hmmm?"

"Thanks."

"Any time."

"I don't make a habit of it." She sniffled. "Got a handkerchief?"

"No."

Reluctant to shift away even slightly, she reached for a tissue on her bedside table. "I guess I figured a man like you would head for the hills when a woman started"—she sniffled again—"blubbering."

"This is different."

She tilted her head back. Her eyes were swollen, her cheeks tear streaked. "Why?"

"It's just different." He brushed a tear from her lashes. Then, though he felt foolish, he let the moisture linger on his thumb. "Feel better?"

"Yes." She did, unaccountably, for she'd never believed tears solved anything. Now that they were shed she felt drained and embarrassed. "I'd, ah . . . appreciate it if we both forgot about this lapse in the morning."

"Never give yourself an inch, do you?"

"I hate to cry."

She said it with such bitter finality that he knew she'd shed hot tears over something before. Or someone. "Me, too."

That made her smile. "You're a nice guy when you put a little effort into it."

"I try not to let it happen often." He stroked her hair again before he shifted her closer. It hadn't been so hard to comfort, he discovered. It wasn't so hard to be needed. "Think you can sleep now?"

"I guess." She closed her eyes, discovering it felt enormously good to let her cheek rest against his.

He ran a comforting hand over her back, then tensed when he felt silk give way to flesh. "Tomorrow's Sunday. You can stay in bed all day."

"I have a photo session at one." With her eyes still closed, she explored the muscles of his shoulders with her fingertips.

"You can cancel it."

"I'll be okay. The photographer's accommodating me because of the shooting schedule."

"Then you'd better get some rest or you'll look like hell."

"Thanks a lot."

"You're welcome."

When he drew her back, she tilted her head up and smiled at him. His fingers tensed on her shoulders, and hers on his, and her smile faded. The need vibrated between them so urgently that it set the air humming.

"I'd better go."

"No." The decision had already been made, she knew, perhaps before they'd even met. Her heart had just accepted it. She loved. There was no changing it. Until now, until him, she hadn't known how much she needed to have the chance to love again. "I want you to stay," She slid her hands over his shoulders. "I want you to make love with me."

The ache that had begun to throb just from looking at her turned sharp and stabbing—a painfully sweet sensation. Her hands felt so cool on his skin. Her eyes looked so warm and dark. The moonlight dappled over her like a dream, but he couldn't afford to forget reality.

"Chantel, I want you so much right now I can hardly breathe. But . . ." He slid his hands up to her wrists. "I don't know if I could live with the fact that this happened between us because you were scared and shaky."

A smile curved her lips as she brought them closer to his. "Haven't you figured out yet that I know what I want?" She turned her head slightly so that her kiss brushed his chin.

"Didn't you say that a man could tell just by the way a woman looked at him? Can't you see the way I'm looking at you?"

"Maybe I only see the way I want you to look." But his fingers had tangled in her hair.

"I want you to stay," she repeated, "not because I'm scared. I want you to stay because of the way you make me feel when you kiss me. When you hold me. When you touch me." She rubbed her cheek against his. "I want you to stay because you can make me forget there's anything outside of this room."

Something snapped inside him. Some would call it control. With an oath, he dragged his hands through her hair and plundered her mouth.

She was everything dark and desperate and desirable. She was pure aphrodisiac. As they knelt on the bed, he let his dreams spring to life and rained kisses over her face, her hair, her throat. The scent that was so much a part of her misted through his brain like a fog. And she trembled. Not on cue but from pleasure, from the pleasure he gave her. Half-mad, he crushed his lips to hers again and tasted her passion.

Never before and, she was certain, never again, would a man bring her to life this way. Never before and never again would she want like this. Her body was like a furnace, pumping heat and energy while her mind was flooded with a brilliant kaleidoscope of sensation. No, never again would a man bring her this, because there was only one man. She'd known it, somehow, from the first.

Everything was so clear. She felt the scrape of his chin over her shoulder, felt the mattress sink under their combined weights as they knelt torso to torso. She could see the moonlight against his skin as she ran her hands over his shoulders and down. His muscles contracted at her touch, and she heard the soft hiss of his indrawn breath. Desperation flavored his kisses and fueled her own need. A kaleidoscope, a whirlwind, a race. The scents from her garden crept into the room. With a gurgle of delight, she lowered her lips to his shoulder and nipped.

A man could lose his mind and his soul to her. Quinn felt his chest constrict as he ran his hands freely over her. Pain and power . . . they were both twined together in his need for her. She made him hurt and made him soar just by being in his arms.

It wasn't just the perfection of form, of face, but the wild, wanton sexuality she had encased in glittering ice. Released, it was a Pandora's box of emotions, some dark, some dangerous, some desperately exciting.

He wouldn't resist her. He couldn't. He could feel her tremble, hear her moan as he touched and tasted and tempted. Her skin was hot, already damp. Her breath caught on his name. Tonight, even if it was just for tonight, he would make her as frenzied as he.

He gathered her hair in his hand, drawing her head back to expose the long white line of her throat. Her pulse beat frantically as he traced his tongue over it. Her hands moved over his chest, then lower, and his stomach muscles quivered at her touch. As she tugged at the snap on his jeans, he found her breast through the thin silk she wore. When he drew both silk and flesh into his mouth, she strained against him, shuddering. Her throat filled with indistinct murmurs of pleasure, she tugged the denim over his hips.

The feel of her hands on him drove every rational thought from his mind. In one crazed movement he ripped the silk from her, rending it down the middle. Her gasp was muffled against his mouth as he dragged her down beneath him.

He couldn't think. He could only feel. When he plunged into her, she was so warm, so moist. He wondered if a man could die from being given his ultimate wish. Then she was wrapped around him, driving him even as he sought to drive her. He could see her, her hair spread out on tumbled white sheets, her eyes half-closed, her lips slightly parted as the breath trembled out.

"Quinn." His name whispered from her as she was tossed by titanic waves of sensation. Heat, light, wind. Nothing had prepared her for this. She tried to tell him, but his lips were on hers again. She was a part of him. Release came in a torrent that left her too stunned for speech.

*   *   *

She didn't know what to say. Would he expect some clever phrase, some easy words? It wasn't possible to explain that she had given herself to only one other man and never, truly never, like this. If it hadn't mattered so much—if he hadn't mattered so much—she was sure she could have come up with something to break the long silence and the tension she felt building again.

He didn't know what to say. He'd taken her like a madman. She deserved better, more care, certainly more finesse. If only he hadn't lost control. But he had, Quinn reminded himself ruthlessly. He couldn't change that any more than he could change the fact that he'd damaged whatever might have been growing between them. He could only hope it wasn't too late to repair it.

Both of them tensed, then turned, then spoke each other's names at the same time. The awkwardness lasted only a moment before they grinned.

"I was thinking you were right," she began, "about me needing a script. I can't think of what I want to say."

"I've been having some trouble with that myself." He took her hand and brought it to his lips. "I guess I was a little rough."

"Were you?" Amused and relieved, Chantel groped for the remains of her silk teddy. Lifting a brow, she dropped it on his chest.

Quinn rubbed the material between his thumb and forefinger. "You could deduct it from my check."

"I intend to. Three hundred and fifty."

"Three hundred and fifty?" He rose on one elbow and examined the ripped silk more carefully. "You've got to be crazy to spend three-fifty on something you sleep in."

"I enjoy indulging myself." To prove her point, she leaned over and nibbled on his lips. "And under the circumstances, I think it only fair that I deduct half the price."

"Half?"

"It was a joint effort." She smiled and ran a fingertip over his chest. "Besides, it was worth it."

"Was it?" His hand came up her leg to rest on her hip. "You sure?"

"Well, I'm a cautious woman, and you know what they say in the business."

"No." Her hair teased his shoulders as she leaned over him. "What do they say in the business?"

"Take two," Chantel sighed, lowering herself to him.

CHAPTER 8

"Quinn, I promise you, this is going to take a good three hours, maybe four." Chantel got out of the car, then leaned over to take her garment bag from the hook by the passenger door.

He noticed how nicely the slim skirt fit over her bottom. "I can be patient."

"A photo session is often very tedious for the people involved, much less for someone who just has to sit there."

"Let me worry about that," he advised, and took the bag from her.

"I have to worry about it. Knowing you're hanging around, grumbling under your breath, is going to make me tense." Chantel pressed a buzzer on the outside door, then tipped down her sunglasses to peer over them. "And tension will show in the pictures. This layout for the *Scene* is very important."

He pushed the glasses back up on her nose. "So are you."

It warmed her. She no longer knew how to pretend it didn't. Chantel rose on her toes to brush a kiss over his lips. "I appreciate that. But I'll be perfectly safe. Margo will be there to do my hair, and the makeup artist is a freelancer I've worked with before. Mrs. Alice Cooke. They have to stay for the whole session. I'll be surrounded by well-meaning women."

"And the photographer," he reminded her. "I'm not letting you alone with this Bryan Mitchell or any other man."

Chantel started to correct him, then thought better of it. A woman was entitled to take every advantage offered. She ran a finger over the collar of his shirt. "Jealous?"

"Cautious."

"Bryan Mitchell." The voice coming through the intercom was low, smooth and feminine.

"It's Chantel O'Hurley for the one o'clock session."

"Right on time."

There was a mechanical buzz from inside the door, and then it unlatched.

"Bryan Mitchell is a tall, gorgeous blonde," Chantel began as they climbed the inside stairs. "We've been friends for years."

Quinn wrapped his fingers around hers. "All the more reason I'm not leaving you alone with him. Until this thing is settled, the only man you're having solitary dealings with is me."

"Well." Chantel paused at the studio door and wrapped her arms around him. "I like that," she murmured, and met his lips with hers.

"I bet you do." Bryan stood in the open doorway, grinning.

"Quinn Doran." Chantel laid a hand lightly on his arm. "Bryan Mitchell."

The photographer was indeed tall, blond and gorgeous. She was also a woman. Quinn shot Chantel a look as she smiled. "Nice meeting you."

Bryan offered him a hand, already wondering if she could convince him to sit for her. "Welcome to chaos," she told them as she gestured them inside. "I'm still setting up. Chantel, you know where the cold drinks are. Hairdressing and makeup are in the back room having an argument about fashion. Personally, I can't get emotionally involved over whether henna is back to stay." As she spoke, she walked over to a set of white umbrellas and adjusted them.

Chantel walked to a cramped little room off the side of the studio and poked in the refrigerator. "Quinn, it's going to be like this for hours. There must be something else you want to do."

He could hear the other two women chattering in the back room. Something about facial packs and eye tucks. "I can think of a couple dozen."

"Then go do them." Chantel set down the bottle of soda to take both of his hands. "Bryan had the security system installed a few months ago when there was a rash of robberies in the neighborhood. No one gets through the outside door unless she releases the lock. I'm surrounded by women who'll be fussing over me for hours, and you'll distract all of us. Go play some handball or something."

She was right. She'd be safe here, and he'd be in the way—as well as unmercifully bored. Then, too, it would help him to have a couple of hours away from her, a couple of hours of pure physical exertion. Would he work her out of his system?

"Gym's a couple of blocks down," he muttered.

"Jim who?"

"*The* gym," he corrected, putting his hands on her hips.

"You mean one of those places with weights and nasty machines that make you grunt and sweat?"

"More or less." Taking out his notebook, he wrote down a name and number. "Call me when you're finished, and I'll come back and pick you up."

"Rizzo's." She kept her face bland as she looked up at him. "Sounds serious."

"Just call." He leaned down to bite her lightly on the bottom lip. "Why don't you go make yourself beautiful?"

She kept her arms around him as she lifted a brow. "Aren't I already?"

He knew she hadn't so much as picked up a tube of mascara that morning. Her eyes were blue and brilliant, her skin luminous and pale. Fresh and dewy, as it was now, her beauty was heartbreaking. He lifted a hand to skim it over her cheek. "Such a hag."

Before she could retaliate he had her close, cutting off her breath in a kiss that seemed to last for hours. He needed to lift weights, Quinn thought. He had to sweat some of the need for her out of his system.

"Try to do something about that face, will you?"

"Take a walk, Doran."

He grinned at her, then slipped back into the studio. Chantel let out a shaky breath and leaned her palms against the cluttered counter beside the refrigerator. There was nothing she could do, and she was nearly ready to admit there was nothing she wanted to do, about the fact that she was in love with him. It was probably a mistake, a desperate one, but it had already been made.

Somehow, if she could somehow draw back a part of herself, she wouldn't be so devastated when he went his own way. And he would, wouldn't he? A man like Quinn lived alone, worked alone, walked alone. When his job was over, he'd kiss her goodbye and go. She caught her bottom lip between her teeth and straightened. No, he wouldn't. Not if she had anything to do with it.

You're going to lose this match, Doran, she promised herself. No way was he going to walk away and leave her.

"Chantel, they're ready for you."

She was ready, too. Chantel left the drink on the counter. She was more than ready.

For two hours she worked nonstop. Her hair was frizzed, smoothed, sprayed and gelled. Her face was painted and powdered. Every time she changed her outfit her hair and face were subtly altered to enhance the look. Bryan worked with a slow, steady enthusiasm, as she always did.

"I haven't asked you how Shade is."

"Put your right hand on your left shoulder," Bryan instructed. "Spread your fingers. Good. Shade's terrific. He's home changing diapers." She caught Chantel's quick, mischievous grin on film.

"That I'd like to see."

"He's great at it. Organized, you know."

"Well, I can tell you, you don't look as though you had a baby two months ago."

"Who has time to eat? Tilt your chin up and try for aloof. That's it." She crouched, shifting angles. "Andrew Colby is a ten-pound slave driver."

"And you're crazy about him."

Bryan lowered her camera and beamed. "He's the most fantastic baby. Between Shade and me, we've taken at least five hundred rolls of film. Every day there's some little change." She tossed her long blond braid behind her back. "You can see how bright he is just by the way he looks at things. Just yesterday he—" She cut herself off with a laugh. "Stop me. It's an obsession."

"No." Chantel smiled, though the quick pang of envy she felt surprised her. "It's lovely."

"It is, you know. I never saw myself as a mother." She lifted the camera back into place. "Now I can't imagine life without Andrew. Or Shade."

"The right man can change your outlook, I guess."

Bryan decided the wistful expression that flitted across Chantel's face would be the best shot yet. "You sure make my work easier."

Bringing herself back, Chantel looked at the camera. "How's that?"

"Turn to the side and look over your shoulder. A bit more. Smolder a little." She pressed the shutter four times in rapid succession. "A face like yours is always a pleasure to shoot, especially when you bring so much to it. But I didn't expect the bonus."

"What bonus?" Chantel asked as she shifted to look over her other shoulder.

"There's nothing more terrific than photographing a woman in love. Close your mouth," she ordered, then lowered her camera to stretch her shoulders.

Slowly Chantel turned to face Bryan again. "It's that obvious?"

"Don't you want it to be?"

"No . . . yes. I don't know." She pushed a hand through her carefully groomed hair. "I don't want to make a fool of myself."

"That kind of goes hand in hand with falling in love, but I think you'll survive it. He's got a great face. I don't suppose you could talk him into sitting for me."

"Maybe if you bound him hand and foot. Bryan, how did you handle Shade?"

Bryan took a chocolate bar out of her back pocket. "*You're* asking *me* for advice on men?"

Chantel accepted a sliver of the chocolate. "Don't let it get around."

"Have you felt like murdering him yet?"

"Several times."

"You're making progress. The best thing I can tell you is to let things happen. We're wrapped here." She bit into the candy. "If I were you, I wouldn't waste what's left of the weekend."

* * *

The gym smelt like men. Damp, athletic men. The air was filled with sweat and swearing. Most of the patrons had stripped down to shorts, and a few had added T-shirts. On a mat, a man with weights on his legs grunted his way through a series of sit-ups. On a bench press, another man swore repetitively every time he extended the bar over his head. The equipment was top-notch, but it had long since lost its shine.

Chantel strolled in and absorbed, both brows lifted. The first one who saw her was a young man pulling weights up the walls with two ropes. He was working steadily, the veins in his neck bulging out as he rotated his arms. His mouth dropped open and the ropes snapped back against the wall. Chantel smiled at him.

Careful to keep her skirts clear, she circled around the bench press. The man stopped swearing as his eyes bugged out. It took less than ten seconds for the noisy, steamy gym to drop into silence. Then she saw Quinn.

He hadn't noticed the sudden quiet. With his back to the room, he was systematically jabbing at a punching bag. Its buffeting noise was the only sound in the room. He looked magnificent, legs spread, eyes intense, his powerful back tensed as he concentrated on his timing. The small brown bag was a blur as his fists never let it rest. Chantel walked over to him, waited a moment, then ran a fingertip down his back.

"Hello, darling."

He swore and spun, his hand still fisted and lifted. Chantel raised a brow, then her chin, as if inviting him to take his best shot.

"What the hell are you doing here?"

"Watching you." She took a finger and pushed at the bag. "Tell me, what's the purpose of beating at this little thing?"

"I told you to call me." He swiped sweat out of his eyes in order to glare at her better.

"I felt like a walk. Besides, I wanted to see where a man like you . . . played." Deliberately she looked over her shoulder and scanned the room. "Fascinating."

Every man in the room sucked in his stomach.

With an oath, Quinn took her by the arm. "You must be crazy. You don't belong in a place like this."

"Why ever not?" As they passed the man on the bench press, Chantel sent him a brilliant smile. The weights clattered against the safety bar.

"Cut that out," he muttered. "Rizzo, I'm using your office."

"Oh, where is he?" As he dragged her out, Chantel glanced back. "I'm dying to meet him."

"Shut up. Do you have to walk in here with legs like that?"

"They're all I have to walk on."

"Sit." He shoved her into a torn plastic chair. "What the hell am I supposed to do with you?"

"Would you like a multiple choice?"

"This isn't a joke, damn it." He pushed at the clutter on

Rizzo's desk until he found a crumpled pack of Camels. "Look, Chantel, we made an arrangement. You were supposed to call. There are reasons." He shook out a cigarette and lit it.

"Quinn, it's a beautiful afternoon and it wasn't far. There isn't much opportunity to stroll in L.A., and I couldn't resist. If you're going to tell me I can't walk two blocks on a public street in broad daylight, I'll scream." She glanced toward the door. "I can't imagine what your, ah, associates would make of that."

He exhaled a long stream of smoke, then crushed the cigarette into a mess of brown tobacco and white paper. "You go nowhere without me. You had instructions, Chantel, and I trusted you to follow them."

"Oh, lighten up." She rose and put her palms on his bare chest.

"I'm sweating like a pig," he muttered, taking her wrists.

"I noticed. I don't know what it is that attracts men to a place that smells like old athletic socks, but if this is how you keep in shape"—she glanced down approvingly—"I might just have to install a gym at home."

"Don't change the subject."

"What subject was that?"

"I don't want anything to happen to you."

She touched her tongue to her upper lip and edged closer. "Why? You've already been paid for this week."

"I don't care about the damn money," he said with violence.

"What do you care about, Quinn?"

"You." He said it between his teeth before he spun away. He'd thought he needed space, just some space and time to get his equilibrium back. There wasn't that much space in the whole world. "Don't pull anything like this again."

"All right. I'm sorry."

"I've got to shower. Stay in here."

When the door slammed at his back, Chantel sat again. He cared. She closed her eyes and hugged the knowledge to her.

He cared about her. If she'd gotten him to say it, the next step was getting him to like it.

* * *

"How long are you going to be angry?"

They were driving home with the top down. Chantel had let the first fifteen minutes pass in silence.

"I'm not angry."

"You're clenching your teeth."

"Consider yourself lucky that's all I'm doing."

"Quinn, I've already said I was sorry. I'm not going to apologize again."

"No one's asking you to." He downshifted around a curve. "What I am asking is that you take the situation you're in seriously."

"You don't think I am?"

"Not after that little stunt of yours this afternoon."

She shifted in her seat. The wind picked up her hair and tossed it as her temper snapped. "Stop treating me like a child. I understand the situation I'm in perfectly. I live with it twenty-four hours a day, every day, every night. Every time the phone rings, every time I go through my mail. When I go to sleep at night, that's what I'm thinking of. When I wake up in the morning, that's what I'm thinking of. If I can't have an hour now and then when I can push it aside, I'll go crazy. I'm trying to survive, Doran. Don't talk to me as though I'm irresponsible."

She shifted away again, and again silence reigned. He was right, Quinn told himself as he slacked his speed. But so was she. There were times, because she put up such a good front, when he believed she'd forgotten she was in any danger. She never forgot, he realized. She just refused to buckle—except in her private moments. He didn't know how to tell her he loved her for that above everything else.

Loved her. That was a tough one to swallow, but then the truth often was. The more his feelings for her grew, the more he worried about her well-being. He knew she worked hard, and for long hours. With the kind of strain she was under, she could only keep up that pace for a limited time. Even a woman as strong willed as Chantel would lose eventually.

Damn it, he wished he had something, anything, to go on. They were moving into their third week, and he was no closer to putting things right than he had been on the first day. He needed to see her safe, secure, content. Even though he was afraid that once she was she'd write him a check and kiss him off.

Quinn's hands tightened on the wheel, then gradually relaxed. She was going to have a fight on her hands when it came to that.

Relax, he told himself. She wasn't going to get away. Moving only his eyes, he took in the stiff, angry way she sat. Angel, he told her silently, I'm just the man to clip your wings.

Quinn tossed his arm casually over the back of the seat. "You're pouting."

"Go to hell."

"You're going to get lines all over your face if you keep that up. Then where will you be?"

"Kiss my—"

"Love to." He pulled over to the side of the road. She didn't even have the chance to snarl at him before he gathered her close. "Why don't I start with that homely face of yours and work my way down?"

"No."

"Okay, if you'd rather I take it from the bottom up."

When he started to shift her, she began to struggle in earnest. "Stop it. I don't want you to kiss me anywhere."

"Are you sure?" He brought her wrist to his lips and brushed them over the inside. "How about there?"

"No."

"Here, then." He pressed his mouth to the side of her throat. She stopped struggling.

"No."

"Well, other options are a little risky on the side of the road, but if you insist—"

"Stop." The laughter bubbled up as she shoved him away. Chantel leaned against the door and crossed her arms. "You creep."

"I love it when you insult me."

"Then you're going to love this," she began, but he was too quick. Whatever she'd had in mind was muffled against his mouth. Response came instantly, from the heart. Her arms went around him and her lips parted. For a moment there was nothing but the warm late-afternoon sun and sheer, unbridled pleasure.

Her eyes stayed closed, seconds after he'd drawn his lips from hers. When they opened, slowly, the irises were dark and clouded. "Are you trying to make up?" she murmured.

"For what?"

Her lips curved as she framed his face with her hands. "Never mind. Let's go home, Quinn."

He touched his lips to hers again, lingering, before he sat back and started the engine. "By the way, Rizzo wanted to know if he could have an autographed picture for his office."

Chantel laughed, then sat back to enjoy the rest of the drive. As they rode by the high wall surrounding her grounds, she began to toy with the idea of a long dip in the pool. Bryan was right. It would be a pity to waste what was left of the weekend. Even as she turned to ask Quinn to join her, he was bringing the car to a fast stop.

"Quinn, we really should wait until we're *inside*."

"There's a car in front of the gates." His tone had her tensing as she looked around. "A man's there, see? Looks like he's causing quite a bit of commotion."

"You don't think that—" She moistened her lips. "He wouldn't come right to the front gate."

"Why don't we find out?" He took the keys from the ignition and unlocked the glove compartment. Chantel watched as he drew out a revolver. It was nothing like her dainty little 22. And she was just as certain it wasn't unloaded.

"Quinn."

"Stay here."

"No, I—"

"Don't argue."

"But I don't want you to . . ." As the argument at the gate heated up, the voices drifted to her. Listening intently, Chantel tightened her grip on Quinn. "I don't believe it." she murmured. She squinted, trying to make out the figure in the distance. "I just don't believe it," she repeated, and sprang out of the car before Quinn could stop her.

"Chantel!"

"It's Pop." Laughing, she spun back to Quinn. "It's Pop. My father." Her long legs flashed as she sped up the rest of the road. "Pop!" Still laughing, she threw her arms wide.

Frank O'Hurley turned from his spirited argument with the guard. His thin face erupted into a grin. "There's my girl." Spry and wiry, he pumped down the remaining distance and caught Chantel close. With a whoop, he spun her in three dizzying circles. "How's my little princess?"

"Surprised." She kissed his baby-smooth face, then hugged him again. He smelled, as he always did, of powder and peppermint. "I didn't know you were coming."

"Don't need an invitation, do I?"

"Don't be silly."

"Well, tell that to the joker on the other side of the gate. The idiot wouldn't let me in even when I told him I was your own flesh and blood."

"I'm sorry, Miss O'Hurley." The stiff-faced man behind the gate speared Frank with a look. The crazy old man had threatened to pull out his tongue and wrap it around his neck. "There was no one here to verify."

"That's all right."

"All right?" Frank piped up. He was primed and ready for

a donnybrook. "All right when your own father's treated like a trespasser?"

"Don't be cranky." Chantel brushed at his lapels. "I've added to the security, that's all."

"Why?" Immediately alert, he cupped Chantel's chin. "What's wrong?"

"It's nothing. We'll get into all that later. Now I'm just glad to see you." She glanced back at the dusty rental car. "Where's Mom?"

"Said she wasn't fit to see anyone until she'd been to the beauty parlor. I wasn't going to sit around cooling my heels while she's getting primped up. She'll be taking a cab out later."

"But tell me what you're doing here, how long you can stay. What—"

"God be praised, girl, can't it wait until a man's washed the dust out of his throat? Drove clear from Vegas today."

"Vegas? I didn't know you had a gig in Vegas."

"You don't know everything." He tweaked her nose, then looked over her shoulder as Quinn pulled up. "Now who might this be?"

"That's Quinn." She shot him a quick look. "Quinn Doran. You're right, Pop, we can talk better inside—especially after you've had a glass of the Irish."

"Now you're talking." Frank hopped back in his car, then sailed through the now-open gates. Chantel saw him look down his nose at the guard.

"Your father?" Quinn asked when she climbed back in the car.

"Yes, I wasn't expecting him, but that's nothing new." Her fingers twisted together. "You put the gun away?"

He lifted a hand to the guard as he drove through. "Don't worry."

"But I am. I didn't want to bring my family into all this." Chantel pressed the bridge of her nose between her thumb and forefinger. "I'm going to have to tell them something. He's seen the guard at the gates. He's bound to notice the men patrolling the grounds."

"Why don't you try the truth?"

"I don't want to worry my parents. Damn, I only get to see them three or four times a year, and now this." She looked at Quinn as he slowed at the end of the drive. "And I have to explain you."

"The truth," he repeated.

"All right. I can't think of anything else." She put a hand on his arm before he could climb out. "But I'll do it my way. I want to play it down as much as possible."

"Well now." Beaming and affable, Frank strolled over to the car. "Looks like you've got yourself a fine strong fellow here, Chantel."

"Quinn Doran, my father, Frank O'Hurley."

"Pleased to meet you." Frank offered a hand and pumped Quinn's exuberantly. "Wouldn't mind helping me in with the bags, would you, son?"

Chantel had to smile when Frank popped open his trunk and took out a small shoulder bag, leaving two large cases for Quinn. "You never change," she murmured, hooking an arm through his to lead him into the house.

"Just leave them there," she told Quinn, gesturing to the base of the staircase. "You can take them up later."

"Thanks."

She met his sarcasm with an easy smile. "Why don't you two go into the living room and have a drink? I want to tell the cook there'll be two more for dinner." Leaving Quinn with a brief warning look, she started down the hall.

"Well, son, I don't know about you," Frank said, giving Quinn a solid slap on the back, "but I could use a drink." He trotted off into the living room and headed directly to the bar. "What's your pleasure?"

"Scotch."

Frank shrugged his narrow shoulders, then poured. "To each his own." Locating the bottle of whiskey, he gave a satisfied grunt and poured a generous three fingers. "Well, now . . . Quinn, is it? Why don't we drink to my girl?" He tapped his glass solidly against Quinn's without regard for the pricey Rosenthal crystal, then swallowed deeply. "Now that's a drink a man can wrap his heart around. Have a seat, son, have a seat." Still playing the congenial host, he gestured to a chair before finding one for himself. "Now . . ." He settled back and sighed. Then, abruptly, his eyes were shrewd and sharp. "Just what are you doing with my daughter?"

"Pop." Grateful for her timing, Chantel strolled into the room, then sat on the arm of her father's chair. "You'll have to excuse him, Quinn. He's never been subtle."

Quinn regarded his Scotch for a moment. "Seems like a reasonable question to me."

"There." Satisfied with what he saw, Frank nodded. "We're going to get along just fine."

"I wouldn't be surprised," she murmured, ruffling her father's hair. "So tell me how it went in Vegas."

"Be glad to." He sipped his whiskey again, appreciating its smooth heat. "Just as soon as you explain why you have a trained gorilla at your front gate."

"I told you, I added some security." But when she started to rise, Frank put a firm hand on her knee.

"You wouldn't try to con an old hand like me, would you, princess?"

It would be useless, she admitted, and settled back. "I've been getting some annoying phone calls, that's all. It seemed wise to take a few precautions."

"What kind of phone calls?"

"Just nuisance calls."

"Chantel." He knew his daughter too well. A few nuisance calls would have been brushed off, laughed off and forgotten. "Is someone threatening you?"

"No. No, it's nothing like that." Realizing she was being backed into a corner, she shot a pleading look at Quinn.

"I still opt for the truth," he said simply.

"Thanks for the help."

"Just be quiet," Frank told her, and there was such uncharacteristic authority in his tone that she closed her mouth instantly. "You tell me what's going on," he ordered Quinn. "And what you have to do with it."

"Quinn—"

"Chantel Margaret Louise O'Hurley, shut your mouth and keep it shut."

When she did, Quinn could only smile. "Nice trick," he said to Frank.

"I use it selectively to keep it fresh." Frank swallowed the rest of his whiskey. "Let's hear it."

Briefly, concisely, Quinn outlined what Chantel was dealing with. As he spoke, Frank's brows lowered, his thin face reddened and the hand still resting on Chantel's knee clenched.

"Slimy bastard." Frank rose out of the chair like a terrier ready to charge. "If you're a detective, Quinn Doran, why in hell haven't you found him?"

"Because he hasn't made a mistake." Quinn set down his glass and met Frank's outraged glare levelly. "But he will, and I'll find him."

"If he hurts my girl—"

"He's not going to get near her," Quinn interrupted flatly. "Because he has to go through me first."

Frank swallowed his fury—it was something he didn't often bother to do—and measured the man in front of him. He'd always prided himself on being a good judge of character. You needed to know whether to raise your fists or laugh and back off. The man in front of him was hard as a rock and mean as they came. If Frank had to trust his daughter to someone, this was the one.

"So. You're staying here, in the house, with Chantel."

"That's right. I'm going to take care of her, Mr. O'Hurley. You have my word on that."

Frank hesitated only a moment before his teeth showed in a smile. "If you don't, I'll skin you alive. And make it Frank."

Cool and regal, Chantel rose. "Perhaps I could say a word now."

"Don't put that face on with me, girl." Frank crossed to her, then gently framed her face in his hands. "You should have come to your family with this."

"There was no point in worrying you."

"Point?" Frank shook his head from side to side. "We're family. We're the O'Hurleys. We stick together."

"Pop, Maddy's getting married at the end of the week. Abby's pregnant. Trace is—"

"You'll kindly leave him out of it," Frank said stiffly. "Family business has nothing to do with your brother. That's his choice."

"Really, Pop, after all this time you should—"

"And don't change the subject. Your mother and me, and your sisters, are entitled to worry about you."

It wasn't the time to go to her brother's defense. And Chantel wasn't entirely sure he'd care one way or the other. Now she wanted to smooth those lines of worry from her father's face.

"All right, then." She kissed him soundly. "Worry all you want, but everything that can be done is being done."

He kept his hand on her shoulder but turned to Quinn. "We're off to New York on Friday to see my daughter married off. You'll be going with us?"

"I didn't think it was necessary to drag Quinn to—"

"I'm going," he interrupted. His eyes met Chantel's in something like a challenge. "I've already made the arrangements."

"You never mentioned it to me."

"Why should I?" he countered for the simple pleasure of watching fury rise in her eyes.

"It hardly seems I'm necessary, does it?" Feeling squeezed from all sides, she bristled. "If you'll both excuse me, I'm going to go soak my head."

"Nasty little number, isn't she?" Frank asked with obvious pride as she stalked out.

"All that and more."

"It's the Irish, you know. We're either poets or fighters. O'Hurleys are a bit of both."

"I'm looking forward to meeting the rest of your family."

And they'll want to get a look at you, Frank said to himself. "Tell me, Quinn," he began in an amiable tone. "Do you intend to, ah, keep your eye on Chantel, so to speak, after this business is settled?"

Quinn studied the man across from him. It seemed it was still time for truths. "Yes. Whether she likes it or not."

Frank gave a quick laugh. "Let's have another drink."

CHAPTER 9

Mom, there's no reason for you to do that." Molly O'Hurley carefully folded a white silk jacket in tissue. "Why should you call a maid up here?" Years of experience had Molly packing Chantel's clothes with a minimum of fuss.

"It's her job."

Molly brushed her objections away with the back of her hand. "I never feel I can speak my mind in front of maids and butlers."

Chantel looked at the suitcase and at her stacks of clothes. She'd spent the first twenty years of her life packing and unpacking. As a matter of principle, she hadn't done so in years. But she'd never been able to win a fight with her mother. Resigned, Chantel began a careful selection of her toiletries.

"I'm sorry we haven't had much time together the past few days."

"Don't be silly." Brisk and practical, Molly rattled more tissue paper. "You're in the middle of that film. Your father and I didn't expect to be entertained."

"Pop seemed to be entertained the day you came to the set."

Chuckling, Molly glanced up. She was a pretty, trim woman who managed to look a decade younger than her years with a minimum of effort. Looking at her, Chantel acknowledged that the rush and craziness of her parents' lifestyle suited Molly just as much as it did Frank. "He did, didn't he? Still, I don't think he should have argued with the director about how to set the scene."

"Mary has a—a sense of humor."

"Good thing." For the next few moments, they packed in silence. "Chantel, we're worried about you."

"Mom, that's exactly what I don't want you to do."

"We love you. You can't expect us to love you and not be concerned."

"I know." She slipped a bottle of perfume into a padded travel box. "That's why I didn't want to tell you about what was going on. You had to worry enough about me when I was growing up."

"You don't expect a parent to turn off the juice just because a child's past the age of twenty-one?"

"No, I suppose not." She smiled and slipped her set of makeup brushes into their cases. "But it seems like you should have less to worry about after a certain age."

"I can only tell you that one day you'll find out differently yourself."

There was that pang again. Chantel's brows drew together as she tried to ignore it. "I don't know about that," she murmured. "I *do* know I don't want this business to affect the family."

"What affects one of us affects all of us. That's that." Molly said it so matter-of-factly, Chantel was forced to smile.

"Your Irish is showing."

"And why shouldn't it?" Molly wanted to know. "Your father and I think we should come back with you after the wedding."

"Back here?" Chantel stopped to stare. "You can't. You have a gig in New Hampshire."

Molly folded a pair of linen slacks by the pleats and said

with a little smile, "Chantel, your father and I have been performing for over thirty-five years. I don't think canceling one
engagement is going to make much of a ripple."

"No." Chantel set down the bottles and pots in her hands to
reach for her mother. "I can't tell you how much it means to
me to know that you would. But what could you do?"

"We could be with you."

"You could hardly even do that. Mom, I'll be filming
for weeks more. You've seen in the last few days how little
I'm home. I'd be a wreck thinking about you sitting around
here twiddling your thumbs when you'd want to be working."

"Sitting around here, as in lounging by the pool?"

Chantel's lips curved, but she shook her head. "If I could
believe you'd be content for more than forty-eight hours, it
would be different. Be logical, Mom. If you stayed, I'd be
worried because you were worried. Pop would drive the staff
crazy, and I wouldn't even be around to enjoy it."

"I told Frank you'd feel this way." With a sigh, Molly
touched Chantel's hair. "I always worried about you the most,
you know."

"I guess I gave you the most cause."

"You did what you had to. And Trace also was going to go
his own way, no matter what. Your father refused to see it, but
it was there from the time he could walk. Somehow I always
knew Abby and Maddy would be all right, even when Abby
was going through the mess of her first marriage and Maddy
was struggling to keep herself in dancing shoes. But you . . ."
Molly caressed her daughter's cheek. "I was always afraid you'd
miss what was beside you because you were always looking
so far ahead. I want you to be happy, Chantel."

"I am. No, I am, really. These past few weeks, even with
this other business hanging over my head, I've found something."

"Quinn."

Chantel made a restless movement before walking to the windows. "It's obvious to everyone but him the way I feel."

Molly had formed her own opinion of Quinn Doran. He wasn't an easy man, nor would he often be a gentle one, but her daughter didn't need an easy, gentle man. She needed one who'd give her a run for her money.

"Men are more thickheaded," Molly commented. She was a woman who knew well just how thickheaded men could be. "Why don't you tell him?"

"No." Chantel turned back, then rested the heels of her hands on the windowsill. "At least not yet. This is going to sound foolish, but I want . . . I need him to respect me. Me," she repeated. "For what I am. I need to be certain he's not just passing the time."

"Chantel, you can't use Dustin Price as a yardstick."

"I'm not." Anger crept into her voice. She managed to control it only because her mother's eyes remained so steady. "No, I'm not. But it isn't something that's easy to forget."

"No, it's impossible. But you can't live your life with that as the foundation. Have you told Quinn about him?"

"No, I can't. Mom, there are so many complications now, why bring up another? It's been nearly seven years."

"Do you trust Quinn?"

"Yes."

"Don't you think he'd understand?"

She pressed her fingers to her eyes for a moment. "If I was sure he loved me, really sure that what's between us is real, I could tell him anything. Even that."

"I wish I could tell you there were guarantees, but I can't." Molly crossed to her and gathered Chantel close. "I can tell you that I wouldn't consider leaving you, not for a minute until everything was resolved, if I wasn't sure Quinn was going to protect you."

"He makes me feel safe. Until I met him, I didn't know anyone could." She squeezed her eyes shut. "I didn't know I needed anyone who could."

"We all need to feel safe, Chantel. And loved." Molly stroked her daughter's hair, the light silver blond locks she'd brushed and braided so often in the past. "There's something I haven't told you. Something I should have told you a long time ago." She embraced Chantel. "I'm very proud of you."

"Oh, Mom." As the tears welled up, Molly shook her head.

"Now, none of that," she murmured. "If we go downstairs with puffy eyes, your father will be pinching at me to find out why we've been sitting up here crying." She kissed Chantel's cheek and held on for another moment. "Let's finish packing."

"Mom."

"Yes, dear."

"I've always been proud of you, too."

"Well." Molly cleared her throat, but her voice was still husky when she spoke. "That's quite a thing to hear from a grown daughter. You're going to be all right?"

"I'm going to be fine. I'm going to be terrific."

"That's my girl. Now let's be about our business." Turning away, Molly made herself busy. "Look at this." Clucking her tongue, she held up a brief nightgown fashioned of black silk and lace. "It looks like sin."

Chantel rubbed a knuckle under her eyes to dry them and giggled. "I can't give it an evaluation yet. I just bought it."

Molly held it up to the sunlight. "I think it speaks for itself."

"You like it." Pleased, Chantel came over, folded it carefully and handed it back to her mother. "A souvenir from Beverly Hills."

"Don't be silly." But Molly couldn't resist rubbing a thumb over the silk. "I couldn't wear a thing like this."

"Why not?"

"I'm the mother of four grown children."

"You didn't pick us from under cabbage leaves."

"Well, your father would . . ." She trailed off, speculating. Chantel watched a wicked gleam come into her eyes. "Thank you, dear." Molly set the nightgown apart from the rest of

Chantel's lingerie. "And I'll thank you from your father in advance."

* * *

By the time they went downstairs again, Frank could be heard picking his banjo.

"He's practicing," Molly said, "so he can play at the reception. They'll have to knock him unconscious to keep him from performing."

"You know Maddy wouldn't have it any other way."

"It's about time, woman." Frank looked up as his family walked in, but his fingers never stilled. "A man needs some backup, you know. This one here"—he jerked his head toward Quinn—"won't sing a note."

"Just doing you a favor," Quinn said easily as he lounged back on the sofa.

"Never heard of a body that wouldn't sing," Frank commented. "Heard plenty who couldn't, but never one who wouldn't. Sit here, Molly, my love. Let's show the man what the O'Hurleys are made of."

Obligingly Molly sat beside him, picked up the count and launched into the song with a strong, practiced voice. Chantel sat on the arm of the sofa beside Quinn and listened to the familiar sound of her parents working together. It was good; it was solid. The tension of the past weeks drained away.

"Come on, princess, you remember the chorus."

Chantel joined in, the words and rhythm of the bright novelty number coming easily. She rarely sang on her own. To Chantel, singing was a family affair. Even now, as she added her voice to her parents', she thought of Trace and her sisters and the countless times they'd all sung that same old song.

She'd surprised him. Quinn sat back, enjoying himself, as Frank merged one tune into another. Chantel wasn't the cool movie star now, nor was she the restless, passionate woman he'd discovered beneath that facade. She was at home with the nonsense songs her father played. She was a daughter, a loving one. The innocence he'd once sensed in her was apparent as she laughed and accused her father of missing a note.

Her scent was there, dark and sultry, in contrast to her relaxed, playful behavior. He'd never seen her like this. Never known she could be like this. He wondered if she realized how much her family meant to her, if she knew how her Hollywood image faded when she was with them.

It had been a good week. Chantel didn't know of the letters that had come, because he'd intercepted them. Nor did she know that they had traced one of the calls to a phone booth downtown. Quinn saw no reason to tell her or to hit her with the fact that two of the letters had begged for a meeting in New York.

He knew her plans.

Quinn lifted a hand and ran it down her arm. Chantel's fingers linked naturally with his. There was no point in telling her. She wouldn't be alone in New York, not for a moment. He'd already arranged for three of his best men to fly to Manhattan. Every step Chantel took would be monitored.

Frank interrupted Quinn's train of thought as he shot a challenging look at his daughter. "Do you still play that thing? Or do you use it as a doorstop?"

Chantel glanced at the white baby grand, then examined her nails. "I manage to hit a few keys."

"With a big, beautiful instrument like that you should be able to do a lot more."

"I don't want to show you up, Pop."

"That'll be the day."

With a shrug, she stood and moved to the piano. Deliberately she fluttered her lashes, sat, then went into a long, complicated arpeggio.

"You've been practicing," Frank accused, then cackled with delight.

Chantel shot a look at Quinn. "I don't spend my evenings darning socks."

Quinn acknowledged the hit with a slight inclination of his head. "Your daughter's full of surprises, Frank."

"No need to tell me that. The stories I could tell you. Why, there was the time—"

"Requests?" Chantel interrupted sweetly. "Unless Pop wants me to tie his tongue in a nice, neat bow."

Always cautious, Frank cleared his throat. "Why don't you do that little number your mother wouldn't let you sing until you turned eighteen?"

"Abby always did that one best."

"True enough." Frank's grin was crooked and amiable. "But you weren't half-bad." Molly managed to hide a smile as Chantel's eyes narrowed.

"Half-bad?" She wrinkled her nose at him as she gave herself a flowing introduction.

The low, torchy ballad prickled along Quinn's skin. Her voice was as smooth as the Scotch in his hand, and just as potent. The words were plaintive, vulnerable, but with her voice they became seductive. She wore white as she sat behind the glossy white piano. But he no longer thought of angels. The room grew warmer just from the sound of her voice. It seemed to weigh on him; pressing down until he was no longer sure he was even breathing.

Then she brought her gaze up from the keys to meet his.

It wasn't a song of love, but of love lost. The thought came to him then that if he lost her, there were no words written that could describe his desperation. She'd made him ache before. And she'd made him burn. Now, for the first time, she made him weak.

She played the last chords with her eyes still locked on his.

"Not half-bad," Frank repeated, pleased with her delivery. "Now if you'd—"

"It's late, Frank." Molly patted his hand, loving him for the knucklehead he was. "We should go up to bed. Tomorrow's going to be a long day."

"Late? Nonsense, it's barely—"

"Late," Molly repeated. "And getting later by the minute. I have a surprise for you upstairs."

"But I was just getting— A surprise?"

"That's right. Come along, Frank. Good night, Quinn."

"Molly." But he couldn't take his eyes off Chantel.

"All right, all right, I'm coming. Good night, you two. Chantel, see if that cook of yours can make waffles in the morning, will you?"

"Night, Pop." She tilted her cheek for his kiss, but her eyes stayed locked on Quinn's.

As he climbed the stairs with his wife, Frank could be heard demanding what his surprise was.

"You were right," Quinn murmured when the room was silent again.

"About what?"

"You are terrific." He rose and came to her. Taking both her hands, he turned them palm up and pressed his lips to the center of each one. "The more I'm with you," he murmured, "the more I know you, the more I want."

With her hands still in his, she stood. Light glowed in her eyes. "I've never in my life felt about anyone the way I feel about you. I need you to believe that."

"And I need to believe it." They were close, very close, to taking that final step. Commitments, promises, dependence. He felt himself teeter on the edge, ready, but was afraid she would pull back and away if he pressed too soon. "Tell me what you want, Chantel."

"You." She could give that answer truthfully enough without demanding more than she thought he was ready to give. "I only want to be with you."

For how long? he wanted to ask, but fear stopped him. He would take today, tonight, and fight for tomorrow. "Come to bed."

Hands linked, hearts lost, they climbed the stairs.

They left a low light burning beside the bed. Odd, she thought, that her pulse should be hammering so hard, that her nerves should be fluttering so wildly when she already knew what they could bring to each other. Why should it feel so different this time? So special. So much, she realized dimly, like the first time. The only time.

She offered her mouth, anticipating the hard demand of his.

He was gentle. He was . . . tender. As he brushed his lips lightly over hers, she felt her muscles go lax and her bones melt. He cupped her face with his hands so that his thumbs traced like whispers, like promises, over her throat. She sighed his name as she felt herself float.

What kind of passion was this that crept in so quietly? Desire was there, already thrumming, but with each caress he soothed it—and stoked it. His mouth was patient, gliding over her face as if he wanted to memorize the essence of her through touch and taste. He strung small, feathery kisses down her cheekbones, then sought her mouth. His tongue traced the outline, then lingered to stroke lazily over her bottom lip. The room began to whirl inside her head.

She was priceless. This time, he promised himself, he would show her. She had a beauty he knew now reached beneath the skin. He would cherish it. He combed his fingers through her hair, delighting in the silken feel of it. He murmured, and she sighed and pressed herself against him.

As his mouth continued to explore, he began to undo the row of buttons at her back. When the material parted, he ran his hands along her spine, gently, as a man touches fragile glass. As the silk slithered to the floor, she trembled. She was warm and naked beneath it. His heart hammered in his throat. It was as though she had waited all evening for this moment with him.

Quinn drew her away to look at her, all of her, in the lamplight. She was so small, so delicate, with skin like porcelain and a form that might have been carved from alabaster. Her hair tumbled over her shoulders, ending just before the curve of her breasts. Her rib cage was narrow. He ran his hands down it, amazed that the strength he knew she possessed came from such delicacy. Her waist tapered so that he could almost span it with his hands before flaring out gently to slender hips and long, slim thighs.

"You're so beautiful." His voice was strained as he brought his gaze back to hers. "You take my breath away."

She stepped forward into his arms.

The material of his shirt was rough against her bare skin. With her eyes half-closed, Chantel moved against him, urging his mouth to take its fill. Her tongue found his and began a silent, exotic seduction. All the while, his fingertips played over her as exquisitely as hers had played over the piano keys.

Through the window the breeze stirred, threatening rain. Chantel inhaled the fragrances of the night as they tangled with the musky scent of passion. Slowly, and with as much care as he had shown her, she undressed Quinn.

She rubbed her palms over the hard, coiled muscles of his shoulders, delighting in the feel. Temptingly she pressed her lips to his chest. There was a power and discipline in his body that urged her to touch, to tease. The ridges of muscles in his torso fascinated her. With a murmur of approval, she bought her lips back to his.

They lowered themselves onto the bed.

No hurry. No rush. The moment was drawn out, dreamlike, as they pleasured each other. Chantel shifted to look down at him. How could she tell him what he'd come to mean to her? How could she explain how much she needed him to be with her—now, tomorrow, forever? Did a man like Quinn believe in forever? She shook her head quickly, thrusting the questions aside. She couldn't tell him; she couldn't ask him. But she could show him.

Softly Chantel brought her mouth to his, then ran her fingertip over it as if to test the warmth she'd elicited. Approving, she brought her lips to his again, to savor.

He hadn't known it could be like this. Even in the wildest rages of passion they'd incited in each other, he hadn't known there could be such wonder. He'd told himself before that she belonged to him, but now, with her pliant and soft in his arms, he could finally believe it. And what was more, he was hers. Completely, utterly. Love fueled by tenderness was more consuming than any madness.

He slipped into her easily, naturally. With a sigh, she accepted him. They rose together in a harmony of movement that was its own kind of beauty.

When there was nothing left to give, they gathered each other close and slept.

* * *

"Don't rush me; don't rush me." With a spring in his step, Frank waltzed in front of the skycap desk. "I'm going to make sure they don't send my banjo to Duluth."

"La Guardia." With a grin, the skycap showed Frank the stubs. "Don't worry about a thing."

"Easy for you to say. I've had that banjo longer than I've had my wife." Then, with a chuckle, he squeezed Molly's shoulder. "Not that you mean less to me, my love."

"But we run neck and neck. Did you take your Dramamine, Frank?"

"Yes, yes, don't fuss."

"Frank's a hideous air traveler," Molly put in as she pocketed the tickets and boarding passes. "That's where Chantel got it from."

Surprised, Quinn stopped in the act of hefting his small carry-on bag. "You don't like to fly?"

"I'm fine." She'd already downed half a roll of antacids and two air-sickness pills.

Molly glanced at the watch on her wrist. "We'd better get moving."

"Women. Always rushing." Frank gave Quinn a slap on the back. "Why do we put up with it, boy?"

"Only game in town."

"Right you are." Delighted with the world in general, Frank cackled as he strolled through the automatic doors.

"You're feeling chipper this morning," Chantel commented dryly, refusing to acknowledge the leaden feeling in her own stomach.

"And why not?" Frank beamed as they rode up the escalator toward their gate. "A good night's sleep's just the ticket." He quirked his brow at Molly and wondered if she'd wear that little black number again anytime soon.

As they passed through gate security, Chantel began the slow and even breathing technique that helped her get on board.

"Angel." Quinn drew her off to the side. "Don't you have a tranquilizer or something?"

"I don't take them." She twisted the strap of her bag in her fingers. "Besides, I'm fine."

He unclenched her fingers and soothed them with his. "Your hands are like ice."

"It's chilly in here."

Quinn noted a man mopping his brow as the room filled with body heat. "I didn't realize you were nervous about flying."

"Don't be silly, I fly all the time."

"I know. It must be rough."

Disgusted with herself, she stared over his shoulder. "Everyone's entitled to a phobia."

"That's right." He brought her hand to his lips. "Let me help."

She started to draw her hand away but found it held firmly. "Quinn, I feel like an idiot. I'd rather you just let it go."

"Fine. But you wouldn't mind holding my hand during the flight, would you?"

"It's six hours," she muttered. "Six incredibly long hours."

He tilted her face to his. "We ought to be able to think of something to pass the time." As he lowered his mouth to hers, neither of them noticed a man wearing dark glasses slip into a seat in the corner of the departure lounge. Neither of them noticed the way his hands clenched into fists as he watched them.

"If we do what you're thinking of, we'll be arrested," Chantel murmured, but the tension in her shoulders eased.

Quinn nipped at her lip. "I'm surprised at you. I was thinking of gin rummy."

"Like hell." When their flight was called, she drew a deep breath and kept her hand in his. "A dollar a point?"

"You're on."

Laughing, she walked with Quinn and her parents through the gate.

The man in dark glasses rose and pulled a low-brimmed hat over his head, then took out his boarding pass. He merged with the crowd that surged onto the plane.

CHAPTER 10

A re you sure you don't mind being drafted into the family?" Chantel carefully zipped a dress into her garment bag. She'd hired one of Hollywood's leading designers to create it, but it wasn't for the stage or the screen. It wasn't every day she was maid of honor at her sister's wedding.

"Is that what you call it?" Amused, Quinn sat on the unmade bed, dressed only in a towel. There was a freshly pressed suit in the closet that he didn't even want to think about.

"I don't know what else." Preoccupied, Chantel checked her makeup bag. If she'd forgotten anything, Maddy was sure to have it—probably still in the box. "Pop said you had to be at Reed's suite an hour before the ceremony." She paused and glanced back at him. "Just what is it men do before a wedding?"

"State secret, and no, I don't mind."

She stopped again, tapping a brush against her palm. "What did you think of Reed, Quinn? I know we only had a few hours together last night, but you must have formed an impression."

"Worried about your sister?"

"It goes with the territory."

He settled back against the pillows and looked at her. Trim slacks, a silk blouse, silver blond hair pulled back from an extraordinary face with hammered-gold combs. Chantel O'Hurley didn't look anything like a mother hen, but he'd learned to see further than skin deep. When it came to her family, she was a marshmallow.

"Dependable, certainly successful. Meticulous, I'd guess. Conservative."

"And Maddy?"

"Scattered, theatrical and a shade wide-eyed."

"That's Maddy," Chantel murmured. "It doesn't seem as though they'd have enough in common for more than a ten-minute conversation. But—"

"But?"

"It feels right." With a sigh, she dropped the brush into her bag. "It just feels right."

"Then what are you worried about?"

"She's my baby sister."

"By how many minutes?" he asked dryly.

"Time has nothing to do with it." She said it with such off-hand certainty that he was sure the question had been put to her before. "She *is* my baby sister, and she's always been the most trusting one, the most loving one. Abby's so . . . solid," she said. "And I've got enough meanness in me to keep my head above water. But Maddy . . . Maddy's the kind of woman who believes the check *is* in the mail, the alarm didn't go off, or the gas gauge was broken."

"I think your sister knows exactly what she wants and how to make it work."

"So do I, really. I guess I'm just being sentimental."

Quinn arched a brow. "Why don't you come over here and be sentimental?"

She sent him a slow smile. "I thought you were waiting for room service."

"Hate to wait alone."

"Quinn, if I get back in that bed . . ."

"Yeah?"

"I'm going to make incredible love to you."

"Threats, huh?" He lay back and crossed his arms behind his head. "Why don't you come over here and say that?"

She tossed her cosmetic bag aside and walked to him. "You haven't got a chance."

"Big talk."

"I can do more than talk," she murmured, and ran her fingertips up his leg to where the towel skimmed the top of his thigh. "Much more."

Before she could prove it, Quinn grabbed her wrist and yanked so that she tumbled across his chest. Her laughter came first, then was muffled to a sigh against his lips.

It didn't seem possible that she could want him as much as she had the night before, when they'd first slipped between the linen hotel sheets, but the excitement was just as new now, just as vital.

The scent of his shower was on him, fresh and tangy. His hair was slightly damp as it brushed across her face. His body was there for her, strong, virile, unclothed. With another laugh, she pressed her lips to his throat.

"Something funny?"

"I feel safe." She tossed back her head to smile at him. "So wonderfully safe."

He brushed the hair away from her face, holding it a moment, then letting it stream through his hands. How had she come to mean so much to him in so short a time?

"Safe's not the only thing I want you to feel."

"No?" She lowered her lips to his shoulder and let her tongue glide across his skin. "What else?"

Love, loyalty, devotion. It was frightening that those were his first thoughts. To protect himself, and maybe to protect her, he didn't tell her that. The physical loving wouldn't hurt either of them—not the way emotions could.

"Why don't I show you?" In one quick move he had Chantel on her back beneath him. The towel around his waist was held in place only by the press of their bodies. When his lips found hers, she began to tug the towel aside. Aroused, he laughed and made quick work of the buttons on her blouse. A knock on the door of the adjoining parlor had them both groaning. Chantel rose on her elbow and tossed her mussed hair back.

"You had to have breakfast, didn't you?"

"Let him bring it back later." Quinn slipped a hand under her skirt to explore her thigh. The knock came again, more insistently this time.

"I'll get it." Shifting away from Quinn, she adjusted her blouse. Then, with a grin, she picked up the towel and tossed it across the room. "You stay here." She kissed him again, quickly. "Right here."

"You're the boss."

"Keep that in mind." Chantel was smiling as she hurried into the parlor. Quinn would have his breakfast, but he was going to eat it cold.

In bed, Quinn reached over and idly turned on the radio. A little music, he thought. With the drapes still drawn, the room was dim. They might be anywhere. For a moment he let himself imagine they were in their bedroom—not in her house, not in his, not in some plush hotel, but in a home they'd made between them. When you loved, he realized, you didn't just think of now, but of always.

Maybe it was time to tell her, time to admit to her, not just to himself, that he loved her and wanted to share his life with her. His life—that meant past, present, future, not just the fleeting urge to satisfy passion, to quench desire. There was passion, but it would never be satisfied. Desire would never be quenched. And more, much more, there was emotion that swelled and expanded every moment he was with her.

He wanted her for his wife. That should have terrified him, but it almost amused him. He wanted her in all the traditional ways, the ways he'd always shrugged aside as restrictive and unimportant. A home, a family, his ring on her finger and hers on his. Quinn Doran, family man. It suddenly seemed to fit.

She might balk. She probably would. He'd just have to apply the right kind of pressure. Thinking of it made him smile a little. Persuading Chantel O'Hurley to marry him might just be the toughest nut he'd ever cracked.

"Quinn."

"Yeah?"

"Would you come out here a minute?"

He heard it in her voice, just a hint of tension. Quinn pushed aside his fantasies and reached for his robe. He saw the flowers as soon as he stepped into the parlor. A dozen bloodred roses with their petals just opened sat on the table by the door. Chantel stood beside them, her face as white as the card she held in her hand.

"He knows I'm here." She managed to keep her voice even, almost calm. "He says he'd follow me anywhere." Her fingers were steady as she handed the card to Quinn, but when his brushed over them, he found them cold. "He says he's waiting for the perfect time."

Quinn took the note and glanced briefly at the message. In the corner of the envelope was the printed name of the florist's shop. "He's made his first mistake," he murmured. "Who brought these up?"

"A bellboy." She stared at the far wall, at a Monet print, and wondered why she felt nothing, nothing at all. "I didn't even tip him."

"Stop it."

His voice snapped her back. After one long shudder, Chantel looked at him. She wouldn't get sympathy from Quinn, or soothing words or empty promises. She didn't want them. She wanted the truth. "He's here, isn't he? He might even be in this hotel."

"Sit down." He started to take her arm, but she backed away.

"I don't need to sit down. I need some answers."

"Chantel—"

At the next knock, she pressed a hand to her mouth to muffle a scream. Swearing, Quinn pushed her into a chair, then went to the door. Through the peephole he saw a room service waiter with a breakfast tray. "It's all right," he tossed over his shoulder. "Just room service."

Quinn opened the door to let the waiter roll the cart to the table by the window. After scrawling his name on the tab, he followed the waiter to the door to take a quick scan of the hall.

"You could use some coffee," Quinn said, moving past Chantel to the breakfast tray.

"No, answers." Though her knees were wobbly, she rose. "I'm not sure why, but I think you have them. You knew he'd be here."

Despite her refusal, Quinn poured two cups. "Yeah."

"Yeah." A dry laugh came from nowhere as she pressed her fingers to her temple. "You're not a man to elaborate, are you, Quinn? How did you know he'd be here? Sixth sense, gut hunch, instinct?"

"Any of those would do." He felt a sick curling in his stomach as he turned to face her again. "I expect him to go where you go, but in addition to that he said he'd be here in the last few notes he sent."

She crossed her arms over her chest. The chill had sprung to her skin quickly. She was beginning to feel now, and feel sharply. "You didn't think I should know?"

"If I'd thought you should know I'd have told you. Why don't you eat something?"

Yes, there were feelings now. They were boiling inside her, threatening to bubble out with the first word she spoke. Chantel walked to the table and, keeping her eyes on Quinn's, picked up a plate and very deliberately dropped it on the floor.

"Just who the hell do you think you are?" Her voice carried more venom when it was low and steady. "How dare you treat me as though I'm some brainless, gutless female who needs to be led around by the nose? I had a right to know he intended to follow me, that things would be the same here as they were on the West Coast."

He could let his temper go or he could control it. Quinn sat down and picked up his coffee. Anger had taken the dazed look out of her eyes. He'd let her take it as far as she could. "I handled it my way. You pay me to handle things my way."

Caught off guard, she stepped back. She paid him. How could she have forgotten he was only doing a job? An arrow of pain passed through her. Even that, somehow, was better than the numbness. "I expect to be kept informed of your progress, Doran."

"Fine." He picked up a piece of toast and began to heap on jelly.

"I'll just leave you to enjoy your breakfast."

"Chantel." His voice was soft, but it had enough punch to stop her before she crossed the room. "You might as well sit down. You're not going anywhere by yourself."

"I'm going down to Maddy's room."

"You can try to leave." He set his knife very deliberately on the side of his plate. "You won't make it. I'll take you down myself as soon as I'm dressed." He sent her a cool, challenging look. "And you'll stay there, inside the room, until I come back for you."

"I don't—"

"I've got a man stationed in the room across the hall, and another in the room across from your sister's. You're perfectly safe inside, but I want to take you down myself."

She was almost angry enough to take her chances. Chantel measured the distance to the door, and the look in Quinn's eyes. Without a word, she dropped down onto a chair and ignored him while he finished his breakfast.

* * *

Quinn found the cramped little flower shop in the West Sixties. In spite of the air-conditioning, the air was sultry inside and heavy with a barrage of floral scents. Three customers were crowded in, two of them in front of a long, chipped counter covered with scraps of papers and a shrilling phone the harried little man behind the counter ignored. Another customer stood in front of a display window and studied arrangements.

"Can't have them there before four. Can't." The owner scrawled on a form and kept shaking his head. He took a credit card and ran it through a machine for authorization. "Yes, it'll be pretty," he answered to the customer's murmured question. "Big pink carnations, some sprays of baby's breath. Tasteful, very tasteful. Sign here."

Quinn wandered to a grouping of lilies while the man dealt with the other customers.

"Okay, okay, you want to buy flowers or just look at them?"

Quinn glanced over to see the man piling the papers on the counter. "Pretty busy today."

"You're telling me nothing." The little man pulled out a handkerchief to wipe the back of his neck. "Got problems with the air conditioner, my clerk gets appendicitis, and too many people are dying." When Quinn lifted a brow, the man settled down a bit. "Funerals. Got a run on gladiolas this week."

"Tough." Quinn skirted a spray of daisies in a watering can. "This one of yours?"

He glanced at the card in Quinn's hand. "Says so right there." The man's squat finger punched at the name. "Flowers by Bernstein. I'm Bernstein. You have a problem with a delivery?"

"A question. Red roses, a dozen, delivered to the Plaza this morning. Who bought them?"

"You ask me who bought them?" Bernstein gave a long, nasal laugh. "Young man, I sell twenty dozen roses this week if I sell one. How am I supposed to know who buys?"

"You keep records?" Quinn gestured toward the register. "Receipts. You should have a receipt for a dozen red roses delivered to the Plaza at, let's say, ten thirty, eleven this morning."

"You want me to go through my receipts?"

Quinn reached in his pocket and drew out a twenty. "That's right."

The little man stood straight. His drooping jowls quivered with indignation. "I don't take bribes. You got twenty dollars, you buy twenty dollars' worth of flowers."

"Fine. How about the receipts?"

"You a cop?"

"Private."

Bernstein hesitated. Then, grumbling, he went into the drawer that held the day's receipts. He mumbled to himself as he flipped through them. "Nobody bought red roses today."

"Yesterday."

That earned Quinn a disgusted look, but Bernstein went into another drawer. "Red roses to Maine, two dozen to Pennsylvania, a dozen to Twenty-seventh Street . . ." He mumbled out a few more addresses. "A dozen to the Plaza Hotel, suite 1203, for delivery this morning."

"Can I take a look at that?" Without waiting for an answer, Quinn plucked it out of his hand. "Paid cash."

"I got no problem taking cash."

But cash meant no signature. Quinn passed the receipt back. "What did he look like?"

"What did he look like?" The man let out another snort of laughter. "How am I going to remember what you look like tomorrow? People come in here and buy their flowers. I don't care if they got an eye in the middle of their forehead so long as their credit's good or their cash is green."

"Just think about it a minute." Quinn pulled out another twenty. "You got some great flowers here."

The florist gave him a shrewd look. "The carnations on display here are getting wilted."

"I happen to be very fond of carnations."

With a nod, the man pocketed the two twenties, then took the slightly drooping carnations from behind the glass. "I remember he said to send the roses to Chantel O'Hurley. Things

were pretty busy here yesterday. They hauled my clerk out
in an ambulance. My other clerk's on vacation, and we've got
two weddings." Because the florist had a genuine love for flowers, he took out a plastic bottle and spritzed the carnations.
"Anyhow, he says to send them to her, so I say, hey, is that the
actress? You know, the wife and I go to the movies a lot. Oh,
yeah, I ask him if he's from California. He was wearing a hat,
one of those panama types, and dark glasses."

"What did he say?"

"I don't think he did. And don't ask me what he looked like
again, 'cause I don't know. I had Mrs. Donahue in here fussing about her daughter's wedding. Rose petals—bags of 'em.
Pink." He shook his head. "He was a guy, and I never saw
much of his face."

"How old?"

"Could've been younger than you, could've been older.
But he wasn't built so big. Nervous hands," he remembered
suddenly, and in a moment of conscience added some fresh
greenery to the carnations.

"Why do you say that?"

"Came in here smoking some foreign cigarette. I don't allow smoking, no matter how classy the tobacco. Not good for
the flowers."

"How do you know it was foreign?"

"How do I know? How do I know? I know an American
cigarette when I see one," the florist said testily. "And this
wasn't one of them. Made him put it out, too. Don't care how
much money you spend in here, you ain't gonna pollute my
flowers."

"Okay, so he had nervous hands."

"Couldn't keep them still once he put the thing out. Look,
I had enough trouble in here yesterday without this character. Mrs. Donahue was driving me to grief, and my clerk was
getting her appendix out. Next thing you know, she'll want to
claim it on workman's compensation."

"Anything else?" Quinn steered him patiently away from his clerk's appendectomy. "Anything he did or said that sticks in your mind?"

"Money clip," he said abruptly. "Yeah, he took the cash out of a clip instead of a wallet. A nice one, nothing you'd pick up on the street. Silver. Monogrammed."

"What initials?"

"Initials?" The florist began to file away his stack of receipts. "What do I know from initials? It had squiggly lines on it."

"Any rings? A watch?"

"I don't know. I notice the clip because the guy's got a nice fat wad tucked into it. Maybe he's got jewelry; maybe he doesn't. I'm taking his cash, not giving him an appraisal."

"Thanks." Quinn took out a card and wrote his number at the hotel on the back. "I'd appreciate it if you'd call if you remember anything else. Or if he comes back."

"He in trouble?"

"Let's just say I'd like the chance to talk to him."

"Don't forget your carnations."

Quinn tucked the arrangement under his arm and headed for the door.

"Guess you get some weirdos out in California," Bernstein commented.

"Our share."

"Movie stars." He gave another quick snort. "Guy said he worked close with Miss O'Hurley. Real close."

Quinn's fingers tightened around the knob. "Thanks." As he stepped onto the sidewalk, he thrust the flowers into the arms of a woman dragging a shopping cart. He didn't look back to see her staring at him. There was a sick feeling starting in his stomach. He knew someone who occasionally carried a silver money clip. A clip that had been a present from Chantel. Matt Burns.

He didn't want to believe it. Matt was a friend, and no one knew better than Quinn how hard it was to make and keep friends in his business. Yet how well did he really know Matt Burns?

He hadn't known about the gambling until he'd dug it up. Matt had betrayed a client then because of a weakness. Didn't that make him first in line to betray Chantel because of another kind of weakness?

A lot of men carried money clips, Quinn reminded himself as he headed away from the hotel rather than toward it. He needed to think things through before going back to Chantel. A lot of men carried silver money clips, Quinn continued, just the way a lot of men smoked foreign cigarettes. But he wondered how many men who knew Chantel, who worked closely with Chantel, did both.

He was being stupid, Quinn decided as he stopped at a phone booth. The word was soft, he corrected. That's what the woman had done to him. It wasn't his job to find reasons why it couldn't be Matt, but find reasons why it could.

Flipping open his notepad, he scanned for Matt's number and dialed.

"Answering for Matt Burns."

"I need to speak with him."

"I'm sorry, Mr. Burns is unavailable until Monday."

"Make him available, sweetheart. It's important."

The voice became very prim. "I'm sorry, Mr. Burns is out of town."

Nerves skimmed down Quinn's spine. "Where?"

"I'm not permitted to give out that information."

"This is Quinn Doran. I'm calling for Chantel O'Hurley."

"Oh, I'm sorry, Mr. Doran. You should have told me who you were. Mr. Burns is out of town, I'm afraid. Should I have him get in touch with you if he checks in?"

"I'll get in touch with him on Monday. Where is he?"

"He flew to New York, Mr. Doran. On some personal business."

"Yeah." He bit off an oath as he hung up the phone. It was

very personal. This was going to hurt her, Quinn thought. And it was going to hurt deep.

* * *

"Three more hours." Maddy O'Hurley jumped up from her chair, paced across the room and plopped onto the sofa. "We should have gotten married in the morning."

"It'll be afternoon soon enough." Chantel sipped at her third cup of coffee and wondered when she would hear from Quinn again. "Shouldn't you be enjoying your last hours as a single woman?"

"I'm too wired to enjoy anything." Maddy was up again, her mop of red hair bouncing with the movement. "I'm so glad you're here." She stopped long enough to give Chantel a quick squeeze. "I'd be going crazy now if you weren't. I wish Abby would come down."

"She will, as soon as she dumps Dylan and the boys on Pop. Think about something else."

"Something else." Maddy's slim dancer's body spun in a circle. "How can I think of something else? Walking down that aisle is the biggest entrance I'll ever make."

"Speaking of entrances, tell me about the play."

"It's terrific." Her amber eyes lighted with love of the theater. "Maybe I'm prejudiced because it was the play that brought Reed and me together, but it's the best thing I've done. I was hoping you'd be able to see it."

"I'll be back in New York shooting on location soon. You'll be back from your honeymoon and onstage." Chantel reached restlessly for a cigarette. "And if the reviews are any indication, the thing's going to be running for years."

Maddy watched her sister toy with, then light, the cigarette. It was something she did rarely, and only when she was tense. "How's the filming going?"

"No complaints."

"And this Quinn? Is it serious?"

Chantel moved her shoulders. "He's just a man."

"Come on, Chantel, this is Maddy. I've seen you with just a man before. Did you have an argument?" She managed to keep herself still long enough to sit on the arm of Chantel's chair. "Last night you seemed so happy. You practically glowed every time you looked at him."

"Of course I'm happy." She gave Maddy's arm a quick pat. "My baby sister's getting married to a man I've decided is nearly worthy of her."

"Don't hedge, Chantel." Abruptly serious, Maddy took Chantel's restless hands in hers. Nerves seemed to leap from one sister to the other. "Hey, something's really wrong, isn't it?"

"Don't be silly, I—" She broke off at the knock on the door. Maddy felt her sister's fingers tense.

"Chantel, what is it?"

"Nothing." Disgusted with herself, Chantel made her muscles relax. "Just make sure who it is, darling. We don't want an overexuberant bridegroom walking in."

Far from satisfied, Maddy rose and walked to the door. "It's Abby," she said as she looked through the peephole. And with Abby's help, Maddy thought, she'd get to the bottom of what was worrying their sister. "How come you're not fat yet?" she accused as she opened the door.

With a laugh, Abby put one hand on her stomach and the other on Maddy's cheek. "Because I have over five months to go. How come you're not getting ready yet?"

"Because the wedding's not for three hours."

"Just enough time." Abby draped a garment bag over the back of a chair and went to Chantel. "Think we can whip her into shape?"

"Maybe. At least if we start on her she can't pace around the suite. Thank God Reed talked you into giving up that apartment. We'd have been sitting on top of each other."

"I still miss it." With a grin, Maddy moved over to wrap an arm around each of her sisters. "I have such a hard time picturing me in a penthouse uptown. Are Dylan and the boys with Pop?"

"I left them at his door. Mom's getting her hair done, and Pop was about to talk Dylan into a prewedding toast. I can't wait to see Ben in his tux again. He looks like such a little man. And Chris is annoyed that we're renting them instead of buying them. He thinks it's just the thing to show off to his friends at home. And by the way"—she gave Chantel a squeeze before she released her—"I liked your Quinn."

"The possessive pronoun's a bit premature," Chantel managed a smile. Then, on impulse, she went to the phone. "I know what's missing here," she told them, punching up room service. "I'd like a bottle of champagne, three glasses. Dom Pérignon '71. Yes, Madeline O'Hurley's suite. Thank you."

Abby arched a brow and leaned her arm on Maddy's shoulder. "It's barely eleven."

"Who's counting?" Chantel wanted to know. "The O'Hurley Triplets are going to celebrate." Without warning, her eyes filled. "Oh, God, sometimes I miss the two of you so much I can hardly stand it."

In an instant they were together, holding close in the bond that had cemented them even before birth. Maddy sniffled, Abby soothed, and then, to her sisters' amazement, Chantel broke down completely.

"Oh, baby." Abby lowered her to the sofa, casting a quick, concerned look at Maddy. "What's wrong, Chantel?"

"It's nothing, nothing." She brushed her tears aside. "Just being sentimental. I guess I'm a little edgy, working too hard. Just seeing the two of you, you with your beautiful family, Abby, and Maddy about to start one of her own. I wonder if things had been different . . ." She let her words trail off with a shake of her head. "No, I made my choices, now I have to deal with them."

Abby brushed the hair from Chantel's face. Her voice was always calm, her hands always gentle. "Chantel, is this about Quinn?"

"Yes— No." She lifted both hands, then dropped them. "I don't know. I'm having a little trouble with an overenthusiastic fan," she said, downplaying her problem. "I hired Quinn to more or less keep him at a distance, and then I fell in love with Quinn and . . ." She trailed off again, letting out a deep breath. "I just said it out loud."

Maddy bent down to kiss the top of her head. "Did it help?"

Some of the tension uncurled. "Maybe. I'm being an idiot." Chantel fumbled for a tissue. "And I'll be damned if I'm going to walk down the aisle as maid of honor with puffy eyes."

"That sounds more like Chantel," Maddy murmured. "And besides, if you're in love with Quinn, everything's going to work out."

"Always the optimist."

"Absolutely. Abby found Dylan, I found Reed, so it's your turn. Now if we could just pin down Trace . . ."

"You're really reaching," Chantel said with a laugh. "If there's a woman out there who can put a hobble on big brother, I'd love to meet her." She started at the knock on the door, but brought herself back quickly. "Must be the champagne." Stuffing the tissue in her pocket, Chantel went to the door but checked the peephole first. "Uh-oh." A smile hovered on her lips as she glanced over her shoulder. "We've got the champagne, all right, but there's more. Abby, drag Maddy into the bedroom. There's a lovesick maniac at the door."

"Reed? Is it Reed?" Maddy was halfway to the door before her sisters headed her off.

"No way." She might be nearly four months pregnant, but Abby was still agile. She had an arm hooked around Maddy's waist. "Bad luck, honey. You get into the bedroom. Chantel and I can transmit any messages."

"This is silly."

"I'm not opening the door until you're out of the room," Chantel said simply, and leaned back on it. "All the way out."

After wrinkling her nose, Maddy slammed the door behind her. As a precaution, Abby posted herself in front of it. With a nod of satisfaction, Chantel pulled open the door to the hall. "Just over there," she told the waiter. "And you"—she put a slender, manicured finger to Reed's chest—"not a step farther."

"I just want to see her for a minute."

Chantel managed to force back a smile and shook her head. She could almost feel the love coming from him, the nerves, the longing. He hadn't changed into his tux yet, and he was wearing a pair of casual slacks and a shirt that reflected his conservative style. He looked like an executive. He *was* an executive, she thought with another shake of her head. And the farthest thing from the type one would have imagined with her free-spirited, bohemian sister. Yet they fit. Chantel imagined Maddy had fallen for those calm gray eyes first. The rest would have been a smooth drop.

"Look, I have something for her." Used to getting his own way, Reed took a step forward, only to be blocked easily by Chantel. "I'll be in and out before you know it."

"You won't be in at all," Chantel corrected. "We're Irish, Reed, and we're theater people. You're not going to find a group more superstitious. You'll see Maddy at the church."

"That's right." Hearing a stirring behind her, Abby hooked her hand firmly around the knob of the bedroom door. "I'm sure you're too much of a gentleman to try to get through both of us." Using the ultimate weapon, she smiled and put a hand to her stomach. "Or should I say all three of us?"

Reed wasn't so sure. He wanted to see Maddy, touch her, if only for a minute, to assure himself it was all real. Abby smiled at him with warm, sympathetic eyes, but she didn't budge. Chantel signed the receipt for the wine without moving from the doorway.

"Go down to the eighth floor and have a drink with Pop," she advised.

"I just want to—"

"Forget it." Then she softened and kissed his cheek. "Just a couple of hours, Reed. Believe me, it'll be worth the wait."

Only minutes before, Reed had managed to talk his way

around Dylan and override Frank's objections. But he knew when he was out of his depth. "Would you give her this?" He took a small box from his pocket. "It was my grandmother's. I was going to give it to her later, but, well, I'd like her to wear it today."

"She'll wear it." She started to hustle him out again, then stopped. "Reed."

"Yeah?"

"Welcome to the family." Then she shut the door in his face. "Lord, another minute of that and I'd have been in tears again. Let her out."

"What did he give you?" Maddy was already nudging past her sister. She took the box from Chantel and opened it. Inside was a tiny heart of diamonds on a thin silver chain. "Oh, isn't it lovely?"

"It's going to look even lovelier against your dress." Abby ran a fingertip over the stones. "Here, I'll clasp it for you."

"Now, *I'm* going to cry." Maddy closed her hand over the heart. He was going to be hers, truly hers, in a matter of hours. And her new life would begin.

"No more tears." Chantel released the cork from the wine with a *swoosh*. It landed on the carpet, to be ignored as she poured wine to overflowing into three glasses. "We're going to get just a little drunk— Well, two of us are going to get a little drunk, and Abby's going to have half a glass. Then, between the three of us, we're going to create the most beautiful bride to ever walk down the aisle at St. Pat's. Here's to you, little sister."

"No." Maddy touched her glass to Chantel's, then to Abby's. "Here's to us. As long as we have each other, we're never alone."

CHAPTER 11

At Chantel's insistence, she and Quinn caught the red-eye to L.A. Saturday night. New York hadn't been the haven she'd hoped for. With the wedding over and her sister off on a Caribbean honeymoon, Chantel could only think of getting home.

The reception had been a strain. She'd caught herself watching strangers, studying familiar faces and wondering. Even when she willed herself to sleep on the plane, she promised herself that the next time she came back to New York, it would be without fear.

And what could she say to Quinn? She felt betrayed by his silence, yet had she, by the extent of her dependence on him, asked for it? Was she so weak, so cowardly, that he felt it necessary to shield her from everything? She wanted his protection, but she also wanted his respect. Had she forfeited that by refusing to listen to his reports, by allowing him to intercept the notes and keep the contents from her? It was time that stopped. All her life, except for one brief period, she had had her hand on the controls. Now, through fear, she'd relinquished them. Starting now, she was taking back the helm.

Quinn wondered how long it would take her to unfreeze. She'd certainly been cool enough throughout the afternoon and evening. Cool, aloof, distant. It was something he had no choice but to accept. Yet when he'd seen her walking down the aisle in front of her sister, wearing that pale blue dress, all filmy and romantic, he'd wanted to step out of his seat, scoop her up and carry her off. Somewhere. Anywhere.

He wondered what it would feel like to stand where Reed Valentine had stood, to watch Chantel, as Reed had watched Maddy, walk toward him wearing white lace. What would it be like to hear her make the promises her sister had made? He shook himself out of the mood.

They were almost ready to land, and Chantel was dozing restlessly beside him. Couldn't she understand that he'd done what he'd done for her sake, because he'd needed so badly to see her relax, even if only for a couple of days? She didn't understand, or wouldn't, and he hadn't tried to explain. He didn't know how.

He didn't have the flair of one of her leading men. He didn't have the words all neatly typed in a script he could memorize. He had only what was inside him, and there didn't seem to be a way to explain that. Words weren't feelings. Phrases weren't emotions. And emotions were all he had.

When they landed, Chantel looked fresh and rested, as though she'd spent eight hours sleeping on a soft bed rather than snatching naps on a plane. They got their luggage without incident and within twenty minutes were riding in the back of a limo toward Beverly Hills.

Chantel lighted a cigarette, then glanced casually at her watch. Right now she felt wired, restless. Jet lag would hit tomorrow, but she would function.

"I'd like to see your reports, all of your reports, by noon tomorrow."

Streetlights flashed intermittently against the windows. His face was in shadow, but Chantel doubted she would have been able to read his expression in any case. "Fine. I have the file at your place."

"I'd also like an update on anything you came up with in New York."

"You're the boss."

"I'm glad you remember that."

He could have strangled her. He thought about ways that were quick and quiet, but instead he simply sat back and bided his time. He stepped out of the limo at the gate. Though Chantel had been gone, he'd thought it best to leave the twenty-four-hour guard in place. A few brief words and he was back in the limo, gliding through the open gates.

At the entrance, Chantel sailed past him. She had reached the head of the main staircase before he caught her.

"Something eating you, angel?"

"I don't know what you're talking about. You will excuse me now, Quinn?" Delicately she peeled his fingers from her arm. "I want to take a long, hot bath."

No one did it better. He had to give her that as he watched her walk down the hall to her room. She could, with a look, with an inflection, slice a man in half without leaving a drop of blood.

He thought he was calm. He thought he was controlled—until the moment he heard the lock click on her door. Then the rage he'd held in throughout the day clawed free. He didn't hesitate. Maybe he wasn't even thinking. Quinn walked to her bedroom door and kicked it in.

She wasn't often speechless. Chantel just stood there. The jacket of her suit had already been discarded, leaving her in a pale pink teddy and a rose-colored skirt. One hand remained frozen on top of her head where she had begun to pin up her hair.

She'd seen fury before, real and simulated, but she'd never seen anything like what was boiling in Quinn's eyes.

"Don't you ever lock a door on me." His voice was so quiet after the crash of splintering wood that she shivered. "Don't you ever walk away from me."

Slowly she lowered her hand so that her hair tumbled to her shoulders. "I want you to leave."

"Maybe it's time you learned even you can't have everything you want. I'm here to stay. You're going to have to do a hell of a lot more than turn a key to keep me out."

When he came toward her, she stiffened but refused to retreat. She was through backing away from anything, even him. He took her hair and wrapped it around his hand.

"You wanted to slap me down, and that's fine. But I'll be damned if I'll take it from you for doing my job."

"I won't be treated like a fool or a weakling." The lace of the teddy trembled over her breasts as she took an unsteady breath. "You knew he was going to follow me to New York. You knew I'd be no safer there than I was here."

"That's right. I knew you didn't. And you had one night when you didn't toss in your sleep."

"You had no right—"

"I had every right." The hand in her hair tightened. She wanted to wince, but she didn't seem to be able to move at all. "I have the right to do anything, everything, to keep you safe, to give you some peace of mind. And I'm going to keep on doing it, because there's nothing that matters to me more than you."

Chantel let out a breath she hadn't been aware she was holding. She'd seen it in his eyes, beneath the anger, beneath the frustration, but she hadn't been certain she could believe it. "Is that your—" She stopped, pressing her lips together. It wouldn't do for her voice to tremble now. She wanted to be strong, for him, as well as herself. "Is that your way of telling me you love me?"

He stared down at her, a good deal more stunned by his announcement than she. He hadn't meant to throw it at her like a threat. He'd wanted to give them both time, to give them both room, so that he could coax her along until she realized she needed him. But he'd never been good at coaxing.

"Take it or leave it."

"Take it or leave it," she repeated in a murmur. How like him. "Would you mind letting go of my hair? I need it for a couple of scenes on Monday. Besides, that way you'd have both arms to put around me."

Before he could, she was pressed against him, holding tight and hard and praying it wasn't a dream.

"I guess this means you're taking it." He buried his face in her hair and wondered how he'd ever survived without her scent, without her touch.

"Yeah. I've been trying to figure out a way to make you fall in love with me so you wouldn't be able to walk away." She tossed her head back to look at him. "Tell me you're not going to walk away."

"I'm not going anywhere." Then he found her mouth and made it a promise. "Let me hear you say it." He took her hair again but drew it back gently until their eyes met. "Look at me and say it. No lights, no camera, no script."

"I love you, Quinn, more than I thought it was possible to love. It scares the hell out of me."

"Good." He kissed her again, harder. "It scares the hell out of me, too."

"We've got so many things to talk about."

"Later." He was already drawing down the zipper of her skirt.

"Later," she agreed, tugging his shirt out of the waistband of his slacks. "Want to take a bath?" As she asked, she yanked his shirt over his shoulders.

"Yeah."

"Before?" With a laugh, she nipped at his chin. "Or after?"

"After." And he pulled her with him onto the bed.

It had been wild before, fierce, violent, passionate, and it had also shimmered with gentleness. But now there was love, felt, spoken, answered. She'd stopped believing that her life would lead her to this—love, acceptance, understanding. In the end she'd only had to open her hand and take it. In a burst of emotion they were caught close, mouths open and hungry, bodies heated and aware. She heard his long indrawn breath as he buried his face in her hair, as if he, too, had just realized what a gift they'd been given.

She thought he trembled. Her hands, pressed against his back, felt the quick tensing of muscle. She didn't want to soothe it. She wanted him to be as she was: stunned, a little afraid and deliriously happy. When she pressed her lips to his throat, she felt the throb of excitement, tasted the heat. In one long, possessive stroke she ran her hands down his back, then up again. He was hers. From this moment, he was hers.

She was there for him, soft, yielding, yet strong enough to hold him. He'd never looked for her. Quinn understood himself well enough to know he'd never looked for anyone to share his life. Still, he'd found her, and in her he'd found everything. A mate. There was something primitive yet soothing in the word. It meant someone to tumble between the sheets with on hot, sultry nights. It meant someone to wake with in the cool, lazy mornings. It was someone to confide in, someone to protect, someone to reach out to.

Just the thought of it made him close his eyes, as if to keep the fantasy trapped forever. With his fingertips he traced her face so that her image hovered there, in his mind.

"So beautiful," he murmured. "Here . . ." His finger lingered on her cheek. "And here." Slowly he slid his hand down her body. Then he opened his eyes to look into hers. "And inside."

"No, I—"

"Don't contradict the man who loves you." He brought her palm to his lips, watching her. He turned her hand over, kissing each finger. A diamond glittered on one, a symbol of what she was to the world. Cool sex, glamour with a hard polish. Her hand trembled like a young girl's.

He brushed kisses along her jawline, and her breath came in slow, quiet gasps. She could almost hear her skin hum as his fingers whispered over it. With each touch she drifted deeper into a dark, liquid world where sensations were her only guide.

Only he could make her forget the boundaries she'd once set for herself. Only he could make her forget that when you loved, you risked. With him she could give without fear, without reservations or restrictions. There would be a tomorrow with Quinn. There would be a lifetime of tomorrows.

He wasn't sure he knew how to show her how he felt. He wasn't used to pampering. Romance was for books, for movies, for the young and foolish. Yet he had a need, a growing one, to show her that his feelings went so far beyond desire that he couldn't measure them.

Rising to his elbow, he brushed the hair carefully away from her face, combing his fingers through it as it fell, silvery blond, over the spread. Gently, as though she might crumble at the slightest touch, he cupped her face in his hand. Could she be more beautiful now? Somehow it seemed so to him as he watched the first beams of daylight steal through the windows and over her skin.

He ran his thumb over her lips, fascinated by the shape, by the softness, by the flavor he imagined would linger on his own flesh. As if it were the first time—and perhaps it was—he touched his lips to hers.

Her body went weak. As his lips lingered, the hand she had pressed to his back slipped down, limp. She'd thought she understood possession, but she'd been wrong. She'd thought she could imagine what it was like to be loved, loved fully. But she'd had no idea. Something fluttered through her, so softly that it might have been a dream. But it expanded within her, and a promise was made.

The heat centered, focused and grew. Strength flooded back into her, and with it a passion so rich that she moaned from the pleasure. Together they rolled until she lay over him. Together they let themselves go.

His hands were quick, but no more urgent than hers. His lips were hungry, but his desperation had met its match. Sanity was discarded as easily as silk and lace. They came together like thunder in a storm that lingered into the morning. As dawn rose, they took each other into the dark.

* * *

"I'm so glad it's Sunday." Chantel eased her shoulders down into the hot, frothy water. She picked up a wineglass from the side of the tub and laughed at Quinn over the rim. "You're

not supposed to scowl at the bubbles. You're supposed to enjoy them."

Quinn shifted to reach for his own glass. Chantel's tub was
easily big enough for two, and the skylight overhead showed a
perfect blue sky. The water that lapped nearly to the edge was
layered with white, fragrant bubbles.

"I'm going to smell like a woman."

"Darling." She touched her tongue to the rim of her glass.
"No one's going to smell you but me."

"With all the stuff you dumped in here, I'll be lucky if it
wears off in a week." He shifted again, and his leg slid over
hers. "But it has its compensations."

"Mmmm." With her eyes half-closed, she leaned back. "For
both of us. I need this. The shooting schedule next week is murder. There are three scenes in particular that I know will leave
me limp. The one where Brad and Hailey nearly die in the fire
is the worst."

"What fire?"

"Read the script," she said lazily, smiling when he tossed
bubbles at her. "I trust special effects, but it doesn't make it any
easier to crawl around in a shack on the back lot or on the set
on the soundstage while they're shooting flames and pumping
smoke in. That's why it's especially nice that it's Sunday, and I
can lie in the tub and think about making love with you." She
looked at him through eyes that were hardly more than slits.
"Again."

"You can lie in the tub *and* make love with me." He twisted
his body, bringing it forward until his face was close to hers.
"At the same time."

Chantel laughed and linked her hands behind his head as
water lapped over the tub and onto the floor. "Too much water."

"You filled it up."

"My mistake. I usually bathe alone."

"Not anymore." Bubbles burst between them as he kissed
her. "Why don't you pull the plug?"

"Can't get to it." She tilted her head to change the angle of the next kiss. "It's, ah, behind me. Now I bet a big strong man like you could manage it all by himself."

"Back here?" His hand trailed over her breast, then slipped to her rib cage.

"Close. Very close." She felt his fingers slide over her hip. "Getting closer. Why don't we—" The words were cut off as she found herself submerged, his mouth hard on hers. Up again, she drew in air, swiped at her face and squinted at him. "Quinn!"

"Slipped." He found the lever easily and flipped it down.

"I bet. Now I've got soap in my eyes." He started to grin, but his mouth went dry when she rose up, magnificent, and let water drain from her skin as she reached for a towel. "Remind me to bring a snorkel next time we take a bath."

"Chantel."

She was holding the towel to her face, but she lowered it with a half smile that faded when he stood beside her. Without a word, he gathered her to him. They stood where they were while the bubbles drained beneath them and dried on their skin.

"I never knew it could be like this," she murmured. "Not like this."

"That makes two of us." He'd found her. It seemed so incredible that he'd found her, found everything, without looking. "You're getting cold." Feeling the chill on her skin, he took a towel and wrapped it around her. "I guess I'd have a lot to answer to if you went to work tomorrow with a red nose."

"I never get a red nose." She took a towel in turn and wrapped it around him. "It's in my contract."

"Think you could take a break when you finish filming?"

"That depends." She smiled again. "On where and with whom."

"With me. We can talk about the where."

"I should be wrapped in three weeks. You pick the where." She started to step from the tub, then braced herself against the wall. "Careful. We've flooded the place."

"Just toss down a couple towels." Quinn plucked another from the shelf and let it fall to the floor to soak up the water.

"My housekeeper's going to love you." Out of habit, Chantel picked up a jar of moisturizer and began to rub a light cover over her skin.

"After we're married, there's going to have to be a change in the rules of the tub." He was hooking the towel at his waist and didn't notice the way her fingers froze in place on her cheek. "Bubbles are okay, but they've got to be unscented. It's one thing for the staff to sniff, but we can't have the kids wondering if their father wears perfume."

Somehow she managed to get the lid back on the jar and set it down without dropping it. "We're getting married?"

He didn't have to look at her to know she'd taken three paces back. He heard it in her voice. "Absolutely."

Her heart was hammering in her throat, but she'd trained herself to speak clearly over nerves. "You want children?"

"Yeah." One by one, the muscles of his stomach knotted. "Is that a problem?"

"I . . . Things are moving pretty fast," she managed.

"We're not teenagers, Chantel. I think we both know what we want."

"I have to sit down." She didn't trust her legs, so she moved quickly back to the bedroom and took a chair. She held the towel together in front of her with hands that had gone white at the knuckles.

Quinn waited a moment. The steam had fogged the wall-length mirror opposite the tub, but he could imagine her sitting there, her beauty reflected, slim, young, perfect. She was a dream, and more, she was a star, someone who lighted up the screen and created fantasies. His jaw was tight when he walked into the bedroom.

"Looks like I pushed the wrong buttons." Digging up his shirt, he found his cigarettes. "I thought that's what you wanted, too." Lighting one, he drew smoke in deeply. "I guess a husband and kids don't go with the image."

She looked up slowly. Her eyes were dry, but he recognized pain, something deep and dull and lasting.

"Chantel—"

"No." She stopped him with a gesture of her hand. "Maybe I deserved that." Rising, she went to the closet and chose a robe. With deliberate motions she dropped the towel, then slipped the robe on and belted it. She linked her fingers a moment, then let them fall to her sides. "My career is important to me, but I've never let it interfere with my personal life—or vice versa. My work is demanding. You've seen for yourself that the hours can be brutal."

"So there's no room for me and a family?"

Something came into her face again. Pain again, but with a touch of anger this time. "My parents raised four children on the road. There was always room, always time for family."

"Then what is it?"

She dipped her hands into her pockets, then took them out again, unable to keep them still. "First, I want to tell you that there's nothing I want more than to marry you and start a family. Please, don't," she said quickly when he started to come to her. "Sit down, Quinn. It would be easier for me if you would sit."

"All right."

When he had, she drew a deep breath. "There are things you have to know before we go any further. It's difficult, at least for me, to admit past mistakes, but you have a right to know. If I'd listened to my mother, I would have told you before. It might have been easier then."

"Look, if you want to tell me you've been with other men—"

Her low laugh cut him off. It was strained. "Not exactly. This doesn't fit the image, either, but I only slept with one other man before you. Surprise," she said quietly when he simply stared. She went to stand at the window. "I was barely twenty when I met him. I was doing commercials, going to acting classes. I even had a part-time job selling magazines on the phone. I kept telling myself it was just a matter of time, and I believed it, but it was tough. Oh, God, it was so tough to be alone. Then Matt called and said he'd gotten me a test for a small part on a feature. *Lawless*, my first real break. The producer was—"

"Dustin Price."

Chantel turned back from the window. Her hand was curled in a fist. "Yes. How do you know that?"

"A lot of movie buffs might, but the fact is, I already know about Price. He turned up when I did a background check on you."

"You did a check on me?" She found herself braced against the windowsill. "On me?"

"It's standard, Chantel. I do a run on you, maybe somebody turns up you've forgotten, or forgotten to mention. Like Dustin Price. He's clean, by the way. Been in England eighteen months."

"Standard," she repeated, letting the rest sift away like sand. "I guess I should have expected it."

"What difference does it make now? So you slept with him. You needed a break; he could give you a break. It was years ago, and I don't give a damn."

Every muscle in her body went rigid. "Is that what you think? You think I slept with him to get a part?"

"I'm telling you I don't care."

"Don't touch me." She whipped away from him as he reached for her. "I don't have to sleep with anyone to get a part, and I never have. I may have made compromises, I may have given up more than I should, but I never prostituted myself."

"I'm sorry." This time he took her arms, ignoring her resistance. "I'm trying to tell you that whatever happened between you and Price doesn't matter."

"Oh, it matters." She pulled away and poured wine into a fresh glass. "It matters. When Matt called me to tell me I had the part, I was so happy. I knew it was the beginning. I was going places. I was going to be somebody." She pressed her fingers to her lips until she was sure she could speak calmly. "Dustin sent me a dozen roses, a bottle of champagne and a lovely letter of congratulations. He said he knew I was going to be a star and suggested we have dinner to discuss the film and my career."

She drank because her throat was dry, then set down the glass, refusing to rely on wine to get her through the story. "Of course, I agreed. He was one of the top producers, riding on a wave of three box office smashes. Of course, he was married, but I didn't think of that." The derision was in her voice again, self-derision, self-disgust.

"Chantel. It was years ago."

"There are some things you never stop paying for. I was going to be sophisticated. We were just having dinner, colleagues. God, he was charming." The memory still hurt, but the pain was dull now, covered with scar tissue. "The flowers kept coming, the dinners. He knew so much about the business, the people. Who to talk to, who to be seen with. All of that was so important to me then. I thought I could handle it. The truth was I was just a naive young girl on her own for the first time.

"I fell in love with him. I believed everything he said about him and his wife living together for appearances only, about the quiet divorce that was already in the works. About the two of us making the best and brightest team Hollywood had seen since the golden age. The whole thing might have run its natural course as I got a little smarter and he a bit bored, but before all that happened, I made a mistake." She ran her damp palms down her robe, then linked them. "I got pregnant." She managed to swallow. "You didn't find that in your background check, did you?"

Rage hit, and he smothered it. "No."

"He had enough money, enough influence, to keep it quiet. And it wasn't an issue for very long."

He was struggling, fighting desperately to understand. "You had an abortion?"

"That's what he wanted. He was furious. I suppose a lot of men would be when their mistress—and that's what I was, really—turns up pregnant and threatens his very comfortable marriage. Of course, he'd never planned on getting a divorce or marrying me. All of that came out when I told him I was going to have his baby."

"He used you," Quinn spit out. "You were twenty years old and he used you."

"No." Strange that she could say it so calmly now. "I was twenty years old, and I pretended I knew all the rules. I pretended very well. I made one mistake, then I made another mistake. I told him he could go to hell, but I was keeping the baby. Things got ugly then. He threatened to destroy my career if I didn't play his way. Well, there's no use going into what was said, except that the affair was over and my eyes were wide open."

"You're still hurting," Quinn said quietly.

"Yes, but not for the reasons you might think. I thought I loved him, but as soon as the glitter washed off, I knew I never had. I called my parents. I was ready to run home and leave everything behind. I bought plane tickets. Quinn, I don't know what I would have ultimately done once I was thinking clearly. That's the worst of it, not knowing. There was an accident on the way to the airport." She took a deep breath, struggling to finish. "Nothing major, the taxi driver had a couple of broken bones, and I—I lost the baby."

With a broken sob, she pressed her fingers to her eyes. "I lost the baby, and I tried to tell myself it was for the best. But all I ever could think was that it had never had a chance. I was only six weeks pregnant. Six weeks. Here, then gone. Matt pulled me out of it, got me back to work almost as soon as I was out of the hospital. Everything clicked for me then, the parts; the people, the fame I'd always wanted. All I had to do was lose a baby."

"Chantel." He came to her, running his hands over her face, her hair, her shoulders. "There's nothing I can say. Nothing I know how to do."

"There's more."

"No more." He started to gather her close, but she backed away.

"When I lost the baby, there were complications. The doctors told me, well, they said it was possible I could have other children, but it wasn't something they could guarantee. Possible, just possible, not even probable. There might never be another baby, another chance. Do you understand?"

He took her hands. "Are you going to marry me?"

"Quinn, aren't you listening? I just told you—"

"I heard you." His fingers linked with hers and held firm. "You might not be able to have children. I want them, Chantel—yours, mine. If we can have them, that's great. But first, always . . ." He bent to touch his lips to hers. "I want you. I need you, angel. The rest is up to chance."

"Quinn, I love you."

"Then let's get married tomorrow."

"No." She put her hands to his chest to hold him off. "I want you to think about this, really think about it. You need some time."

"I need you," he corrected. "I don't need time."

"I feel I owe it to you. Let's leave things as they are. A few days."

He could have pushed. He could have won. But the hurt seemed too close to the surface just then. "A very few days. Come here." This time she went willingly into his arms. "I'm not going to let anyone hurt you again," he murmured.

She closed her eyes, hoping she could promise him the same thing, even if she were speaking of herself.

CHAPTER 12

The day started at six and never let up. Filming began at a shack on the back lot. The interior was no more than that, a small frame building that had been used in a handful of films. For *Strangers* it had been given a facelift, a false front that had turned it into a rustic cabin in the woods of New England. In a climactic scene, special effects would burn it down, the fire starting under mysterious circumstances with Hailey and Brad inside.

The interior scenes would be shot later, on a two-story set on the soundstage, but the morning was spent on exteriors. Chantel drove Hailey's Ferrari to the deserted cabin. She was older now but still caught between the man she had married and the man who had betrayed her. The scene called for her, on the verge of a breakdown, to seek solace in the remote cabin, searching for the roots of her art, which she'd lost in the tangle of success.

All the scenes were shot out of sequence and then would be edited together. For several hours of this shoot there was no dialogue. She was filmed unloading her art equipment, setting an easel on the narrow porch, walking through the door and out again with costume changes. There was a long, lingering close-up of her leaning on the porch rail with a cup of coffee in her hand. Without words, Chantel could use only her face to show the turmoil her character was feeling.

She painted on the porch, sketched on the porch steps, planted flowers. Through posture and gestures and by relaxing the set of her face, Chantel showed her character's gradual healing.

From the sidelines, Quinn watched her and felt his pride in her grow. He didn't know the story, but he understood the woman she became for the cameras. And he began to root for Hailey.

There was a poignant scene in which Hailey sat on the porch and poured out her heart to a stray dog. It was the examination of a life, with all its flaws, its wrong turns, its regrets. Even when it was reshot to change the angle, the emotion generated remained intense. Quinn saw more than one member of the crew wipe their eyes.

Before lunch they had wrapped a number of scenes, including a short, vicious argument between Hailey and Brad on the porch. During an hour's break Chantel took a quick, necessary nap, then shored up her energy with fruit, cheese and a protein drink before going to the soundstage for the interiors.

The set was as rustic as the outside of the cabin had promised, but there were a few of Hailey's paintings on the wall. The props included a large carved music box that had been a wedding present from her husband. The earlier tension was back in her character as Chantel opened the box and let the strains of the "Moonlight Sonata" out.

Dissatisfied with the way the scene was going, Chantel and the director went into a discussion on mood and motion.

"What do you think of our little story?"

James Brewster appeared beside Quinn. The two of them watched Larry Washington bring Chantel a glass of juice.

"Hard to say when you see it chopped up this way." Quinn kept his eye on Larry as the young man hovered around Chantel, ready to jump at the tiniest gesture. "But I expect it'll sell. It has it all—sex, violence, melodrama."

"You don't write a bestseller by leaving them out," Brewster said easily. "Of course, Hailey is the key, the hinge. What she does, what she feels, affects every character. When I started the book, I thought I was telling a tale of betrayal and birth. But it became a story of how one woman—and what happens to her—determines the destiny of everyone she touches." He broke off with a laugh. "It sounds pretentious, and perhaps it would be without Chantel. She is Hailey."

"She does make you believe," Quinn murmured.

"Exactly." Pleased, Brewster gave a quick nod. "As a writer, there's no greater reward than watching one of your characters come to life, particularly one you feel strongly about. I nearly killed her in the fire, you know."

Quinn stiffened. "What do you mean?"

Brewster laughed again and drew out a cigarette. "You're a very literal man, Mr. Doran. I meant I nearly ended the book here, in this cabin, with Hailey losing everything, including her life, in a fire set by the only man who really loved her. I found it impossible. She had to go on, you see, and survive."

They both watched as the stage was set for the next take. "An extraordinary woman," Brewster murmured. "Every man here is just a little bit in love with her."

"And you?"

A wry smile in his eyes, Brewster turned. "I'm a writer, Mr. Doran. I deal in fantasies. Chantel is very much flesh and blood."

At the assistant director's signal, the set fell silent and filming began again.

Quinn watched Brewster carefully. The writer seemed less nervous than he had in the early days of shooting. Perhaps he was pleased with the progress. It was Larry Washington who seemed on edge now. Chantel's assistant was never still for long, was always moving from one spot to the next. Did the tension Quinn felt on the set come from him? It was there. Quinn sensed it sparking the air, something nervy and desperate. Yet, everywhere he looked, people were going about their jobs with the drum-tight efficiency the director insisted on.

Perhaps the tension was just within himself. There was plenty of cause. Chantel was still just out of reach, not yet ready, or not yet able, to commit herself. When a man who had lived his life avoiding commitments finally found one he wanted, he was bound to be impatient. So Quinn told himself as he watched Chantel listen to the music box with pain and indecision in her eyes.

Were her thoughts on him, he wondered, or was she in character? Her talent made it nearly impossible to separate the actress from the role.

Every eye was on her, but she was alone, in a cabin in the woods, at a turning point in her life.

"Cut. Print. Wonderful." Mary Rothschild straightened from her position behind the camera operator. "Really wonderful, Chantel."

"Thanks." She drew a deep breath and tried to shake off the emotion that had carried her through the scene. "I'm glad I don't have to do that again."

"We're going to go to the confrontation with Brad." As she spoke, Mary began to knead Chantel's shoulders. "You know what you're feeling. You still want him. After everything he's done, everything you know, you can't quite remove yourself from the young woman who fell in love with him. You want to love your husband, you've tried, but the only thing you've managed to do is hurt him. You're on the edge of your life here. You know if you go with Brad, you'll never survive. Yet you're drawn."

"I'm fighting myself more than him."

"Exactly. Let's run through it."

They worked until six. Before it was over, special effects had pumped smoke onto the set. Hailey, dazed by the smoke, terrified of the fire that had begun to roar through the cabin, crawled along the wooden floor in a desperate search for the door. All she carried was the music box.

*　*　*

"Hell of a day," Quinn commented later when they were in Chantel's trailer.

"Tell me about it." Weary, she creamed off the streaks of soot makeup had smeared her face with. "I don't even want to eat, just sleep."

"I'll tuck you in."

She smiled and, after drying her face, swung her bag over her shoulder. "Tuck me in? I prefer having someone to snuggle against."

"You'll have that, too, in a few hours." They walked out of the trailer, past the soundstage, where the director and cinematographer were having an impromptu meeting.

"Going somewhere?"

"I've got some business." He thought of Matt, his friend, and of Chantel, the woman he loved. "I'll tell you about it when I get back."

"I'd rather you told me now." When they were outside, Chantel headed straight for the waiting limo. "Quinn, I don't want to be protected this way. Not anymore."

She was right, and he'd known that sooner or later he'd have to tell her. When she settled into the limo, he slid his arm behind, ready to comfort her.

"I didn't want to get into it in New York. You had your sister's wedding, and we had our own problems to deal with. Yesterday . . ." He hesitated, still not sure how to describe what that one twenty-four-hour period had meant to him. "I wanted yesterday for both of us."

"I understand." She lifted a hand to his. "So, what is it, Quinn?"

"I got a lead on the man who ordered the flowers." He felt her tense but didn't try to soothe her. She wouldn't want soothing now. "He paid cash, so there's no record. The florist couldn't give me much of a description. The guy wore dark glasses and a hat. There were a couple of things the florist noticed, though." He hesitated, hating to be the one to destroy a trust and a friendship. She was more important than both.

Than anything. "He smoked a foreign brand of cigarette and carried a monogrammed silver money clip."

For a moment her mind was blank. Slowly, the meaning came through. Rather than disillusionment, he saw a quick flash of determination. "A lot of men prefer foreign tobacco and clips."

"A lot of men don't work closely with you. This one said he did."

"He could have been lying."

"Could have been. We both know he wasn't. All along the one thing we could bank on was that this man knows you, and you know him. Chantel, you gave a silver money clip to someone who works with you."

"It's not Matt."

"Angel, it's time to separate what you want from what is, or at least what might be."

"It doesn't matter what you say, I won't believe it."

"I called Matt while we were in New York." He lifted a hand to cup her face. His grip was firm. "He was out of town, Chantel."

"So he was out of town." There was a quick flutter just beneath her heart, but she ignored it. "A lot of people go out of town on weekends."

"He was in New York on personal business."

She paled, but just as quickly shook her head.

"Quinn—"

"I have to go talk to him."

"I don't want you to accuse—" A look from him cut her off. "All right," she murmured, turning her head to stare out the window. "I'm not supposed to tell you how to do your job."

"That's right, angel. Look." He took her shoulder and turned her toward him. "Look at me." When she did, he swore under his breath and brushed the hair back from her face. "I don't want this to hurt you."

"You're telling me that my closest friend is your top suspect. I can't help but be hurt."

"Go home." He leaned closer and touched his lips to hers. "Go to bed. Stop thinking about it tonight. For me," he said before she could speak. "I love you, Chantel."

"Stay home and show me."

"No." He caught her face in his hands. "I won't be long. And this is going to be over. I promise you that."

They went through the gate and up the long, quiet drive. "I trust you," she told him, and forced herself to relax. "I'm going to wait for you."

"Wait for me in bed," he murmured, hoping for her sake that she'd fall asleep quickly.

They stepped out of the limo. "You'll be careful?"

"I'm always careful."

She started up the steps, then stopped and turned back. "I hate this, but I can't regret it anymore, because it brought you. Come back soon." She walked into the house without looking back.

She wouldn't think. The day's work had drained her body, and she would concentrate on that. She'd have a late supper brought upstairs when Quinn came back. For now, she would wind down with a swim and a whirlpool.

If it was Matt, it could all be over tonight. Over. For a moment, her hope centered there. Abruptly she felt the sickness hit the pit of her stomach. No, she wouldn't wish for that. Running away from her own thoughts, she hurried upstairs to change.

* * *

I'm glad I caught you in."

"Even superagents don't party every night." Matt was dressed in a casual sweater and slacks and comfortable boat shoes, and was wound tight as a spring. "Actually, I'm having a quiet dinner at home tonight. I didn't expect to see you. Want a drink?"

"No. Thanks."

Matt set the decanter down. "How's Chantel?"

"She's fine." Rather, he was going to see that she was fine, no matter what he had to do. "Funny, I thought you'd be checking a bit more closely on that yourself."

"I figured she'd be in good hands with you." Matt rocked back and forth on his heels, not sitting, not offering Quinn a chair. "And I've been a little tied up on some personal business."

"The business take you into New York over the weekend?"

"New York?" Matt's brows drew together. "What makes you think that?"

"The florist got a pretty good look." Quinn drew out a cigarette, watching Matt as he lighted it.

"Yeah?" With a half laugh, Matt finally sat. "What the hell are you talking about, Quinn?"

"The roses you sent to Chantel. You made a mistake this time. The envelope for the card had the florist's name on it."

"Roses I sent?" Matt dragged a hand through his hair as he shook his head. "I don't know what you're getting at. I—" He stopped then, as understanding came into his eyes. "Good God, you think I've been doing this to her? You think it's me? Damn it, Quinn." He sprang out of the chair. "I thought we knew each other."

"So did I. Where'd you spend the weekend, Matt?"

"None of your damn business."

Blowing out smoke, Quinn remained in his chair. "You can tell me, or I can find out. Either way, I'm going to see to it that you're out of her life."

Fury showed in clenched fists. Quinn glanced at them, almost hoping Matt would put them to use. A physical outlet would be more to his taste than this psychological sparring, hoping to wear down his opponent's resistance. "I'm her agent. I'm her friend. When she hit rock bottom, I was there for her. If I'd had those kind of feelings, I could have acted on them then."

"Where were you over the weekend?" Quinn demanded, determined to play this through to the bitter end.

"I was out of town," Matt snapped. "Personal business."

"You've had a lot of personal business going lately. You haven't shown up at all during the filming. You're such a good friend of Chantel's, but you've only seen her twice since you found out what was going on."

Guilt flashed briefly in his eyes, but then temper obscured it. "If Chantel had wanted me, she would have called me."

"I wonder if it's you who's been calling her."

"You're crazy." But Matt's hands shook a bit as he went to pour a drink.

"You use a money clip, Matt. A silver one," Quinn continued. "One Chantel gave you. The florist picked up on a couple little details like that."

"You want to see my money clip?" Furious, Matt reached into his pocket and yanked out a wad of bills held together by a small metal clip. It hit the table with a quiet thud.

Frowning, Quinn picked it up. It was gold, not silver, with Matt's initials engraved on it.

"I've been using that for two months, since you're so interested. Ever since Marion gave it to me." He picked up his drink and tossed it back. "If it wasn't for Chantel, I'd take a shot at tossing you out."

"You're entitled to try." Quinn dropped the clip again. "Maybe you'd be smarter to level with me. Where were you over the weekend, Matt?"

"New York." Swearing, he walked to the window and back. "Brooklyn. From Friday night until Sunday afternoon—I was meeting Marion's parents. Marion Lawrence, a twenty-four-year-old schoolteacher. Twenty-four," he repeated under his breath, rubbing a hand over his face. "I met her about three months ago. She's twelve years younger than me, bright, innocent, trusting. I should have walked away. Instead, I fell in love with her." After sending Quinn a furious look, he fumbled for a cigarette of his own.

"I've spent the last three months thinking about how I relate to houses with picket fences. This young, beautiful woman is going to marry me, and I spent the weekend trying to convince her conservative and very concerned parents that I wasn't some Hollywood playboy out to take their daughter for a ride. I'd rather have faced a firing squad." He puffed on his cigarette without inhaling.

"Listen, Quinn, if I haven't been around as much as Chantel needed, it was because I've lost my head over an elementary school teacher. Look at her." Matt flipped a photograph out of his billfold. "She looks like she could still *be* in school. I've been living on nerves for weeks."

Quinn believed him. With a mixture of relief and frustration, Quinn shut the billfold. It could have been a lie, but one man in love easily recognizes another. "What the hell does she see in you?"

Matt gave a shaky laugh. "She thinks I'm terrific. She knows about the gambling, about everything, and she thinks I'm terrific. I want to marry her before she finds out any different."

"Good luck."

"Yeah." Matt put the billfold away. His temper was gone, as were his embarrassment and his nerves. But guilt remained. "If we've got that straightened out, I'd like you to fill me in about Chantel. This character sent her flowers in New York?"

"That's right."

"He looked like me?"

"I don't know what he looked like."

"But you said—"

"I lied."

"You always were a bastard," Matt said without heat. "How's she holding up?"

"She's struggling. She's going to be better knowing you're clear."

"Let me ride out with you." He rubbed the back of his neck. "I would've told her about Marion before, but I felt—I guess I felt like an idiot. Here lies Matt Burns, agent of the stars, knocked unconscious by a woman who helps kids tie their shoelaces all day."

* * *

With her hair wet and loose, Chantel came into the pool house after a quick swim. The water and exercise had helped clear her head. Now all she wanted was to soothe her body. Hitting the switch for the whirlpool, she sent the bubbles gushing. A sigh of gratitude purred out as she lowered her body into the hot, churning water.

Quinn would be back soon, and one way or the other they would work things out. She had to concentrate on that, and not on the circumstances that had brought them together. Not on the circumstances that had taken him away tonight.

Beams from the setting sun came through the ribbon of high windows. The skylights above were the deep blue of early evening. Chantel let the jets of water beat the fatigue out of her muscles and soothe the lingering tension from her limbs.

She was on the verge of having everything she wanted. She had only to say yes to Quinn. He loved her. Chantel closed her eyes on that thought. He loved her for what she was, not what she appeared to be on the surface. No one but her family had ever accepted her totally, with her flaws, her insecurities, her mistakes. Quinn did. A woman could live a lifetime and not find a man who loved what she was on the inside.

What held her back from taking what she needed was the fear that she might not be able to give him everything—not a family of his own.

She wanted children. His children. What if she ultimately disappointed him that way? What if he, too, had to pay for her past mistakes? If she didn't love him so much, it would be so easy to say yes.

She wanted him to come back, to be with her now. If he could just hold her now, she'd know, somehow, the right answer to give him. Chantel closed her eyes and let herself sink a little deeper. When he came back to her, she would know, and whatever she did would be right for both of them.

She heard a sound, a soft one, at the back of the pool house. Straightening, Chantel pushed the wet hair away from her face. "Quinn? Don't say anything now." She closed her eyes again. "Just come here."

Then she heard the music, and her heart shot to her throat.

It was quiet, lovely, with the bell-like quality only the best music boxes achieve. The sky was nearly dark as the strains of the "Moonlight Sonata" flowed over the sound of churning water.

"Quinn." But she said his name knowing he wasn't there. Her hand shook as she reached over and turned off the jets. In the silence, the music box continued to play. Putting the heels of her hands behind her, Chantel pushed herself out of the tub.

"I've waited so long for this."

At the whisper, the air clogged in her throat. She had to breathe, she told herself. If she was to get to the door she had to breathe, and the door was so far away. The lights dimmed, and the fear raced along her skin.

"You're so beautiful. So incredibly beautiful. Nothing I could imagine or create could be as perfect. Tonight, we'll finally be together."

He was in the shadows near the rear door. Chantel forced herself to look, but even then she couldn't see who it was. "There are guards outside." She balled her hand into a fist, refusing to allow her voice to quiver. "I could scream."

"There's only the guard at the gate, and he's too far away. I had to hurt the others. Sometimes you have to hurt when you love."

She gauged the distance to the front door. "How did you get in?"

"Over the wall by the tennis courts. You haven't been using the tennis courts. I've been watching for you."

"The alarm—"

"I took care of the alarm. I have some knowledge. My reputation for careful research is well deserved." Brewster stepped out of the shadows with the music box in his hands.

"James." The air in the pool house was sultry, but Chantel began to shiver. "Why are you doing this?"

"I love you." His eyes were glazed, and she could see no emotion in them as he walked closer. "When you first formed in my mind, I knew I had to have you. Then you were there, flesh, blood. Real. I had this made for you."

He held out the music box, and Chantel stepped back.

"Don't be afraid of me, Hailey."

"James, I'm Chantel. Chantel."

"Yes, yes, of course." He smiled at her, then set the box down on a little table beside the tub. It continued to play, romantic and sweet. "Chantel O'Hurley, with the perfect face. I've dreamed of you for months. I can't write. My wife thinks I'm agonizing over my new book. But there is no book. There'll never be another book. Chantel, you wouldn't keep my flowers."

"I'm sorry." Quinn would be back, she told herself. The nightmare would be over. She felt exposed in her brief suit, so she reached for her wrap. Training kept her gestures casual, even as her heart roared in her head. "It was the way you sent them, James. You frightened me."

"I never meant to. Hailey—"

"Chantel," she corrected, a flutter of panic in her voice. "I'm Chantel. James, I think we should go into the house and talk about this."

"Chantel?" He looked momentarily puzzled. "No, no, I want to be alone with you. I've waited too long for tonight. The perfect night, when the moon is full. The song." He looked at the music box. "It was meant for you."

"Why didn't you just talk to me?"

"You would have rejected me. Rejected me," he repeated in a rising voice. "Do you think I'm a fool? I've seen you with those young men, all muscles and smooth faces. But none of them love you like I do. You've driven me mad with waiting. You were obsessed with Brad. It was always Brad."

"There is no Brad!" she shouted. "He's a character. There is no Hailey. You made them up. They're not real."

"You're real. I've seen you with him. I've watched the way you look at him, let him touch you, when it should be me. But I've been patient. Tonight." He started toward her. "I've waited for tonight."

Chantel raced for the front door, knowing that if she could beat him she'd have a chance. Grabbing the knob, she pulled, but it held firm.

"I locked it from the outside," Brewster told her quietly. "I knew you'd try to run away. I knew you'd throw my love back in my face."

Chantel spun around, pressing her back to the door. "You don't love me. You're confused. I'm an actress; I'm not your Hailey."

He winced as if in pain and pressed his fingers to his eyes. "Such headaches," he murmured. "No, don't," he warned when she edged toward the back door. He blocked her way, then stepped back into the shadows to pick something up. "I know what I have to do, and there's no running for either of us now, Hailey."

"I'm not—"

"It's too late," he said viciously. "Too late. I guess I've always known. I hate what you've done to me." He pressed his fingers to his temple as tears welled up in his eyes. "But as God is my witness, I can't let another man have you. You're mine. From the first moment, you were mine. If you could only understand that."

"James." She was afraid to touch him, but she took a small step closer. "Please, come into the house with me. I'm—I'm cold," she said quickly. "I'm wet. I need to change. Then we can sit down and talk."

He looked at her but saw only what he wanted to see. "You

can't lie to me. I created you. You're going to try to leave. You want to see them put me away. My doctor wants to put me away, but I know what I have to do. For both of us. It ends here, Hailey."

He held up the can, and she smelled the gasoline. "Oh, God, no."

"You were meant to die in the fire before, but I couldn't do it then. Now I have to."

He turned the can over as she lunged at him. It hit the floor with a clatter, then skidded, gas soaking into the wood. She fought to get past him. Chantel heard him sob as he shoved her down, and her head hit the table. Suddenly there were shooting stars in front of her eyes.

* * *

"Chantel's going to want to open a bottle of champagne."

"I think we could all use it," Matt commented as they walked into the house. "Quinn, I'd appreciate it if you'd let me tell her."

"You're entitled." He looked around the cool, quiet hall. "You were entitled to take a swing at me back there."

"You're bigger than I am," Matt said easily.

"I overreacted, Matt. I'm not used to that." He thought about Chantel waiting for him upstairs, and what he would have done, would continue to do to keep her safe. "The thing is I jumped on you with both feet because it was the first solid lead I've had in this whole mess."

"From what you told me, it looks like everything the florist told you fit me."

"What fits you fits someone else. I'm missing it," Quinn murmured. "I'm missing it because I'm too close. You know what the first rule of law enforcement, private or public service, is? Don't get involved."

"A little late for that I take it."

"Way too late. She believed in you," he added. "I think you

should know that. Even after I spelled it all out for her, she stood behind you."

Touched, Matt fiddled with the lapel of his jacket. "She's a very special woman."

"She's the most beautiful woman I've ever met, inside and out. Integrity. You don't see the integrity when you look at her, or the guts, or the loyalty. It's taken me a while to get under the surface and see all there is to her." He moved his shoulders, restless, dissatisfied. "Maybe if I'd had a little more of her faith in the people she cares for, I wouldn't have chased down a blind alley."

Matt followed Quinn's gaze up the stairs. If Quinn had overreacted, he thought, then he himself had underreacted. The past few weeks he'd been too involved with his own world to give one of his closest friends the kind of time and attention she needed. He turned the bottle in his hand. He was going to start making up for it now.

"Look, I was pretty steamed before, but I think you're as crazy about Chantel as I am about Marion. I probably would have done the same thing myself."

"Maybe." Quinn glanced at the stairs again. He didn't want champagne. He only wanted to be alone with Chantel, but she needed to see Matt, needed to talk to him. She'd be relieved, and yet he wondered if she would feel the same frustration he was experiencing. They'd come so far, yet they'd gone nowhere. "I hate what she's going through."

"So do I." Matt laid a hand on his shoulder. "The past couple months have taught me that love can drive anybody crazy. I guess it's like Brewster said in that interview."

"What interview?"

"It was in the paper tonight. They did an article on *Strangers*, focusing on Hailey. The way he described her, hell, you'd have thought she was real. But he said something that rang true—about how when a man really loves a woman, he sees her as no one else does; no matter what he accomplishes, what he fails at, she stays at the center of his life, rules it just by being. I guess I was feeling sentimental when I read it," Matt said with a trace of embarrassment. "But I thought I knew what he meant. He even got Chantel and Hailey's names mixed up once."

"What?"

"You could tell the reporter got a charge out of that. He played up how Chantel must be turning in an Emmy-winning performance to have the writer confuse the actress with the character."

"Damn." Quinn slammed his fist against the newel post and started up the stairs. "He practically confessed this afternoon. He all but spit it in my lap."

"What are you—" But Quinn was gone. Matt just shrugged and wondered if he had time to telephone Marion.

"Call the fire department," Quinn shouted, taking the steps three at a time. "The pool house is going up."

"It's on fire?"

"She's in there." Quinn was at the door before Matt picked up the phone. "He's got her in there."

* * *

Chantel shook her head to try to clear it. The room swam, and she struggled to her hands and knees. She smelled the smoke first, thick and pungent, as it had been that afternoon during the filming. But this wasn't special effects, she remembered. She heard the crackle of flames and looked over to see the floor turn to fire.

He was still blocking the back door, standing there as if hypnotized by the fire, which was spreading fast. He wasn't trying to leave. He would die here, he wanted to die here. And he would take her with him.

Chantel stood, choking on smoke as she looked around frantically. Her head throbbed and spun, but she couldn't allow herself the luxury of passing out. The windows were too high. She'd never get out that way. The front door was barred.

There was only one exit. She had to get past him before the fire closed it off.

Her breath came in a fit of coughing, but he didn't hear. The flames held his attention as they ate greedily at the far wall. The heat was growing, visible in waves that shimmered between her and the door. Moving fast, Chantel grabbed a towel and dumped it in the tub. Then, draping it over her face, she looked for a weapon.

The music box sat on the table, playing though the tune was muffled by the sound of flames. She took it and, on legs that threatened to buckle, walked behind Brewster.

He was crying. She heard it now as she raised the heavy wooden box over her head. Tears were streaking her own face, blurring her vision. It was so much like the scene she had studied, rehearsed, tried to understand.

Hailey, she thought as smoke clouded her brain. It was the cabin, her New England retreat. She was Hailey, and she'd brought tragedy on herself, on those who had loved her. Past mistakes, past loves, past lives. If only she hadn't given her love and her innocence to Brad. . . . To Dustin?

Her vision went gray, and she fought to clear it. There was no Brad. Only Quinn. Quinn was real and she was Chantel. An O'Hurley. O'Hurleys were survivors.

Weeping, she smashed the box down on Brewster's head.

When he crumpled at her feet, she could only crouch, panting, struggling to find air in a room consumed by smoke and flame.

Had she killed him? She looked at the doorway, framed now by flames. Her only way out. Survival. She took a step forward, stopped, then bent over Brewster.

He'd loved her. Mad or sane, whatever he'd done had been tied to her. Somehow, later, she would sort it out, but she couldn't save herself without trying to save him.

She snatched off the towel and covered his face with it. The ceiling gave an ominous crack, but she didn't dare look. She didn't think. Everything was centered on living. Hooking her hands under his armpits, Chantel began to drag him toward the door and closer to the flames.

She was losing. There was no air to fill her lungs as she dragged the deadweight of Brewster's unconscious body. The fire was winning, edging closer. She felt the furnace blast of heat on her skin and wished desperately that she'd taken the time to wet some towels.

Inches from the door, she stumbled and fell, lightheaded from lack of oxygen. A little farther, she demanded, dragging herself and Brewster across the floor. Oh, God, just a little farther.

She watched, too dazed to be frightened, as a beam fell, flaming, into the hot tub.

"Chantel!"

She heard the shout dimly as her consciousness started to waver. Somehow she managed to gain another two inches.

Quinn kicked in the front door and saw nothing but a wall of flame. He screamed for her again and heard nothing but fire. The roof was going. He ran for the doorway, but the heat drove him back. It was then he saw her, or thought he did, slumped by the far wall, with the flames separating them.

Coughing on the smoke he'd swallowed, he raced around the building, praying for the first time in his adult life.

She'd almost made it. That was his first thought as he saw her, collapsed against Brewster near the door. Burning wood showered from the ceiling as he hurled his body over hers. He felt it hit and sear his hand before he dragged her out onto the grass.

"In the name of God—" Matt began as he raced to them.

"Brewster's in there," Quinn managed. "Take care of her."

Quinn fought the heat again, nearly giving way at what had been the back doorway. Crawling on his belly, he inched closer, until he managed to grip Brewster's wrist. If there was a pulse, he couldn't feel it, but he dragged him back. As the roof collapsed inward, he left Brewster lying on the grass and rolled onto his back to draw in air.

"Chantel." Still coughing, he crawled to her. Her face was smeared with soot. He heard the sirens as she opened her eyes to look at him.

"Quinn. He—"

"I got him out. Don't try to talk now." She began to shiver, though the heat was still intense. Quinn stripped off his shirt and covered her. "She's in shock," he said tersely. "Smoke inhalation. She needs the hospital."

"I told them to send an ambulance." Matt peeled off his sweater and added it to Quinn's shirt. "She's going to be all right. She's tough."

"Yeah." Quinn cradled her head in his lap. "Yeah."

"He thought I was Hailey." She groped for his hand as she wavered in and out of consciousness.

"I know. Shhh." He took her hand and squeezed. The pain from his burns was real. She was real. And they were alive.

"I . . . for a little while in there, so did I. Quinn, tell me who I am."

"Chantel O'Hurley. The only woman I've ever loved."

"Thanks," she whispered, and drifted off.

* * *

By the time he was allowed to see her, Quinn had gone twenty-four hours without sleep. He'd refused to leave the hospital to change, and his clothes were streaked and reeking of smoke. Throughout the night he'd paced the halls and driven the nurses crazy.

She'd been treated for shock and smoke inhalation. The doctors had assured him that all she needed was rest. He intended to see and speak to her himself before he went anywhere. And when he went, she was going with him.

At dawn the day after the fire, Chantel awoke from a drugged sleep. When the doctor came out of her room, he was shaking his head. He looked at Quinn, noting his bandaged hand and singed clothing. "You can see her now. I'm going to process her discharge papers, though if you have any influence, you should talk her into staying one more day for observation."

"I can take care of her at home."

The doctor sent a dubious look in the direction of the door. "Maybe you can. Mr. Doran?"

Quinn stopped with his hand on the knob. "Yes?"

"She's a very strong-willed woman."

"I know." For the first time in hours, Quinn smiled. He opened the door to see Chantel sitting up in bed, frowning into a mirror.

"I look horrible."

"Beauty's only skin deep," he said as she lowered the mirror to look at him.

"It's a good thing, because you look worse than I do. Oh, Quinn . . ." She spread her arms wide. "You're really here," she whispered as she used all her strength to squeeze. "It's all right now, isn't it? Everything's going to be all right."

"It's over. I should have taken better care of you."

"I'll dock your pay."

"Damn it, Chantel, it's not a joke."

"You saved my life," she told him as she drew away.

"When I think of what might have happened—"

"No." She put her fingertips to his mouth. "I don't want to think of 'what ifs' anymore, Quinn. I'm safe and so are you. That's all that matters now. And . . . and James . . ."

"He'll live," Quinn said, answering her unspoken question. He stood and began to prowl the room. "He's going to be put away, Chantel. I'm going to help see to that."

"Quinn, he was so pathetic, so confused. He created something that overwhelmed him."

"He would have killed you."

"He would have killed Hailey," she corrected. "I can only pity him."

"Forget him," Quinn told her, knowing he would have to if he didn't want to be eaten alive by bitterness. "Your family's coming."

"Here? All of them?"

"Your sisters, your parents. Nobody knows how to reach Trace."

"Quinn, I don't want to disrupt Maddy's honeymoon. And everyone else—"

"Wants to make sure you're all right. That's what families are for, right?"

"Yes." She folded her hands. "It is. Quinn, you deserve a family, your own family."

He turned to her, ready to fight for what he needed. "I know what I want, Chantel."

"Yes, I think you do." She'd made her decision when she'd opened her eyes on the grass and seen his face. "Quinn, before all of this happened last night, I was waiting for you. I knew when you came back and held me, I'd make the right choice, for both of us." She glanced around the room, then into the mirror. With a grimace she set it facedown on the table beside her. "This isn't exactly how I expected things to be, but it would help a lot if you'd come here and put your arms around me."

He sat on the bed beside her and gathered her close. "Listen, I have to tell you this. When I got there last night and the pool house was burning, I knew you were inside because my heart had stopped. If I had lost you, it would never have started again."

"Quinn." She lifted her head, searching for his lips. Finding them, she found all the answers she needed. "I'd like a short engagement," she said, smiling. "Very, very short."

Irish Rose

CHAPTER 1

Her name was Erin, like her country. And like her country, she was a maze of contradictions—rebellion and poetry, passion and moodiness. She was strong enough to fight for her beliefs, stubborn enough to fight on after a cause was lost, and generous enough to give whatever she had. She was a woman with soft skin and a tough mind. She had sweet dreams and towering ambitions.

Her name was Erin, Erin McKinnon, and she was nervous as a cat.

It was true that this was only the third time in her life she'd been in the airport at Cork. Or any airport, for that matter. Still, it wasn't the crowds or the noise that made her jumpy. The fact was, she liked hearing the announcements of planes coming and going. She liked thinking about all the people going places.

London, New York, Paris. Through the thick glass she could watch the big sleek planes rise up, nose first, and imagine their destinations. Perhaps one day she'd board one herself and experience that stomach-fluttering anticipation as the plane climbed up and up.

She shook her head. It wasn't a plane going up that had her nervous now, but one coming in. And it was due any minute. Erin caught herself before she dragged a hand through her hair. It wouldn't do a bit of good to be poking and pulling at

herself. After thirty seconds more, she shifted her bag from
hand to hand, then tugged at her jacket. She didn't want to look
disheveled or tense . . . or poor, she added as she ran a hand
down her skirt to smooth it.

Thank God her mother was so clever with a needle. The
deep blue of the skirt and matching jacket was flattering to her
pale complexion. The cut and style were perhaps a bit conservative for Erin's taste, but the color did match her eyes. She
wanted to look competent, capable, and had even managed to
tame her unruly hair into a tidy coil of dark red. The style
made her look older, she thought. She hoped it made her look
sophisticated, too.

She'd toned down the dusting of freckles and had deepened
the color of her lips. Eye makeup had been applied with a
careful hand, and she wore Nanny's old and lovely gold cres-
cents at her ears.

The last thing she wanted was to look plain and dowdy. The
poor relation. Even the echo of the phrase in her head caused
her teeth to clench. Pity, even sympathy, were emotions she
wanted none of. She was a McKinnon, and perhaps fortune
hadn't smiled on her as it had her cousin, but she was determined to make her own way.

Here they were, she thought, and had to swallow a ball of
nerves in her throat. Erin watched the plane that had brought
them from Curragh taxi toward the gate—the small, sleek
plane people of wealth and power could afford to charter.
She could imagine what it would be like to sit inside, to drink
champagne or nibble on something exotic. Imagination had
always been hers in quantity. All she'd lacked was the means
to make what she could imagine come true.

An elderly woman stepped off the plane first, leading a
small girl by the hand. The woman had cloud-white hair and a
solid, sturdy build. Beside her, the little girl looked like a pixie,
carrot-topped and compact. The moment they'd stepped to the
ground, a boy of five or six leaped off after them.

Even through the thick glass, Erin could all but hear the woman's scolding. She snatched his hand with her free one, and he flashed her a wicked grin. Erin felt immediate kinship. If she'd gauged the age right, that would be Brendon, Adelia's oldest. The girl who held the woman's hand and clutched a battered doll in the other would be Keeley, younger by a year or so.

The man came next, the man Erin recognized as Travis Grant. Her cousin's husband of seven years, owner of Thoroughbreds and master of Royal Meadows. He was tall and broad-shouldered and was laughing down at his son, who waited impatiently on the tarmac. The smile was nice, she thought, the kind that made a woman look twice without being sure whether to relax or brace herself. Erin had met him once, briefly, when he'd brought his wife back to Ireland four years before. Quietly domineering, she'd thought then. The kind of man a woman could depend on, as long as she could stand toe-to-toe with him.

On his hip he carried another child, a boy with hair as dark and thick as his father's. He was grinning, too, but not down at his brother and sister. His face was tilted up toward the sky from which he'd just come. Travis handed him down, then turned and held out a hand.

As Adelia stepped through the opening, the sun struck her hair with arrows of light. The rich chestnut shone around her face and shoulders. She, too, was laughing. Even with the distance, Erin could see the glow. She was a small woman. When Travis caught her by the waist and lifted her to the ground, she didn't reach his shoulder. He kept his arm around her, Erin noticed, not so much possessive as protective of her and perhaps of the child that was growing inside her.

While Erin watched, Adelia tilted her face, touched a hand to her husband's cheek and kissed him. Not like a long-time wife, Erin thought, but like a lover.

A little ripple of envy moved through her. Erin didn't try to avoid it. She never attempted to avoid any of her feelings, but let them come, let them race to the limit, whatever the consequences.

And why shouldn't she envy Dee? Erin asked herself. Adelia Cunnane, the little orphan from Skibbereen, had not only pulled herself up by the bootstraps but had tugged hard enough to land on top of the pile. More power to her, Erin thought. She intended to do the same herself.

Erin squared her shoulders and started to step forward as another figure emerged from the plane. Another servant, she thought, then took a long, thorough look. No, this man would serve no one.

He leaped lightly to the ground with a slim, unlit cigar clamped between his teeth. Slowly, even warily, he looked around. As a cat might, she thought, a cat that had just leaped from cliff to cliff. She couldn't see his eyes, for he wore tinted glasses, but she had the quick impression that they would be sharp, intense and not entirely comfortable to look into.

He was as tall as Travis but leaner, sparer. Tough. The adjective came to her as she pursed her lips and continued to stare. He bent down to speak to one of the children, and the move was lazy but not careless. His dark hair was straight and long enough to hang over the collar of his denim shirt. He wore boots and faded jeans, but she rejected the idea that he was a farmer. He didn't look like a man who tilled the soil but like one who owned it.

What was a man like this doing traveling with her cousin's family? Another relative? she wondered, and shifted uncomfortably. It didn't matter who he was. Erin checked the pins in her hair, found two loose, and shoved them into place. If he was some relation of Travis Grant's, then that was fine.

But he didn't look like kin of her cousin's husband. The coloring might be similar, but any resemblance ended there. The stranger had a raw-boned, sharp-edged look to him. She remembered the picture books in catechism class, and the drawings of Satan.

"Better to rule in hell than to serve in heaven."

Yes . . . For the first time, a smile moved on her lips. He looked like a man who'd have similar sentiments. Taking a deep breath, Erin moved forward to greet her family.

The boy Brendon came first, barreling through the doorway with one shoe untied and eyes alight with curiosity. The white-haired woman came in behind him, moving with surprising speed.

"Stand still, you scamp. I'm not going to lose track of you again."

"I just want to see, Hannah." There was a laugh in his voice and no contrition at all when she caught his hand in hers.

"You'll see soon enough. No need to worry your mother to death. Keeley, you stay close now."

"I will." The little girl looked around as avidly as her brother, but seemed more content to stay in the same place. Then she spotted Erin. "There she is. That's our cousin Erin. Just like the picture." Without a hint of reserve, the girl crossed over and smiled. "You're our cousin Erin, aren't you? I'm Keeley. Momma said you'd be waiting for us."

"Aye, I'm Erin." Charmed, Erin bent down to catch the little girl's chin in her hand. Nerves vanished into genuine pleasure. "And the last time I saw you, you were just a wee thing, all bundled in a blanket against the rain and bawling fit to wake the dead."

Keeley's eyes widened. "She talks just like Momma," she announced. "Hannah, come see. She talks just like Momma."

"Miss McKinnon." Hannah kept one hand firmly on Brendon's shoulder and offered the other. "It's nice to meet you. I'm Hannah Blakely, your cousin's housekeeper."

Housekeeper, Erin thought as she put her hand in Hannah's weathered one. The Cunnanes she'd known might have been housekeepers, but they'd never had one. "Welcome to Ireland. And you'd be Brendon."

"I've been to Ireland before," he said importantly. "But this time I flew the plane."

"Did you now?" She saw her cousin in him, the pixielike features and deep green eyes. He'd be a handful, she thought, as her mother claimed Adelia had always been. "Well, you're all grown up since I saw you last."

"I'm the oldest. Brady's the baby now."

"Erin?" She glanced over in time to see Adelia rush forward. Even heavy with child she moved lightly. And when she wound her arms around Erin, there was strength in them. The recognition came strongly—family to family, roots to roots. "Oh, Erin, it's so good to be back, so good to see you. Let me look at you."

She hadn't changed a bit, Erin thought. Adelia would be nearly thirty now, but she looked years younger. Her complexion was smooth and flawless, glowing against the glossy mane of hair she still wore long and loose. The pleasure in her face was so real, so vital, that Erin felt it seeping through her own reserve.

"You look wonderful, Dee. America's been good for you."

"And the prettiest girl in Skibbereen's become a beautiful woman. Oh, Erin." She kissed both her cousin's cheeks, laughed and kissed them again. "You look like home." With Erin's hand still held tightly in hers, she turned. "You remember Travis."

"Of course. It's good to see you again."

"You've grown up in four years." He kissed her cheek in turn. "You didn't meet Brady the last time."

"No, I didn't." The child kept an arm around his father's neck and eyed Erin owlishly. "Faith, he's the image of you. It's a handsome boy you are, Cousin Brady."

Brady smiled, then turned to bury his face in his father's neck.

"And shy," Adelia commented, stroking a hand down his hair. "Unlike his da. Erin, it's so kind of you to offer to meet us and take us to the inn."

"We don't often get visitors. I've got the minibus. You know from the last time you came that renting a car is tricky, so I'll be leaving it with you while you're here." While she spoke, Erin felt an itch at the base of her neck, a tingle, or a warning. Deliberately she turned and stared back at the lean-faced man she'd seen step off the plane.

"Erin, this is Burke." Adelia placed a hand on her skirt at the stirrings within her womb. "Burke Logan, my cousin, Erin McKinnon."

"Mr. Logan," Erin said with a slight nod, determined not to flinch at her own reflection in his mirrored glasses.

"Miss McKinnon." He smiled slowly, then clamped his cigar between his teeth again.

She still couldn't see his eyes but had the uneasy feeling that the glasses were no barrier to what he saw. "I'm sure you're tired," she said to Adelia, but kept her gaze stubbornly on Burke's. "The bus is right out front. I'll take you out, then we'll deal with the luggage."

* * *

Burke kept himself just a little apart as they walked through the small terminal. He preferred it that way, the better to observe and figure angles. Just now, he was figuring Erin McKinnon.

A tidy little package, he mused, watching the way her long, athletic legs moved beneath her conservative skirt. Neat as a pin and nervous as a filly at the starting gate. Just what kind of race did she intend to run? he wondered.

He knew snatches of the background from conversations on the trip from the States and from Curragh to this little spot on the map. The McKinnons and Cunnanes weren't first cousins. As near as could be figured, Adelia's mother and the mother of the very interesting Erin McKinnon had been third cousins who had grown up on neighboring farms.

Burke smiled as Erin looked uneasily over her shoulder in

his direction. If Adelia Cunnane Grant figured that made her and the McKinnons family, he wouldn't argue. For himself, he spent more time avoiding family connections than searching them out.

If he didn't stop staring at her like that, he was going to get a piece of her mind, Erin told herself as she slid the van into gear. The luggage was loaded, the children chattering, and she had to keep her wits about her to navigate out of the airport.

* * *

She could see him in the rearview mirror, legs spread out in the narrow aisle, one arm tossed over the worn seat—and his eyes on her. Try as she might, she couldn't concentrate on Adelia's questions about her family.

As she wound the van onto the road, she listened with half an ear and gave her cousin the best answers she could. Everyone was fine. The farm was doing well enough. As she began to relax behind the wheel, she dug deep for bits and pieces of gossip. Still, he kept staring at her.

Let him, then, she decided. The man obviously had the manners of a plow mule and was no concern of hers. Stubbornly avoiding another glance in the rearview mirror, she jabbed another loose pin back in her hair.

She had questions of her own. Erin expertly avoided the worst of the bumps on the road and trained her eyes straight ahead. The first of them would be who the hell was this Burke Logan. Still, she smiled on cue and assured her cousin again that her family was fit and fine.

"So Cullen's not married yet."

"Cullen?" Despite her determination, Erin's gaze had drifted back to the mirror and Burke. She cursed herself. "No. Much to my mother's regret, he's still single. He goes into Dublin now and again to sing his songs and play." She hit a rough patch that sent the van vibrating. "I'm sorry."

"It's all right."

Turning her head, she studied Adelia with genuine concern. "Are you sure? I'm wondering if you should be traveling at all."

"I'm healthy as one of Travis's horses." In a habitual gesture, Adelia put a hand on her rounded belly. "And I've months to go before they're born."

"They?"

"Twins this time." The smile lit up her face. "I've been hoping."

"Twins," Erin repeated under her breath, not sure whether she should be amazed or amused.

Adelia shifted into a more comfortable position. Glancing back, she saw that her two youngest were dozing and that Brendon was putting up a courageous, if failing, battle to keep his eyes open. "I've always wanted a big family like yours."

Erin grinned at her as the van putted into the village. "It looks like you're going to match it. And may the sweet Lord have mercy on you."

With a chuckle, Adelia shifted again to absorb the sights and sounds of the village she remembered from childhood.

The small buildings were still neat, if a bit rough around the edges. Patches of grass were deep and green, shimmering against dark brown dirt. The sign on the village pub, the Shamrock, creaked and groaned in a breeze that tasted of rain from the sea.

She could almost smell it, and remembered it easily. Here the cliffs were sheer and towering, slicing down to a wild sea. She could remember the times she'd stood on the rock watching the fishing boats, seeing them come in with their day's catch to dry their nets and cool dry throats at the pub.

The talk here was of fishing and farming, of babies and sweethearts.

It was home. Adelia rested a hand against the open window and looked out. It was home—a way of life, a place she'd never been able to close out of her heart. There was a wagon filled with hay, its color no brighter, its scent no sweeter than that of the hay in her own stables in America. But this was Ireland, and her heart had never stopped looking back here.

"It hasn't changed."

Erin eased the vehicle to a stop and glanced around. She knew every square inch of the village, and every farm for a hundred miles around. In truth, she'd never known anything else. "Did you expect it would? Nothing ever changes here."

"There's O'Donnelly's, the dry goods." Dee stepped out of the van. Foolishly she wanted to have her feet on the ground of her youth. She wanted to fill her lungs with the air of Skibbereen. "Is he still there?"

"The old goat will die behind the counter, still counting his last pence."

With a laugh, Dee took Brady from Travis and cuddled him as he yawned and settled against her shoulder. "Aye, then he hasn't changed, either. Travis, you see the church there. We'd come in every Sunday for mass. Old Father Finnegan would drone on and on. Does he still, Erin?"

Erin slipped the keys of the van in the pocket of her purse. "He died, Dee, better than a year ago." Because the light went out of her cousin's eyes, Erin lifted a hand to her cheek. "He was more than eighty, if you remember, and died quietly in his sleep."

Life went on, she knew, and people passed out of it whether you wanted them to or not. Dee glanced back at the church. It would never seem exactly the same again. "He buried Mother and Da. I can't forget how kind he was to me."

"We've a young priest now," Erin began briskly. "Sent from Cork. A hell-raiser he is, and not a soul sleeps through one of his sermons. Put the fear of God into Michael Ryan, so the man comes sober to mass every Sunday morning." She turned to help with the luggage and slammed solidly into Burke. He put a hand on her shoulder as if to steady her, but it lingered too long.

"I beg your pardon."

She couldn't stop her chin from tilting forward or her eyes

from spitting at him. He only smiled. "My fault." Grabbing two hefty cases, he swung them out of the van. "Why don't you take Dee and the kids in, Travis? I'll deal with this."

Normally Travis wouldn't have left another with the bulk of the work, but he knew his wife's strength was flagging. He also knew she was stubborn, and the only way to get her into bed for a nap was to put her there himself.

"Thanks. I'll take care of checking in. Erin, we'll see you and your family tonight?"

"They'll be here." On impulse, she kissed Dee's cheek. "You'll rest now. Otherwise Mother will fuss and drive you mad. That I can promise."

"Do you have to go now? Couldn't you come in?"

"I've some things to see to. Go on now, or your children will be asleep in the street. I'll see you soon."

Over Brandon's protest, Hannah bundled them inside. Erin turned to grip another pair of cases by the handles and began unloading. It passed through her mind that expensive clothes must weigh more when she found herself facing Burke again.

"There's just a few more," she muttered, and deliberately breezed by him.

Inside, the inn was dim but far from quiet. The excitement of having visitors from America had kept the small staff on their toes all week. Wood had been polished, floors had been scrubbed. Even now old Mrs. Malloy was leading Dee up the stairs and keeping up a solid stream of reminiscence. The children were cooed over, and hot tea and soda bread were offered. Deciding she'd left her charges in good hands, Erin walked outside again.

The day was cool and clear. The early clouds had long since been blown away by the westerly wind so that the light, as it often was in Ireland, was luminescent and pearly. Erin took a moment to study the village that had so fascinated her cousin. It was ordinary, slow, quiet, filled with workingmen and women and often smelling of fish. From almost any point in town you could see the small harbor where the boats came in with their daily catch. The storefronts were kept neat. That was a matter of pride. The doors were left unlocked. That was a matter of custom.

There was no one there who didn't know her, no one she didn't know. Whatever secrets there were were never secrets for long, but were passed out like small treasures to be savored and sighed over.

God, she wanted to see something else before her life was done. She wanted to see big cities where life whirled by, fast and hot and anonymous. She wanted to walk down a street where no one knew who she was and no one cared. Just once, just once in her life, she wanted to do something wild and impulsive that wouldn't echo back to her on the tongues of family and neighbors. Just once.

The van door slammed and jolted her back to reality. Again she found herself looking at Burke Logan. "They're all settled, then?" she asked, struggling to be polite.

"Looks like." He leaned back against the van. With his ankles crossed, he pulled out a lighter and lit his cigar. He never smoked around Adelia out of respect for her condition. His eyes never left Erin's. "Not much family resemblance between you and Mrs. Grant, is there?"

It was the first time he'd spoken more than two words at a time. Erin noted that his accent wasn't like Travis's. His words came more slowly, as if he saw no reason to hurry them. "There's the hair," he continued when Erin didn't speak. "But hers is more like Travis's prize chestnut colt, and yours"—he took another puff as he deliberated—"yours is something like the mahogany stand in my bedroom." He grinned, the cigar still clamped between his teeth. "I thought it was mighty pretty when I bought it."

"That's a lovely thought, Mr. Logan, but I'm not a horse or a table." Reaching into her pocket, she held out the keys. "I'll be leaving these with you, then."

Instead of taking them, he simply closed his hand over hers, cradling the keys between them. His palm was hard and rough as the rocks in the cliffs that dropped toward the sea. He enjoyed the way she held her ground, the way she lifted her brow, more in disdain than offense.

"Is there something else you're wanting, Mr. Logan?"

"I'll give you a lift," he said simply.

"It's not necessary." She clenched her teeth and nodded as two of the town's busiest gossips passed behind her. The evening news would have Erin McKinnon holding hands with a stranger in the street, sure as faith. "I've only to ask for a ride home to get one."

"You've got one already." With his hand still on hers, he pushed away from the van. "I told Travis I'd see to it." After releasing her hand, he gestured toward the door. "Don't worry, I've nearly got the hang on driving on the wrong side of the road."

"It's you who drive on the wrong side." After only a brief hesitation, Erin climbed in. The day was passing her by, and she'd have to make every minute count just to catch up.

Burke settled behind the wheel and turned the key in the ignition. "You're losing your pins," he said mildly.

Erin reached behind her and shoved them into place as he drove out of the village. "You'll take the left fork when you come to it. After that it's only four or five kilometers." Erin folded her hands, deciding she'd granted him enough conversation.

"Pretty country," Burke commented, glancing out at the green, windswept hills. There were blackthorns, bent a bit from the continual stream of the westerly breeze. Heather grew in a soft purple cloud, while in the distance the mountains rose dark and eerie in the light. "You're close to the sea."

"Close enough."

"Don't you like Americans?"

With her hands still folded primly, she turned to look at him. "I don't like men who stare at me."

Burke tapped his cigar ash out the window. "That would narrow the field considerably."

"The men I know have manners, Mr. Logan."

He liked the way she said his name, with just a hint of spit in it. "Too bad. I was taught to take a good long look at something that interested me."

"I'm sure you consider that a compliment."

"Just an observation. This the fork?"

"Aye." She drew a long breath, knowing she had no reason to set her temper loose and every reason to hold it. "Do you work for Travis?"

"No." He grinned as the van shimmied over ruts. "You might say Travis and I are associates." He liked the smell here, the rich wet scent of Ireland and the warm earthy scent of the woman beside him. "I own the farm that borders his."

"You race horses?" She lifted a brow again, compelled to study him.

"At the moment."

Erin's lips pursed as she considered. She could picture him at the track, with the noise and the smells of the horses. Try as she might, she couldn't put him behind a desk, balancing accounts and ledgers. "Travis's farm is quite successful."

His lips curved again. "Is that your way of asking about mine?"

Her chin angled as she looked away. "It's certainly none of my concern."

"No, it's not. But I do well enough. I wasn't born into it like Travis, but I find it suits me—for now. They'd take you back with them if you asked."

At first it didn't sink in. Then her lips parted in surprise as she turned to him again.

"I recognize a restless soul when I see one." Burke blew out smoke so that it trailed through the window and disappeared. "You're straining at the bit to get out of this little smudge on the map. Though if you ask me, it has its charm."

"No one asked you."

"True enough, but it's hard not to notice when you stand on the curb and look around as though you wished the whole village to hell."

"That's not true." The guilt rose in her because for a moment, just a moment, she'd come close to wishing it so.

"All right, we'll alter that to you wishing yourself anywhere else. I know the feeling, Irish."

"You don't know what I feel. You don't know me at all."

"Better than you think," he murmured. "Feeling trapped, stifled, smothered?" She said nothing this time. "Looking at the same space you saw the day you were born and wondering if it's the last thing you'll see before you die? Wondering why you don't walk out, stick out your thumb and head whichever way the wind's blowing? How old are you, Erin McKinnon?"

What he was saying hit too close to the bone for comfort. "I'm twenty-five, and what of it?"

"I was five years younger when I stuck my thumb out." He turned to her, but again she saw only her own reflection. "Can't say I ever regretted it."

"Well, it's happy I am for you, Mr. Logan. Now, if you'll slow down, the lane's there. Just pull to the side. I can walk from here."

"Suit yourself." When he stopped the van, he put a hand on her arm before she could climb out. He wasn't sure why he'd offered to drive her or why he'd started this line of conversation. He was following a hunch, as he had for most of his life. "I know ambition when I see it because it looks back at me out of the mirror most mornings. Some consider it a sin. I've always thought of it as a blessing."

What was it about him that made her throat dry up and her nerves stretch? "Have you a point, Mr. Logan?"

"I like your looks, Erin. I'd hate to see them wrinkled up with discontent." He grinned again and tipped an invisible hat. "Top of the morning to you."

Unsure whether she was running from him or her own demons, Erin got out of the van, slammed the door, and hurried down the lane.

CHAPTER 2

She had a great deal to think about. Erin sat through dinner at the inn, with her family talking on top of each other, with laughter rolling into laughter. Voices were raised to be heard over the clatter of tableware, the scrape of chair legs, the occasional shout. Scents were a mixture of good hot food and whiskey. The lights had been turned up high in celebration. The group filled Mrs. Malloy's dining room at the inn, but wasn't so very much bigger than a Sunday supper at the farm.

Erin ate little herself, not because one of her brothers seemed to interrupt constantly to have her pass this or that, but because she couldn't stop thinking about what Burke had said to her that afternoon.

She *was* dissatisfied, though she didn't like the idea that a stranger could see it as easily as her family had always overlooked it. Years before she'd convinced herself it wasn't wrong to be so. How could it be wrong to feel what was so natural? True, she'd been taught that envy was a sin, but . . .

Damn it all, she wasn't a saint and wouldn't choose to be one. The envy she felt for Dee sitting cozily beside her husband felt healthy, not sinful. After all, it wasn't as if she wished her cousin didn't have; it was only that she wished she had as well. She doubted a body burned in hell for wishes. But she didn't think they grew wings for them, either.

In truth, she was glad the Grants had come back to visit. For a few days she could listen to their stories of America and picture it. She could ask questions and imagine the big stone house Dee lived in now and almost catch glimpses of the excitement and power of the racing world. When they left again, everything would settle back to routine.

But not forever, Erin promised herself. No, not forever. In a year, maybe two, she would have saved enough, and then it would be off to Dublin. She'd get a job in some big office and have a flat of her own. Of her very own. No one was going to stop her.

Her lips started to curve at the thought, but then her gaze met Burke's across the table. He wasn't wearing those concealing glasses now. She almost wished he was. They'd been disturbing, but not nearly as disturbing as his eyes—dark gray, intense eyes. A wolf would have eyes like that, smoky and patient and cunning. He had no business looking at her like that, she thought, then stubbornly stared right back at him.

The noise and confusion of the table continued around them, but she lost track of it. Was it the amusement in his eyes that drew her, or the arrogance? Perhaps it was because both added up to a peculiar kind of knowledge. She wasn't sure, but she felt something for him at that moment, something she knew she shouldn't feel and was even more certain she'd regret.

* * *

An Irish rose, Burke thought. He wasn't sure he'd ever seen one, but was certain they would have thorns, thick ones with sharp edges. An Irish rose, a wild rose, wouldn't be fragile or require careful handling. It would be sturdy, strong and stubborn enough to grow through briers. It was a flower he thought he could respect.

He liked her family. They would be called salt of the earth, he supposed. Simple, but not simple-minded. Apparently their farm did well enough, as long as they worked seven days a week. Mary McKinnon had a dressmaking business on the side, but seemed more interested in discussing children with Dee than fashion. The brothers were fair, except for the oldest, Cullen, who had the looks of a Black Irish warrior and the voice of a poet. Unless Burke missed his guess, Erin had her softest spot there. Throughout the meal he watched her, curious to see what other soft spots he might discover.

By the time dinner was over, Burke was glad he'd let Travis talk him into an extra few days in Ireland. The trip had been profitable, the visit to the track at Curragh educational, and now it seemed it was time to mix business with a little pleasure.

"You'll play for us, won't you, Cullen?" Adelia was already reaching across the table to grip Erin's oldest brother's hand. "For old times' sake."

"He'll take little enough persuading," Mary McKinnon put in. "You'd best clear a space." She gestured to her two youngest sons. "It's only fitting that we dance off a meal like that."

"I just happen to have my pipe." Cullen reached in his vest pocket and drew out the slim reed. He stood, a big man with broad shoulders and lean hips. The fingers of his workingman's hands slid over the holes as he lifted the instrument to his lips.

It surprised Burke that such a big, rough-looking man could make such delicate music. He settled back in his chair, savored the kick of his Irish whiskey and watched.

Mary McKinnon placed her hand in her youngest son's and, without seeming to move at all, set her feet in time to the music. It seemed a very restrained dance to Burke, with a complicated pattern of heels and toes and shuffles. Then the pace began to pick up—slowly, almost unnoticeably. The others were keeping time with their hands or occasional hoots. When he glanced at Erin, she was standing with a hand on her father's shoulder and smiling as he hadn't seen her smile before.

Something shimmered a bit inside him—shimmered, then strained, then quieted, all in the space of two heartbeats.

"She still moves like a girl," Matthew McKinnon said of his wife.

"And she's still beautiful." Erin watched her mother whirl in her son's arms, then spin with a flare of skirt and a flash of leg.

"Can you keep up?"

With a laugh that was only slightly wistful, Erin shook her head. "I've never been able to."

"Come now." Her father slid an arm around her waist. "My money's on you."

Before she could protest, Matthew had spun her out. His grin was broad as he held her hand high and picked up the rhythm of the timeless folk dance she'd been taught as soon as she could walk. The pipe music was cheerful and challenging. Caught up in it and her family's enthusiasm, Erin began to move instinctively. She put her hands on her hips and tossed up her chin.

"Can you manage it?"

Adelia looked up at her eighteen-year-old cousin. "Can I manage it?" she repeated with her eyes narrowed. "The day hasn't come when I can't manage a jig, boyo."

Travis started to protest as she joined her cousins on the floor, but then he subsided. If there was one thing his Dee knew, it was her own strength. The depth of it continued to surprise him. "Quite a group, aren't they?" he murmured to Burke.

"They're all of that." He drew out a cigar, but his eyes remained on Erin. "I take it you don't jig."

With a chuckle, Travis leaned back against the wall. "Dee's tried to teach me and labeled me hopeless. I'm inclined to believe you have to be born to it." He saw Brendon go out to take his place as his mother's partner. His mother's son, Travis thought with a ripple of pride. Of all their children, Brendon was the most strong-willed and hardheaded. "She needed this more than I realized."

Burke managed to tear his eyes from Erin long enough to study Travis's profile. "Most people get homesick now and again."

"She's only come back twice in seven years." Travis watched her now, her cheeks pink with pleasure, her eyes laughing down at Brendon as he copied her moves. "It's not enough. You know, she'll take you to the wall in an argument—half the time an argument no sane man can understand. But she never complains, and she never asks."

For a moment Burke said nothing. It still surprised him after four years that his friendship with Travis had become so close, so quickly. He'd never considered himself the kind of man to make friends, and in truth had never wanted the responsibility of one. He'd spent almost half his thirty-two years on his own, needing no one. Wanting no one. With the Grants, it had just happened.

"I don't know much about women." At Travis's slow smile, Burke corrected himself. "Wives. But I'd say yours is happy, whether she's here or in the States. The fact is, Travis, if she loved you less I might have made a play for her myself."

Travis continued to watch her as his mind played back the years. "The first time I saw her I thought she was a boy."

Burke drew the cigar out of his mouth. "You're joking."

"It was dark."

"A poor excuse."

His chuckle was warm and easy as he looked back. "She seemed to think so, too. Nearly took my head off. I think I fell for her then and there." He heard her laugh and looked over as she shook her head and stepped away from the dancers. She came to him, hands outstretched. The jeweled ring he'd put on her finger years before still glimmered.

"I could go for hours," she claimed, a little breathlessly. "But these two have had enough." With her free hands, she covered her babies. "Are you going to try it, Burke?"

"Not on your life."

She laughed again and put a hand on his arm with the simple generosity he'd never quite gotten used to. "If a man doesn't make a fool of himself now and again, he's not living." She took a couple of deep, steadying breaths, but couldn't keep her foot from tapping. "Oh, it's like magic when Cullen plays and all the more magic to be here, hearing it." She brought Travis's hand to her lips, then rested her cheek on it. "Mary McKinnon can still outdance anyone in the county, but Erin's wonderful, too, isn't she?"

Burke took a long sip of whiskey. "It's not a hardship to watch her."

Laughing again, Adelia rested her head against her husband's arm. "I suppose as her elder cousin I should warn her about your reputation with women."

Burke swirled the whiskey in his glass and gave her a bland look. "What reputation is that?"

With her head still nestled against Travis, she smiled up at him. "Oh, I hear things, Mr. Logan. Fascinating things. The racing world's a tight little group, you know. I've heard murmurs that a man not only has to watch his daughters but his wife when you're about."

"If I was interested in another man's wife, you'd be the first to know." He took her hand and brought it to his lips. Her eyes laughed at him.

"Travis, I think Burke's flirting with me."

"Apparently," he agreed, and kissed the top of her head.

"A warning, Mr. Logan. It's easy enough to flirt with a woman who's five months along with twins and who knows you're a scoundrel. But mind your step. The Irish are a clever lot." She stood on her toes and kissed his cheek. "If you keep staring at her like that, Matthew McKinnon's going to load his shotgun."

He glanced back as Erin stepped away from the group. "No law against looking."

"There should be when it comes to you." She snuggled

against Travis again. "Looks like Erin's going outside for a breath of air." When Burke merely lifted a brow, she smiled. "You'd probably like to light that cigar, maybe take a little walk in the night air yourself."

"As a matter of fact, I would." He nodded to her, then sauntered to the door.

"Were you warning him off or egging him on?" Travis wanted to know.

"Just enjoying the view, love." She turned her mouth up for a kiss.

*　*　*

Erin drew her jacket tightly around her. Nights were coldest in February, but she didn't mind now. The air was bracing and the moon half-full. She was glad her father had pressured her to dance. It seemed too seldom now that there was time for small celebrations. There was so much work to be done, and not as many hands to do it now that Frank had married and started his own family. And within a year she expected Sean to marry the Hennessy girl. With Cullen more interested in his music than milking, that left only Joe and Brian. And herself.

The family was growing, but at the same time spreading out. The farm had to survive. Erin knew that was indisputable. Her father would simply wither away without it. Just as she knew she would wither away if she stayed much longer. The only solution was to find a way to ensure both.

She hugged herself with her arms to ward off the wind. It brought with it the scent of Mrs. Malloy's wild roses and rhododendrons. She wouldn't think of it now. In a short time the Grants would be gone and her own yearnings for more would fade a bit. When the time was right, something would happen. She looked up at the moon and smiled. Hadn't she promised herself that she'd make something happen?

She heard the scrape and flare of a lighter and braced herself.

"Nice night."

She didn't turn. The little jolt to her system teased her. No, she hadn't wanted him to come out, she told herself. Why should she? Since he had, she would hold her own. "It's a bit cold."

"You look warm enough." She wouldn't give an inch. It only gave him the pleasure of taking it from her. "I liked the dancing."

She turned to walk slowly away from the inn. It didn't surprise her when he fell into step beside her. "You're missing it."

"You stopped." The end of his cigar grew bright and red as he took another puff. "Your brother has a gift."

"Aye." She listened now as the music turned from jaunty to sad. "He wrote this one. Hearing it's like hearing a heart break." Music like this always made her long, and fear, and wonder what it would be like to feel so strongly about another. "Are you a music lover, Mr. Logan?"

"When the tune's right." This one was a waltz, a slow, weepy one. On impulse he slipped his arms around her and picked up the time.

"What are you doing?"

"Dancing," he said simply.

"A man's supposed to ask." But she didn't pull away, and her steps matched his easily. The motion and the music made her smile. She turned her face up to his. The grass was soft beneath her feet, the moonlight sweet. "You don't look like the kind of man who can waltz."

"One of my few cultural accomplishments." She fit nicely into his arms, slender but not fragile, soft but not malleable. "And it seems to be a night for dancing."

She said nothing for a moment. There was magic here, starlight, roses and sad music. The flutter in her stomach, the warmth along her skin, warned her that a woman took chances waltzing under the night sky with a stranger. But still she moved with him.

"The tune's changed," she murmured, and drew out of his arms, relieved, regretful that he didn't keep her there. She turned once again to walk. "Why did you come here?"

"To look at horses. I bought a pair in Kildare." He took a puff on his cigar. He'd yet to realize himself what his horses and farm had come to mean to him. "There's no match for the Thoroughbreds at the Irish National Stud. You pay for them, God knows, but I've never minded putting my money on a winner."

"So you came to buy horses." It interested her, though she didn't want it to.

"And to watch a few races. Ever been to Curragh?"

"No." She glanced up at the moon again. Curragh, Kilkenny, Kildare, all of them might have been as far away as the white slash in the sky. "You won't find Thoroughbreds here in Skibbereen."

"No?" He smiled at her in the moonlight, and the smile made her uneasy. "Then let's say I'm just along for the ride. It's my first time in Ireland."

"And what do you think of it?" She stopped now, unwilling to pass out of the range of the music.

"I've found it beautiful and contradictory."

"With a name like Logan, you'd have some Irish in you."

Unsmiling, he glanced down at his cigar. "It's possible."

"Probable," she said lightly. "You know, you said you were a neighbor of Travis's, but you don't sound like him. Your accent."

"Accent?" His mood changed again with a grin. "I guess if you want to call it that it comes from the West."

"The West?" It took her a moment. "The American West? Cowboys?"

This time he laughed, a full, rich laugh, so that she was distracted enough not to protest when his hand touched her cheek. "We don't carry six-guns as a rule these days."

Her feathers were ruffled. "You don't have to make fun of me."

"Was I?" Because her skin had felt so cool and so smooth, he touched it again. "And what would you say if I asked you about leprechauns and banshees?"

She had to smile. "I'd say the last to have seen a leprechaun in these parts was Michael Ryan after a pint of Irish."

"You don't believe in legends, Erin?" He stepped closer so that he could see the moonlight reflected in her eyes like light in a lake.

"No." She didn't step back. It wasn't her nature to retreat, even when she felt the warning shiver race up her spine. Whether you won or went down in defeat, it was best to do it with feet firmly planted. "I believe in what I can see and touch. The rest is for dreamers."

"Pity," he murmured, though he had always felt the same. "Life's a bit softer the other way."

"I've never wanted softness."

"Then what?" He touched a finger to the hair that curled at her cheekbones.

"I have to go back." It wasn't a retreat, she told herself. She felt cold all at once, cold to the bone. But even as she started to turn, he closed a hand over her arm. She looked at him, eyes clear, not so much angry as assessing. "You'll excuse me, Mr. Logan. The wind's up."

"I noticed. You didn't answer my question."

"No, because it's no concern of yours. Don't," she said when his fingers closed lightly over her chin, but she didn't jerk away.

"I'm interested. When a man meets someone he recognizes, he's interested."

"We don't know each other." But she understood him. When he'd brought his arms around her in the waltz, she'd known him. There was something, something in both of them that mirrored back. Whatever it was had her heart beating hard now and her skin chilling. "And if it's rude I have to be, then I'll say it plain. I don't care to know you."

"Do you usually have such a strong reaction to a stranger?"

She tossed her head, but his fingers stayed in place. "The only reaction I'm having at the moment is annoyance." Which was one of the biggest lies she could remember telling. She'd already looked at his mouth and wondered what it would be like to be kissed by him. "I'm sure you think I should be flattered that you're willing to spend time with me. But I'm not a silly farm girl who kisses a man because there's a moon and music."

He lifted a brow. "Erin, if I'd intended to kiss you, I'd have done so already. I never waste time—with a woman."

She felt abruptly as foolish as she'd claimed not to be. Damn it, she would have kissed him, and she knew he was well aware of it. "Well, you're wasting mine now. I'll say good night."

Why hadn't he kissed her? Burke asked himself as he watched her rush back to the inn. He'd wanted to badly. He'd imagined it clearly. For a moment, when the moonlight had fallen over her face and her face had lifted to his, he'd all but tasted her.

But he hadn't kissed her. Something had warned him that it would take only that to change the order of things for both of them. He wasn't ready for it. He wasn't sure he could avoid it.

Taking a last puff, he sent the cigar in an arch into the night. He'd come to Ireland for horses. He'd be better off being content with that. But he was a man on whom contentment rarely sat easily.

* * *

She'd come late on purpose. Erin rolled her bike to the kitchen entrance of the inn and parked it. She knew it was prideful, but she simply didn't want Dee to know she worked there. It wasn't the paperwork and bookkeeping that bothered her—that made her feel accomplished. It was her kitchen duties she preferred to keep to herself.

Mrs. Malloy had promised not to mention it. But she tut-tutted about it. Erin shrugged that off as she entered the kitchen. Let her tut-tut, as long as that was all she let out of her mouth.

Dee and her family were visiting in town through the morning. That had given Erin time to clear up her chores at home, then ride leisurely from the farm to handle the breakfast dishes and the daily cleaning. Since the books were in order, she'd be able to take a few hours that afternoon to drive out to the farm where her cousin had grown up.

It wasn't being deceitful, she told herself as she filled the big sink with water. And if it was, it couldn't be helped. She wouldn't have Dee feeling sorry for her. She was working for the money; it was as simple as that. Once enough was made, she could move on to that office position in Cork or Dublin. By the saints, the only dishes she'd have to clean then would be her own.

She started to hum as she scrubbed the inn's serviceable plates. She'd learned young when there was work to be done to make the best of it, because as sure as the sun rose it would be there again tomorrow.

She looked out the window as she worked, across the field where she'd walked with Burke the night before. Where she'd danced with him. In the moonlight, she thought, then caught herself. Foolishness. He was just a man dallying with what was available. She might not be traveled or have seen big cities, but she wasn't naive.

If she'd felt anything in those few minutes alone with him, it had been the novelty. He was different, but that didn't make him special. And it certainly didn't warrant her thinking of him in broad daylight with her arms up to the elbows in soapy water.

She heard the door open behind her and began to scrub faster. "I know I'm late, Mrs. Malloy, but I'll have it cleared up before lunch."

"She's at the market, fussing over vegetables."

At Burke's voice, Erin simply closed her eyes. When he crossed over and put a hand on her shoulder, she began to scrub with a vengeance.

"What are you doing?"

"I'd think you'd have eyes to see that." She set one plate to drain and attacked another. "If you'll excuse me, I'm behind."

Saying nothing, he walked over to the stove and poured the coffee that was always kept warm there. She was wearing overalls, baggy ones that might have belonged to one of her brothers. Her hair was down, and longer than he'd imagined it. She'd pulled it back with a band to keep it out of her face, but it was thick and curly beyond her shoulders. He sipped, watching her. He didn't quite know what his own feelings were at finding her at the sink, but he was well aware of hers. Embarrassment.

"You didn't mention you worked here."

"No, I didn't." Erin slammed another plate onto the drainboard. "And I'd be obliged if you didn't, either."

"Why? It's honest work, isn't it?"

"I'd prefer it if Dee didn't know I was washing up after her."

Pride was another emotion he understood well. "All right."

She sent him a cautious look over her shoulder. "You won't tell her?"

"I said I wouldn't." He could smell the detergent in the hot water. Despite the years that had passed, it was still a scent that annoyed him.

Erin's shoulders relaxed a bit. "Thank you."

"Want some coffee?"

She hadn't expected him to make it easy for her. Still cautious, but less reserved, she smiled. "No, I haven't the time." She turned away again because he was much easier to look at than she wanted him to be. "I, ah, thought you'd be out by now."

"I'm back," he said simply. He'd intended to grab a quick cup and leave, take a leisurely walk around town or duck into the local pub for conversation. He studied her, her back straight at the sink, her arms plunged deep into the soapy water. "Want a hand?"

She stared at him this time, caught between astonishment and horror. "No, no, drink your coffee. I'm sure there're muffins in the pantry if you like, or you might want to go out and walk. It's a fine day."

"Trying to get rid of me again?" He strolled over and picked up a dishcloth.

"Please, Mrs. Malloy—"

"Is at the market." He picked up a dish and began to polish it dry.

He was standing close now, nearly hip-to-hip with her. Erin resisted the urge to shift away, or was it to shift closer? She plunged her hands into the water again. "I don't need any help."

He set down the first dish and picked up another. "I've got nothing else to do."

Frowning, she lifted out a plate. "I don't like it when you're nice."

"Don't worry, I'm not often. So what else do you do except wash dishes and dance?"

It was a matter of pride, she knew, but she turned to him with her eyes blazing. "I keep books, if you want to know. I keep them for the inn and for the dry goods and for the farm."

"Sounds like you're busy," he murmured, and began to consider. "Are you any good?"

"I've heard no complaints. I'm going to get a job in Dublin next year. In an office."

"I can't see it."

She had a cast-iron skillet in her hand now and was tempted. "I didn't ask you to."

"Too many walls in an office," he explained, and lowered the pan into the water himself. "You'd go crazy."

"That's for me to worry about." She gripped the scouring pad like a weapon. "I was wrong when I said I didn't like you when you were nice. I don't like you at all."

"You know, you've only to ask and Dee would take you to America."

She tossed the pad into the water, and suds lapped up over the rim of the sink. "And what? Live off her charity? Is that what you think I want? To take what someone is kind enough to give me?"

"No." He stacked the next plate. "I just wanted to see you flare up again."

"You're a bastard, Mr. Logan."

"True enough. And now that we're on intimate terms, you ought to call me Burke."

"There's plenty I'd like to be calling you. Why don't you be on your way and let me finish here? I've got no time for the likes of you."

"Then you'll have to make some."

He caught her off guard, though she told herself later she should have been expecting it. With her arms still elbow deep in water, he curled a hand around her neck and kissed her. It was quick, but a great deal more of a threat than a promise. His lips were hard and firm and surprisingly warm as he pressed them against hers. For a second, for two. She didn't have time to react, and certainly no time to think before he'd released her again and picked up another dish.

She swallowed, and beneath the soapy water her hands were fists. "You've a nerve, you do."

"A man doesn't get very far without any—or a woman."

"Just remember this. If I want you touching me, I'll let you know."

"Your eyes say plenty, Irish. It's a pleasure to watch them."

She wouldn't argue. She wouldn't demean herself by making an issue of it. Instead, she pulled the plug on the sink. "I've the floor to do. You'll have to get your feet off it."

"Then I guess I'd better take that walk." He laid the cloth down, spread open so it would dry. Without another word or another glance, he strolled out the back door. Erin waited a full

ten seconds, then gave herself the satisfaction of heaving a wet
rag after him.

* * *

Two hours later, after a quick change into a skirt and sweater,
Erin met the Grants in the public room of the inn. Joe's
overalls were bundled into a sack tied on the back of her bike,
and she'd used some of Mrs. Malloy's precious cream to offset
the daily damage she did to her hands. Burke was there. Of
course he was, she thought, and deliberately ignored him as he
bounced young Brady on his knee.

"Ma sent this." Erin handed Dee a plate wrapped tightly in
a cloth. "It's her raisin cake. She didn't want you to think Mrs.
Malloy could outcook her."

"I remember your mother's raisin cake." Dee lifted the corner of the cloth to sniff. "Now and then she'd bake an extra and
have one of you bring it by the farm." The scent brought back
memories—some sweet, some painful. She covered the cake
again. "I'm glad you could come with us today."

"You remember it's only on the condition that you come by
and visit. Ma's counting on it."

"Then we'd best be rounding up the brood. Burke, if you
give the lad chocolate you deserve to have him smear it on you.
Brendon, Keeley, into the van now. We're going for a ride."

They didn't have to be told twice.

First they went to the cemetery, where the grass was high
and green and the stones weathered and gray. Flowers grew
wild, adding the promise of life. Some of Erin's family was
buried there; most she barely remembered. She'd never lost
anyone close or grieved deeply. But she loved deeply when it
came to her family, and thought she could understand how
wrenching it would be to lose them.

Yet it had been so long ago, Erin thought as she watched her
cousin stand between the graves of her parents. Didn't a loss

like that begin to fade with time? Adelia had been only a child when they'd died, nine or ten. Wouldn't her memory of them have dimmed? Still, though she could imagine a world away from her family, she couldn't imagine one where they didn't exist.

"It still hurts," Dee murmured as she looked down at the stones that bore her parents' names.

"I know." Travis ran a hand down her hair.

"I remember Father Finnegan telling me after it happened that it was God's will, and thinking to myself that it didn't seem right. It still doesn't." She sighed and looked up at him. "I'll never be able to figure it out, will I?"

"No." He took her hand in his. There was a part of him that wanted to gather her up and take her away from the grief. And a part of him that understood she'd been strong enough to deal with it years before they'd even met. "I wish I'd known them."

"They'd have loved you." She let the tears come, but smiled with them. "And the children. They'd have fussed over the children, spoiled them. More than Hannah does. It comforts me that they're together. I believe that, you know. But it's painful that they missed knowing you and the babies."

"Don't cry, Momma." Keeley slipped a hand into Adelia's. "Look, I made a flower. Burke showed me. He said they'd like it even though they're in heaven."

Dee looked at the little wreath fashioned of twigs and wild grass. "It's lovely. Let's put it right in the middle, like this." Bending, she placed it between the graves. "Aye, I'm sure they'll like this."

What a strange man he was, Erin thought as she sat beside Burke in the van and listened to Brendon's chattering. She'd seen him sit in the grass and twine twigs together for Keeley. Though she'd kept herself distant enough that she hadn't heard what he'd said, she'd been aware that the girl had listened attentively and had looked at him with absolute trust.

He didn't seem to be a man to inspire trust.

She knew the road that led to the farm that had been the Cunnanes'. She remembered Dee's parents only as the vaguest of shadows, but she did remember Lettie Cunnane well, the aunt Dee had lived with when she'd been orphaned. She'd been a tough, stern-faced woman, and because of her Erin had kept her visits to the farm few and far between. That was behind them now, she reminded herself as she gestured toward the window for Brendon. "You see, just over this hill is where your mother grew up."

"On a farm," he said knowledgeably. The patches of green pasture and yellow gorse meant little to him. "We have a farm. The best one in Maryland." He grinned at Burke as if it was an old joke.

"It'll still be the second best when I'm finished," Burke answered, willing to rise to the bait.

"Royal Meadows has been around for gener . . . gener . . ."

"Generations," Burke supplied.

"Yeah. And you're still wet behind the ears 'cause Uncle Paddy said so."

"Brendon Patrick Grant." It was all the warning Hannah had to give. She turned her stern eye on Burke. "And you should know better than to encourage him."

Burke merely grinned and tousled the boy's hair. "Doesn't take much."

"Burke won his farm in a poker game," Brendon supplied as the van shuddered to a halt. "He's teaching me to play."

"That's so when Royal Meadows belongs to you, I can win that, too." He pushed open the sliding door, then grabbed the giggling boy around the waist.

"Did he really?" Erin asked in an undertone as Hannah took Keeley's hand. "Win his horse farm gambling?"

"So I'm told." Hannah stepped a bit wearily out of the van. "Rumor is he's lost and won more than that." She glanced over as Burke settled Brendon on his shoulders. "It's hard to hold it against him."

She wouldn't, Erin thought as she joined the others. She was too Irish to turn her nose up at a gambler, especially a successful one. Trailing behind Dee, she looked over the rise to the farm below.

It hadn't changed much, not in her memory. Oh, the milking parlor was new, and a fresh coat of paint had been slapped on the barn a year or so before. It was the only farm in sight. To the east, the hills rose up and blocked the view. The vegetable garden was already tilled and planted, and a smattering of the dairy cows could be seen in the strip of pasture. There was smoke spiraling out of the chimney of the little stone cottage, which was a great deal like her own. The good, rich smell of peat carried on the wind.

"The Sweeneys are a nice family," she said at length because her cousin stared down so long without speaking. "I know they wouldn't mind if you wanted to go down and look about."

"No." She said it too quickly, then softened the refusal with a touch of her hand. "I don't mind looking from here." The truth was she couldn't bear to go any closer to what had been and was no longer her own. "Do you remember, Erin, when Aunt Lettie was so sick and you and your mother came visiting?"

"Yes, you gave Ma one of the roses from the bush there." The bush had been her mother's, Erin remembered, and she linked her fingers briefly with Dee's. "The roses still bloom every summer."

She smiled at that. "Such a little place. Smaller now than even I remember. Look, Keeley, see that window there." She crouched down to show her daughter. "That was my room when I was your age."

Adelia stood again. There was only her and Travis now as the others strolled down the side of the road. "Dee, I've told you before, you can have it back if you want. We can make the Sweeneys a good offer for it."

She continued to look down, remembering. Then, with a little sigh, she slipped an arm around Travis's waist. "You know, when I left here all those years ago, I thought I'd lost everything." She tilted her head back and kissed him. "I was wrong. Let's walk a little ways. It's such a beautiful day."

Erin watched them. There was a small meadow that was green now but would be choked with wildflowers in only a matter of weeks. She heard Burke behind her and spoke without thinking.

"If I were to go, to leave here and find something else, I'd never look back."

"If you don't look over your shoulder once in a while, things catch up with you faster than you think."

"I don't understand you." She turned, and her hair fluttered around her face and shoulders, free of bonds. "One minute you sound like a man without any roots at all, and the next you sound as though you've just transplanted them where it's convenient."

"But not too deep." He caught the ends of her hair in his fingers. He was becoming more and more fascinated by it. It wasn't silk; it was too wild and untamed for silk. "Maybe that's the trick, Irish, not letting them sink too deep. You can yank yours up because you'll damn well strangle if you don't, but you'll take some of this with you."

He reached down and took up a handful of soil. "Seems like a good enough base."

"And what's yours?"

He looked down at the rich dirt in his hand. "Have you ever seen the sand in the desert, Irish? No, no, you haven't. It's thin. It'll slip right out of your hands, no matter how hard you hold on to it."

"Grains of sand have a habit of clinging to the skin."

"And are easily brushed away." He glanced around as Brady let out a squeal of laughter at a gull that had glided in from the sea.

"Why did you kiss me before?" She hadn't wanted to ask. Rather, she hadn't wanted him to know it mattered. He smiled at her again, slowly, with the amusement only a hint in his eyes.

"A woman should never wonder why a man kisses her."

Annoyed with herself, she shrugged and turned away. "It wasn't a proper one, anyway."

"You want a proper one?"

"No." She continued to walk, but the devil on her shoulder took over. She glanced around, a half smile on her face. "I'll let you know when I do."

CHAPTER 3

There was a storm coming. Erin could feel it brewing inside her, just as she could see it brewing in the clouds that buried the sun and hung gloomily over the hills. She worked quickly, routinely, pulling the pins off the line and dropping the dry, billowing clothes in the basket at her feet.

She didn't mind this kind of monotonous, mindless work. It left her brain free to think and remember and plan. Just now, with the wind tossing sheets away from her and the sky boiling, she liked the simple outside chore. She wanted to see the storm break, to be a part of it when the wind and rain raised hell. When it was over, things would settle back into the quiet routine she knew was slowly driving her mad.

What was wrong with her? Erin yanked one of her brother's work shirts from the line and, out of ingrained habit, folded it to ward off wrinkles. She loved her family, had friends and work to keep the wolf from the door. So why was she so restless, so edgy? She couldn't blame it all on her cousin's visit or on the unexpected appearance of one Burke Logan. She'd been feeling restless before they'd come, but for some reason their presence—his presence—intensified it.

She couldn't talk to her mother about it. Erin stripped down one of her mother's aprons and buried her face in the cool, fresh scent of the material. Her mother simply couldn't understand discontent or yearnings for more, not when there was a sturdy roof over the head and food enough for everyone. Time and again Erin had wished herself as serene a heart as her mother's. But it wasn't meant to be.

She couldn't go to her father, though Erin knew he would understand the storm inside her. He wasn't a calm, easy man. From the stories she'd heard he'd been a hellion in his youth, and it had taken marriage to his Mary and a couple of babies before he'd begun to take hold. But while her father would understand, Erin knew he would also be distressed. If she wanted more, needed more, he would take it to mean he hadn't given her enough.

There was Cullen. She'd always been able to talk to Cullen. But he was so busy just now, and her feelings were so mixed, the longings so indistinct, that she wasn't sure she could articulate them in any case.

So she would wait, let the storm come and the wind blow.

* * *

He'd been watching her for some time. Burke never considered that it was rude to stand and observe people without their knowledge. You learned more about people when they thought they were alone.

She moved well. Even doing something so simple, there was an innate sensuality in her movements. She had more fire than showed in her hair. Inside her there was a flame smoldering. He recognized it because he'd been born with one himself. That kind of heat, of passion, could and would break free. It only took the right elements falling into place. Time, place, circumstance.

She didn't hum as she worked now, but occasionally looked up at the sky as if daring it to open and pour its fury on her. Her hair blew back from her face, fighting against the band that held it. Just as she fought whatever held her. He'd wondered what the results would be when she finally broke free. He'd already decided he wanted to be around to see for himself.

"I haven't seen a woman do that for a long time."

Erin spun around, her heels digging into the soft ground, a pillowcase clutched in her hand. He looked so at home, she thought, with the collar of his jacket up against the wind, the buttons undone in contradiction. He had his thumbs hooked in his pockets and that damned devil smile on his face. She'd never known a man to look better or more suited to the raw air and the warring skies. She turned away to snatch another clothespin because she knew her reaction to him would bring her nothing but trouble.

"Don't women take down the wash where you come from?"

"Progress often stamps out tradition." He moved to her with the easy stride of a man used to walking toward what he wanted. He unhooked a cotton slip—her cotton slip—folded it and dropped it in the basket. Erin clamped her teeth together and told herself only a foolish chucklehead would be embarrassed.

"There's no need for you to be putting your hands on the wash."

"Don't worry, they're clean enough." As if to prove it, he held them out. For the first time she noticed a thin, jagged scar across his knuckles.

"What are you doing here?"

"I came to see you."

She said nothing for a moment. He didn't make it easy when he didn't invent comfortable excuses. "Why?"

"Because I wanted to." He took down a pair of serviceable white panties, folded those, too, without a blush, then laid them on top of the slip.

Erin felt a slow, uncomfortable curling in her stomach. "Shouldn't you be with Travis and Dee?"

"I think they'll survive the afternoon without me. I liked your farm when we were here yesterday." He glanced around now at the neat buildings. The cottage was nearly half again as large as the one where Adelia Grant had grown up, but the roof had the same bleached yellow thatching and sturdy stone walls. There were flowers here as well. The Irish seemed happy to let them grow as they chose—gay, untamed and sturdy. A hedge of wild fuchsia was already blooming. It made him think of home and the snow covering the fields.

The roof of the barn showed fresh patching. The paint on the silo was peeling and no longer white, but the chickens in the coop were fat and clucking. He imagined the McKinnons worked seven days a week to maintain the place. Such was the life of a farmer. "This is a fine piece of land. Apparently your father knows what to do with it."

"It's his life," Erin said simply as she took down the last of the wash.

"What about yours?"

"I don't know what you mean."

He lifted the basket before she could. "It's a good farm, a good life for some. You weren't meant for it."

"You don't know me well enough to say what I'm meant for." She took the basket from him and walked toward the kitchen door. "But I've already told you I'm going north to an office job in a year or so." Taking a deep breath, she swung the door open. Her mother would be horrified if she didn't ask the man in and at least offer him a cup of tea. She turned to him, but before she could issue the invitation he was taking the first step.

"Let's take a walk. I have a proposition for you."

Erin leaned back against the door and studied him coolly. "Oh, I'll just bet you do."

He took the basket from her again, set it inside the door and gave it a little shove. "You're getting ahead of yourself, Irish. Let's just say when I want you in bed I won't ask."

And he wouldn't, she thought as they watched each other. He wasn't the type to court a woman with flowers and pretty words, any more than he was the type to coax a woman gently into his arms. Well, she wasn't the type who wanted to be coaxed, but neither would she be steamrollered. "Just what is it you're wanting, Burke?"

"Let's take a walk," he repeated, but this time he closed his hand over hers.

She could have refused, but then she wouldn't know what it was he had to say. Erin decided that if she shook free and shut the door in his face, he'd tuck his hands in his pockets and stroll off, leaving her the one who was fuming.

There was no harm in walking with him, she told herself as she stepped down beside him. Her mother was in the house, and her father, along with a couple of her brothers, was somewhere on the farm. Added to that was the fact that she had every confidence she could take care of herself.

"I don't have much time," she said briskly. "There's a lot more to be done today."

"This won't take long." But he said nothing more as they walked away from the house. He didn't seem to look, but he saw everything—the care, the sweat that went into the farm, the long hours and the hope. He counted thirty cows. A man could make a living off less, he imagined. It hadn't been so many years since he'd worked backbreaking hours. He hadn't forgotten, just as he never forgot that fate could take what he had just as easily as it had given it to him.

"If it was a tour of the farm you were wanting—" Erin began.

"I had one yesterday, remember?" He paused a moment to look out over a field. He knew what it was to haul rocks from them, to ride sweating over them at baling time and to curse the land as much as you worshiped it. "You grow grain here for the stock?"

"Aye. It'll be plowing time soon."

"You work the fields?"

"I've been known to."

Burke turned her hand palm-up and studied it. It wasn't raw and cracked, but toughened with a ridge of callus. The nails were trimmed short and left unpainted. "You haven't pampered them."

"What good would that do me? I'm not ashamed of the work they've done."

"No. You're too practical for that." He turned her hand over again and looked at her face. "You're not the kind of woman who daydreams about white knights."

She could smile at that, though the intensity of his eyes made her uneasy. "I've always thought white knights would be painfully dull, and the last thing I want is to be a lady in distress. I'd rather be slaying my own dragons."

"Good. I don't have much use for a woman who wants to be taken care of." He still had her hand, as he watched the wind whip furiously through her hair. "Why don't you come back to America with me, Erin?"

She stared at him, speechless. The skies opened up. They were both soaked in a matter of seconds. She might have stood there, wide-eyed and openmouthed, but he grabbed her arm and yanked her inside a shed.

Inside it was dim and smelled of soil and damp. Tools for the vegetable garden lined the walls. Her mother's peat pots and seeds were stacked on shelves waiting for planting. Rain beat on the tin roof, and the wind snaked through the cracks in the boards and moaned.

Erin stood shivering just inside the door, her hair plastered to her head, her sweater dripping at the hem. But her senses had come back, full force.

"You're a madman, Burke Logan. By the saints, you're as mad as a hatter. Do you think I'd just bundle up my skirts and cross an ocean with you?" She still shivered, but the more she spoke, the hotter her temper became. "Sure and it's a conceited ox you are to believe all you have to do is crook your finger to have me tagging after you. I don't even know you." She swiped a hand over her face to dry it, then went one better and shoved him hard in the chest. "And it's the God's truth that I have no desire to."

She turned to the shed door and would have yanked it open if he hadn't caught her by the shoulders.

"Take your hands off me, you snake." On impulse, she grabbed a rake and turned on him with it. "Touch me again and I'll slice you into pieces, little ones that won't be put back together easily."

So she'd slay her dragons with a garden rake, he thought, lifting both hands, palms out, in a gesture of peace. "You don't have to defend your honor, Irish. I'm not after it—yet. This is business."

"What business would I be having with you?" When he took a step toward her, she gestured with the rake. "Come closer and I promise you'll be missing an ear at the very least."

"Fine." He made as if to take a step back. Then he moved quickly. Erin cursed him when he wrenched the rake out of her hands. Even as it clattered to the floor, her back was against the wall. "You'll have to learn not to drop your guard." His face was close, so close she could see his eyes, smoky and dark, and little else. She twisted, but his fingers only dug in harder. "Hold still a minute, will you? You're making a fool of yourself."

Nothing he could have said would have struck the light to her temper faster. She all but bared her teeth and snarled. "There'll come a time and there'll come a place when you'll pay for this."

"Everyone pays, Irish. Now take a deep breath, shut your mouth and listen. I'm offering you a job, that's all." She stopped wriggling to stare at him again. "I need someone sharp, someone clever with figures, to run my books."

"Your books?"

"The farm, expenses, payroll. The man I had was a little too creative. Since he's going to be a guest of the state for the next few years, I need someone else. I want someone I know, someone I can see and talk to, handling my money rather than a big shiny company that doesn't give a damn about the farm or me."

Because her head was whirling, she took one long breath before she spoke again. "You want me to come to America and keep your books?"

He smiled because she sounded almost disappointed. "I'm not offering you a free ride. You're a pleasure to look at, Erin, but at the moment all I intend to pay for is your brain."

"Move back," she ordered in a voice that was suddenly firm. "I can't breathe with you pushing me through the wall."

"No more attacks with garden tools?"

Her chin came up. "All right. Just move aside." When he did, she took a couple of deep breaths. She had to keep a clear head now. She didn't mind taking a new road; in fact, she'd often fretted to do just that. She only wanted to study all the curves and angles of it first. "You want to hire me?"

"That's right."

"Why?"

"I've just told you."

She shook her head, still cautious. "You told me you need a bookkeeper. I imagine there're plenty of them in America."

"Let's just say I like your style." Bending, he picked up the rake and replaced it. He wondered briefly if she would have used it. Yes, indeed, he thought, grinning to himself. Oh, yes, indeed.

"For all you know, I can't add two and two."

"Mrs. Malloy and O'Donnelly at the dry goods say differently." He leaned back against a workbench. Studying her from there, he decided he'd spoken no less than the truth. Even wet and dripping, she was a pleasure to look at.

"Mrs. Malloy. You've spoken to her? You went to Mr. O'Donnelly and asked questions about me?"

"Just checking your references."

"No one told you to go poking about the town asking questions about me."

"Business, Irish. Strictly business. What I found out is that you're neat as a pin and dependable. Your figures tally and your books are clean. That's good enough for me."

"This is crazy." Struggling against a surge of excitement, she dragged a hand through her still-dripping hair. "A body doesn't hire someone they've known only a few days."

"Irish, people are hired after a ten-minute interview."

"That's not what I mean. This isn't a matter of me giving you a résumé, then catching a bus to take a new job across town. You're talking about me coming to America and taking on a job that's bigger than the inn, the farm and the dry goods put together."

He only moved his shoulders. "It's just a matter of more figures, isn't it? You're talking about going north in a year, I'm giving you a chance to go to America now. Make the break."

"It's not so simple." Along with the excitement was a growing panic. Wasn't this what she'd always wanted? Now that it was nearly as close as a handspan, she was terrified.

"It's a gamble." He was watching her again in that quiet, intense way. "Most things worth winning are. I'll pay for your ticket as a sign of good faith. You'll start out at a weekly salary." He considered a moment, then named a figure that had her mouth dropping open. "If it works out, there'll be a ten percent raise in six months. For that you take care of all the details, all the figures, all the bills. I'll want a weekly report. We'll leave in two days."

"Two days?" She was numb now, so numb she could only stare at him. "But even if I agreed, I could never be ready to leave by then."

"All you have to do is pack and say your goodbyes. I'll handle the rest."

"But I—"

"You have to make up your mind, Erin. Stay or go." He stepped toward her again. "If you stay, you'll be safe, and you'll always wonder what if."

He was right. The question was already nagging at her. "If I go, where will I live?"

"I've got plenty of room."

"No." On this she would have to be firm, right from the start. "I won't agree to that. I may say I'll work for you, but I won't live with you."

"It's your choice." Again he moved his shoulders as if it

didn't matter. He'd already anticipated her balking there. "I don't imagine Adelia would have any problem putting you up. In fact, I think you know she'd love to have you with her. It wouldn't be charity," he said, keeping one step ahead of her. "You'd be bringing in a wage. You could get your own place, for that matter, but I think you'd be more comfortable with your cousin at first. And our farms are close enough to make it convenient."

"I'll talk to her." Sometime during the last two minutes her mind had been made up. She was going. Her bridges might not be burning behind her, but they were certainly smoking. "I'll have to speak to my family, as well, but I'd like to accept your offer."

She held out her hand. Burke took it just as casually, though he wondered about the wild surge of relief that coursed through him. "I expect a day's work for a day's pay. I don't doubt you'll give it to me."

"That I will. I'm grateful for the chance."

"I'll remind you of that after you've spent a few days sorting through the mess my last bookkeeper left me with."

She stood very still for a moment, letting it all soak in, layer by layer. Then she spun in a quick circle and laughed. "I can't believe it. America! It's like some kind of a mad dream. I've hardly been more than fifty kilometers from Skibbereen, and now I'm going thousands in the blink of an eye."

He liked to see her this way, her face flushed with pleasure, her eyes lit with it. And the rain still drummed on the roof. "It takes a bit longer than that to cross the Atlantic."

"Don't be so literal." But she was too excited to take offense. "In a matter of days I'll be in a new country, a new place, a new job. New money."

He started to reach for a cigar, then thought better of it. "The money puts a gleam in your eye."

"Anyone who's ever been poor gleams a bit when they've got enough money."

He acknowledged this with a nod. He'd been poor, but he

doubted Erin would understand that degree of poverty. He appreciated money, though if he lost it, as he had before, he would simply shake the dust off his shoes and make more. "You'll earn it."

"I wouldn't be having it any other way." She stopped as reality began to seep through. "But I need a passport and the green card that allows you to work. There must be a pile of papers that have to be processed."

"I told you I'd see to it." He drew a paper out of his pocket. "Fill this out and drop it off at the inn tonight. It's an application," he explained as she studied it. "I've already arranged to have it processed tomorrow. Your passport and whatever else you need will be in Cork when we get there."

She tapped the paper slowly against her palm. "You were damn sure of yourself, weren't you?"

"It pays to be. You'll need a picture they can use, too. A recent one."

"What if I'd said no?"

He simply smiled. "Then you'd have been a fool and I'd have thrown the application away."

"I can't figure you." She tucked the application in the pocket of her baggy pants, but shook her head at him. "You've made me a very generous offer, and you're giving me the opportunity to do something I've wanted to do for as long as I can remember. But even as you're doing it, it doesn't seem to matter to you one way or the other."

He remembered the surge of relief, but chose to ignore it. "Things matter too much to people. That's how they get hurt."

"Are you saying that things don't matter to you? Nothing at all? What about your farm?"

He shifted a bit, surprised that the question, when she asked it, made him uncomfortable. "It's a place. A comfortable and fairly profitable one at the moment. But that's all it is. I don't have the ties to it that you have to the land here, Erin. That's why if I leave it, I will leave without a second glance. When you leave Ireland, no matter how much you want to go, you're going to hurt."

"There's nothing wrong in that," she murmured. "It's my home. It's only right to miss your home."

"Some people don't make homes. They just live somewhere and leave it at that."

She saw more clearly now, though the light was still dim. She saw, though she'd told herself she didn't care, that there were places inside him no one, no woman, would ever touch. "That's a cold and sorry way to live."

"It's a choice," he corrected. Then he pushed the subject aside. "Make sure you get me the application tonight. I'm leaving for Cork first thing in the morning."

"But you said we weren't going for a couple of days."

"I'll meet you there."

"All right, then. I should be getting along. There's a lot to be done."

"There's something else I think we should get out of the way." He rocked back on his heels a moment, then stunned her by grabbing both her arms and dragging her against him. "This has nothing to do with business."

Infuriated, she brought her hands to his chest and gave him one hard shove. It didn't budge him an inch. Then he clamped his mouth down on hers, rough and ready and with no patience at all.

She would have ripped and clawed at him. She would have struggled and bit and cursed. That was what she told herself she would have done if she hadn't been so stunned by the heat. His lips were firm. That she already knew. But she hadn't known they could be so hot, so passionate, so tempting.

Her head filled with sounds—louder, deeper sounds than the rain that drove furiously on the roof above. Her hands were trapped between their bodies so that she could feel the pounding of a heart without knowing which of them it came from.

This is what the apple must have tasted like when Eve took the first forbidden bite, she thought giddily. Succulent, tart, unbearably delicious. Nothing else ever tasted would be as satisfying. Lost in the flavor, she parted her lips and let him take more.

He'd known what he'd wanted but hadn't been sure what to expect. If she'd hissed at him, he would have ignored her and taken his fill. If she'd struck out at him in anger, he would have taken her struggles in stride and enjoyed the fury. He'd fought or gambled for everything he'd wanted all of his life. For days he'd been trying to convince himself that Erin McKinnon was no different. But she was.

She gave. After the first stunned instant she gave passionately, with the kind of desperation that left him shaken and edgy for more. Her mouth was avid and mobile, her body taut and trembling. He could feel the raw, jagged need raging through her, rising, speeding up to meet and match his own.

He wanted to take her there, on the damp floor with the smell of rain and earth everywhere. He wanted her to touch him, to feel those capable hands on his flesh. To hear her say his name. To watch her eyes go dark as midnight as he covered her body with his. It could be now. He could feel it in the press of her body against his, in the give of her mouth.

It could be now. There had been times, and there had been women with whom he wouldn't have hesitated. Why he did so now he couldn't be sure. But he drew her away, though his hands stayed on her shoulders and his eyes stayed on hers as they slowly fluttered open.

She couldn't speak, not for a moment. The feeling was so immense it left no room for words. She'd never known that a body could be filled so quickly with sensations or that a mind could be emptied of them just as swiftly. She knew now. If anyone had told her that the world could change in the single beat of a heart, she would have laughed. Now she understood.

He didn't speak. Erin struggled to find her footing as he kept his silence. She couldn't allow herself that kind of madness, not again. If she were to travel an ocean with him, work for him, understand him just a little, she couldn't let this happen again. Not with a man like him. Taking a deep breath, she steadied herself. No, never with him. If the past few moments had taught her anything, it was that he was a man who knew women and who understood their weaknesses very well.

"You had no right to do that." She didn't unleash her temper, knowing she hadn't the energy left for it.

He was shaken, down to the bone, down to the heart, but it wasn't the time to dwell on it. "It wasn't a matter of right but of want. That was a proper kiss, Irish, and we needed to get it out of our systems whether you were coming with me or not."

She nodded, hoping she sounded as casual as he. She'd rather have died on the spot than have admitted her own inexperience. "Now that our systems are clear, there'll be no need for it to happen again."

"Don't ask me for promises. You'll be disappointed." He strolled to the door, pushing it open so that the wind and rain lashed their way in. It helped cool his head and steady his heart rate. "You can talk to Dee and Travis when you bring the papers in. Give your family my best."

Then he was gone, into the storm. Though Erin dashed to the door, he was only a quickly fading shadow in the gloom.

A shadow, she thought, whom she knew nothing about. And she would be going with him to America.

CHAPTER 4

Amerca. Erin wasn't naive enough to believe the streets were paved with gold, but she was determined to make it the land of opportunity. Her opportunity.

It was the speed of things that struck her first, the hurry every living soul seemed to be in. Well, she was in a bit of a hurry herself, she decided as she sat in the back of her cousin's station wagon and tried not to gawk.

The cold had surprised her, too, a numbing, bone-chilling cold she'd never experienced in the mild Irish climate. But the snow was novelty enough to make it a small inconvenience. Piles of it, more than she'd ever seen, rolling over the gentle hills and heaped on the sides of the road. It was a different sky above, different air around her. So what if she gawked, Erin thought to herself, and she smiled as she tried to see everything at once.

Burke had been true to his word. The paperwork had gone so smoothly that in a matter of days after he'd offered her the job she'd been across the Atlantic. He'd left her with her cousin's family at the airport in Virginia, with a casual comment that he'd see her in a couple of days, after she'd settled in. Just like that. Erin was still trying to catch her breath.

She'd hoped he'd say more. She'd hoped—perhaps foolishly—that he would seem more pleased that she was there.

She'd even waited to see that half smile, that dark amusement in his eyes, or to feel the flick of his finger down her cheek. But he'd only dismissed her as an employer dismisses an employee. Erin reminded herself that was precisely what they were now. There would be no more waltzes or wild embraces.

Did she wish there would be? The devil of it was she'd done just as much thinking about Burke Logan as she had about coming to America. Something had told her that they were both chances—the man and the country. Sometime, somehow, she'd begun to mix them together and had discovered she wanted both. She knew she was being foolish again and resolved to settle for the land.

It was beautiful. The mountains dark in the distance reminded her just enough of home to make her comfortable, while the whiz of the cars beside them in three lanes were foreign enough to add excitement. Erin found it a palatable combination and was already hoping for more.

Adelia shifted in her seat so that she could smile back at her cousin. "I remember my first day here, when Uncle Paddy picked me up at that same airport. I felt like I'd been plopped down in the middle of a circus."

"I'll get used to it." Erin smiled and took another long look out the window. "I'll get used to it very quickly, as soon as I believe I'm really here."

"I for one am grateful to Burke." Distracted a moment, Dee murmured to Brady, who was fretting in his car seat, then soothed him with a stuffed dog. "It was never in my mind when we went to Ireland that we'd be bringing family back with us."

The guilt tingled a little, shadowing the pleasure. "I know it was all very sudden, and I'm beholden to you, Dee."

"Oh, what a pack of nonsense. I feel like a girl again, having my best friend come to stay. We'll have a party." The minute the thought struck, Adelia rolled with it. "A proper one, too, don't you think, Travis?"

"I think we could handle it."

"I don't want you to go to any trouble," Erin put in.

"If you don't let Dee go to any trouble, you'll break her heart," Travis said without embellishment. They crossed over the line into Maryland. "Nearly home now, love."

"I'm as excited to be back as I was to leave. Brendon, if you don't stop teasing your sister you'll be seeing nothing but the four walls of your room until morning." Dee sighed a bit and shifted.

"All right?" Travis sent her a quick, concerned glance.

"They're just active." She patted his hand to make light of the discomfort. "Probably squabbling between themselves already."

"I'd like to help with the children." The closer they came, the more Erin's nerves began to jump. "Or however else I can to pay you back for taking me in this way."

"You're family," Adelia said simply. Then she sat up straighter as they drove between the stone pillars that led to home. "Welcome to Royal Meadows, cousin. Be happy."

Erin didn't know what she'd been expecting. Something grand, surely. She wasn't disappointed. The sun shone hard on the February snow, causing the thin crust to glitter and shine. Acres of it, Erin thought. This world was white and gleaming. Even the trees were coated with it, their bare black branches mantled with snow and dripping with cold, clear ice. Like a fairyland, she mused, then called herself foolish.

When the house came into view, she could only stare. She'd never seen anything so big or so lovely. The stone rose up as sturdy as it was majestic from the white base of snow. Charm was added by the wrought-iron-trimmed balconies that graced the windows.

"It's beautiful," Erin murmured. "It's the most beautiful house I've ever seen."

"I've always thought so, too." Dee reached over to unhook Brady as Travis brought the car to a halt. "And it's so good to see it again. Come now, my lad, we're home."

"Uncle Paddy!" From the backseat, both Brendon and Keeley began to shout. Then they were out and kicking through the snow. A short, stocky man with wiry gray hair and a face like an elf spread his arms wide for them.

"Give me the baby, missy," Hannah told Dee. "You're already carrying two. And we'll let the men handle the bags while you come in for a nice cup of tea and put your feet up."

"Stop fussing," Dee said. Then she laughed as her uncle grabbed her in a fierce hug.

"How's my best girl?"

"Fit as a fiddle and glad to be home. Look what we brought back with us from Skibbereen." Still laughing, she held out a hand to Erin. "You remember Erin McKinnon, Uncle Paddy. Mary and Matthew McKinnon's daughter."

"Erin McKinnon?" His face seemed to scrunch together as he thought back. Then, with a hoot, he was beaming. "Erin McKinnon, is it? Faith, lass, the last time I saw you you were no more than a baby. I used to raise a glass with your da now and then, but you wouldn't be remembering that."

"No, but they still speak of Paddy Cunnane in the village."

"Do they now?" He grinned as if he knew exactly what was said. "Well, get inside out of the cold."

"I can help with the bags," Erin began as Adelia started to shoo her children indoors.

"I'd appreciate it if you'd go with Dee, let her show you your room." Travis was already pulling out the first of the luggage. Even as he set them in the drive, his gaze was following his wife. "She doesn't like to admit she gets tired, and having you to fuss over will keep her from overdoing."

Erin stood a moment, torn between carrying her own weight and doing what was asked of her. "All right. If you like."

"It wouldn't hurt if you told her you'd like to sit down with a cup of tea."

Quietly domineering, Erin thought again. On impulse, she leaned over and kissed Travis's cheek. "Your wife's a fortunate woman. I'll see that she rests without knowing she's been maneuvered into it." Still, she picked up one of the cases and took it inside with her.

The warmth struck her immediately, not just the change of temperature but the colors and the feel of the house itself. The children were already racing through the rooms as if they wanted to make sure nothing had changed in their absence.

"You'll want to go up first, see your room." Dee was already stripping off her gloves and laying them on an ornamental table in the hall. Hooking her arm through Erin's, she started up the stairs. "You'll tell me if it suits you or not, and if there's anything else you want. As soon as you feel settled in, I'll show you the rest."

Erin only nodded. The space alone left her speechless. Adelia opened a door and gestured her inside.

"This is the guest room. I wish we'd had time to have some flowers for you." She glanced around the room, regretting she hadn't been able to add a few more personal touches. "The bath's down the end of the hall, and I'm sorry to say the children are always flinging wet towels around and making a mess of it."

The room was done in gray and rose with a big brass bed and a thick carpet. The furniture was a rich mahogany with gleaming brass pulls and a tall framed mirror over the bureau. There were knickknacks here and there, a little china dog, a rose-colored goblet, more brass in a whimsical study of a lion. The terrace doors showed the white expanse of snow through gauzy curtains, making a dreamlike boundary between warmth and cold. Unable to speak, Erin gripped her case in both hands and just looked.

"Will it suit you? You're free to change anything you like."

"No." Erin managed to get past the block in her throat, but her hands didn't relax on the handle of the case. "It's the most beautiful room I've ever seen. I don't know what to say."

"Say it pleases you." Gently Dee pried the case from her. "I want you to feel comfortable, Erin, at home. I know what it's like to leave things behind and come to someplace strange."

Erin took a deep breath. She wasn't able to bear it, not for another second. "I don't deserve this."

"What foolishness." Businesslike, Dee set the case on the bed with the intention of helping her cousin unpack.

"No, please." Erin put her hand over Dee's, then sat. She didn't want her cousin to tire herself, and she didn't want her to see what a pitiful amount she'd brought with her. "I have to confess."

Amused, Dee sat beside her. "Do you want a priest?"

With a watery laugh that shamed her, Erin shook her head. "I've been so jealous of you." There, it was out.

Dee considered a minute. "But you're much prettier than I am."

"No, that's not true, and that's not it, in any case." Erin opened her mouth again, then let out a long breath. "Oh, I hate confession."

"Me, too. Sinning just comes natural to some of us."

Erin glanced over, saw both the warmth and humor and relaxed. "It comes natural enough to me. I was jealous of you. Am," she corrected, determined to make a clean breast of it. "I'd think about you here in a big, beautiful house, with pretty things and pretty clothes, your family, all the things that go with it, and I'd just near die with envy. When I met you at the airport that day, I was resentful and nervous."

"Nervous?" She could pass over resentment easily. "About seeing me? Erin, we all but grew up together."

"But you moved here, and you're rich." She closed her eyes. "I've a powerful lust for money."

A smile trembled on Dee's lips, but she managed to control it. "Well, that doesn't seem like a very big sin to me. A couple of days in purgatory, maybe. Erin, I know what it is not to have and to wish for more. I don't think less of you for envying me—in truth, I'm flattered. I suppose that's a sin, too," she added after a moment's thought.

"It's worse because you're so kind to me, all of you, and I feel like I'm using you."

"Maybe you are. But I'm using you as well, to bring Ireland a little closer, to be my friend. I have a sister—Travis's sister.

But she moved away about two years ago. I can't tell you how much I miss her. I guess I was hoping you'd fill the hole."

Because her conscience was soothed by the admission, Erin touched a hand to Dee's. "I guess it's not so bad if we use each other."

"Let's just see what happens. Now I'll help you unpack."

"Let's leave it. I'd really like to go down and have a cup of tea."

As Erin rose, Adelia eyed her. "Did Travis tell you to keep me off my feet?"

"I don't know what you're talking about."

"Lying's a sin, too," Dee reminded her, but she smiled as she led her downstairs.

* * *

She dreamed of Ireland that night, of the heady green hills and the soft scent of heather. She saw the dark mountains and the clouds that rushed across the sky ahead of the wind. And her farm, with its rich plowed earth and grazing cows. She dreamed of her mother, telling her goodbye with a smile even as a tear slid down her cheek. Of her father, holding her so tight her ribs had ached. She heard each of her brothers teasing her, one by one.

She cried for Ireland that night, slow, quiet tears for a land she'd left behind and carried with her.

But when she woke, her eyes were dry and her mind clear. She'd made her break, chosen her path, and she'd best be getting on with it.

The plain gray dress she chose was made sturdily and fit well. Her mother's stitches were always true. Erin started to pin her hair up, then changed her mind and tamed it into a braid. She studied herself with what she hoped was a critical and objective eye. Suitable for work, Erin decided, then started downstairs.

She heard the hoopla from the kitchen the moment she'd

reached the first floor. At ease with confusion, she headed toward it.

"You'll have plenty to tell your friends at school." Hannah was at the stove, lecturing Brendon as she scooped up scrambled eggs.

"You've missed two weeks, my lad." At the kitchen table, Dee was fussing with a ribbon in Keeley's hair. "There's no reason in the world you shouldn't go back to school today."

"I have jet lag." He made a hideous face at his sister, then attacked the eggs Hannah set in front of him.

"Jet lag, is it?" With an effort, Dee kept a straight face. After kissing the top of Keeley's hair, she nudged her daughter toward her own breakfast. "Well, if that's the truth of it, I suppose we have to forget those flying lessons when you're sixteen. A jet pilot can't be having jet lag."

"Maybe it's not jet lag," Brendon corrected without missing a beat. "It's probably some foreign disease I caught when we were in Ireland."

"Bog fever," Erin said from the doorway. Clucking her tongue, she walked over to rest a hand on Brendon's brow. "Sure and that's the most horrible plague in Ireland."

"Bog fever?" Dee made sure there was a tremor in her voice. "Oh, no, Erin, it couldn't be. Not my baby."

"Young boys are the ones who catch it easiest, I'm afraid. There's only one cure, you know."

Dee shuddered and closed her eyes. "Oh, not that. Poor darling, poor little lad. I don't think I could bear it."

"If the boy has bog fever, it has to be done." Erin put a hand on his shoulder for comfort. "Nothing but raw spinach and turnip greens for ten days. It's the only hope for it."

"Raw spinach?" Brendon felt his little stomach turn over. He wasn't sure precisely what turnip greens were, but they sounded disgusting. "I feel a lot better."

"Are you sure?" Dee leaned over to check his brow herself. "He seems cool enough, but I don't know if we should take any chances."

"I feel fine." To prove his point, he jumped up and grabbed his coat. "Come on, Keeley, we don't want to miss the bus."

"Well, if you're sure . . ." Dee rose to kiss his cheek, then Keeley's. "Uncle Paddy's going to drive you to the end of the lane. It's cold, so stay in the car until the bus comes."

Dee waited until the door slammed behind them before she lowered herself in the chair again and howled with laughter. "Bog fever? Where in the blue heaven did you dig that up?"

"Ma always used it on Joe. It never failed."

"You've a quick mind." Hannah chuckled as she turned around. "What can I fix you for breakfast?"

"Oh, I don't—"

"If you think Mrs. Malloy can cook, wait until you taste Hannah's muffins." Understanding her cousin's embarrassment, Dee took the cloth off a little wicker basket. "Why don't you have some eggs to go with it? I have the appetite of a hog when I'm carrying, and I hate to eat alone."

"Coffee?" Hannah was by her shoulder with the pot.

"Please. Thank you. Ah, is Travis not up yet?"

"Up and gone," Dee said comfortably. "He's been down at the stables for more than an hour. When he travels on business, I'm never sure if he misses me or the horses more." She glanced at the muffins, lectured herself, then took another anyway. After all, she was eating for three. "Brendon's in the first grade now, and Keeley goes mornings to kindergarten. So there's only Brady." She gestured to the high chair where he sat, his face covered with oatmeal as he sang to his fingers. "He's the best-tempered child in the world, if I do say so myself. Now what would you like to do today?"

"Actually, I thought I'd go over to Mr. Logan's and begin work."

"Already?" Dee smiled her thanks at Hannah as the breakfast plates were set in front of them. "You've only just got here. Surely Burke's willing to give you a day or two to get your bearings."

"I know, but I'm anxious to get started, to see what there is to be done. And to make certain I can do it."

"I can't imagine Burke Logan putting anyone on his payroll who didn't know their business."

"It's different for me. Even thinking in dollars instead of pounds is different. If I'm in the middle of it working my way out, I won't worry so much about making a mess."

Dee remembered how anxious she herself had been to begin work when she'd come to America, to prove to herself she was still competent and able to make her own way. "All right, then, I'll drive you over myself after breakfast."

"Not on your life, missy," Hannah said from the stove.

"Oh, for pity sakes, I can still fit behind the wheel of a car."

"You're not driving anywhere until you have your next checkup and the doctor clears it. Paddy can take Miss McKinnon."

Dee wrinkled her nose at Hannah's back, but subsided. "I'm a prisoner in my own house. If I go down to the stables, Travis has every hand on the place watching me like a hawk. You'd think I never had a baby before."

"Twins come early, as you know very well."

"The sooner the better." Then she smiled. "Well, I'll just stay in and plan the party. And Brady and I can build block houses, can't we, love?"

In answer, he squealed and slapped his hand into his oatmeal.

"After he has a bath."

"Why don't I take care of that?" Rising, Erin moved over to free Brady from his high chair.

"You're not going to start pampering me, too. I'll go mad."

"Nothing of the kind. I just think it's time this handsome young man and I got better acquainted."

By the time she was finished, Erin had to clean the oatmeal off herself as well. Bundled inside a cardigan and a coat, she drove with Paddy Cunnane to Burke's neighboring horse farm.

The nerves were back. She could feel them tense in her fingers as she curled them together.

It was a waste of time to be nervous about the likes of him, she told herself. What had happened on that stormy morning in the shed was over and done with. Now they were nothing more than boss and employee. He'd said he expected a day's work for a day's pay, and she intended to give it to him.

Whatever other feelings she'd had had been born of the moment. Lust, she said firmly, telling herself she was mature enough to face that as a fact of life. Just as she would be strong enough to resist it.

She was a bookkeeper now. Her nerves were suddenly tinged with excitement. A bookkeeper, she repeated silently, with a good job and a good wage. Within the month she could start sending money home, with enough left over to buy . . . Lord, she couldn't begin to think what would be first.

Paddy turned the Jeep under an arch. The sign was large, wrought iron, strong rather than fancy with its block letters. Three Aces. Erin caught her lip between her teeth. Was that the hand he'd won it with, or the hand the former owner had lost it with?

The snow lay here as well, but the rise of hill wasn't as gentle. She saw a willow, old and gnarled, with its leaves dulled and yellow from winter. Perhaps in the summer it would look peaceful and lovely, but for now it looked fierce. Then she saw the house. She'd thought nothing could surprise her after the Grants'. She'd been wrong.

It had cupolas, like a castle, and the stone was dull and gray. The windows were arched, some of them with little parapets. Across from the steps and circled by the drive was an oval island that was now covered with untrammeled snow.

"Do people really live in places like this?" she said half to herself.

"Cunningham, he'd be the owner before Logan, liked to think of himself as royalty." Paddy sniffed, but Erin wasn't entirely sure if the sound was directed at the present or the former owner. "Put more money into fancying up this place than into the stables and the stock. Got a pool right inside the house."

"You're joking."

"Indeed not. Right inside the house. Now you've only to call when you've finished here. I'll come fetch you, or one of the boys will."

"I'm obliged to you." But her fingers seemed frozen on the handle.

"Good luck to you, lass."

"Thanks." Screwing up her courage, she pushed out of the Jeep. She was grateful it stayed parked where it was as she climbed the stone steps to the front door.

And what a door, she thought. As big as a barn and all carved. She ran a hand over it before she pulled back the knocker. Erin counted slowly under her breath and waited. It was opened by a dark-haired woman with big eyes and a small, erect figure. Erin swallowed and kept her chin up.

"I'm Erin McKinnon, Mr. Logan's bookkeeper."

The woman eyed her silently, then stepped back. Erin managed to throw a smile to Paddy over her shoulder before she stepped inside.

By the saints, she thought, tongue-tied again as she stood in the atrium. She'd never seen anything to match it, with its high ceilings and lofty windows. It seemed the sun shone in from all directions and slanted over the leaves of thick green plants. A balcony ran all the way around in one huge circle, the rail gleaming and carved as the door had been. The heels of her sensible shoes clicked on the tile floor, then stopped as she stood, uncertain what to do next.

"I'll tell Mr. Logan you're here."

Erin only nodded. The accent sounded Spanish, making her feel more out of place than ever. Erin wiped her hands on her skirt and thought she knew what Alice had felt like when she'd stepped through the looking glass.

"Are you eager to work, or did you just miss me?"

She turned, knowing she'd been caught gaping. He was in jeans and boots, and the smile was the same. The confidence she'd lost when she'd stepped inside came flooding back. It was the best defense.

"Eager to work and earn a wage."

The cold and excitement had heightened the color in her cheeks and darkened her eyes. As she stood in the center of the big open room, Burke thought she looked ready and able to take on the world.

"You could have had a day or two to settle in."

"I could, but I didn't want it. I'm used to earning my way."

"Fine. You'll certainly earn it here." He lifted a hand and gestured her to follow. "Morita, my last bookkeeper, managed to embezzle thirty thousand before the cage shut on him. In the process, he made a mess of the records. Your first priority is to straighten them out again. While you're doing that, you're to keep up the payroll and the current invoices."

"Of course." Of course, a little voice inside her said mockingly.

Burke pushed a door open and led her inside. "You'll work here. Hopefully you won't have to ask me a bunch of annoying questions, but if something comes up, you can call Rosa on the intercom and she'll pass it on to me. Make a list of whatever supplies you think you'll need, and you'll have them."

She cleared her throat and nodded. Her office was every bit as large as O'Donnelly's entire storeroom. The furniture was old and glossy, the carpet like something out of a palace. Determined not to stare again, Erin walked over to the desk. He had been right about one thing. It was a mess. For the first time since she'd approached the big stone house, she felt relief. Here was something familiar.

Ledgers and books and papers were piled together in one heap. There was an adding machine, but it was nothing like the clunky manual one she'd used before. Besides the clutter, there was a phone, a china holder stuffed with pencils and a basket clearly marked In and Out.

Burke moved behind the desk and began opening and closing drawers. "You've got stamps, stationery, extra worksheets, and checkbooks. Since Morita, nothing goes out without my signature."

"If you'd taken that precaution before, you'd be thirty thousand dollars richer."

"Point taken." He didn't add that Morita had worked for him for ten years, during lean times and better. "Set your own pace, as long as it's not sluggish. Rosa will fix you lunch. You can take it in here or in the dining room. There may be times I'll join you."

"Are you here most of the day?"

"I'm around." He settled a hip on the corner of the desk. "You didn't sleep well."

"No, I . . ." But her fingers had automatically lifted to the slight smudges under her eyes. "The time change, I guess."

"Are you comfortable at the Grants'?"

"Aye, they're wonderful to me. All of them."

"They're extraordinary people. You won't find many like them."

"You're not." She hadn't meant to say it, but told herself it was too late to be sorry she had. "You've an edge to you."

"Then be careful you don't get too close. Edges can be sharp."

"I've already seen that for myself." She said it lightly as she reached for the first stack of papers. He closed his hand slowly and firmly around her wrist.

"Are you trying to provoke me, Irish?"

"No, but I don't imagine it takes much."

"You're right there. It might be fair to tell you that I have a short fuse, and a dangerous one."

"I'm so warned." She looked amused, but when she tried to free her hand, his fingers only tightened.

"One more warning, then. Since you've moved into our

little community, you'll hear it from others soon enough. When I find a woman who attracts me, I find a way to have her. Fair means or foul, it doesn't mean a damn to me."

It wasn't a warning, Erin realized. It was a threat. Beneath his fingers, her pulse was beating hard and fast, but she kept her eyes even with his. "I didn't have to be told to know that, nor have I any intention of attracting you."

"Too late." He grinned but released her hand. "I find you intriguing enough to dance in the moonlight with, desirable enough to kiss in a garden shed, and passionate enough to imagine making love to."

Her stomach knotted with fear, with longing. "Well, a woman's head could be turned clear around with such flattery, Mr. Logan. Tell me, did you bring me to America to sleep with you or to fix your books?"

"Both," he said simply, "but we'll deal with business first."

"Business is all we'll deal with. Now I'd like to begin."

"Fine." But instead of leaving, he ran his hands up her arms. Erin stiffened, but didn't back away. She wouldn't play the fool and struggle. Though she braced herself for the hot passion she'd experienced before, he only brushed a kiss over her cheek.

He'd thought of her and little else since he'd come home again. He'd thought of how she'd felt in his arms, of how his system reacted when she smiled, of how her voice flowed, warm and sweet, so that a man didn't care what the words were as long as she spoke again.

He knew he could have her. Her response had been too quick and too encompassing before for either of them to pretend otherwise. He knew she wanted him, though it didn't sit well with her. Even now, as he kissed her lightly, avoiding her lips, her breath was beginning to tremble. He'd never known a woman whose passion was so close to the surface. Now that she was here, in his home, he knew he wouldn't rest until he had all of it.

But she would come to him. His pride demanded it. So he

teased her with his lips, knowing he stirred her. He teased her with his lips, knowing he was slowly killing himself.

"Fair means or foul," he murmured, nipping gently at her earlobe. "I want you."

Her eyes were closed. How was it possible to be swept away so quickly, to want so desperately what you knew you shouldn't have? She put a hand to his chest, willing it to be steady. "And you're used to taking what you want. I understand that. I won't deny you move something in me, but I'm not here for the taking, Burke."

"Maybe not," he murmured. Some women were only there for the earning. "I can be patient, Irish. When a man's got the cards, he's got to know when to hold and when to lay them on the table." Thoughtfully he ran a finger down her braid. "We'll play out this hand sooner or later. I'll let you get started."

Erin waited until he'd left before she let out a long breath. How was it he could be that arrogant and still make her want to smile? With a shake of her head, she sat behind the desk in a plush leather chair that made her sigh.

Burke was right about one thing, she mused. They would play out the hand sooner or later. The problem was Erin feared that even if she won, she'd lose.

CHAPTER 5

Within a week, Erin had developed a routine that pleased her. In the mornings she rose early enough to help Dee ready the children for school, then drove a borrowed car to the Three Aces to report to work by nine.

The mess of Burke's bookkeeping had been an enormous understatement. So had her estimate of his wealth. As she tallied figures and pored over ledgers, she tried to think of it in simple, practical terms. Numbers, after all, were just numbers.

She was rarely interrupted, and took her lunch from the silent Rosa at her desk. By the end of the first week, she'd made enough headway to feel pleased with herself. Only once or twice had she been made to feel foolish. She'd had to ask Burke for the instruction book on the adding machine. Then she'd asked him to supply her with a pencil sharpener. He'd simply picked up a cylinder with a hole in it and handed it to her.

"And what good is this?" she'd demanded. "It doesn't even have a crank."

He'd picked up a pencil and shoved it in the hole; then, damn him, had laughed when she'd jumped at the grinding. "Batteries," he'd said, "not magic."

She'd gotten over that small humiliation by burying her face in the account books. Maybe she wasn't used to gadgets, but by the saints, she'd balanced his books. Now she sat at the little electric typewriter and wrote up her weekly report. After tidying her desk, Erin picked up her report and went to find Burke.

His house was still almost completely uncharted territory to her. In the atrium, Erin hesitated. She could have called for Rosa on the intercom, but talking into the blasted thing always made her feel foolish. Instead, Erin set off in what she hoped was the general direction of the kitchen.

The place went on forever, she thought, and found it increasingly difficult not to open doors and peek inside as she went. Hearing a hum, she turned in that direction. Dishwasher, she thought, or a washing machine. With a shrug, she decided she'd find Rosa at the end of it.

The woman was a mystery, Erin thought as she walked. Rosa rarely spoke and always seemed to know precisely where to find Burke. Though the housekeeper referred to Burke as Mr. Logan, Erin sensed something less formal between them. She'd wondered, though it hadn't brought her any pleasure, if they were or had been lovers. Pushing the thought aside, she moved to the south end of the house.

But it wasn't the kitchen she found, or the laundry room. As she pushed open one of a pair of double doors, Erin entered the tropics. The pool was an inviting blue, sparkling under the sun that poured through the glass roof and walls. There were trees here the likes of which she'd never seen, planted in huge pottery urns. And flowers. She stepped in farther, overwhelmed by the heady scent when she could still see the snow through the glass. There were rich red petals, brilliant orange and yellow, exotic blues. If she closed her eyes, she imagined, she'd hear the chatter of parrots. Paradise, she thought, smiling as she walked farther.

With his eyes half-closed and his body just beginning to relax, Burke watched her. She didn't look sultry like the room, but fresh, untouched. The sun was all over her hair, drawing out the fire, licking at the layers of light. She'd pulled it back in a band as he'd seen her wear it in Ireland. And he could remember very well, too well, what it felt like to run his fingers through its mass.

He saw her reach for a flower as if her fingers itched to pick it, then draw back her hand and bury her face in the blooms instead. Her laugh was quiet, delighted, and he knew she thought herself alone.

So the Irish rose had a weakness for flowers, he thought, then watched her shake her head and look wonderingly, longingly around. And for money. At the latter, he shrugged his shoulders. It was difficult for someone in his position to blame her.

He could blame her, however, for the fact that his body was no longer even close to relaxing.

"Want a swim, Irish?"

At the sound of his voice, she whirled around. She'd forgotten about the hum. She saw its source now, and Burke in the middle of it. Another pool—no, not a pool, she corrected. She wasn't a complete dunderhead. She'd seen pictures of spas with their jets and bubbles and steamy water. And she couldn't help, for just a moment, wondering what it felt like to lower one's body into it.

"Want to join me?"

Because he grinned when he said it, Erin merely shrugged. "Thank you, but I'll be leaving for home in a few minutes. I've finished for the day and brought you your first report."

He nodded, but merely gestured to a white wicker chair beside the spa. "Have a seat."

Biting off a sigh, Erin did as he asked. "You may be a man of leisure yourself, but I've things to do."

Burke stretched his arms along the edge of the spa. He didn't mention that he'd been up and at the stables since dawn, or that he'd strained every muscle in his body overseeing the mating between a stud and a particularly high-strung mare. "You've still got a few minutes on the clock, Irish. So how are my finances?"

"You're a rich man, Mr. Logan, though how that might be

with the mess your books were in amazes me. I've done a bit of studying and come up with a new system." The truth was she'd spent two nights burning the midnight oil with books on accounting. "If you like, I'll wait until you've finished and go over it with you."

"It'll keep."

"Suit yourself. By the end of next week I should have everything running smoothly enough."

"That's good to know. Why don't you tell me how?"

He stretched his shoulders. Erin watched the muscles ripple along the damp skin, then deliberately shifted her gaze above his head. This was no place for her to be, she told herself, especially when her mind was wandering away from accounting. "It's all in this report, if you'd care to pull yourself out of the tub there and have a look at it."

"Have it your way." Burke pushed the button that shut off the jets, then stood. Erin's limbs went weak as she saw he wore no more than he'd been born with. She was grateful color didn't rise to her cheeks, though she couldn't prevent some from leaving.

Burke took a towel and swung it easily over his hips as he stepped from the spa.

"You've no shame, Burke Logan."

"None at all."

"Well, if you'd meant to shock me, I'll have to disappoint you. I've four brothers, if you'll remember, and . . ." She glanced over again, prepared to look at him without interest. It was then she noticed the darkening bruise just under his left ribs. "You've hurt yourself." She was up immediately and laying gentle fingers on it. "Oh, it's a nasty one." Without thinking, she took her fingers up over his ribs, carefully checking. "You didn't break anything."

"Not so far," he murmured. He was standing very still, the amusement he'd felt completely wiped out. Her fingers felt so cool, so tender on his skin. She touched him as if she cared. That was something he'd learned to live a long time without.

"It'll look worse yet tomorrow," she said with a cluck of her tongue. "You should put some liniment on it." Then she realized her fingers were spread over his chest, and his chest was hard and smooth and wet. Erin snatched her hand away and stuck it behind her back. "How'd you come by it?"

"The new colt I picked up in Ireland."

She closed her hand into a fist. It was damp from his skin. "You'll have to give him more room next time." The shudder inside her came as no surprise and was quickly controlled.

"I intend to. I have the highest respect for the Irish temper."

"And so you should. If you'd look over the report now, I could answer any questions you might have before I leave."

Burke picked up the neatly typed sheets. Erin found it necessary to clear her throat as she turned to look out through the glass, now lightly fogged from the steam of the spa. But she didn't see the snow. She could still see him—the long arms roped with muscle, the hard chest glistening with water, the narrow hips leading to taut thighs.

A fine specimen, some would have said, herself included. And she could have murdered him for making her want.

"It seems clear enough." She jolted a bit, then cursed herself. "You know your business, Erin, but then I wouldn't have hired you if I hadn't believed that." No, he wouldn't have, but he'd have found some other way to bring her back with him. "Got anything in mind for your first paycheck?"

"A thing or two." She relaxed enough to smile at him, schooling her gaze to go no lower than his neck. Half the money would be on its way to Ireland in the morning. And the rest . . . She couldn't begin to think of it. "If you're satisfied, I'll be going home now."

"I'm a long way from satisfied," Burke said under his breath. "Listen, did you ever think the bookkeeping would be more interesting if you knew more about the stables, the racing?"

"No." Then she moved her shoulders as the thought he'd planted took root. "I suppose it might, though."

"I've got a horse running tomorrow. Why don't you come along, see where the money comes from and where it goes?"

"Go to the races?" She caught her lip between her teeth as she thought of it. "Could I bet?"

"There's a woman after my heart. Be ready at eight. I'll take you around the stables and paddock first."

"All right. Good day to you." She started out, then glanced over her shoulder. "I'd put some witch hazel on that bruise."

*   *   *

Erin paced the living room. It was her first day off, and she was going to spend it at the races. There would be mobs of people she'd never met; she'd hear dozens of voices for the first time. She ran a hand down her hair and hoped she looked all right. Not for Burke, she thought quickly. For herself, that was all. She wanted to look nice, to feel she looked nice when she stood in the midst of all those people.

The minute she heard Burke's car, she was racing out of the house. She hesitated on the steps, staring down at the fire-red sports car with its long, sleek hood. She made a mental note of the make so she could write home and tell Brian.

"You're prompt," Burke commented as she climbed in beside him.

"I'm excited." It didn't seem foolish to admit it now. "I've never been to the races before. Cullen has, and he told me the horses are beautiful and the people fascinating. Faith, look at all these dials." She studied the dash. "You'd have to be an engineer to drive it."

"Want to try?"

When she glanced at him and saw he was serious, she was sorely tempted. But she remembered all the cars that had been on the highway when they'd driven from the airport. "I'll just watch for now. When does the racing start?"

"We've got plenty of time. How's Dee?"

"She's fine. The doctor gave her a clean checkup but told

her she had to stay off her feet a bit. She grumbles because she can't spend as much time down at the stables, but we're keeping her busy. The snow's melting."

"A few more days like we've been having and it'll be gone."

"I hope not. I like to look at it." She settled back, deciding that riding in the sports car was like riding on the wind. "Are you going to be warm enough?" she asked, looking at his light jacket and jeans. "There's still a bite in the air."

"Don't worry. So what do you like best about America so far, besides the snow?"

"The way you talk," she said instantly.

"Talk?"

"You know, the accent. It's charming."

"Charming." He glanced over at her, then laughed until the bruise began to throb. Still chuckling, he rubbed a hand over it absently.

"Is that troubling you?"

"What, this? No."

"Did you use witch hazel?"

He knew better than to laugh again. "I couldn't put my hands on any."

"I'd imagine you'd have a case or two of horse liniment down in the stables. Oh, look at the little planes." When he turned into the airport, she looked over at him. "What are we doing here?"

"Taking a ride on one of the little planes."

Her stomach did a quick flip-flop. "But I thought we were going to the races."

"We are. My horse is racing at Hialeah. That's in Florida."

"What's Florida?"

Burke paused in the act of swinging his door closed. On the other side of the car, Erin stared at him. "South," he told her, and held out a hand.

Too excited to think, too terrified to object, Erin found herself bundled onto a plane. The cabin was so small that even she had to stoop a bit, but when she sat the chair was soft and roomy. Burke sat across from her and indicated the seat belt. Once hers was secured, he flipped the switch on an intercom. "We're set here, Tom."

"Okay, Mr. Logan. Looks like smooth sailing. Skies are clear except for a little patch in the Carolinas. We ought to be able to avoid most of them."

When she heard and felt the engines start, Erin gripped the arms of the chair. "Are you sure this thing's safe?"

"Life's a gamble, Irish."

She nearly babbled before she caught the amusement in his eyes. Deliberately she made her hands relax. "So it is." As the plane started to roll, she looked out the window. Within minutes the ground was tilting away under them. "It's quite a sight, isn't it?" She smiled, leaning a little closer to the window. "When all of you landed in Cork, I looked at the plane and wondered what it would be like to sit inside. Now I know."

"How is it?"

She gave him a sideways smile. "Well, there's no champagne."

"There can be."

"At half past eight in the morning?" With a laugh, she sat back again. "I think not. I should have thanked you for asking me to go today. The Grants have been nothing but kind to me, so I'm really grateful to give them a day to themselves."

"Is that the only reason you should have thanked me?" He stood and went into a little alcove.

"No. I appreciate the chance to go."

"You want cream in this coffee?"

"Aye." He could have said you're welcome, she thought, then let it pass. Nothing was going to spoil her mood. When he sat, she took the cup but was too wound up to drink. "Will you give me an answer if I ask a question that's none of my business?"

Burke drew out a cigar and lit it. "I'll give you an answer, but not necessarily the truth." He kicked out his legs, then rested his ankles on the seat beside her.

"Did you really win Three Aces in a poker game?"

He blew out smoke. "Yes and no."

"That's not an answer at all."

"Yes, I played poker with Cunningham—quite a bit of poker with Cunningham—and he lost heavily. When you gamble you have to know when to stick and when to walk away. He didn't."

"So you won the farm from him."

She'd like that, he thought, watching her eyes. He imagined she saw a smoky, liquor-scented room with two men bent over five cards each and the deed to the farm between them. "In a manner of speaking. I won money from him, more money than he had to lose. He didn't have enough cash to pay me, or for that matter to pay certain other parties who were growing tired of holding IOUs. In the end, I bought the farm from him, dirt cheap."

"Oh." It wasn't quite as romantic. "You must have been rich before then."

"You could say my luck was on an upswing at the time."

"Gambling's no way to make a living."

"It beats sweeping floors."

Since she could only agree, Erin fell silent a moment. "Did you know about horses before?"

"I knew they had four legs, but when you've got your money riding on a game, you learn fast. Where did you learn to keep books?"

"Arithmetic came easily to me. When I could I took courses in school, then I started to run the books at the farm. It was more satisfying than morning milking. Then, because everyone knows what everyone else is up to back home, I found myself working for Mrs. Malloy, then Mr. O'Donnelly. I worked for Francis Duggan at the market for a time, too, but his son Donald thought I should marry him and have ten children, so I had to let that job go."

"You didn't want to marry Donald Duggan?"

"And spend my life counting potatoes and turnips? No, thank you. It came to the point where I knew I had to either black both his eyes or give up the job. It seemed easier to give up the job. What are you smiling at?"

"I was just thinking that Donald Duggan was lucky you didn't carry a rake."

Erin tilted her head as she studied him. "It's you who're lucky I held myself back." Comfortable now, she tucked her legs under her and sipped her cooling coffee. "Tell me about the horse you're racing today."

"Double Bluff, he's a two-year-old. Temperamental and nervy unless he's running. He's proved himself from his first race, took the Florida Derby last weekend. That's the biggest purse in the state."

"Aye, I heard Travis mention it. He seems to think this horse is the best he's seen in a decade. Is it?"

"Might be. In any case, he'll be my Derby entry this year. His sire won over a million dollars in purses in his career, and his dam was the offspring of a Triple Crown winner. Likes to come from behind, on the outside." He took another puff, and again Erin noticed the scar along his knuckles.

"You sound as though you're fond of him."

He was, and that fact was a constant surprise. Burke only shrugged. "He's a winner."

"What about the one you bought in Ireland, the one who kicked you?"

"I'm going to start him off locally—Charles Town, Laurel, Pimlico, so I can keep an eye on him. If my hunch is right, he'll double what I paid for him in a year."

"And if your hunch was wrong?"

"They aren't often. In any case, I'd still consider my trip to Ireland paid off."

She wasn't completely comfortable with the way he looked at her. "Being a gambler," she said evenly, "you'd know how to lose."

"I know how to win better."

She set her coffee down. "How did you get the scar on your hand?"

He didn't glance at it as most people would, but tapped out his cigar as he watched her. "Broken bottle of Texas Star in a bar fight outside of El Paso. There was a disagreement over a hand of seven-card stud and a pretty blonde."

"Did you win?"

"The hand. The woman wasn't worth it."

"I suppose it makes more sense to gash your hand open over a game of cards than it does for a woman."

"Depends."

"On what? The woman?"

"On the game, Irish. It always depends on the game."

* * *

When they arrived, Erin stepped off the plane into another new world. Burke had told her to leave her coat on the plane, but even so she hadn't been expecting the warmth or the glare of the sun.

"Palm trees," she managed, then laughed and grabbed Burke's hands. "Those are palm trees."

"No fooling?" Before she had a chance to be annoyed, he swung an arm over her shoulders and swept her away. There was a car waiting for them. Erin slipped inside, wanting to pretend she did such things every day. "There's no handle for the window," she began. Burke leaned over and pressed the button to lower it. "Oh." After ten seconds, she gave up trying to be poised. "I can't believe it. It's so warm, and the flowers. Oh, my mother would die for the flowers. It's like that room in your house with all the glass. Two weeks ago I was scrubbing Mrs. Malloy's floor, and now I'm looking at palm trees."

He drove competently, without asking directions or checking a map. Erin realized this life wasn't new to him. Here she was babbling and sounding like a fool. She made one attempt to restrain herself, then gave it up. It didn't matter how she sounded.

He hadn't realized he'd get such enjoyment out of seeing

someone take little things and make them special. For a moment he wished they could just keep driving so that she would go on talking, laughing, asking questions. He'd nearly forgotten there were people who could still find things fresh and new no matter how often they'd been used.

Traveling was a profession to him, and like most professional travelers he'd long ago stopped looking at what was around him. Now, with Erin pointing out white sand, young skateboarders and towering hotels, he began to remember what it was like to see something for the first time.

They knew him at the track. Erin noticed as they walked over the green lawn toward the spread of stables that people nodded in his direction or greeted him as Mr. Logan. There were jockeys and trainers and grooms already preparing for the afternoon races.

"Logan."

Erin glanced over and saw a big, potbellied man in a straw hat. She saw the flash of a diamond on his finger and the light film of sweat the heat had already drawn on his face. "Durnam."

"Didn't know you were coming down for a look-see."

"I like to keep an eye on things. Your horse ran well last week."

"At Charles Town. I didn't know you were there."

"I wasn't. Erin McKinnon, Charlie Durnam. He owns Durnam Stables in Lexington."

"Real horse country, ma'am." He took her hand and flashed her a smile. "A pleasure, a real pleasure. Nobody picks the fillies like Logan."

"I won't be running any races, Mr. Durnam," she told him, but she smiled, judging him harmless.

"From Ireland, are you?"

"She's Adelia Grant's cousin." Burke spoke mildly, giving Durnam a straight look until he released Erin's hand.

"Well, ain't that something? I tell you, ma'am, any friend of the Grants is a friend of Charlie Durnam's. Fine people."

"Thank you, Mr. Durnam."

"I'm going to go check on my horse, Charlie. See you around."

"Take a look at Charlie's Pride while you're at it," he called after them. "That's a real piece of horseflesh."

"What a funny man," Erin murmured.

"That funny man has one of the best stables in the country and a roving eye."

She glanced back over her shoulder and chuckled. "His eye can rove all it pleases. I can't imagine he has much luck on a landing."

"You'd be surprised the kind of luck ten or fifteen million can buy." Burke nodded to a groom. "I'm running against him today."

"Is that so?" Erin tossed her hair back and was sure the sun had never shone brighter. "Then you'll just have to beat him, won't you?"

With a grin, Burke put his arm around her shoulders again. "I intend to." He walked by a few stalls. Erin cautiously kept on the far side of him. The smell of horse and hay was familiar, and so was the little knot in her stomach. Ignore it, she told herself, stepping up beside Burke as he stopped at a stall.

"This is Double Bluff."

She judged the dark bay to be about fifteen hands, broad at the chest and streamlined for speed. The beauty of him struck her first; then she froze when he tossed his head. "He's a big one." Her throat had gone bone-dry, but she forced herself to take one step closer.

"Ready to win?" With a laugh, Burke reached up to stroke his nose. The colt's ears came forward in acknowledgment, but he continued to prance. "Impatient. This one hates to wait. He's an arrogant devil, and I think he might just win Three Aces its first Triple Crown. What do you think of him?"

"He's lovely." Erin had taken a step backward the first time the colt had looked in her direction. "I'm sure he'll do you proud."

"Let's have a closer look, make sure the groom's done his job." Burke opened the stall door and stepped in. Erin steeled herself, and with her heart pounding walked to the opening. "You look good, fella." Burke ran his hands over the colt's flank, then dipped under him to check the other side. He lifted each hoof, then nodded in approval. "Clean as a whistle. Wait until they put a saddle on him. The minute they do, he's ready. You have to hold him back from the starting gate."

As if he understood, Double Bluff pawed the ground. He tossed up his head and whinnied as Burke laughed. Erin fainted dead away.

When she surfaced, there was an arm supporting her. Something cool and wet was being urged through her lips. She swallowed reflexively, then opened her eyes. "What happened?"

"You tell me." Burke's voice was rough, but the hand that stroked her cheek was gentle.

"Probably too much sun." Erin heard the drawled pronouncement and shifted her gaze beyond Burke's shoulder. She saw a young face and a thatch of sandy hair.

"That's right," she said, grabbing the excuse. "I'm fine now."

"Just sit still." Burke held her down as she tried to get up. "It's okay, Bobby, I'll handle it from here."

"Yes, sir, Mr. Logan. You take it easy now, miss, stay in the shade."

"Thank you. Oh . . ." Erin closed her eyes and cursed herself for seven kinds of a fool. "I'm sorry I caused a scene. I don't know what could have happened."

"You were fine one minute and in a heap the next." And nothing, absolutely nothing in his life, had ever scared him so badly. "You're still pale. Why don't we take Bobby's advice and get you up and into some shade?"

"Aye." She let out a breath of relief. Just as Burke started to help her up, Double Bluff stuck his head out again and shook the stall door. With a muffled cry, Erin threw her arms around Burke's neck and clung.

It took him only a moment to put one and one together. "For

God's sake, Erin, why didn't you tell me you were afraid of horses?"

"I'm not."

"Nitwit," he muttered, hauling her unceremoniously into his arms.

"Don't carry me. I've had enough humiliation already."

"Shut up." When he judged they were far enough away from the stables, he set her down under a palm. "If you'd had the brains to tell me, you wouldn't have shaved ten years off my life." With another oath, he dropped down beside her. His heart had yet to resume its normal rhythm.

"The last thing I'm wanting from you is a lecture." She would have stood and stormed away, but she knew her legs weren't ready to carry her. "Besides, there was nothing to tell. I thought I was over it."

"You thought wrong." Then, because she was still pale, he relented and took her hand. "Why don't you tell me about it?"

"It's childish."

"Tell me anyway."

"We had some field horses, two good ones." She let out a long breath. He could hardly think her any more of a fool than he did now. "We had them out, and a storm was coming up. Brian unhooked the one to take him back to the barn. There was a lot of thunder and lightning, so the horses were nervous. Joe was unhooking the second, and I was at the head trying to calm him, I don't know, it happened fast, lightning spooked him and he reared. God, those hooves are big when they're over your head." She shuddered once. "I fell, and he ran right over me."

"Oh, God." Burke tightened his fingers on her hand.

"I was lucky, it wasn't that bad. A couple of broken ribs, some bruises, but I've just never been able to get too close to one without panicking."

"If you'd told me I never would have brought you."

"I thought I'd beaten it by now. It was more than five years ago. Stupid." She ran a hand over her face, then tucked back her hair. "I've been making excuses all week to Dee and Travis why I don't go down to the stables."

"Why don't you just tell them?" When she only shrugged, he shifted closer. "It's not half as stupid to be afraid as it is to be ashamed of it."

Her chin came up; then she sighed. "Maybe." Avoiding his eyes, she plucked a blade of grass. "Don't tell them."

"More secrets?" Patiently he caught her chin in his hand and turned her face to his. It was far more difficult to resist her now when her cheeks were pale, her eyes a little damp and the vulnerability like a sheen on her skin. "You shouldn't worry so much about what people think of you. I know you wash dishes and faint at the sight of horses, but I still like you."

"Do you?" A reluctant smile tugged at her mouth. "Really?"

"Well enough." Unaccustomed to resisting any desire for long, he lowered his mouth to hers, to taste, to nibble, to explore. She lifted a hand to his chest as if to hold him off, but then her fingers simply curled into his shirt and held him there.

His other kisses hadn't made her feel peaceful or secure. Anything but. Yet this one was different. Even as excitement shimmered warm in her stomach, she felt safe. Maybe it was the way his hand curved around her neck, with his fingers gentle and soothing. Or maybe it was the way his lips made hers feel soft and tingly.

He wanted to draw her close, to cuddle her, to rock her on his lap and murmur foolish things. He'd never had that urge with a woman before. It was an odd and uneasy sensation, and at the same time . . . comforting.

He drew away slightly, but kept her close. "I'll take you home."

"Home? But I want to see the races." For some reason she felt as though she could face anything at that moment. "I'm fine, I promise you. Besides, maybe if I can learn to watch them from a distance I won't freeze up when I'm near one." She stood, grateful that her legs were sturdy again. "Come now, Burke, we didn't fly all the way to—where are we?"

"Florida," he told her, and rose.

"Aye, Florida to turn right around and go home again. That great beast in there is going to win, isn't he?"

"I've got my money on him."

"And I've got ten more on the nose."

With a laugh, he accepted the hand she held out. "Let's go get a seat."

The stands were already filling up. In them, Erin indeed saw many faces, tanned and sunburned ones, faces with lines spreading out from the eyes and more with skin as smooth as new cream. Some people pored over racing forms, others smoked fat cigars or sipped from plastic cups.

But in the boxes was elegance, the kind that spoke of confidence and poise. Sheer summer dresses in pastels mixed well with light cotton suits and straw hats. She saw more than one tanned, slender woman tilt a head in Burke's direction. Now and then he lifted a hand, but he made no effort to mix with them.

From Burke's box in the front, she could see the wide brown oval where the horses would run and the lush green infield filled with tropical flowers and pink flamingos. Still farther away were more stands with more people. Every minute, more were filing in.

"I've never seen so many people in one place at one time. And they're all here to watch the race."

"Want a beer?"

Erin nodded absently and continued to take in everything as Burke left her. She spotted Durnam not far away, talking to a woman in the tiniest pair of shorts Erin had ever seen. Erin passed over him and looked at the electronic board that was beginning to flash with numbers and odds for the first race.

"I want you to explain to me what it all means up there," Erin began before Burke had a chance to sit down again. "So I'll know best how to bet."

"If you want a tip, you'll wait for the third race, bet on number five."

"Why?"

"The horse is out of Royal Meadows. Sentiment aside, he's a strong runner. Record's a little shaky, but he looks good today. First race is anybody's game. So far the odds aren't spectacular."

"Are you betting on it?"

"No."

"I thought you were a gambler."

"I like to pick my own game."

Erin sat back and listened to the announcements for the first race. "Crystal Maiden sounds pretty."

"Pretty names don't win races. Hold on to your money, Irish."

She settled back and contented herself with absorbing the sounds and sights around her. By the time the horses were brought to the starting gate, she was leaning forward in her chair. "They *are* beautiful," she said, but she felt a great deal better when Burke's hand rested lightly on hers.

Her pulse was hammering. He gauged it to be almost as much from excitement as nerves. He'd been right about the contradictions in her. As the gates opened, her fingers linked hard with his, but she didn't cringe.

"What a noise," she murmured, while her heart beat almost as loudly as hooves on turf. As they rounded the first turn, she strained to keep following them. That was power, she thought, both raw and controlled. They might well have made it a business, but she could see why it had been and was still the sport of kings.

When it was over, she laid a hand on her breast. "My heart's still pounding. Don't smile at me like that," she warned, but laughed with it. "It's the most wonderful thing I've ever seen. All those colors, all that energy. Can you imagine doing this every day?"

"There are plenty who do."

But she only shook her head. Today was special, a once-in-a-lifetime day. "I want to bet on the next one."

"Third race," Burke repeated, and sipped his beer.

When her time came, she insisted on betting herself. Erin put the stub in the pocket of her shirt, then changed her mind and tucked it carefully in her billfold. Seated beside Burke again, she fretted until the horses were brought to the gate.

"I don't mind losing," she said with a quick grin, "but I'd sure as hell like to win better."

When they were off, she stood and leaned against the rail. "Which one is he?" she demanded, grabbing Burke's hand to drag him forward with her.

"Fourth back on the inside. Red-and-gold silks."

"Aye." She watched, urging him on. "He runs well, doesn't he?"

"Yes."

"Oh, look, he's moving up."

"Better hang on, Irish. They've got half a mile to go."

"But he's moving up." She gave a hoot of laughter as she pointed. "He's in second now."

There was shouting all around her, competing with the announcer and the thundering of hooves. Erin strained to hear all three as she grabbed Burke's shirt and tugged.

"He's taken the lead. Look at him!" She spun away from the rail and into Burke's arms as he finished half a length ahead. "He won! *I* won!" Laughing, she kissed Burke hard. "How much?"

"Mercenary little witch."

"It's nothing to do with mercenary and everything to do with winning. I'm going home and tell Dee I bet on her horse and won. How much?"

"The odds were five to one."

"Fifty dollars?" She gave another peal of laughter. "I'll buy the next beer." She took him by the hand. "When does your horse race?"

"In the fifth."

"Thank goodness. It'll give me time to recover."

She bought him a beer, then went one better and bought

them both hot dogs. The only time she could remember spending such a frivolous day was at a fair. This seemed like one to her, with the noise and smells and colors. She had another ticket in her pocket and Burke's sunglasses on by the time the fifth race was announced.

"I really hope he wins," she told him with her mouth full. "Not just because I bet on him, either."

"That makes two of us."

"How does it feel to own one?" she wondered. "Not just a horse, but a horse from a great line."

"Most of the time it's like having an expensive lover, one you have to keep happy and lavish money on for moments of intense gratification."

Erin turned and, tipping the glasses down, looked at him over them. "You're full of blarney."

"At the very least."

He turned and watched his horse charge through the gate. How did it feel? Burke asked himself. How did it feel for a dirt-poor bastard from New Mexico to sit and watch his six-figure horse come flying by? Incredible. So incredible he couldn't begin to describe it and wasn't sure he wanted to. It could all be gone tomorrow.

And what of it?

He'd taught himself long ago that when you held on to something too tightly it squeezed through your fingers. He was giving Three Aces the best he had, though he'd never intended to get involved with the running of it. He'd certainly never intended to get attached to it. He worked better on the move. Yet he'd been in one place for four years.

Just recently he'd been telling himself that maybe it was time for him to get a manager for the place and take an extended vacation. Monte Carlo, San Juan, Tahoe. If a man stuck with one game too long, didn't he get stale? But then he'd gone to Ireland. And had come back with Erin.

The damnedest thing was, he wasn't thinking about Monte

Carlo or playing the wheel anymore. It was becoming easier and easier to stay in one place. And think about one woman.

"You won!" Suddenly she was laughing and her arms were around his neck. "You won by two lengths, maybe three, I couldn't tell. Oh, Burke, I'm so pleased for you."

"Are you?" He'd forgotten the race, the horse and the bet.

"Of course I am. It's wonderful that your horse won, and he looked so beautiful doing it. And I'm happy for me, too." She grinned. "The odds were eight to five."

Then he stunned her by dragging her closer and kissing her with a power and passion that left her limp. She didn't protest but, held trapped in his arms, allowed herself to be buffeted by the storm.

"The hell with the odds," Burke muttered, and kissed her again.

CHAPTER 6

She didn't know what to think. No one could have been kinder than Burke the day Erin had spent with him. She'd watched the races, the strong, beautiful horses striving for speed. She'd seen women dressed in elegant clothes and jockeys in brilliant silks. She'd heard the noises that came from thousands of people in the same place. She'd seen exotic birds and flowers, had sipped champagne in a private plane. But her clearest memory of the day was of sitting on the grass in Burke's arms.

She didn't know what to think.

Since then, the days had passed routinely. Erin had to remind herself she was doing exactly what she'd set out to do—making a wage, starting a life, seeing new things. But Burke's visits to her office had become few and far between. She began to catch herself watching the door and wishing it would open.

She told herself that her feelings for him were surface ones. He made her laugh, showed her exciting things and could be kind enough when it suited him. He was just arrogant enough to keep an edge on without alienating her. A woman could like a man like that without putting her heart at risk. Couldn't she? A woman could even kiss a man like that without falling too deep. Wasn't that right?

And yet she knew she'd come to the point where she thought of him a bit too easily and watched for him far too often.

* * *

He'd stayed away from her long enough. That was what Burke told himself as he came in through the back of the house from the stables. He'd stayed away from her since their quick trip to Florida because his feelings were mixed. He was used to clear thinking and well-defined emotions, not this jumbled mess of needs and restraint.

He couldn't stop thinking about the way she'd looked at the track, watching the horses race by. She'd been vivid, excited, exciting. The kind of woman he could handle. Yet he couldn't stop thinking about the way she'd looked when she'd fainted all but at his feet. She'd been pale and helpless, frightened. He'd needed to protect and soothe.

He'd never wanted the responsibility of a woman who needed protection or care. Yet he wanted Erin. She wasn't the kind of woman you took to bed for a night of mutual enjoyment, then strolled away from. Yet he wanted her. For all her strong talk, she was a woman who would put down roots and sink them deep. He'd never wanted the restriction or the responsibility of a home in the true sense. Yet he still wanted Erin McKinnon.

And he'd stayed away from her long enough.

When he walked into the office, she was marking in the ledger in her clear, careful hand. She knew it was him—even without looking she knew—but made herself finish before she glanced up.

"Hello. I haven't seen much of you lately."

"I've been busy."

"That's clear from the papers on my desk. I've just paid your vet bill. Dr. Harrigan back home could live a year off what you pay a month. Are the new foals well?"

"They'll do."

"I see you've hired a new stable boy."

"My trainer sees to the hiring."

Erin lifted a brow. So he was going to play master of the estate, was he? "I see your Ante Up ran well at Santa Anita."

"Reading the sports page these days?"

"I figure living with the Grants and working for you I should keep up." Erin picked up her pencil again. "Now that we've had such a pleasant little talk I'll get back to work, unless there's something you're wanting."

"Come with me."

"What?"

"I said come with me." Before either of them had a chance to think it through, he took her arm and hauled her to her feet. "Where's your coat?"

"Why? Where are we going?"

Instead of answering, he glanced around and spotted it folded on a chair. "Put this on," he told her. Then, even as he thrust it at her, he began to walk.

"A fine thing," Erin began breathlessly as he pulled her down the hall. "Interrupting my work in the middle of the day, dragging me off without any explanation. Just because you pay me, Burke Logan, doesn't mean I have to jump at your bidding. An employee has rights in this country. Which reminds me, I've been meaning to ask you about my paid holidays."

"You learn fast," he muttered as he pushed the door open.

"If you don't let go of my arm, I won't be able to put it in my coat." When he did, Erin rammed her arm in the sleeve but left the coat unbuttoned. "Sure and it's a fine day. The ground's a bit of a mess with the snow melting, but that's all the better for spring growing. If that was all you wanted to show me, I'll go back to work."

She managed to hiss out a protest when he grabbed her arm and began walking again.

"Burke, what the devil's got into you? If there's something you want me to do or see, fine, but there's no need to strong arm me."

"How long have you been working for me?"

"Three weeks." Giving up, Erin matched her stride to his.

"And in three weeks you've barely poked your head out of the office."

"I work in the office," she reminded him.

"Did it ever occur to you that you can't understand the work if you've never looked at where the money comes from or where it goes?"

"I thought that's why we went to the races."

"There's more to this place than one race."

"Why do I have to understand as long as the figures tally?"

He wasn't sure of the answer himself, but he knew he wanted her to see what was his, to understand it, to move closer to it.

Pushing the hair out of her eyes, she glanced up at him. His profile was set, and she thought she detected a shadow in his eyes. "Is there something troubling you?"

"No." He said it sharply, almost defensively, then made himself relax. "No, nothing." Except the need tethered tight inside him that strained hard at the scent of her. What the hell was happening to a man who could only think of one woman, of one voice, of one taste?

She continued to walk beside him in silence, but she noticed the crocuses—big fat purple ones that pushed their way up through the soggy ground, unmindful of the patches of snow. She saw the way the land sloped, the way the sun slanted over it. And she saw the stables, with their white wood gleaming in the sunlight. She saw the checkerboard of paddocks and the long oval track where even now a horse was being ridden.

"Why, it's lovely," she murmured. "Like something out of a book. You must be proud that it's yours."

He wasn't sure he had been, but he stopped and looked out as she did. He'd won it fairly, but then he'd won and lost a great deal in his life. It had never been his intention to stay, but rather reorganize so that the gamble paid off. He'd come into this knowing little about horses and nothing about racing or breeding, and had told himself he'd better learn in order to turn a true profit.

That had been four years ago, and he was still here. Looking out with Erin beside him, he began to understand why. It was lovely, it was his, and it was and would always be a gamble.

Keeping Erin's hand in his, he began to walk again. "We've got thirty horses, two of which are studs that do nothing but please the ladies."

"And themselves," Erin added.

"Two of the mares just foaled, and we've two more that are due any day. Nearly half of what's left are being trained for next year. At the moment I've got five prime two-year-olds and a few veterans that have another season or two in them before they go out to stud or retirement. There, you see the horse being exercised now? That's one of the pair I picked up in Ireland."

Erin looked back at the track. The rider was up in the stirrups and bent low, but he earned no more than a glance. The horse was magnificent, a chestnut with a slash down his face like white lightning. Already his legs were spreading out in a rhythm that picked up speed and pounded on the soggy track.

"He's fast."

"And mean as hell."

"That would be the one that kicked you." Erin looked back again. Beautiful he might be, but she'd keep her distance. "If he's bad-tempered, why did you buy him?"

"I liked his style." As he started to walk again, Erin held back.

"I'd just as soon not be on closer acquaintance."

"I want to show you something else."

Erin told herself to relax as she walked with him. "If you'd told me we were going tramping around the yard, I'd have worn boots."

He glanced down but kept walking. "You could use some new shoes anyway."

"Thank you very much."

"I'd have thought you'd have gone shopping by now with a couple of paychecks under your belt."

"I'm thinking about it." They passed the stables, where the scent of horses and wet grass was strong. She could hear men talking inside. Erin braced herself, but he continued to walk. Then she saw the paddock where the mare was standing nursing a fawn-colored foal.

"That's one of the newest residents of Three Aces."

Cautiously Erin approached the fence. "They're sweet when they're little, aren't they?" She relaxed enough to curl her hands over the top rail and lean a little closer. The air was mild, with just a hint of spring. It wasn't the green or the scent of Ireland, but she found herself suddenly content. "We never had much time to think of an animal as any more than a means to an end." She smiled as the foal burrowed deeper and sucked. "Joe was always the one for animals, cooing at them and stroking. He'd love to see this."

"You miss your family."

"It's strange not seeing them every day. I hadn't realized . . ." She let the words trail off. "Word from home is everyone's fine. Cullen's back in Dublin playing at one of the clubs, and Brian's taken a fancy to Mary Margaret Shannesy. Ma says he's making a fool of himself, but that's to be expected."

The foal, having had his fill, began to scamper around the paddock. Erin watched him absently, thinking of home. "Frank's wife's nearly ready to have the baby. I could be an aunt already. It's funny, most mornings when I wake up I think it's time to go down to the henhouse. But there's no henhouse here."

The foal came over to the fence to sniff at her. Without thinking, Erin reached out a hand and rubbed between his ears.

"Do you wish there were?"

"I suppose I could live my life happily enough without gathering eggs again." She glanced down and, focusing on the foal, started to draw her hand back automatically. Burke set his on top of hers and rested it on the foal's head.

"Trusting little soul, isn't he?"

"Aye, but his mother—"

"Is probably relieved that he's distracted, for a few minutes. Sometimes if you're afraid it's best to face it in small doses."

"I suppose." The foal was soft as butter and nuzzled its nose between the rails to nip at her coat. "Find something else to chew on," she said laughing. "It's all I brought with me." Finding nothing of interest, the foal scampered away to race around his mother. "Will he be a champion?"

"If it's in the cards."

Erin stepped away from the fence and, dipping her hands in her coat pockets, looked at him. "Why did you bring me out here?"

"I don't know." He didn't think about the men walking around the yard and going in and out of the stables. He thought only of her as he lifted a hand to her cheek. "Why should it matter?"

Had it come so far, so fast, that it only took the touch of his fingers on her skin to send her heart racing? Inside her pockets, the palms of her hands grew damp. "I think it does, and I think I should go back in."

"You've faced one fear today, why not face another?"

"I'm not afraid of you." That was true, and she felt a surge of relief that it was. Her heart might not be steady, but it wasn't in fear that it raced.

"Maybe not." He slid his hand from her cheek to the back of her neck as he drew her closer. He was afraid, afraid of what she was doing to him without his planning, without his calculations.

She yearned toward him. She strained away. "I don't think it's wise for you to kiss me that way again."

"All right. We'll try another way."

So he nibbled, teasing, tempting, tormenting. She felt the scrape of his teeth, then the moist trace of his tongue. Her hand went to his cheek and rested there as she opened herself for an emotional assault like nothing she'd ever experienced.

So he could be sweet and patient and alluring. She hadn't known. Her fingers crept into his hair as her lips parted and invited. No, she wasn't afraid, not of him. If what he brought to her was more than she'd ever imagined, then she was willing, even eager to accept it. With a sigh she tilted her head back and let him take.

He held himself back. The more generosity she showed him, the more wary he became of accepting. Burning inside him was a desire to sweep her away to some dim, private place where they could both take their fill. To touch her. He pressed his lips over hers and imagined how it would be to fill his hands with her. No barriers. While her teeth nipped gently, he imagined what it would feel like to have her flesh slide warm over his.

There was such a flavor here, warm and wild and willing. But he wanted more than her mouth. As her sigh whispered into him, he knew he needed more.

He took his hand to her hair and held her close against him. "I want you to stay with me tonight."

"Stay?" She floated up out of the dream and was stunned by the heat and passion that had turned his eyes to smoke.

"Stay," he repeated. "Tonight. Damn it, more than tonight. Get your things and bring them here."

The thrill moved through her. There was something in the command, in the look in his eyes as he gave it, that called to her even as it raised her hackles. "Move in with you?" She lifted her hands to his chest and struggled to keep her voice calm. "You want me to live under your roof, eat your food, sleep in your bed?"

"I want you with me. You know damn well I've wanted that since the first time I put my hands on you."

"Aye, maybe I did. But what I agreed to do was work for you." She tilted her head back again, but not in surrender this time. Yes, she'd been willing to accept the feelings he stirred in her, but not to compromise her principles for them. "Do you think I'd be your mistress? Do you think I'd let you keep me in your fine house?"

"No one's talking about keeping."

"No, you're not a man for keeping, are you, but for taking, enjoying and moving on. I'll tell you now, no matter how you make me feel, how you make me want, I'll not be any man's mistress."

It was foolish to be hurt, ridiculous to be insulted, but she was both. Erin jerked out of his hold and stood with her feet planted. "If I kiss you, it's because it pleasures me to do so, and nothing more. I'll not live in your house, shaming my family, until you're tired of me." She tossed back her hair and crossed her arms. "I'll be going back to work now, and you'd best keep out of my way unless you want to explain to your men why the payroll isn't done."

She turned on her heel and strode away. Burke leaned back against the paddock fence. A smart man would have folded his cards and pushed away from the table. He figured he'd stay for the next hand and see where the chips fell.

* * *

Whether she was feeling festive or not, Erin was swept along in her cousin's plans for the party. And what better day to celebrate than St. Patrick's Day? Erin decided if there'd been a dog around, she'd surely have kicked it.

No "come live with me and be my love" from the likes of Burke Logan, she thought. She attacked a silver platter with a polishing cloth as though she could have rubbed through the metal. Oh, no, with him it was just "pack your things and be quick about it." Hah!

As if she'd want pretty words from that swine of a man. The truth of it was Erin McKinnon didn't want pretty words from anyone. What she wanted was to be left alone to pursue her new career. In six months she'd have a place of her own and a new job altogether, she decided. She'd find a job where she didn't have to put up with a man who made her laugh one minute and steam the next. And steam in more ways than one, she added as she tossed the polishing cloth aside.

Turning the platter over, she studied her own reflection. He was toying with her, he was. Hadn't she known that right from the beginning? Well, what was fine for him was fine for her. She could do some toying herself, and tonight was as good a time as any to start it. From what Dee had told her, there would be plenty of men at the party tonight. Including a certain snake in the grass.

"Have you finished scowling at yourself?" From the other side of the table, Dee set aside another tray.

"Almost."

"That's good, then, because we've only a couple more hours." Rising, she stacked the bowls and platters beside the crystal. Between Hannah and the caterers, the rest could be easily handled. "Is there anything you'd like to talk to me about?"

"No."

"Nothing that might have to do with why you've been muttering to yourself for the past week or so?"

Erin set her teeth, then dropped her chin on her hand. "I think American men are even more rude and arrogant than Irish men."

"I've always thought it was a draw." Adelia came over to lay a hand on her shoulder. "Has Burke been troubling you?"

"To say the least."

Something in the way Erin said it caused Dee to smile. "He has a way with him."

"Not my way."

"Well, then, we won't be worrying about him anymore. We've a party to get ready for."

Erin nodded as she rose. She'd known she was in trouble as soon as she'd seen the silver and crystal. Things had only gotten worse when she'd watched the team of caterers descend to fuss over things like salmon mousse and goose-liver pâté.

She'd seen the cases of champagne delivered. Cases, by God. Then there was the black caviar she'd managed to sample while no one was looking. And there were the flowers, tubs of them that were being arranged even as she walked with Dee down the hall.

"A madhouse, isn't it?" Dee began when they started up the stairs. "Later, if you've had your fill of hearing about horses and tracks and stud fees, just send me a sign."

"I like listening. It's a bit like learning a new language."

"It's all of that." Dee moved into her room and took a large box off the bed. "Happy St. Patrick's Day."

Automatically Erin put her hands behind her back. "What is it?"

"It's a present, of course. Aren't you going to take it?"

"There's no need for you to give me presents."

"No, but I didn't think of it as a need." Pride was something Adelia understood too well. Her own had been bruised repeatedly. "I'd like you to have it, Erin, from all of us as a kind of welcome to a new place. When I came here I had only Uncle Paddy. I think I understand now how happy it made him to share with me. Please."

"I don't mean to seem ungrateful."

"Good, then you'll pretend to like it even if you don't." Dee sat on the bed and gestured with both hands. "Open it. I've never been long on patience."

Erin hesitated only another moment, then laid the box on the bed to draw off the top. Under a cushion of tissue paper was dark green silk. "Oh. What a color."

"It's expected today. Well, take it out," she demanded. "I'm dying to see if it's right on you."

Cautiously Erin touched the silk with her fingertips, then lifted the dress from the box. The material draped softly in the front and simply fell away altogether in the back to a slim skirt. Dee rose to hold the dress in front of her cousin.

"I knew it!" she said, and her face lit up. "I was sure it was right. Oh, Erin, you'll be dazzling."

"It's the most beautiful thing I've ever seen." Almost reverently she brushed her fingers over the skirt. "It feels like sin."

"Aye." Then, with a laugh, Dee stepped back for a better viewpoint. "It'll look like it, too. There won't be a man able to keep his eyes in his head."

"You're kinder to me than I deserve."

"Probably." Gathering up the box, she handed it to Erin. "Go put it on, fuss with yourself awhile."

Erin kissed her cheek. Then, letting her feelings spread, she gave her cousin a hard, laughing hug. "Thank you. I'll be ready in ten minutes."

"Take your time."

Erin paused at the door. "No, the sooner I have it on, the longer I can wear it."

* * *

The party was already underway when Burke drove up. He'd nearly bypassed it altogether. Restless and edgy, he'd thought about driving up to Atlantic City, placing a few bets, spinning a few wheels. That was his milieu, he told himself, casinos with bright lights, back rooms with dim ones. A party with the racing class, with their old money and closed circles, wasn't his style.

He told himself he was here because of the Grants. The fact that Erin would be there hadn't swayed him. So he told himself. Since their last encounter he'd nearly talked himself out of believing there was something between them. Oh, a spark, certainly, a frisson, a lick or two of flame, but that was all. That overwhelming and undesirable feeling that there was something deeper, something truer, had only been his imagination.

He hadn't come tonight to prove that, either. So he told himself.

It was Travis who let him in. Burke could hear voices raised in the living and dining rooms along with the piping Irish music that set the tone.

"Dee was worried about you." Travis closed the door on the nippy mid-March air outside.

"I had a few things to see to."

"No problems?"

"No problems," Burke assured him. But if that was true, he wondered why his shoulders were tensed, why he felt ready to jump in any direction.

"You'll know just about everyone here," Travis was saying as he led him into the living room.

"You've got quite a crowd," Burke murmured, and was already searching through it, though he didn't move beyond the doorway.

"I think you'll see that Dee's outdone herself in more ways than one." With the slightest gesture, Travis had Burke's gaze traveling to the far end of the room and Erin.

He hadn't known she could look like that, coolly sexy, polished. She was sipping champagne and laughing over the rim of her glass at Lloyd Pentel, heir to one of the oldest and most prestigious farms in Virginia. Flanking her were two more men he recognized. Third- and fourth-generation racing barons, with Ivy League educations and practiced moves. Burke felt his blood heat as one of them leaned close to murmur something in her ear.

Both amused and sympathetic, Travis laid a hand on Burke's shoulder. "Beer?"

"Whiskey."

He downed the first one easily, appreciating its bite. But it did nothing to relax his muscles. He took a second and sipped it more slowly.

Erin was perfectly aware that he was there. She doubted he'd been in the room ten seconds before she'd felt his presence. She smiled and flirted with Lloyd and the others who wandered her way, and told herself she was having a wonderful time. But she never stopped watching Burke and the women who gravitated to him.

Adelia had been right—the talk was horses. Purses, the size

of which made the head reel, were discussed and the politics of racing dissected. Erin took it in, determined to hold her own, but as she nursed her single glass of champagne her gaze kept roaming.

The man didn't even have the courtesy to say "how do you do," she decided. But then he seemed more interested in the leggy blonde than in manners. Erin accepted a dance with Lloyd, and if he held her a bit too close she ignored it. And watched Burke.

It didn't appear to bother her to have the young Pentel stud pawing her, Burke noted as he swirled his whiskey. And where in the hell had she gotten that dress? Setting down his whiskey, he lit a cigar. She was nothing to get worked up over, he reminded himself. If she wanted to wear a dress that was cut past discretion and bat her baby blues at Pentel, that was her business.

The hell it was. Burke crushed out his cigar and, leaving the blonde who had snuggled up beside him staring, walked over to Erin.

"Pentel."

Annoyed, but as well-bred as his father's prize colt, Lloyd nodded. "Logan."

"I have to borrow Erin a minute. Business."

Before either of them could object, Burke had maneuvered his way between them and had Erin in his arms.

"You're a rude, shameless man, Burke Logan." She was delighted.

"I wouldn't talk about shameless while you're wearing that dress."

"Do you like it?"

"I'd be interested to hear what your father would say about it."

"You're not my father." Though she smiled, there was more challenge than humor in the curve of lips. "Doesn't a man like you worry about luck, Burke? No wearing of the green on St. Patrick's Day?"

"Who says I'm not?" His eyes tossed the challenge right back.

"Money doesn't count."

"I was talking about something more personal than money. If you want to go somewhere private, I'll be happy to show you where I'm wearing my green."

"I'm sure you would," she murmured, and tried not to be amused. "Now, what business do we have?" He wasn't holding her as close, not nearly as close as Lloyd had been, but she felt the pull of him.

"You've come a long way from dancing in moonlit fields, Irish."

"Aye." Some of the pleasure went out of her as she studied him. "What does that mean?"

"You're an ambitious woman, one who wants things, big things." God, it was driving him mad to be this close, to smell her as he had once before in a dim garden shed with rain pelting the roof.

"And what of it?"

"Lloyd Pentel's not a bad choice to give it to you. He's young, rich, not nearly as shrewd as his old man. The kind of man a smart woman could twist easily around her finger."

"It's kind of you to point that out," she said in a voice that was very low and very cold. She didn't know what possessed her to go on, but whatever it was, she swore she wouldn't regret it. "But why should I settle for the colt when I can have the stallion? The old man's a widower."

Burke's mouth thinned as he smiled. "You work fast."

"And you. The skinny blonde's still pouting after you. It must be rewarding to walk into a room and have six females trip over themselves to get to you."

"It has its compensations."

"Well, why don't you get back to them?" She started to pull away, but his hand pressed into her back so that their bodies bumped. The flame that was never quite controlled flared at the contact. "Damn you," she said from the heart as he tightened his fingers on hers.

"I'm tired of playing games." He had her across the room and into the hall before she found the breath to speak.

"What are you doing?"

"We're leaving. Where's your coat?"

"I'm not going anywhere, and I—"

He merely stripped off his jacket and tossed it over her shoulders before he yanked her outside. "Get in the car."

"Go to hell."

He grabbed her then, hard and fast. "There'll be little doubt of that after tonight." When his mouth came down on hers, her first reaction was to fight free, for this was a man to fear. But that reaction was so quickly buried under desire that she moved to him.

"Get in the car, Erin."

She stood at the base of the steps a moment, knowing no matter how strong, how determined he was, the choice would be hers. She opened the door herself and got in without looking back.

CHAPTER 7

Had she lost her mind? Erin sat in Burke's car, watching his headlights cut through the night, and heard nothing but the sound of her own heart pounding in her ears. She must be mad to have thrown all caution, all sense, any pretense of propriety to the winds. Why had no one ever told her that madness felt like freedom?

She'd never been self-destructive. Or had she? she asked herself, almost giddy from the speed and the night and the man beside her. Perhaps that was one more thing he'd recognized in her. A need to take risks and damn the consequences. If that wasn't true, why didn't she tell him to stop, to turn back?

Erin gripped her fingers together until the knuckles turned white. She wasn't at all sure he'd listen, but that wasn't the reason she didn't speak. No, the reason she didn't speak was that she'd lost more than her mind. Her heart was lost as well.

Perhaps one was the same as the other, Erin thought. Surely it was a kind of madness to love him. But love him she did, in a way she'd never imagined she could love anyone. There was a ferocity to it, an edgy sort of desperation that didn't swell the heart so much as tighten it. Indeed, it felt like a hard, hot lump beneath her breast even now.

Was this the way love should feel? Shouldn't she know? There should be a warmth, a comfort, a sweetness—not this wild combination of power and terror. Though she searched, she could find no tenderness in her feelings. Perhaps they were a reflection of his. At a glance she could see no gentleness in the man beside her. His hands gripped the wheel tightly and he looked nowhere but straight ahead.

Erin pressed her lips together and told herself not to be a romantic fool. Love didn't have to be gentle to be real. Hadn't she known all along that her emotions when it came to Burke would never be ordinary or simple? She didn't want them to be. Still, she would have liked to have laid a hand over his, to have offered some word to show him how deep her feelings went and how much she was willing to give. But more than her heart was involved. There was pride and spirit as well. She had to be realistic enough to understand that just because she loved didn't mean he loved in return.

So she said nothing as they drove under the sign and onto his land.

* * *

Why did he feel as though his life had just changed irrevocably? Burke saw the lights of his house in the distance and tensed as though readying for a blow. He wanted her, and if the need was stronger than he wanted to admit, at least tonight it would be assuaged. She hadn't said a word. His nerves neared the breaking point as he rounded the first curve in the drive. Did it mean so little to her, could she take what was happening between them so casually that she sat in silence?

He didn't want this. He wanted it more than he'd ever wanted anything in his life.

What was she feeling? Damn it, what was going on inside her? Couldn't she see that every day, every hour he'd spent with her had driven him closer and closer to the brink? Of what? Burke demanded of himself. What line was he teetering on that he'd never crossed before? What would his life and hers be like once he'd stepped over it?

The hell with it. Burke braked at the base of the steps and

without sparing her a glance, slammed the door and got out of the car.

Legs trembling, Erin got out and started up the steps. The door looked bigger somehow, like a portal to another world. With one long breath, she passed through.

Was it always so silent and angry when lovers came together? she wondered as she started up the staircase. Her hand on the banister was dry—dry and cold. She wished he'd reached for it, held it, warmed it in his own. That was nonsense, she told herself. She wasn't a child to be coddled and soothed, but a woman.

He walked into the bedroom ahead of her, waiting for her to smile, to offer her hand, to give him some sign that she was happy to be with him. But when the door closed at her back she simply stood, chin up, eyes defiant.

The hell with it, he thought again. She didn't need sweetness and neither did he. They were both adults, both aware and willing. He should have been glad she didn't want coaxing and candlelight and the promises that were so rarely kept.

So he pulled her against him. Their eyes met once, acknowledging. Then his mouth was on hers and the chance for quiet words and gentle caresses was past.

This was enough, Erin told herself as the heat rose like glory. This had to be enough, because she would never have more from him. Accepting, she pressed against him, offering her mind and body along with her heart he didn't know was already his. There was no hesitation now as her lips parted, as their tongues met in a hot, greedy kiss. When his hands roamed over her back, pressed into her hips, she only strained closer. She was prepared to trust him to show her the art of intimacy. She was prepared to risk self-destruction as long as he was part of the gamble.

Her fingers trembled only slightly as they dug into his arms. The strength was there, an almost brutal kind of strength that had her heart racing and her body yearning.

Good God, no woman had ever taken him so close to

desperation so quickly. It only took a touch, a taste. When she kissed him avidly for one sweet moment he could almost believe he was the only one. That was its own kind of madness. A sane man would think of just this one night, but like a drug she was seeping into his system, making his heart race and his mind swirl.

He tugged on her dress and she moved against him, murmuring. He recognized the excitement, the tremble of anticipation, but not the modesty. When her flesh was freed for him he took, with rough hands that incited both desire and panic. No one had ever touched her like this, as if he had a right to every part of her. No one had ever caused this hard fist of need to clench inside her so that she was willing to cede to him that right.

Then she was naked, tumbling to the bed so that his body covered hers. His hands found her, sent her spiraling so that she arched against him even as the fear of the unknown began to brew. Her breath caught with the sensation of being pressed under him, vulnerable, dizzy with desire. Her own body seemed like a stranger's, filled with towering emotions and terrifying pleasures. She wanted a moment, just one moment of reassurance, one soft word, one tender touch. But she was beyond asking, and he beyond listening.

Greedy, impatient, he took his lips over her as he wrestled out of his shirt. He wanted the feel of her flesh against his. How many times had he imagined them coming together this way, urgently, without questions? She was murmuring his name in a breathy, desperate whisper that had his passion snowballing out of control. He dragged at his clothes, swearing, hardly able to breathe himself and far beyond the capacity to think.

Her body was like a furnace beneath his, and with each movement she stoked the flames higher. She dug her nails into his shoulders; he fused his mouth with hers. Past all reason, he plunged into her.

* * *

She was curled away from him, trembling. Burke lay in the dark and tried to clear his head. Innocent. Dear God, he'd taken her with all passion and no care. And he was the first. He should have known. Yet from the first time he'd held her she'd been so ripe, so ready. There had been the strength, the hotheaded passion, the unquestioning response. It had never crossed his mind that she hadn't been with anyone else.

He ran his hands over his face, rubbing hard. He hadn't seen because he was a fool. The innocence had been there in her eyes for any man to see who'd had the brains to look. He hadn't looked, perhaps because he hadn't wanted to see. Now he'd hurt her. However careless, however callous he had been with women in the past, he'd never hurt one. Because the women he'd chosen before had known the rules, Burke reminded himself. Not Erin. No one had ever taught them to her.

Searching for a way to apologize, he touched her hair. Erin only drew herself closer together.

She wouldn't cry. She squeezed her eyes tight and swore it. She was humiliated enough without tears. What a fool he must think her, sniffling like a baby. But how could she have known loving would be all heat and no heart?

The hell of it was he was lousy at words. Burke reached down to the foot of the bed and drew a cover over her. As he tried to sort through and pick the best ones, he continued to stroke her hair.

"Erin, I'm sorry." By God, he *was* lousy with words if those were the pick of the litter.

"Don't apologize. I can't bear it." She turned her face into the pillow and prayed he wouldn't do so again.

"All right. I only want to say that I shouldn't have . . ." What? Wanted her? Taken her? "I shouldn't have been careless with you." That was beautiful, he thought, detesting himself. "I hadn't realized that you hadn't—that tonight was your first time. If I'd known, I would have . . ."

"Run for cover?" she suggested, pushing herself up. Before

she could climb out of the bed, he had her arm. He felt her withdrawal like a blade in the gut.

"You've every right to be angry with me."

"With you?" She turned her head and made herself look at him. He was hardly more than a silhouette in the dark. They had loved in the dark, she thought, unable to see, unable to share. Perhaps it was best it was dark still so that he couldn't see the devastation. "Why should I be angry with you? It's myself I'm angry with."

"If you'd told me—"

"Told you?" She sniffed again, but this time there was more than a little derision in it. "Of course. I should have told you, while we were rolling around on the bed naked as the day we were born, I might have said, *'Oh, by the way, Burke, you might be interested in knowing I've never done this before.'* That would have put a cap on it."

He was amazed to find himself smiling even as he reached for her hair again and she jerked her head away. "Maybe the timing could have been a bit better than that."

"It's done, so there's no sense pining over it. I want to go home now before I humiliate myself again."

"Don't."

"Don't what?"

"Don't go." That was a tough one. He hadn't known he'd had it in him to ask. "What happened wasn't wrong, it was just done badly. And that's my fault." He caught her chin in his hand as she started to turn away. "Look, I'm not good at asking, but I'd like you to let me make it up to you."

"There's no need." She wasn't aware that it was the gentleness in his voice that was calming her. "I told you I'm not angry with you. It's true it was my first time, but I'm not a child. I came here of my own free will."

"Now I'm asking you to stay." He took her hand and, turning it palm up, pressed his lips to the center. When he looked up at her again she was staring, her lips parted in surprise. He cursed himself again. "I'll draw you a bath."

"You'll what?"

"Draw you a bath," he said, snapping off the words. "You'll feel better."

When he disappeared into the adjoining room, Erin simply continued to stare after him. What in the world had gotten into him? she wondered. She gathered the blanket around her and stood as Burke came back in. He was wearing a robe tied loosely at the waist. The light from the bath angled out onto the floor. She could hear the sound of water running and sensed— but surely she was mistaken—a hesitation in him.

"Go ahead in and relax. Do you want something? Tea?"

Mutely she shook her head.

"Take your time, then. I'll be back in a few minutes."

Not a little baffled, Erin walked in and lowered herself into the tub. The water was steaming so that she felt the tension and the ache begin to diminish almost immediately. Sinking down, she closed her eyes.

She wished she had another woman to talk to, another woman to ask if this was all there was to lovemaking. She wished there was someone she could talk to about her feelings. She loved Burke, yet she felt no fulfillment after being with him. It had been exciting. The way he had touched her, the way his body had felt against hers, made her tremble and ache. But there had been no glorious glow, no beautiful colors, no feeling of rightness and contentment.

She was probably a fool for imagining there would be. After all, it was the poets and dreamers who promised more. Pretty words, pretty images. She was a practical woman, after all.

But Burke had been right. The bath had made her feel better. There was no reason for humiliation or for regret. If she was no longer innocent, she had brought about the change herself, willingly. One thing her parents had always told her was to follow what was in your heart and to blame no one.

Steadier, she stepped from the bath. She would face Burke now. No tears, no blushes, no recriminations.

Seeing no other cover, she wrapped the towel securely around her and stepped into the bedroom.

He'd lighted candles. Dozens of them. Erin stood in the doorway, staring at the soft light. There was music, too, something quiet and romantic that seemed to heighten the scent of wax and flowers. The sheets on the bed were fresh and neatly turned down. Erin stared at them as all the confidence she'd newly built up began to crumble.

He saw her glance at the bed and saw the quick, unmistakable flash of panic that went with the look. It brought him guilt and a determination to erase it. There were other ways, better ways. Tonight he would show both of them. Rising, he went to her and offered a rose he'd just picked in the solarium.

"Feel better?"

"Aye." Erin took the rose, but her fingers nearly bit through the stem.

"You said you didn't want tea, so I brought up some wine."

"That's nice, but I—" The words jammed in her throat as he lifted her into his arms. "Burke."

"Relax." He pressed a kiss to her temple. "I won't hurt you." He carried her to the bed and laid her against the pillows. Taking two glasses already filled with pale wine, he offered her one. "Happy St. Patrick's Day." With a half smile, he touched his glass to hers. Erin managed a nod before she sipped.

"This is a fine room . . ." she began lamely. "I didn't notice . . . before."

"It was dark." He slipped an arm around her shoulders and settled back even as she tensed.

"Aye. I've, ah, wondered what the other rooms were like."

"You could have looked."

"I didn't want to pry." She sipped a little more wine and unconsciously brushed the rose over her cheek. Its petals were soft and just on the verge of opening. "It seems like a big place for one man."

"I only use one room at a time."

She moistened her lips. What was this music? she wondered.

Cullen would know. It was so lovely and romantic. "I heard Double Bluff won his last race. Travis said he beat Durnam's colt by a length. Everybody's talking about the Kentucky Derby already and how your horse is favored." When she realized her head was resting against his shoulder, she cleared her throat. She would have shifted away, but he was stroking her hair. "You must be pleased."

"It's hard not to be pleased when you're winning."

"And tonight at the party, Lloyd told me that Bluff was the horse to beat."

"I didn't tell you how wonderful you looked tonight."

"The dress. Dee gave it to me."

"It made my heart stop."

She was able to chuckle at that. "What blarney."

"Then again, you managed to stop it wearing overalls."

She slanted a look up at him. "Aye, now I'm sure there's some Irish in you."

"I discovered I had a weakness for women taking in the wash."

"I'd say it's more a matter of a weakness for women in general."

"Has been. But just lately I've preferred them with freckles."

Erin rubbed rueful fingers over her nose. "If you're trying to flirt with me, you ought to be able to do better."

"Works both ways." Lifting the hand that still held the rose, he kissed her fingers. "You could say something nice about me."

Erin caught her lip between her teeth and waited until he glanced up. "I'm thinking," she said, then laughed when his teeth nipped her knuckle. "Well, I suppose I like your face well enough."

"I'm overwhelmed."

"Oh, I'm picky, I am, so you should be flattered. And though you haven't Travis's build, I'm partial to the wiry type."

"Does Dee know you've had your eye on her husband?"

Erin laughed into her glass. "Surely there's no harm in looking."

"Then look here." Tilting her face up to his, he kissed her. His lips lingered softly, more a whisper than a shout.

"There's the way you do that, too," she murmured.

"Do what?"

"Make my insides curl all up."

With his lips still hovering over hers, he took the glass from her and set it aside. "Is that good?"

"I don't know. But I'd like you to do it again."

With a hand to her cheek, he nuzzled. Drawing on a tenderness he hadn't known he possessed, waiting for her lips to warm and soften beneath his. She hesitantly touched a hand to his shoulder. She knew his strength now, what it was capable of, and yet . . . and yet his mouth was so patient, so sweet, so beautifully gentle. When he increased the pressure, her fingers tensed. Immediately he drew back to nibble again until he felt her begin to relax.

He wanted to take care, and not just for her, he realized, but for himself. He wanted to savor, to explore, to open doors for both of them. He'd never been a man to bother with candlelight and music, had never looked for the romance of it. Now he found himself as soothed and seduced by it as she was.

The scent of her bath was on her skin; fresh, clean. On her his soap seemed feminine, somehow mysterious. Her skin was smooth but not frail. Beneath it were firm muscles, honed by an unpampered life. He would never have found frailty as appealing. Still, he could feel the nerves jangle inside her. Now he would treat her as though she'd never been touched. Where there was innocence there should be compassion. Where there was trust there should be respect.

And somehow, wonderingly, he felt as though it was his own initiation.

She heard the rustle of the sheets as he shifted. Her body hammered with need even while her fears held her back. It was natural, she reminded herself. And now that she wasn't expecting, she wouldn't be disappointed. Then her breath caught as a new thrill coursed over her skin. Confused, she brought a hand to his chest.

"I won't hurt you again." He drew away from her to brush the hair from her face. His fingers weren't steady. God, he had to be steady now, he warned himself. He couldn't afford to lose control, to lose himself a second time. "I promise I won't hurt you."

She didn't believe him. Even as she opened her arms in acceptance, he saw she didn't believe him. So he lowered his mouth to hers again and thought only of Erin.

He'd never been a selfish lover, but he'd never been a selfless one, either. Now he found himself ignoring his own needs for hers. When he touched her, it wasn't to fulfill his own desire but to bring her whatever passion he was able. He felt the change in her start slowly, a gradual relaxation of the limbs, a dreamy murmuring of his name.

She'd waited, braced, for the speed, the pressure, the pain. Instead he gave her languidness, indulgence and pure pleasure. He moved his hands over her freely, as he had before, but this time there was a difference. He stroked, caressed, lingered until she felt as though she was floating. The sensation of vulnerability returned, but without the panic. Light and sweet, he brought his mouth to her breast to nibble and suckle so that she felt the response deep inside, a pull, a tug, a warmth that spread to her fingertips.

With a moan she wrapped her arms around him, no longer simply accepting but welcoming.

My God, she was sweet. With his lips rubbing over her skin he discovered she had a taste like no other, a taste he would never be able to do without again. Her body was so completely responsive under his that he knew he could have her now and satisfy them both. But he was greedy in a different way this time. Greedy to give.

Reaching for her hand, he linked his fingers with hers. Even that, just that, was the most intimate gesture he'd ever made. In the candlelight he saw her face glow with pleasure, the soft, silky kind that could last for hours.

So he came back to her mouth to give them both time.

She tasted the wine, just a hint of it, on his tongue. Then she felt his lips move against hers with words she heard only in her heart.

Here was the glow she'd once imagined, and all the bright, beautiful colors the poets had promised. Here was music flowing gently and light soft as heaven. Here was everything a woman who'd given her heart could ask in return.

She'd loved him before. But now, experiencing the compassion, the completeness, she fell deeper.

Slowly, carefully, he began to show her more, finding all the pleasure he could want from her response. Her body shuddered and strained toward him without hesitation, without restrictions. When he nudged her over the first peak, he saw her eyes fly open with shock and dark delight.

Breathless, she clung to him. It felt as though her mind was racing to keep pace with her body. And still he urged her on in ways she'd never dreamed existed. The next wave struck with a force that had her rearing up. There couldn't be more. The colors were almost too bright to bear now, and need and pleasure had mixed to a point that was both sharp and sweet.

She held him, moaning out his name. There couldn't be more. But he filled her and showed her there was.

* * *

She was trembling again, but she wasn't curled away from him. This time she was turned to him, her face pressed against his shoulder, her arms holding tight. Because he was more than a little dazed himself, he kept her close and said nothing.

He was no novice at this game, Burke reminded himself. So why did he feel as though someone had just changed the rules? The candlelight flickered its shadows around the room so that he shook his head. It looked as if he'd changed them himself. Soft light, soft music, soft words. That wasn't his style. But it felt so damn right.

He was used to living hard, loving hard and moving on. Win, lose or draw. Now he felt as though he could go happily to the grave if he never moved beyond this spot. As long as Erin stayed with him.

That thought had several small shock waves moving through him. Stayed with him? Since when had he started thinking along those lines? Since he'd laid eyes on her, he realized, and let out a long, none-too-steady breath. Good God, he was in love with her. He'd gone through his life without taking more than a passing interest in any woman. Then someone had opened the chute, and he'd fallen face first in love with a woman who hadn't had time to test the waters.

He didn't have time for this. His life was unsettled, the way he wanted it. His days, his decisions, his moves were his own. He had plans, places to go. He had . . . nothing, he thought. Absolutely nothing without her.

Closing his eyes, he tried to talk himself out of it. It was crazy, he was crazy. How did he know what it meant to love someone? There had only been one person he'd loved in his life, and that was long ago. He was a drifter, a hustler. If he'd stayed in one place a little too long, it was only because . . . because there hadn't been a better game, that was all. But he knew it was a lie.

He should do them both a favor and take that trip to Monte Carlo. He should leave first thing in the morning. The hell with the farm, the responsibilities. He'd just pick up and go, the way he always had. Nothing was keeping him.

But her hand was resting on his heart.

He wasn't going anywhere. But maybe it was time he upped the stakes and played out his hand.

"You okay?" he asked her.

Erin nodded, then lifted her face to look into his. "I feel . . . You'll think I'm foolish."

"Probably. How do you feel?"

"Beautiful." Then she laughed and threw her arms around his neck. "I feel like the most beautiful woman in the world."

"You'll do," he murmured, and knew in that moment that no matter how hard he struggled he was already caught.

"I never want to feel any different than this." She drew him closer to press kisses along his jawline and throat.

"You will, but there's no reason you can't feel like this as often as possible. We'll bring your things over tomorrow."

"What things?" Still smiling, her arms still around his neck, she drew back.

"Whatever things you have. There's no reason to bother moving tonight. Tomorrow's soon enough."

"Moving?" Slowly she unwound her arms. "Burke, I told you once before I won't live here with you."

"Things have changed," he said simply, reaching for the wine. He wished it was whiskey.

"Aye, but that hasn't. What happened tonight . . ." Had been beautiful, the most beautiful experience of her life, and she didn't want it spoiled by talk of sharing a life with him that wouldn't be a true one. "I want to remember it. I'd like to think that there may be a time when we might—when we might love each other this way again, but that doesn't mean I'll toss my beliefs aside and move in as your mistress."

"Lover."

"The label doesn't really matter." She started to move away, but he grabbed her shoulders. The glass tilted to the floor and shattered.

"I want you, damn it, don't you understand? Not just once. I don't want to have to drag you away from the Grants every time I want an hour with you."

"You'll drag me nowhere." The afterglow of love was replaced by angry pride. "Do you think I'll move in here so it'll be convenient for you when you have an urge to wrestle in bed? Well, I won't be a convenience to you or any man. The hell with you, Burke Logan."

She pushed away and had swung her legs off the bed when she went tumbling backward to find herself pinned under him. "I'm getting tired of you wishing me to hell."

"Well, get used to it. Now take your hands off me. I'm going home."

"No, you're not."

Her eyes narrowed. "You'll not keep me here."

"Whatever it takes." Then she twisted under him. Before he realized her intent, her teeth were sunk into his hand. He swore, and they rolled from one end of the bed to the other before he managed to pin her again.

"I'll draw blood next time, I swear it. Now let me go."

"Shut up, you crazy Irish hothead."

"Name-calling, is it?" Erin sucked the breath between her teeth. The words she uttered now were Gaelic.

This was hardly the time to be amused, he reminded himself. But there was no help for it. "What was that?"

"A curse. Some say my granny was a witch. If you're lucky, you'll die fast."

"And leave you a widow? Not a chance."

"Maybe you'll live, but in such pain you'll wish . . . What did you say?"

"We're getting married."

Because her mouth went slack and her bones limp, he released her to suck on his wounded hand.

"It's a relief to know you've got good teeth." He reached to the bedside table for a cigar. "Nothing to say, Irish?"

"Getting married?"

"That's right. We could fly to Vegas tomorrow, but then Dee would give me grief. I figure we can get a license and do it here in a few days."

"A few days." She shook her head to clear it, then sat up. "I think the wine's gone to my head." Or he had, she thought. "I don't understand."

"I want you." He lit the cigar, then spoke practically, deciding it was the style she'd relate to best. "You want me, but you won't live with me. It seems like the logical solution."

"Solution?"

Calmly, as if his life wasn't on the line, he blew out smoke.

"Are you going to spend the rest of the night repeating everything I say?"

Again she shook her head. Trying to keep calm, she watched him, looking for any sign. But his eyes were shuttered and his face was closed. He'd played too many hands to give away the most important cards he'd ever held.

"Why do you want marriage?"

"I don't know. I've never been married before." He blew out another stream of smoke. "And I don't intend to make a habit of it. I figure once should do me."

"I don't think this is something you can take lightly."

"I'm not taking it lightly." Burke studied the end of his cigar, then leaned over to tap it out. "I've never asked another woman to marry me, never wanted one to. I'm asking you."

"Do you . . ." Love me? she wanted to ask. But she couldn't. Whatever answer he gave wouldn't be the right one, because she'd posed the question. "Do you really think that what we had here is enough for marriage?"

"No, but we're good together. We understand each other. You'll make me laugh, keep me on my toes, and you'll be faithful. I can't ask for more than that." And didn't dare. "I'll give you what you've always wanted. A nice home, a comfortable living, and you'll be the most important person in my life."

She lifted her head at that. It could be enough. If she was indeed important to him. "Do you mean that?"

"I rarely say what I don't mean." Because he needed to, he reached for her hand. "Life's a gamble, Irish, remember?"

"I remember."

"Most marriages don't make it because people go into them thinking that in time they'll change the other person. I don't want to change you. I like you the way you are."

He took her fingers to his lips, and her heart simply spoke louder than her head. "Then I guess I'll have to take you the way you are as well."

CHAPTER 8

"This is all happening so fast." Dee sat in Erin's bedroom, where even now a dressmaker was pinning and tucking a white satin gown on her cousin. "Are you sure you don't want a little more time?"

"For what?" Erin stared out the window, wondering whether if one of the dressmaker's pins slipped and pierced her skin she would discover it was all a dream.

"To catch your breath, think things through."

"I could have another six months and still not catch my breath." She lifted a hand to her bodice and felt the symphony of tiny freshwater pearls. Who would have thought she'd ever have such a dress? In another two days she would put it on to become Burke's wife. Wife. A chill ran up her spine, and at her quick shudder the dressmaker murmured an apology.

"Have a look, Miss McKinnon. I think you'll be pleased with the length. If I do say so myself, the dress is perfect for you. Not every woman can wear this line."

Holding her breath, Erin turned to the cheval mirror. The dress was the real dream, she thought. Thousands of pearls glimmered against the satin, making it shimmer in the late-afternoon light. She thought it was something a medieval princess would wear, with its snug sleeves coming to points over her hands and its miles of snowy skirts.

"It's beautiful, Mrs. Viceroy," Adelia put in when her cousin only continued to stare. "And it's a miracle indeed that you could have it ready for us in such a short time. We're beholden to you."

"You know you've only to ask, Mrs. Grant." She eyed Erin as she continued to stare into the glass. "Is there something you'd like altered, Miss McKinnon?"

"No. No, not a stitch." She touched the skirt gingerly, just a fingertip, as if she was afraid it would dissolve under her hand. "I'm sorry, Mrs. Viceroy, it's only that it's the most beautiful thing I've ever seen."

More than placated, Mrs. Viceroy began to fuss with the hem. "I think your new husband will be pleased. Now let me help you out of it."

Erin surrendered the dress and stood in the plain cotton slip Burke had once unhooked from the clothesline. As the wedding gown was packed away, she slipped into her shirtwaist and thought she understood what Cinderella must have felt like at midnight.

"If I might suggest," the dressmaker continued, "the dress and veil would be most effective with the hair swept up, something very simple and old-fashioned."

"I'm sure you're right," Dee murmured as she continued to watch her cousin. Erin was staring out the window as if she was looking at a blank wall.

"And, naturally, jewelry should be kept to the bare minimum."

"She'll have my pearl earrings for something borrowed."

"What a sweet thought."

"Thank you again, Mrs. Viceroy," Dee said, rising. "I'll show you out."

"No need for you to go up and down those stairs in your condition. I know the way. The dress will be delivered by ten, day after tomorrow."

Day after tomorrow, Erin thought, and felt the chill come back to her skin. Would it always be now or never when it came to Burke?

"A lovely lady," Dee said after she closed the bedroom door. "It was kind of her to come here."

"Kind is one thing, business another." Since the weight of the twins seemed to grow heavier every day, she sat again. "She would hardly pass up the opportunity to please the future Mrs. Burke Logan. Erin . . . I'm happy for you, of course. Oh, I feel like a mother hen. Are you sure this is what you want?"

"I'm not sure of anything," Erin blurted out, then sank onto the bed. "I'm scared witless, and I keep thinking I'll wake up and find myself back on the farm and this all something I dreamed up."

"It's real." Dee squeezed her hand. "You have to understand that everything happening now is as real as anything can be."

"I do, and that only scares me more. But I love him. I wish I knew him better. I wish he'd talk to me about his family, about himself. I wish Ma was here and my father and the rest of them. But . . ."

"But," Dee coaxed as she moved over to sit beside her.

"But I love him. It's enough, isn't it?"

"Enough to start." She remembered that in the beginning all she'd had was a blind, desperate love for Travis. Time had given her the rest. "He's not an easy man to know."

"But you like him?"

"I've always had a soft spot for Burke. He's got a kind heart, though he'd rather no one noticed. He's a tough one, but I believe he'd do his best not to hurt someone he loved."

"I don't know if he loves me."

"What's this?"

"It doesn't matter," Erin said quickly, and rose to pace. "Because I love him enough for the two of us."

"Why would he want to marry you if he didn't love you?"

"He wants me." Better to face it now, head-on, she told herself as she turned back to Dee.

"I see." And because she did, she chose her words with care. "Marriage is a mighty big step for a man to take only for a want, a bigger step yet for a man like Burke. If the words are hard to come by, it might be that he hasn't learned how to say them."

"It doesn't matter. I don't need words."

"Of course you do."

"Aye, you're right." She turned back with a sigh. "But they can wait."

"Sometimes a person needs to feel safe before he can speak what's in his heart."

"You're good for me." Erin reached out both hands and grasped Dee's. "I'm happy, and despite the both of us I'm going to make him happy."

*   *   *

Brave words aside, when she stood at the top of the staircase two days later, clinging to Paddy's arm, Erin wasn't sure she could walk as far as the atrium, where the ceremony would take place. The music had begun. In truth, she could hear nothing else. She took one step and stopped. Then she felt Paddy's comforting pat on her hand.

"Come now, lass, you look beautiful. Your father would be proud of you today."

She nodded, took two slow, easy breaths, then descended.

Burke thought the tux would strangle him. If he'd had his way, they would have walked into the courthouse, said a few words and walked out again. Mission accomplished. It had been Dee who had browbeaten him into a wedding. Just a simple one, she'd said, Burke thought with a grimace. A woman was entitled to white lace and flowers once in her life. She herself hadn't been given the choice, but she wanted it for Erin. He'd relented because he'd been certain she couldn't pull it off in the two weeks he'd given her. Of course, she had.

The simple wedding she'd promised had swelled into what he considered a sideshow, with two hundred people eager to watch him juggle. The house was full of white and pink roses, and he'd been forced to pull himself into a tux. She'd ordered a five-tiered wedding cake and enough champagne to fill his pool. Wasn't it enough that he was about to make a lifetime commitment without having a trio of violins behind him?

Burke stood with his hands at his side and his face carefully blank and wondered what in the hell he was doing.

Then he saw her.

Her hair was glowing, warm and vibrant under layers of white tulle. She seemed pale, but her eyes met his without hesitation. How was it he'd never noticed how small she was, how delicate, until now, when she was about to become a permanent part of his life? Permanent. He felt the quick sliver of panic. Then she smiled, slowly, almost questioningly. He held out a hand.

Her fingers were icy. It was a relief to find his equally cold. She held tight and turned to face the priest.

It didn't take long to change lives. A few moments, a few words. She felt the ring slip onto her finger, but she was looking at him. Her hand was steady when she took the gold band from Dee and placed it on Burke's finger.

And it was done. He lifted the veil and touched the warm skin beneath. He brought his lips to hers, lightly, then more strongly. With a laugh, Erin threw her arms around his neck and held him. And it was sealed.

Then, almost from the moment she became his wife, she was spun away to be congratulated, complimented and envied.

It became like a dream, full of music and strangers and frothy wine. She was toasted and fussed over. Cameras flashed. There was caviar and elegant little hors d'oeuvres and sugared fruit that sparkled like diamonds under the lights. Erin found herself answering questions, smiling and wishing herself a hundred miles away.

Then she was dancing with Burke, and the world snapped back into focus.

"This didn't seem real. Until now." She rested her cheek against his and sighed. "I always dreamed of a day like this. Are we really married, or am I still imagining?"

He lifted her hand, running a finger over her ring. "Looks real to me."

Smiling, she looked down and caught her breath. "Oh, Burke, it's beautiful." Stunned, she turned her hand so that the layers of diamonds and sapphires glittered. "I never expected anything like this."

"You've had it on for an hour. Haven't you looked?"

"No." It was foolish to cry now, but she felt the tears sting her eyes. "Thank you." She was grateful the music stopped while she still had control. "I'll be back in just a minute."

"You'd better be. I'll be damned if I'll deal with this crowd alone."

She tucked her thumb into her fist so that she could run it along the ring as she hurried upstairs. She just needed a minute, Erin told herself. To compose, to adjust, to believe.

Stepping inside the bedroom, she leaned back against the door and caught her breath. Tonight, she thought, this would be her room, just as Burke would be—was—her husband. She would sleep in this bed, wake in it, tidy the sheets, fuss with the curtains. And one day it would become usual.

No, she thought with a laugh, and hugged herself. It would never become usual. She wouldn't let it. From this day on her life would be special. Because she loved and belonged.

Touching her cheeks to be certain they were cool and dry, she started to open the door. A trio of women were passing on their way downstairs.

"Why, for his money, of course." This from a woman Erin recognized from Adelia's party, one with beautiful white hair and a watered-silk suit. "After all, she hardly knew the man. Why else would she marry him? You don't think she came all the way from Ireland to settle for keeping his books."

"It seems strange that Burke would marry her, a nobody, when he could have had his pick of some of the most acceptable women in the area." The leggy blonde from the party fussed with the snap of her purse.

"I thought they made a lovely couple." The third woman

merely shrugged as the white-haired matron looked down her nose. "Really, Dorothy, a man hardly marries without reason."

"No doubt she's got a few tricks up her sleeve. It's one thing to get a man into bed, after all, and another to get him to the altar. Men are charmed easily enough, and bore just as easily. I imagine he'll be finished with her in a year. If she's as smart as I think she is, she'll tuck away a nice settlement—starting with that ring he gave her. Ordered it from Cartier's, you know. Ten thousand. Not a bad start for a little farm girl from nowhere."

The blonde fussed with her hair as they approached the head of the stairs. "It should be interesting to see her struggle to climb the social ladder in the next few months."

"She's not one of us," the white-haired woman announced with a flick of the wrist.

Erin stood with her hand on the knob and watched them descend the stairs. Not one of them? Through the first shock came the tremble of anger. Well, damned if she wanted to be. They were nothing but a bunch of gossiping old broody hens with nothing better to do than make cruel remarks and speculate on the feelings of others.

For his money? Did everyone really believe she'd married Burke for his money? Did he? she wondered with a sudden and very new shock. Anger drained as she let her hand slip off the knob. Oh, sweet God, did he? Was that what he'd meant when he'd said he could give her what she wanted?

She put her hands to her cheeks again, but they were no longer cool. Could he believe that her feelings were tied up in what he had instead of what he was? She hadn't done anything to show him otherwise, Erin realized with a sinking heart.

But she would. Lifting her head, she started out of the room. She would show him, she would prove to him that it was the man she had married, not his fine house or his rich farm. And to hell with the rest of them.

When she descended the steps this time, she didn't look like the pale, innocent bride. Her color was high, her eyes dark. She might not be one of them, she thought, but she would find a way to fit in. She would make Burke proud of her. Forcing a smile, she walked directly to the woman in watered silk.

"I'm so glad you could come today."

The woman gave Erin a gracious nod as she sipped champagne. "Wouldn't have missed it, my dear. You do make a lovely bride."

"Thank you. But a woman's only a bride for a day, and a wife for a lifetime. If you'll excuse me." She crossed the room, her dress billowing magnificently. Though Burke was surrounded, she moved directly to him and, putting her arms around him, kissed him until the people around them began to murmur and chuckle. "I love you, Burke," she said simply, "and I always will."

He hadn't known he could be moved by words, at least not such well-used ones. But he felt something shift inside him as she smiled. "Is that a conclusion you just came to?"

"No, but I thought it past time I told you."

* * *

He thought he'd never nudge the last guest out the door. No one loved a party and free champagne like the privileged class.

Erin stood in the center of the atrium with her hands clasped together. "It's going to take an army to put this place to rights."

"No one's walking through that door for twenty-four hours."

She smiled, but the fatigue and nerves were beginning to show. "I should go up and change."

"In a minute." Before she could move, he took both her hands. "I should have told you how beautiful you are. I can't remember ever being as nervous as I was when I stood down here waiting for you."

"Were you?" Her smile came fully now as she pressed against him. "Oh, I was scared to death. I nearly picked up my skirts and bolted."

"I'd have caught you."

"I hope so, because there's no place I want to be but here with you."

He framed her face with his hands. "You haven't had much chance to compare."

"It doesn't matter."

But he wondered. He was the only man she'd ever known. Now he'd done his best to be certain he was the only one she ever would. Selfish, yes, but a desperate man takes desperate measures. He kissed her again and then, while his lips were on hers, lifted her into his arms. "There's no threshold to carry you over."

Her eyes laughed at him. "There's one in the bedroom."

"I told you that you were a woman after my heart," he said, and carried her up the stairs. Rosa had champagne chilling in a bucket and two glasses waiting.

"Burke, I wonder, would you mind giving me ten minutes?"

"Who's going to help you out of that dress?"

"I can manage. I'm sure it's bad luck for the bridegroom to do so. Just ten," she repeated when he set her down. "I'll be quick."

With a shrug, he pulled a robe out of his closet. "I suppose I can get out of this straitjacket somewhere else."

"Thank you."

He didn't give her a minute more than that, but she was ready. She was still in white, but this gown was like a cloud, wisping down, shifting with each breath she took. Her hair was loose over the shoulders, fire against snow. He closed the door quietly behind him and looked his fill.

"I didn't think you could be more beautiful than you were this afternoon."

"I wanted tonight to be special. I know we've already . . . we've already been together, but—"

"This is the first time I'll make love to my wife."

"Aye." She held out her hands. "And I want you to love me. I want you more now than I did before. If you could—" It was foolish to blush now. She was a married woman. "If you could teach me what to do."

"Erin." He didn't know what to say. He simply didn't have the words. But he took her hand and pressed a kiss to her brow. "I have something for you."

When he took a box out of his pocket and handed it to her, she moistened her lips. "Burke, I don't want you to feel obliged to buy me things."

"If I don't, how am I going to please myself by looking at you wear them?" So he opened the box himself. Inside was a rope of diamonds holding one perfect sapphire.

"Oh, Burke." She wanted to cry because it was so lovely. She wanted to cry because she was afraid he thought she required it. "It matches my ring," she managed.

"That was the idea." But he was watching her, frowning at the look in her eyes. "Don't you like it?"

"Of course I do, it's like something out of a palace. I think I'm afraid to wear it."

He laughed at that and turned her toward the mirror. "Don't be silly. It's made to be worn. See?" He held it up around her throat. The sapphire gleamed dark against her skin and the wink of diamonds. "What good are pretty stones if a woman doesn't wear them? You'll need more than this before it's done. We can pick up some things on our honeymoon." He kissed the curve of her throat. "Where do you want to go? Paris? Aruba?"

Ireland, she thought, but was afraid he'd laugh at her. "I was thinking maybe we should wait awhile for that. After all, this is one of the busiest times of year for you, with the Derby coming up. Could we wait a few months before we go away?"

"If you like." He placed the necklace back in the box before turning her to face him. "Erin, what's wrong?"

"Nothing. It's just all so new and . . . Burke, I swear to you I won't do anything to cause you shame."

"What the hell is this?" Patience gone, he took her by the

arm and set her on the bed. "I want to know what you've got into your head and how it got there."

"It's nothing," she said, furious with herself that she was always an open book to him while she could never dig beneath the top layer. "It's just that I realized today that I don't really fit in with your people and lifestyle."

"My people?" His laugh wasn't amused and had her tensing. "You don't know anything about my people, Irish, and you can consider yourself fortunate. If you mean the people who were here today, two-thirds of them aren't worth the snap of your fingers."

"But I thought you liked them. You've friends among them, and associates."

"Associates, for the most part. And that can change at any time. We can go to parties, and you can join any clubs or committees you like. But if you want to thumb your nose at the lot of them, it wouldn't matter to me."

"You're part of the racing world," she insisted. "And married to you, so am I. I won't have anyone saying you married some little nobody who can't fit in."

"And someone did," he murmured. She didn't have to confirm with words what he could see so clearly in her eyes. "You listen to me. It only matters what we think. I married you because you were what I wanted."

"I'm going to be." She lifted her hands to his face. "I swear to you." She brought her mouth to his with all the passion, love and longing she had.

She wanted the night to be special, but that meant more than champagne and white lace. It meant showing him what was in her heart, what she was just beginning to understand for herself. That she loved him unrestrictedly. With her arms around him, her mouth on his, she lowered onto the bed. Their marriage bed.

He had shown her what loving could be. Now she hoped she could give some of that beauty back to him. Since experience wasn't hers, she could only act on what was in her heart. She had no idea if a man could feel more than need and satisfaction, but she wanted to try to give him some of the sweetness, some of the comfort he had given to her.

Hesitant, unsure, she pressed her lips to his throat. His taste was darker there, potent, and she could feel the beat of his pulse beneath her mouth. Its rhythm quickened. She smiled against his skin. Yes, she could give him something.

She liked the way he felt under her hands, the muscles that bunched and flowed as she moved her fingers over them. Tentatively she parted his robe. When she felt him tense, she retreated immediately, an apology forming on her lips.

"No." With a half laugh, he took her hand and brought it back to him. "I want you to touch me."

He kept his own hands gentle, though each hesitant stroke of her fingertips drove him mad. He was already caught in the innocence and passion of her, in her willingness to be taught, her eagerness to please and be pleased.

So they loved slowly, taking time to teach, to learn. There was no shyness on her part when he drew the lace from her shoulders, but rather a wonder that he found her so desirable. In answer, she slipped his robe away and let herself marvel at the strength and beauty that was her husband.

Perhaps it didn't make sense, but it was more exciting now that he belonged to her. The hard fist of need hadn't lessened; the trembles of anticipation and anxiety were just as sharp. But now, along with desire, was the simple joy that the man who held her was the man who would hold her night after night. This was only the beginning, she thought. Laughing, she rolled over him.

"Something funny?" he managed. He felt as though his body was stretched beyond the breaking point.

"I'm happy." She brought her mouth down hard on his, then, incredibly, felt her bones liquify. With a soft moan, she took him into her. When the whirlwind started, she could only hold her breath and grip his hands tight. Her body took control now, moving with his instinctively as pleasure built and crested and built again.

Her head was thrown back. He thought she looked like a goddess, red hair streaming over white shoulders, her slender body strong and agile as it merged with his. He wanted to hold her like this, to see her like this again and again in his mind's eye. Then the pleasure was so complete that it blinded him.

* * *

Erin woke on her first day as Mrs. Logan to a gray morning lashed by spring rain. She thought it was beautiful. Smiling, she shifted over to reach for Burke. And found him gone. Terrified she'd dreamed it all, she sat straight up.

"Do you always wake up like that?" Across the room, Burke hooked his belt and watched her.

"No, I thought . . ." It wasn't a dream. Of course, it wasn't. She laughed at herself and shook her head. "Never mind. Where are you going?"

"Down to the stables."

"So early?"

"It's seven."

"Seven." She rubbed her hands over her eyes as she struggled up. "I'll fix your breakfast."

"Rosa'll see to it. You should get some more sleep."

"But I—" She wanted to fix his breakfast. It was one of the small and very vital things a wife could do for her husband. She wanted to sit in the kitchen with him, talking of the day to come and remembering the night that had passed. But he was already pulling on his boots. "I'm not tired. I could go down and start on the books."

"You've gotten them in good enough shape to take a couple of days off. In fact, we haven't talked about it, but you don't have to continue with that if you don't like."

"Well, of course I'll continue with it. That's why I came here."

He lifted a brow as she tugged on a robe. "Things have changed. I don't want my wife to have to close herself up in an office all day."

"If it's all the same to you, I'd like to work." Uncomfortable, she began to tug on the sheets. "If you don't want me to be doing your books anymore, I'll find another job."

"I don't care if you work on them or not, I just want you to know you have a choice. What are you doing?"

"I'm making the bed, of course."

Crossing over, he caught her hand in his. "Rosa takes care of the bed-making, as well."

"There's certainly no need for her to make mine—ours."

"That's her job."

He kissed her brow, then changed his mind and drew her close against him. "Good morning," he murmured against her lips.

Hers curved just slightly. "Good morning."

"I'll be back in a few hours. Why don't you take a swim?"

When the door closed behind him, Erin crossed her arms. Take a swim? On her first day as a wife, she wasn't supposed to cook breakfast or make a bed but to take a swim? Walking over to the mirror, she stared at herself. She didn't look so very different. But feelings didn't always show. Wasn't it odd that she'd refused to be Burke's mistress, but now she was feeling more like that than a wife?

Married him for his money.

Erin pushed away from the mirror. The hell with that. It was past seven and she had work to do.

Rosa wasn't any more cooperative than Burke. There was no reason for the *señora* to do that. There was no reason for the *señora* to do this. Perhaps the *señora* would like to take a book into the solarium. In other words, Erin thought, you're of no use here. That was going to change, she decided.

She threw herself into her paperwork. When Burke didn't

return for lunch, Erin took matters into her own hands. Filling a pail with hot water and detergent, she took it and a mop to the atrium. Glasses and plates had already been cleared away, but Rosa hadn't yet gotten to the tiles. Erin felt a stab of satisfaction at having beaten her to it.

This is my house, she told herself as she sloshed out soapy water. My floor, and I'll damn well wash it if I like.

* * *

Burke strode through the streaming rain, thinking that the horse he had entered at Charles Town that night would have an edge on the muddy track. His second thought was that Erin might get a kick out of taking the trip to West Virginia to see the run. It would give him a chance to show her off a bit.

God, she'd looked beautiful that morning, all heavy-eyed and dewy-skinned. He was far from certain he'd done the right thing for her by rushing her into marriage, but he was more certain than ever that he'd done the right thing for himself. He couldn't remember ever being at peace before or ever feeling as though each day had a solid purpose to it.

He could give her the things in life she'd always wanted. The money didn't matter to him, so he didn't give a hang how she spent it. In turn she was giving him a solid base, something he hadn't known he'd wanted.

Inside, he shook the rain out of his hair and went to look for her. When he entered the atrium, he stopped. She was on her hands and knees, scrubbing. Even as she heard his steps and glanced up, he was dragging her to her feet.

"What in hell are you doing?"

"Why, I'm washing the floor. It took a beating yesterday. You'd be amazed what people can drop and what they don't bother to pick up again. Burke, you're hurting my arm."

"I don't ever want to see you down on your knees again. Understand?"

"No." Studying him, she rubbed her arm. She knew real anger when she looked it in the face. "No, I don't."

"My wife doesn't scrub floors."

"Now wait a minute." As he turned on his heel, she caught him. "She'll scrub them if she pleases, and she won't be called *my wife* as though she were something shiny to be kept in a box. What's the matter with you?"

"I didn't marry you so you could scrub floors."

"No, nor that I could cook your breakfast or make the bed, that's plain. Just why did you marry me, then?"

"I thought I'd made that clear."

"Aye." She dropped her hand from his arm. "I suppose you did. So I'm to be your mistress after all, it's just a matter of being a legal one."

He made an effort, an enormous one, to block off the anger. It didn't work. "Don't be a fool. And leave that damn bucket where it is."

"You'll remember the word in the ceremony was changed from *obey* to *cherish*." Scowling at him, she gave the bucket a kick and sent soapy water pouring over the tiles. "But I'll be happy to leave it just where it is."

"Where the hell are you going?"

"I don't know," she said over her shoulder. "Surely I can walk through the house even though I'm not allowed to touch anything in it."

"Stop it." He caught her as she stormed down the hall, but she only shook him off and kept going. "Damn it, Erin, you can touch whatever you like, just don't clean it."

"I can see it's time we had the rules straight." She pushed through the doors into the solarium. The heat was like a wall and suited her mood perfectly. "Touching and looking are allowed."

"Stop acting like an idiot."

"Me?" She turned on him and nearly upset a pot of geraniums. "It's me who's an idiot, is it? Out there it's a fool I am and in here an idiot. Well, it wasn't me who went into a rage because the floor was getting washed."

"I thought you came here to get away from that, because you wanted more out of life than washing dishes."

Slowly she nodded. "Aye, I came to America for that, but it's not why I married you. Maybe I can handle others thinking I married you because of your money and your fine house, but not you. I told you yesterday that I loved you. Don't you believe me?"

"I don't know." He ran a hand over his face and struggled for calm, for clear thinking, for the kind of controlled logic that had always brought him out on top of any game he chose. "Why does it matter?"

She had to turn away because it hurt too much to face him. "I didn't lie when I said it, but you can think whatever you like. It doesn't matter at all." Very deliberately she picked up a pottery bowl and sent it crashing to the tiles. "You needn't worry, I won't clean it up."

"Are you finished?"

"I haven't decided." Crossing her arms, she stared at the clear water of the pool.

He put his hand on her shoulder. Perhaps she did love him a little. It would take a bigger fool than he to push her away. "My mother spent more than half of her life on her knees scrubbing other people's floors. She was barely forty when she died. I don't want you on your knees for anyone, Erin."

When he started to draw his hand away, she clasped it in her own. "That's the first thing you've trusted me with." She turned to put her arms around him. "Don't you see you'll drive me mad if you shut me out?"

"You agreed to take me for what I am."

"I have. I will. I do love you, Burke."

"Then let me see you enjoy yourself."

"But I am." Tilting her head back, she grinned at him. "I like to fight."

He ran a finger down her nose. "Then I'm glad to oblige you. Did you take that swim?"

"No, I had the books, and then I argued with Rosa for a while."

"Busy day. Let's take one now."

"I can't."

"More arguing to do?"

"No, I've done with that, but I don't want to swim."

"Can't you?"

Her chin angled as he'd expected. "Of course I can, but I don't have a suit."

"That's okay." Lifting her up, he walked to the edge as she giggled and shoved against him.

"You wouldn't, and if you try, by God, you'll go in with me."

"I never intended it any other way." They went in together, fully dressed.

CHAPTER 9

Before she had been married a full month, Erin had taken trips to New York and Kentucky and back to Florida. She grew used to the look and feel of the racetracks, whether they were earthy or glamorous. She grew used to, but never less fascinated by, the people who inhabited them, from the young grooms still shiny with ambition to the older hands who lived from race to race and bet to bet.

The contrasts were a constant curiosity. From her box she could watch the other owners, their families and friends. Seersucker suits and picture hats. While against the rail, elbow to elbow, were the masses who came for the fun or the money. She learned that wagering had its own scent, often a desperate one, always a little sweaty. Away from the stands were the horses, the scales, the tack and the riders. Only a few who watched knew the thrill and the anxiety of ownership.

In Lexington she visited horse farms with Burke and saw stables grander than she had ever thought any house could be. She saw the races of the Thoroughbred world, grew to know the people whose lives were tied to them, and she learned.

At cocktail parties, dinner parties and small celebrations she listened to discussions on breeding, on training, on strategy. She grew to understand that owners often thought of their horses as possessions, while trainers more often than not thought of a horse in their care as an athlete to be disciplined and pampered in the peculiar way of the sportsman. But above all, the horse was the focus, for envy or for pride.

After a time she drew together the courage to go as far as the paddocks, where she could watch the horses being examined and saddled for the races. Though the scent and sounds of horses still disturbed her, she was determined that Burke's associates would never twitter about his wife being afraid.

She grew more accustomed to the parties, the lavish ones that only the successful and the privileged could attend. The talk there was of horses and the people who owned them. Not so different from Skibbereen, she began to think. Certainly this life was more glamorous, but at home the talk had often been just as narrow.

She studied, poring over books on Thoroughbreds, racing and the history of both. She learned that every Thoroughbred descended from three Arabian studs and that the most expensive horseflesh in the world was to be found in Ireland at the Irish National Stud. She'd had to smile at that, not only from home pride but because two such horses were in Burke's stables.

She learned to wager wisely and to win, a skill that never failed to amuse her husband. He'd been right when he'd said she would make him laugh. Erin found more pleasure in that than in all the pretty stones he bought her or the new clothes that hung in her closet. She'd discovered something in a month of marriage. The things she'd thought she'd always wanted weren't important after all.

And she was pregnant.

The knowledge both thrilled and terrified her. She was carrying a child, Burke's child, one that had been conceived on their first night together. In a matter of months they would no longer be just husband and wife but a family. She couldn't wait to tell him. She was afraid of what he would say.

They'd never discussed children. But then, there had been time to discuss little. She hardly knew more of him now than she had when she'd married him. True, she had come to understand that, unlike many of his associates, his horses were neither possessions nor pets. Nor were they the game of chance he claimed them to be. They had his pride and his affection, and Erin came to see that they had his admiration for simply being what they were. It wasn't just the winning but the heart that made champions.

There was this and little more she had learned of him. He'd never spoken of his mother or his family again. Though she'd tried to question him gently, he'd simply ignored her. Not evaded, Erin thought now, just ignored.

It didn't matter, she told herself as she went to find him. She'd seen him with Dee's children, and he'd been gentle and kind and caring. Surely he would be only more so with a child of his own. She would tell him and he would hold her tight and tell her how happy he was. They would laugh and she would show him all the pamphlets the doctor had given her on childbearing classes and diet. Then they would plan the nursery, all pinks and blues like a sunrise.

She found him in the library and had to bite back an impatient oath when she saw he was on the phone.

"I'm not interested in selling," he said as he gestured her in. "No, not at that price, not at any. If you want to get back to me in a few years and talk stud fees . . . Yes, that's a firm no. Tell Durnam none of my stock's for sale at the moment. Yeah, you'll be the first to know." He hung up and pulled a hand through his hair.

"Problems?" Erin crossed over to kiss his cheek.

"No. Charlie Durnam's interested in buying one of the new foals. Makes me think he's the one with problems. So what did you buy?"

"Buy?"

"You said you were going shopping."

"Oh, yes. I didn't buy anything." She rested her cheek against his hair a moment. "Burke, I've something I want to tell you."

"In a minute. Sit down, Erin."

It was the tone that had her retreating. He used that odd flat voice when she'd annoyed him. "What's wrong?"

"I've had a letter from your father."

"From Da?" She was up again almost before she sat. "Is something wrong? Is someone sick?"

"No, nothing's wrong. Sit down." He swiveled in his chair, and for the first time in a month she felt as though they were back on terms of business. "He wrote to welcome me into the family and to express what I suppose is fatherly concern that I take good care of you."

"What nonsense. He knows very well I can take care of myself." She relaxed again, unconsciously resting a hand low on her stomach. "Was that all?"

"He also thanked me for the money you've been sending over. He says it's been a great help." Burke paused a moment as he flipped through the papers on his desk. "Why didn't you tell me you've been sending more than half your money over to Ireland?"

"I never thought of it," she began. Then she stopped. "How do you know how much I'm sending?"

"You keep excellent and very clear books, Erin." He pushed away from the desk to pace to the window.

"I don't understand why you're angry. The money's mine, after all."

"It's yours," he murmured. "Damn it, Erin, there's a checkbook in the office. If you'd felt the need to send money home, why didn't you just take what you wanted and be done with it?"

"There's more than enough out of my wages."

"You're my wife, damn it, and that entitles you to whatever you want. You're past the point where you have to draw wages."

She was silent a moment, and when she spoke, she spoke carefully. "That's it, isn't it? You still believe that I'm here because of your fat checkbook."

He didn't know what he thought, Burke admitted as he stared out the window. She was perfect, warm, loving. And the longer she was with him, the more he was certain there had to be a catch. No one gave unconditionally. No one gave without wanting something back. "Not entirely," he said after a moment. "But I don't believe you'd have married me if I didn't have one. I told you before it doesn't matter. We suit well enough."

"Do we?"

"The point is the money's there and you may as well make use of it. You never know how long it'll last." With a half smile, he lit a cigar. "That's a bridge we'll cross when we come to it. Enjoy it, Irish, it's all part of the bargain."

She thought of the child inside her and could have wept. Instead she stood. "Is there anything else?"

"I want you to go write out a check for whatever your family needs."

"All right. Thank you."

"We'll be leaving for Kentucky in a few days. The Bluegrass Stakes and the Derby." He turned and leaned back against the sill. "You should enjoy it. It's quite a show."

"I'm sure it's wonderful." She took a long breath and watched him carefully. "It's a pity Dee's too far along to travel so she and Travis won't be there."

"That's the price you pay for having a family." He shrugged and moved back to his desk.

"Aye," she said quietly, but the light had gone out of her eyes. "I'll let you get back to work."

"Wasn't there something you wanted to tell me?"

"No. It was nothing." Erin closed the door behind her, then covered her face with her hands. Hadn't she told him she loved him? Hadn't she showed him in every way she knew? And now she was carrying physical proof of her feelings, but none of it mattered to him.

Then it would have to matter to her even more. Erin straightened her shoulders and walked away from the door, unaware that Burke stood on the other side, hesitating, his hand on the knob.

He hadn't meant to be angry. She'd looked so happy when she'd come into the room. She'd smiled at him as though . . . as though she loved him. Why couldn't he get past the block and just accept? Because he didn't believe in that kind of love, not even when he felt it himself.

He did believe that she would stay with him, happily enough, as long as he continued to provide her with what she needed. When he'd met her, he'd recognized the hunger for more he himself had always felt. He'd recognized the need to see new things, climb new mountains and win. It was just fortunate for both of them that he was in a position to show her those things, to provide her with the means to taste and hear and see the fantasies she'd had.

She could love him for that, and that he could understand.

But what about the man who had come from nothing? What about the man who could be back to nothing at the toss of the dice? What would her feelings be for him? He couldn't afford to find out, because the man who thought love only existed for convenience was desperately in love with his wife.

* * *

She was far from aware of it. As Erin walked into the kitchen, she was certain Burke only wanted her as long as she did nothing to upset the balance of his lifestyle. Sooner or later, he would be aware that together they already had.

Rosa was washing crystal in the sink but stopped the moment Erin walked in the room.

"Is there something you want, *señora*?"

"I'm just going to fix some tea."

"I'll heat the water."

"I can do it myself," Erin snapped as she slammed the kettle onto the stove.

"As you like, *señora*."

Erin leaned her palms against the stove. "I'm sorry, Rosa."

"*De nada.*"

As Rosa went back to her crystal, Erin found a cup and saucer. What kind of wife was it, she wondered, who didn't even know which cupboard held her dishes? How could she be so happy and so unhappy at the same time?

"Rosa, how long have you worked for Mr. Logan?"

"Many years, *señora.*"

"Before he came here to this house?"

"Before that."

Like pulling teeth, she thought, determined to pull harder. "Where did you work with him before that?"

"In another house."

Erin turned from the stove. "Where, Rosa?"

She saw the housekeeper's lips tighten. "In Nevada. In the West."

"What did he do there?"

"He had much business. You should ask Mr. Logan yourself."

"It's you I'm asking. Rosa, don't you think I have a right to know who my husband is?"

She saw the brief hesitation before Rosa began to polish glasses. "It's not my place, *señora.*"

"I need something." With an angry flick of her wrist, she shut off the flame. "I don't care what he did, what he was. If he's done something wrong it doesn't matter. How can I get through to him if I don't understand him?"

"*Señora.*" Carefully Rosa set down the first glass and picked up another. "I'm not sure you would understand even if you knew."

"Tell me, and let me try."

"Some things are better left alone."

"No!" She wanted to throw something, anything, but managed to hold the need back. "Rosa, look at me. I love him." When the housekeeper turned, Erin spoke again. "I love him and I can't stand being kept apart from who he is. I want to make him happy."

Rosa stood silently a moment. Her eyes were very dark and very clear. For a moment Erin felt a stab of recognition. Then it passed. "I believe you."

"It's Burke who needs to believe."

"For some, believing such things doesn't come easily."

"Why? Why for Burke?"

"Do you know what it's like to be hungry? Truly hungry? For food, for knowledge, for love?"

"No."

"He grew up with nothing, less than nothing. When there was work, he worked. When there was not, he stole." She moved her shoulders and picked up the next glass. "Not such a bad life for some. Hell for others. He never knew his father. His mother was not married, you understand?"

"Yes." Erin sat and made no objection when Rosa moved over to the stove to fix her tea.

"His mother worked very hard, though she was never well. But in such places a person always owes much more than they could ever have. At times he went to school, but more often he worked in the fields."

"On a farm?" she asked, remembering the way Burke had looked over hers.

"*Sí.* He lived on one for a while so that he could give his mother his pay."

"I see." And she was beginning to.

"He hated the life, the dirt and the stench of it."

"Rosa, how did you know him when he was a child?"

She set the tea down in front of Erin. "We had the same father."

Erin stared. Then, when Rosa would have walked away, she grabbed her arm. "You're Burke's sister?"

"Half sister. My father took me to New Mexico when I was six. He met Burke's mother. She was pretty, frail and very innocent. After Burke was born he left me with her, promising to send for us all when he had a job. He never did."

"Something might have happened to him. He might—" She stopped when she saw the look in Rosa's eyes.

"Burke's mother discovered he'd met another woman in Utah. That was his way. So she worked, washing up other people's dirt, for twenty years. Then she died. She had done her best for him, but Burke was always wild and restless. The day she was buried, he left. It was five years before I saw him again."

"He found you?"

"No, I found him." Rosa went back to her glasses. "Burke is not a man who looks for anyone. He owned part of a casino in Reno. Because I wouldn't take the money he offered, I went to work for him. He's never been comfortable with it, but he doesn't send me away."

"He couldn't. You're his sister."

"Not to him. Because to him our father never existed. There is no family in Burke's life, no roots, no home."

"That can change."

"Only Burke can change it."

"Aye." Nodding, she stood. "Thank you, Rosa."

* * *

She didn't tell him about the baby. Over the next few days she fretted over the secret but didn't speak it. There were races to prepare for. Important ones. Now, as she watched Burke handle his business and deal with his horses, she watched from a different perspective.

How had his early life shaped him? She took note of the way he treated those who worked for him. He was firm and demanding but never unreasonable. Not once had she heard him raise his voice to any of his men. Because he knew what it was like to be abused by an employer? she wondered. Because he understood how it felt to be dependent for your existence on another?

He loved the horses. She wasn't sure he was aware of it himself, but she could see it in the way he watched them take to the track, the way he supervised their grooming. Perhaps it was true that when he'd won the farm it had been only another game, but he'd made a life out of it whether he realized it or not. That alone gave Erin hope.

The time came for them to fly to Kentucky. Erin vowed she would tell him about the baby when they returned.

* * *

There was something different about her, Burke thought as he fixed himself a drink in the parlor of their hotel suite. He just couldn't quite put his finger on it. Her moods were like a roller coaster—up, down and sideways as quick as a wink. Not that he didn't find them interesting. He'd never been one who wanted to settle in too comfortably, and a man would hardly do that with a wife who was raging one minute and smiling sweetly the next. She was always doing the unexpected these days, cuddling up against him and falling into long, thoughtful silences or racing down to the stables to drag him back for a picnic under the willow.

She was the same in public, playing the dignified wife one moment and a flirtatious woman the next. And she didn't always flirt with only him. He couldn't deny it made him jealous, but he was fully aware that was her intent.

He found her daydreaming one minute and rushing around talking about redecorating the next. At times he worried that she was becoming restless again, but then she would reach for him at night, and no one had ever seemed so content.

He'd noticed she seemed to have lost her taste for champagne, though they attended the spring parties with regularity. She'd taken to sipping plain juice and discussing bloodlines and the pros and cons of certain tracks.

Then there had been the day he'd given her the earrings, sapphires to match her necklace. She had opened the box, burst into tears and fled, only to come back an hour later to gather him close and thank him.

The woman was driving him crazy, and he was enjoying every minute of it.

* * *

"A re you almost ready, or do you want to be fashionably late?" he asked as he strolled toward the bedroom.

"Almost ready. Since we're going to win the race tomorrow, I thought I should look my best for the pictures they'll be taking tonight. I've never known people with such love for taking pictures at parties."

"You didn't complain about having yours in the paper," he began, then stopped to stand in the doorway. She smiled when she saw him and turned a slow circle.

She'd chosen the dress carefully, knowing that before too many more weeks she would be showing and wouldn't feel proper wearing something daring. The midnight blue was shot through with silver threads so that she shimmered even standing still. It left her shoulders bare, then slithered down her body without drape or fold. Without the slit up the skirt, she wasn't sure she could have moved in it.

"Well, do you like it? Mrs. Viceroy said I should have something to show off my necklace."

"Who's going to notice the necklace?" He came to her and, in the way he had of making her heart stop, took both her hands to kiss them. "Irish, you're gorgeous."

"It's sinful for me to want the other women to be jealous, isn't it?"

"Probably."

"But I do. I want them to look at you and think he's the most wonderful man here. And she has him." Laughing, she spun another circle. "Then I can just look at them and smile, sort of pitying."

"It's a shame I won't be able to notice, because I won't be able to take my eyes off you."

She turned back to touch his cheek. "You know, when you say things like that, it still makes my insides curl up. Burke . . ." She wanted to tell him she loved him, but she knew he would only smile and kiss her forehead. Then her heart would break a little because he wasn't able to give the words back to her. "Did you ever think these parties are a little—slow?"

"I thought you liked them."

"Well, I do." She moved closer to run a finger down his lapel. "But sometimes, sometimes I find myself in the mood for something that takes a little more energy." She smiled as she looked up at him under her lashes. "A lot more energy. You smell very nice."

"Thanks." He lifted a brow as she loosened his tie. "Are you trying to start something?"

"And what if I am?" She pushed his jacket off his shoulders.

"Just checking," he murmured while she unbuttoned his shirt. "This isn't going to make all those women jealous."

With a laugh she ran her hands up his chest. "That's what you think." Grinning, she shoved him onto the bed and jumped in after him.

* * *

For the first time since she'd fainted, Erin insisted on going down to the stables with Burke. She told him it was a matter of pride, and it was. Pride in him.

She wasn't able to bring herself to go in, but urged him to as she stood in the sun and watched the people.

A long way from Skibbereen indeed, she thought. The air was warm with springtime, and flowers were already in bloom. Trainers and exercise boys she'd come to know by

sight nodded or tipped their hats as they passed her and
greeted her as Mrs. Logan.

There was excitement in the air as well, the kind that
hummed before an important race. Before long, it would be
the race. The Derby. But for now everyone's attention was on
today and the Bluegrass Stakes. A win here added to Double
Bluff's record would make him the favorite. Erin smiled as
she thought that would lower the odds, but odds didn't matter. She wanted Burke to win, today and at Churchill Downs.
She could almost taste the satisfaction of having Double
Bluff named Horse of the Year. More than she'd wanted
anything, she wanted that for Burke, for him to know he'd
done something special, something only the best could ac-
complish.

"Good day to you, Mrs. Logan."

"Paddy." Pleased to see him, Erin opened her arms for a hug.
"Oh, it's a fine day, isn't it? How's Dee?"

"Right as right and mean as a bear. She told me to tell you
if Travis's Apollo doesn't win, Burke's Double Bluff better."

"And who are you betting on?"

"Now who do you think? I trained Apollo myself. But if I
was hedging my bets, I'd lay some money on the colt out of
Three Aces."

"A smart man would put his money down on Charlie's
Pride." Durnam came up behind them and slapped Paddy on
the shoulder.

"Well, now, it's a fine colt you have there, Mr. Durnam, and
that's the truth. But I think I'll stick with my own."

"That's your choice. Hello there, Mrs. Logan. You're looking as pretty as ever."

"Thank you. Good luck to you today."

"You don't need luck when you've got the best." He pulled
at the brim of his straw hat and moved on.

"We'll see who's the best," Erin said under her breath.

"Got the fever, do you?" Chuckling, Paddy slipped an arm
around her shoulders. "There's a powerful competition in this

business. Can't be otherwise when money and prestige change hands in a matter of minutes."

"How do you know when you've got a winner?"

"Well, now, there's breeding and training and a matter of attitude. There's feed and grooming. There's the jockey that sits on top and finding the right man for the right mount. But what it comes down to, darling, is blood. It's in the blood or it isn't, just like with people."

"Aye, the blood." She looked toward the stables and thought of Burke. "So you think that someone could be denied the proper care and feeding, the training, and still be a winner?"

"We talking horses or people?"

"Does it matter?"

"Not much." He gave her shoulder a quick squeeze. "It's in the blood and it's in the heart. I've got to tend to my boy now."

"I'll wave to you from the winner's circle, Paddy Cunnane," she called after him.

"You sound sure of yourself," Burke commented as he crossed to her.

"Sure of you." She gripped his hands as they headed for the stands. "You don't have to walk me up. I know you want to stay to see your jockey weighed in and watch Double Bluff saddled."

"The last time I didn't go with you I found you surrounded by reporters."

"I know how to handle them now. Besides, I did like seeing my picture in the paper."

"You're a vain woman, Irish."

"Aye, and why not?" She brushed a finger over his cream-colored shirt and found herself pleased he didn't go in for the seersucker of his associates. "Whether it's pride or vanity, I find it exciting to see my picture on the society page. Did you know, Mr. Logan, you're a very important man?"

"Is that so?"

"Aye, 'tis so, and so I'm told often enough. Then, by rights, I have to be an important woman."

"You could pass for one today," he decided, taking a quick study of her pale blue suit and pearls. She'd added a plain wide-brimmed straw hat, then had tilted it at an angle so it could no longer be called demure.

"I decided the day called for dignified." Then she laughed and touched the brim of her hat. "Sort of. Burke, I'll be fine, really, I know you want to stay close to the horse."

"I'd rather stay close to you. Mind?"

"No." She hooked her arm through his and grinned. "Why don't I buy you a beer?"

She thought it was a perfect day. The most perfect day of her life. The sky was cloudless, a soft spring blue that made her smile just to look at it. She noticed the woman from her wedding as she stepped into the box, and made sure she tilted her head and smiled coolly in greeting.

"Why do I feel you're always sticking pins in Dorothy Gainsfield?"

"Because I am, darling." She stood on tiptoe and kissed him. "Long, sharp ones. I didn't know until the other day that the skinny blonde who was hanging all over you on St. Patrick's Day was Mrs. Gainsfield's favorite niece." She laughed again, figuring it meant another day in purgatory. "Life can be sweet."

"You'll have to fill me in on all this later."

"In ten or twenty years, perhaps. Look, Burke, television cameras. Can you imagine?"

Delighted with the world in general, she took her seat. Now and then she spotted someone she knew, and waved to Lloyd Pentel, to Honoria Louis, to the elderly Mrs. Bingham.

"Do you know, I've met as many people in a month's time as I've known all of my life. It's an odd and wonderful feeling." She turned to see he was smiling at her. "Why do you look at me like that?"

"It's an education to watch you in a place like this, soaking it all up, storing it away. I wonder what you'll look like when we go to Paris or Rio."

"Probably stand around with my mouth hanging open the whole time and humiliate you."

"There's that." He only laughed when she jabbed him with her elbow. "Try to behave yourself. It's almost post time."

"Oh, Lord save us, so it is, and I haven't bet."

"I bet for you while you were buying my beer and trying to decide if you were going to eat a cheeseburger or two hot dogs. Living in America's improved your appetite."

It wasn't only that that was increasing her appetite, she thought, and wondered when she would work up the nerve to tell him. "It wasn't my fault we missed breakfast," she reminded him. "Where's my ticket?"

Watching the horses being led to the starting gate, he reached in his pocket. Erin took the stub and was about to tuck it away when she noticed the amount.

"A thousand dollars?" Her voice squeaked so that a few interested heads turned. "Burke, where would I be getting a thousand dollars to bet on a horse?"

"Don't be ridiculous." He didn't spare her a glance. His trainer had moved to Double Bluff's head as the colt reared and danced. "Seems a little more wired than usual," he murmured as two grooms stepped up to help.

"But, Burke, a thousand dollars."

"Afraid you'll lose?"

"No." She stopped. Then, closing the ticket tight in her hand, she said a quick prayer. "No, of course not."

The bell sounded. The gate was released. The horses plunged forward.

She recognized the Pentel colt in the lead. He was a fast starter, she remembered, but he didn't have stamina. With the ticket still clutched in her hand, she put a fist to her breast. The pack was hardly more than a blur, but she could see the green-and-white silks of Burke's jockey. Rounding the first turn he was in fourth, with Travis's colt on his left. The crowd was already shouting so that she could no longer hear the announcer.

It didn't matter. With her free hand she gripped the sleeve of Burke's linen shirt and held on.

"He's making his move," Burke murmured.

She saw the whiz of crops, the strain of speed as the jockeys leaned low. Double Bluff moved to the outside. His stride lengthened, eating up distance. It seemed that before her eyes he grew bigger, his coat glossier, his legs longer.

A champion, she thought again, was in the heart. Hers was with the colt. It was more than a race, she knew, more than prestige and certainly more than money. It was Burke's pride. She understood what it was like to come from little, then to have a chance for everything.

The Pentel colt began to lag. As they came down the stretch it was a race between three, leaving the pack behind. Charlie's Pride held first, with Travis's colt and Double Bluff vying for second. She could see the dirt flying and the sweat. All around her there was one huge, bellowing roar.

"He's going to do it!" She didn't even realize she was shouting as she watched Double Bluff gain on Charlie's Pride. They were nose to nose for what seemed forever. And then he was ahead, by a neck, by half a length, by a length, with his speed only increasing. He was two lengths ahead at the wire.

"Oh, Burke, he did it. You did it!" She hadn't been aware of standing, but found herself on her feet as she turned to throw her arms around him. "Sure and he's the most beautiful horse ever born. I'm so proud of you."

"I wasn't racing."

She drew back to caress his cheek. "Yes, you were."

"Maybe I was," he murmured as he kissed the tip of her nose. He continued to watch as his jockey took the horse around for the victory lap. "Can you manage to stand in the winner's circle with me?"

"I think so." People were congratulating them, and though Erin acknowledged them, her thoughts were already moving forward to standing beside Burke as he accepted the win.

Her arms were still around him when the official winner was declared. Charlie's Pride. Double Bluff had been disqualified.

"Disqualified? What do they mean?"

"We'll find out." Taking her hand, Burke moved out of the stands. The murmurs had already started.

"Burke, they can't say he didn't win. For heaven's sake, I saw it with my own eyes. He was well in the lead. There's a mistake."

"Wait here." Leaving her, he walked over to the paddock area where Double Bluff was being held. She saw a bald man in a suit approach Burke, then two other men join them. It looked so official, she thought. The bald man was talking calmly, pointing to the horse, then to a piece of paper. As he spoke, both the jockey and the trainer began to argue furiously, but Burke simply stood, listening.

She began to feel the heat as she stood there, so she moved over into the shade. It was a mistake, of course, she told herself as she removed her hat to stir air into her face. No one would take away what Burke had earned, what he needed, what she needed for him.

"What is it?" she demanded as Burke strode back.

"Amphetamines. Someone gave the horse amphetamines."

"Drugs? But that's ridiculous."

"Apparently not." His eyes were narrowed as he looked over at the paddock. "Someone wanted him to win very badly. Or to lose."

CHAPTER 10

"What do you mean you're sending me home? I'm not a package to be wrapped and stamped." Erin rushed after Burke as he strode from the parlor to the bedroom of the suite. "You've barely said a word to me since we left the track, and now all you can say is you're sending me home."

"There's nothing else to say, not at the moment."

"Nothing to say?" Because she was breathless after struggling to keep pace with him, she sat. "Double Bluff was just disqualified from one of the most important races of the year because someone gave him drugs. That's plenty to talk about to start."

"It's not your concern." He pulled a suitcase out of the closet and set it open on the bed. "Pack."

She kept her seat and, just barely, her temper, but her eyes narrowed. "Oh, I see. So this is one more thing I'm not to touch."

Pausing only a moment, Burke studied her. He could see the temper beginning to brew. As far as he was concerned, she was better off angry than dealing with the tempest of the next few days. He'd never considered himself a man of great virtues, but he'd protect his wife.

"You can look at it that way or any other way you like. I've got some calls to make. Pack your things while I see that your flight's changed."

"Just one bloody minute." She was up and after him again

as he walked into the next room. "I'm sick to death of orders from you. Almost as sick as I am of talking to your back. If you don't put down that phone, Burke Logan, it'll pleasure me to wrap the cord around your neck."

"Erin, I've got enough to deal with at the moment without you adding one of your tantrums."

"Tantrums." Her hands clenched into fists as she walked toward him. "Oh, I've a flash for you, I do. You haven't seen a tantrum yet. Now sit." Taking both hands, she shoved him into a chair. "And it's time you unplugged your ears and listened for a change."

He could have risen again and struck back with his own temper. He decided against it, in the same way he might have decided to bluff his way to a pot with a pair of deuces. The quickest way to have her out and on her way was to show disinterest. "Is this going to take long?"

"As long as needs be."

"Then would you mind if I had a drink?"

Seething, she went behind the bar and grabbed a bottle and a glass. She slammed them down on the table beside him. "Go ahead, have the whole bottle. Drown yourself in it."

"Just one'll do." He poured two fingers, then lifted the glass in a half salute. "Say what's on your mind, Irish. I have a few things to see to before your flight."

"If I said half what was on it, your ears would be ringing from now till Gabriel blew his horn. Answer me this, are you going to take this business lying down?"

He lifted the glass and sipped, watching her steadily over the rim. "What do you think?"

"I think you're going to fight, and I think you won't be resting until you find out who's behind this. Then I think you're going to carve them up in little pieces."

He toasted her again, then downed the rest of the whiskey. "That about covers it."

"And I'm not going home to twiddle my thumbs while you're about it."

"That's exactly what you're going to do."

"Did it ever occur to you that I could help?"

"I don't want your help or need it, Erin."

"No, you don't need anyone." She swung away to pace the room, wishing she knew a better way than shouting to handle an argument. "All you need are a few paid servants to deal with the little details while you go on your merry way. You certainly don't need a wife, a partner, to tend to your shirts or hold your hand when there's trouble."

The urge to get up, to hold on to her, was so strong he had to press his fingers into the glass until his knuckles whitened. Because she was wrong. She was very, very wrong about what and whom he needed. "I didn't marry you to do my laundry."

"No, you married me to sleep with, and I know it well enough. But you got more than you bargained for, because I'm not running back home like some weakhearted, whiny female who can't face a spot of trouble."

Pride, he thought, and nearly laughed. It always seemed to be his pride or hers on the line. "No one's insulting your valor, Erin. It would simply make things easier if I didn't have you to deal with."

"You won't have to deal with me. In private I'll stay out of your way and you can do your business however you please. But in public I'm going to be there."

"The loyal and trusting wife?"

"What's wrong with that?"

"Nothing." He sat back, determined to study her calmly. She looked like a comet about to go into orbit. "It matters to you what these people think, what they say?"

"And why shouldn't it?"

Why shouldn't it indeed? he thought as he stared into his empty glass. She was worried about her position, and hers walked hand in glove with his own. "Have it your way, then. I can hardly drag you to a plane and tie you on. But I warn you, it won't be pretty."

"You've said you understand me, almost from the first

moment we met you said it, and I believed you. Now I see that you really don't understand me at all." There was no more anger. It had been smothered by a rising despair. If they'd really been married, in the true sense, they would have been able to talk about what had happened, they would have been able to fight together, rage together instead of at each other. "You can make your calls, I'm going for a walk."

But he didn't pick up the phone when she left. It was more than being unused to having someone stand beside him, more than his own penchant for handling his own in his own way. He'd wanted her to go, away from the murmurs and sly looks. He didn't want her to be a part of the suspicion that had already fallen over him and his.

She'd never even asked. Burke scrubbed his hands over his face and tried to get beyond his own fury. It wasn't losing the purse or the race so much as knowing that someone had violated what was his. And she'd never asked if he'd arranged it himself. Could she really believe so blindly in him, or was it a matter of her not caring how he won?

However she felt, he couldn't shield her from the gossip. And gossip there would be, he thought grimly. Once she had a taste of it, he figured she'd be happy enough to go back to the quiet of Three Aces. In the meantime, he was going to find out who'd messed with him. Pushing the bottle aside, Burke picked up the phone.

*　*　*

The action moved to Churchill Downs and Derby week. Erin made certain she attended each function and every qualifying race. She held her head up and, when she heard a whisper, only held it higher.

Not everyone seemed inclined to believe that Burke had had a hand in the drugging of his horse. For every snub and murmur there was someone else to offer support. But the only one who mattered had closed himself off from her. She didn't try to break through the barrier. It took all the energy she had to hold up the pretense of a united couple. The strain was taking its toll, all the more because she worked hard to make sure Burke didn't see it.

He rose early, so she rose early. He went to the track to oversee Double Bluff's morning exercise, so she spent her mornings at the track. There were days when by noon she was so weary she wanted to crawl off into a corner and sleep. But there were races and luncheons and functions, often back-to-back. She refused to miss even one.

Erin McKinnon Logan wasn't hiding in some dim corner until the trouble passed. She would face it, shoulders straight, and dare even one person to look her in the eye and make an accusation. It was hard, and grew harder, so that every day she had to force herself to put in an appearance. There were whispers and knowing looks behind smiles. There were eyes that turned away rather than meet hers. And there were a few who preferred to cloak their insults in manners.

She dressed carefully for a formal dinner party near the end of Derby week. Erin had always felt that a strong outer appearance helped tap the inner strength. Attending alone was only more difficult, but Burke had been called to a meeting at the last minute.

She could have stayed at the hotel, just as Burke had asked. The truth was that a quiet evening, a tray in bed and a good book was exactly what she would have preferred. But that would have been cowardly. So she wore her midnight-blue silk and hung her sapphire around her neck like a badge.

While others sipped cocktails, she nursed orange juice and made conversation. More than ever she was grateful for Paddy. He stayed close, keeping her spirits up and her mind busy with stories of Ireland. But he couldn't shield her from everything, nor from everyone.

"My dear, what a pretty dress." Dorothy Gainsfield swept toward her, her eyes as cold as her diamonds.

"Good evening, Mrs. Gainsfield."

"Tell me, are you enjoying your first Derby week? It is your first, isn't it?"

"Aye, it's my first." If Erin had learned one thing, it was how to return a meaningless smile. "I'm sure you've been coming here for many years."

"Indeed," she said repressively, refusing to be insulted by one so beneath her station. "I don't see your husband."

"He couldn't make it."

"That's understandable, isn't it?"

Erin felt Paddy start forward, and laid a hand on his arm. "With the race only a couple of days away, Burke is busy."

"I'm sure he is." The older woman gave a dry laugh and sipped her champagne. "You know, I'm rather surprised he's being allowed to enter after that . . . mishap, shall we say, at the Bluegrass Stakes."

"The racing commission feels Double Bluff's record speaks for itself and for Burke. Once the investigation's complete, that, too, will speak for itself."

"Oh, I don't doubt it, my dear, not for a minute. It isn't unusual for someone to get a bit too enthusiastic about winning. This wouldn't be the first time the method's been used to lower the odds."

"Burke doesn't cheat. He doesn't have to."

"I'm sure you're right." Mrs. Gainsfield smiled again. "But then, I wasn't speaking of your husband . . . Mrs. Logan." Satisfied with the dig, Mrs. Gainsfield moved away.

"That dough-faced old cow," Paddy began as he fired up. "I'll give her a piece of my mind."

"No." Again Erin put a hand on his arm. "She's not worth it." Erin watched her mingle with the crowd. "When Double Bluff wins, it'll be enough."

* * *

Erin was determined that by the end of the week they would have discovered who was responsible for Double Bluff's disqualification and the cloud on Burke's reputation would be gone. She was even more determined that on Sunday, when Churchill Downs opened for the Derby, Burke would win what was rightfully his.

Once that was done, she would face the cracks and scars on her marriage. Perhaps Burke had been wrong when he'd said most marriages didn't work because one person tried to change the other. She knew now that if changes weren't made—in both of them—their marriage would never survive.

She watched him now as he stood near the oval with his trainer. It was barely dawn, with a light so sweet and fragile that it turned the white steeples pink. The air was cool, quiet enough to carry voices to her, if not the words. All around her the stands were empty. In twenty-four hours they would be filling, section by section, until they and the infield grass were packed with bodies. The race would last only a matter of minutes, but for those few minutes, every square inch would be crammed with excitement, with pumping hearts and with hope.

"It has its own magic, this time of day."

"Travis." Erin was up and swinging her arms around him. She hadn't realized until that moment how badly she'd needed someone to hold on to. "Oh, it's so glad I am to see you. But you shouldn't be here." She drew away just as quickly. "What about Dee? Is she all right?"

"All right enough to throw me out. She told me she could use a couple of days without my hovering over her."

"That's nonsense and I know it, but I'm grateful to both of you." She looked beyond his shoulder to her husband. "He needs his friends now."

"How about you?"

She gave a quick laugh and a shake of her head. "Oh, he doesn't seem to need me."

"I don't believe that, but it isn't what I meant. How are you holding up?"

"I'm tough enough to get through a few rough spots yet."

"You're a bit pale," he murmured, then took her chin in his hand. "More than a bit."

"I'm fine, really. Could use a bit more sleep, that's all." Then she swayed against him. Before she could pull herself back, he was settling her into a seat.

"Just sit back. I'll get Burke."

"No." She gripped his hand and held hard. "I'll be all right in a second. I just need to close my eyes."

"Erin, if you're ill—"

"I'm not ill." She laughed and unconsciously laid a hand on the child that was growing inside her. "I promise you."

He lifted his brow as he studied her. "Then congratulations."

Erin opened her eyes slowly. "You're a sharp one."

"I've been through it a few times." He stroked her hand until a hint of color returned to her face. "How does Burke feel about starting a family?"

"He doesn't know." Steadier, she sat up and was relieved to see Burke's back was still to them. "He has enough to worry about right now."

"Don't you think this would more than balance the scales?"

"No." Letting out a sigh, she faced Travis again. "No, I don't, because I'm not sure he wants children at all. And right now he doesn't want anything more than for me to leave him alone."

"You're underestimating him."

"You're his friend."

"And yours."

"Then stand up with him until this is over. Let me tell him about the baby when the time's right."

"All right. If you promise to take better care of yourself."

She smiled and kissed his cheek. "After tomorrow, I'll sleep for a week."

"Travis." Burke slipped under the rail. "I didn't expect to see you down here."

"Hate to miss a Derby. How are things going?"

Burke glanced over his shoulder to where the horse was being walked and cooled. "The colt's in top form. You can say we're both ready to put things right."

"The investigation?"

"Slow." That was true, at least of the official one. His own was moving quite a bit faster. Now that Travis was here, he would have someone he could trust to listen to his theory. Though he wore his tinted glasses, Erin felt his eyes on her. With a nod of acknowledgment, she rose.

"I'll leave you to discuss business."

"She's worried about you," Travis murmured as Erin walked away from the stands.

"I'd prefer she didn't. What I'd prefer is that she went back to the Three Aces until this is cleared up."

"If you'd wanted a quiet, obedient wife, you shouldn't have picked an Irish one."

Burke pulled out a cigar and contemplated it. "How many times have you been tempted to throttle Dee?"

"In the last seven years or in the last week?"

For the first time in days, Burke smiled and meant it. "Never mind. Do me a favor and keep an eye on her, will you? I don't think she's feeling well."

"You could try talking to her yourself."

"I'm not much good at talk. I'd like you to take her back with you after the race tomorrow."

"Aren't you coming back?"

"I might have to stay in Kentucky a few more days."

"Got a lead?"

"A hunch." He lit the cigar and blew out smoke. "Trouble is the racing commission likes proof."

"Want to talk about it?"

He hesitated, only because it still seemed unnatural to confide in another. "Yeah. You got a few minutes?"

* * *

Erin wasn't sure why she felt the sudden need, but she walked toward the stables. Maybe if she could prove to herself that she was strong and capable, Burke would begin to believe it. She'd faced the gossip, she'd stood tall against the innuendos. She'd held her own. But there was one thing she'd yet to face, one fear she'd yet to vanquish. So she would do it. Then, tomorrow, she would walk easily beside Burke into Double Bluff's stall, and she would stand beside him without a quiver in the winner's circle.

Three yards from the stables, she stopped to give herself another lecture. It was foolish to be afraid after all this time. It was useless to cling to a feeling that had been caused years before by an accident. She'd been around animals all her life. Married to Burke, she would continue to be around them. And the child . . . She rested a hand on her stomach. Her child would be raised without fear of his inheritance.

She would walk in alone. Then, tomorrow, even if Burke wished her to hell and back, she would walk in beside him.

She went closer. The scents were there—the hay, the sweet smell of grain, the pungent smell of horse and sweat. The sounds, too—hooves scraping over concrete, harness jingling, the sighs and lazy whinnies of horses at rest. She'd be quiet and go carefully, remembering that each step was one step closer.

The light changed almost from the moment she stepped inside. It was dimmer, softer, and now there was the scent of leather as well.

Most of the horses had already been exercised, and the grooms were indulging in their own breakfasts before it came time to brush and rub and wrap. She'd chosen this time, the least busy time, so that if she bolted no one would see.

But she didn't bolt. One of the horses dipped its head over the gate and she jumped a little, but she stood her ground. She could touch him, Erin told herself. The gate was latched. She could lay her hand on him just as easily as she had with Burke's foal.

Her fingers trembled a little, but she laid them gingerly

against the horse's cheek. He eyed her, but when he shifted his weight she jerked back.

"I'll have to do better than that," she muttered, then laid her hand more firmly on his neck. Her palm was damp and she didn't move a muscle, but she felt a little thrill of victory.

He was a fine-looking animal, she told herself as she made her hand move just a little over his neck. It was the Pentel colt, one she'd seen race nearly as often as she'd seen Bluff.

"There, now," she managed with a sigh. "It's not so bad. My heart's thumping, but I'm here." I'm here, she repeated silently, and I'm coming back every day. Each time it would be a little easier. She drew her hand back, then made herself reach out again. And it was easier. Just as it would become easier to face and overcome her insecurities with Burke. She wasn't going to go through life being cowed and miserable because her husband was too stubborn to accept her love and her support. She might have taken him the way he was, but there would be some changes made. And soon.

When she heard voices, she drew her hand back again, embarrassed. She didn't want one of the grooms wandering in to find her. She didn't think she was quite ready to stand in the stables and hold a conversation. Erin wiped her damp palm on her slacks and fixed a casual smile on her face.

She'd started out when the tone of the voices stopped her. There was anger in them and, though they remained quiet, more than a little desperation. Because she hesitated, she had time to recognize one of them.

"If you want your money, you'll find a way."

"I tell you the horse isn't alone for five minutes. Logan's got him locked up like the crown jewels."

Erin's lips parted, then firmed. She took a step back into the shadows and listened.

"You've got a job to do, one you're paid well for. If you can't get to the horse, get to his feed. I want him out of the running for tomorrow."

"I ain't poisoning no horse and I'm tired of taking all the risks."

"You didn't have any qualms about using a hypodermic or taking ten percent of the purse from the Bluegrass Stakes."

"Amphetamines is one thing, cyanide's another. That horse dies and Logan's not going to rest until somebody hangs for it. It ain't going to be me."

"Then use the drugs." The voice was impatient, dismissive. Erin found her hands balled into fists. "Find a way, or you won't see a penny. If the colt's found drugged in the Derby, he's out for the season. I need this race."

And she needed to get to Burke. Erin stayed still and waited for them to pass on. But luck wasn't with her. As she saw the two figures enter the stables, she straightened her shoulders and moved forward. It was a gamble, but the best she could hope for was a bluff.

"Good day to you, Mr. Durnam." She made her lips curve even when she saw the shock come into his eyes. She glanced at the groom, too, one of the new ones Burke's trainer had hired.

"Mrs. Logan." Durnam smiled in return but was already calculating. "We didn't see you in the stables."

"Just thought I'd look over the competition. If you'll excuse me, Burke's waiting."

"I think not." He took her arm as she tried to pass. Because she'd been half expecting it, Erin was already primed to scream. With surprising speed, his hand clamped over her mouth.

"Good God almighty, what are you doing?" the groom demanded. "Logan'll have your head."

"He'll have yours as well if she goes to him and blabs. She heard everything, you idiot." Because Erin's struggles were making him pant, Durnam thrust her at the groom. "Hold on to her. Let me think."

"We've got to get the hell out of here. If someone comes in—"

"Shut up. Just shut up." Durnam's face was already sheened with sweat. He took out a white handkerchief and mopped it. He was a desperate man who had already taken desperate measures. Now it was time to take another. "We'll put her in the van until the race is over tomorrow. By then I'll have thought of something." Taking the handkerchief, he pulled it around her mouth. As an extra precaution, he took the groom's grimy bandanna and tied it over her eyes. "Get some rope. Hurry, tie her hands and feet."

Erin choked on the gag and struggled against both of them, but she was already aware she'd lose. On a desperate impulse she worked her wedding ring off her hand and let it fall to the ground. Then ropes bit into her wrist and she was smothered inside a blanket.

She felt herself being lifted but could do no more than squirm. Even that was futile as the more she resisted, the harder it was to breathe. She heard a door open just before she was lifted up and set inside on a hard floor.

"What the hell are we going to do with her?" the groom demanded as he stared down at the heap inside the blanket. "The minute we let her go, she'll talk."

"Then we won't let her go." Durnam leaned against the side of the van and this time mopped his brow with his sleeve. Everything was going to go his way, he told himself. He'd come too far, risked too much to have one woman destroy it.

"I ain't having no part in murdering a woman."

Durnam dropped his arm and gave the groom a long, narrow look. "You just take care of the horse and leave the woman to me."

They were going to kill her. Erin struggled to work the blanket from her face as she heard them shut the van door and walk away. She'd heard that in his voice. Even if he'd promised the groom that he'd cause her no harm, she would have known. Whatever had pushed Durnam to this point, he wouldn't hesitate to do away with any obstacle.

Her baby. With a half sob, Erin twisted her wrists and fought against the rope. Mother of mercy, she had to protect her baby. And Burke.

The panic welled up, and for a moment she lost herself in it completely. Before she'd regained control, her wrists were raw and her shoulders bruised. Panting, Erin lay quiet in the dark and tried to think. If she could get up somehow and find the door, she might find a way of forcing it open. She inched her way over to the wall; then, using it as a brace, she managed to get to her knees. She was soaked with sweat by the time she'd struggled to her feet. Keeping her back to the wall, she slid along it, groping with her fingers.

She almost wept when she found the knob. She twisted, straining on her toes before she could fit her fingers around it. Locked. She had to shake her head to keep the tears from coming. Of course it was locked. Durnam might be a brute, but he wasn't a fool. She tried thudding against the door, hoping to draw some attention, but trussed up tightly she was unable to get the momentum to make more than a quiet bump. Erin slid to the floor again and, closing her mind to both panic and pain, continued to work at the ropes.

* * *

Have you seen Erin?"
Travis continued to run his hands down his colt's leg as he looked up at Burke. "Not since this morning. I assumed she'd gone back to the hotel."

"Maybe. She could have taken a cab." It was logical, Burke reminded himself. There was no reason for the sick feeling in his stomach. "We came in together this morning. She usually waits."

"She was looking a little tired." Travis straightened. "She could have gone back to get some rest before tonight."

"Yeah." It made sense. She was probably soaking in a hot tub right now, thinking about the party that night. "I think I'll drive back and check on her."

"Ask her if she'll take pity on a lonely man and save a few dances for me."

"Sure."

"Burke?"

"Yeah?"

"Something wrong?"

His hands were cold. Ice-cold. "No, nothing. See you in a couple hours."

They stayed cold as he drove from the track toward the hotel. It wasn't like Erin to simply go off without a word. But then, they hadn't been exchanging a great many words lately. His fault. He accepted that with a shrug. He didn't feel right about her being there. And he hated seeing her brace herself against the gossip that would certainly swell before it diminished.

If she wasn't so damn stubborn about maintaining a social position . . . but then, that was one of the things he'd promised her when they'd married. He couldn't help but be grateful that she was sticking by him, whatever her reasons, but with gratitude came only more guilt and responsibility.

He was no fonder of responsibility now than he'd ever been. Maybe it would be a relief to head the car west and keep going. To start from scratch as he'd done so many times before. Nothing had ever held him back before. But then, there hadn't been an Erin before.

Once the race and the scandal were behind them, they would talk. The air had to be cleared, the rules had to be reset. Maybe, just maybe, after it was all done, he'd tell her about his past. The way he'd grown up, the things he'd filled his life with. It was better to have it out, to make it clean now and let her walk away, than to continue waiting for her to find out for herself.

He'd never thought of his past as anything to be ashamed of. That was something else she'd done to him. She'd forced him to look back at his past a little too hard. And he didn't like what he saw.

His mood hadn't improved by the time he reached the hotel. He knew it was ridiculous for him to be angry with her for leaving the track when he'd demanded she leave altogether. But, damn it, she'd made him depend on her. The days were easier to get through when he knew he could look around and see her. He didn't care for that, either.

By the time he walked into their suite, he was primed for a fight. It had been too long since they'd developed a polite veneer and no substance. He was going to shout at her and let her shout back. Then they'd both vent the rest of their frustrations in bed.

"Erin?" He slammed the door behind him, but had gone no farther than the center of the parlor before he knew she wasn't there. And his hands were cold again.

Cursing himself, he walked into the bedroom. Had she left him? Had he pushed her away far enough, consistently enough, that she'd decided to take that final step? He didn't want to lose her. That admission left him shaken as he reached for the closet door. No, he didn't want to lose her any more than he wanted to need her.

He had to make himself pull open the door of the closet, and was nearly dizzy with relief when he saw her clothes undisturbed.

She'd gone shopping, he told himself. Or to have her hair done. But those thoughts didn't relieve his mind as he closed the closet door.

He was pacing the suite nearly thirty minutes later when the phone rang. Burke pounced on it, ready to rail at her no matter what her explanation.

"Burke, it's Travis."

"Yeah?"

"Is Erin back at the hotel?"

"No." And now his mouth was dry. "Why?"

"Lloyd Pentel just brought me her wedding ring. He found it on the floor in the stables."

"What? The stables?" He was lowering himself into a chair,

unaware that he'd moved at all. "That's not right. She wouldn't go in the stables. She's afraid of horses."

"Burke." Travis kept his voice calm. "Has she been back to the hotel?"

"No, she hasn't been here. I want to talk to Pentel."

"I already have. He hasn't seen her. Burke, we may be jumping the gun, but I think you should call the police."

* * *

She'd lost track of the time. Once she'd thought the ropes had loosened, but had had to accept it as wishful thinking. More than her wrists hurt now. There were bumps and bruises all over from a fall she'd taken while trying to maneuver standing up. Because the fall had scared her badly with the thought of what might have happened to the baby, she no longer tried to stand. For a time she closed herself off and thought of Burke, as if she could will him to find her.

Would he be worried? Had enough time passed that he would begin to wonder where she was? Would he care? She may have prayed, then slept a little while, dreaming first of Ireland and the farm. Why had she wanted to leave so badly what had been safe and secure? Then she dreamed of Burke and knew that part of the answer was that she'd been meant for him.

"Mrs. Logan."

Her body jackknifed as a hand touched her shoulder. The blindfold was loosened, and she had to blink and struggle to focus. In the dim light she made out the face of the groom, and panic flooded back. He'd come to kill her. And her baby.

"I brought you some food. You gotta promise to be quiet. Durnam would have my hide for coming in here like this. If you promise not to scream, I'll take the gag off so you can eat. If you make noise, I put it back and you get nothing."

She nodded, then drew in fresh air when her mouth was free. It wasn't easy to smother the instinct to cry out, but she could still taste the gag he'd pulled from her mouth. "Please, why are you doing this? If it's money you want, you can have it."

"I'm in too deep." He had a sandwich that was rapidly going stale. "Eat some or you'll get sick."

"What difference does it make?" Just the smell of the meat between the bread made her stomach turn. "You're going to kill me anyway."

"Now, I don't have nothing to do with that." She saw the panic in his eyes and the sweat beading on his lip. He was as afraid as she was. If she could use that, she might yet have a chance.

"You know what Durnam's going to do. He can't let me go."

"He just wants to win, that's all. He needs to. Got himself in some financial trouble, and his stable isn't as good as it was. Charlie's Pride is his best shot, but Logan's colt is better. That's why he had me hire on at Three Aces, so I could keep an eye on things and make sure the race went wrong. But that's it," he added, glancing around. He was talking too much. He always talked too much when he got nervous. And he wanted a drink. The saliva in his mouth had dried to nothing. "I just sweetened the horse some. That's what Durnam wanted. He just needs to put him out of the running. You gotta understand, this is business. Just business."

"You're talking about races. I'm talking about murder."

"I don't want to hear about it. I got nothing to do with that. Now you eat."

"Mr. . . . I don't know your name."

"It's Berley, ma'am. Tom Berley." Ridiculous as it was, he lifted his fingers to his cap.

"Mr. Berley, I'm begging you for my life. And not just for mine, but for the baby I'm carrying. You can't let him kill my baby. Now you'll only be in trouble about the horse, but this is murder. An innocent child, Mr. Berley."

"I'm not going to hear no more talk about killing." His voice had roughened, but his hands weren't steady when they pulled the gag up again. He no longer wanted a drink, he needed one desperately. He started to replace the blindfold, but the look in her eyes had him hesitating. There was nothing for her to see anyway, he told himself. The back of the van was windowless, and the cab was blocked off by a wooden partition.

"You don't want to eat, that's your business. I've got my own to see to." He stuffed the sandwich in his pocket. Erin saw him look both ways before he stepped out the door again and left her in the dark.

CHAPTER 11

I'd prefer if you'd go out and look for my wife, Lieutenant, rather than sitting here asking me questions."

Lieutenant Hallinger was nearly sixty, and after thirty-seven years on the force he figured he'd seen it all and heard twice as much. He'd certainly experienced more than his share of frustrated and angry spouses. It seemed to him that the man in front of him was both.

"Mr. Logan, we have an APB out on your wife right now, and several officers are asking questions at the track." Though he envied Burke his cigar, he didn't mention it. "It would help clear things up, and give us a better chance of locating your wife, if you'd fill me in."

"I've already told you Erin hasn't come back to the hotel. No one's seen her since this morning, and her wedding ring was found at the stables at Churchill Downs."

"Some people are careless with jewelry, Mr. Logan."

Some people. What the hell was this business about some people? They were talking about Erin, his Erin. Where the hell was she? He looked back at Hallinger again and spoke precisely. "Not Erin. And not with her wedding ring."

"Um-hmm." He made a notation in his book. "Mr. Logan, occasionally this sort of thing comes down to a simple misunderstanding." He could have written a book, Hallinger thought. Yeah, he could've written a book on misunderstandings alone. "Did you and your wife quarrel this morning?"

"No."

"It's possible she rented a car and decided to do a little sightseeing."

"That's ridiculous." He glanced up as Travis handed him a cup of coffee. Burke accepted it but set it aside. "If Erin had wanted to go for a drive, she would have taken the car we've already rented. She would have told me she was leaving and she would have been back two hours ago. We had plans for this evening."

He'd had plans himself, which had included a nice quiet evening with his own wife. And a footbath. Hallinger wriggled his aching toes inside his shoes. "Derby week can be chaotic. It might have slipped her mind."

"Erin's the most responsible person I know. If she's not here, it's because she can't get here." He thought again of the hateful and terrifying calls he'd already made to the hospitals. "Because someone's keeping her from getting here."

"Mr. Logan, kidnapping usually prompts a ransom call. You're a wealthy man, yet you tell me you haven't been contacted."

"No, I haven't been contacted." But he still broke out in a sweat every time the phone rang. "Look, Lieutenant, I've told you everything I know. And I'm damn sick of going over the same ground when you should be out doing your job. I'd go out and look myself, but I feel it's more important for me to stay here and . . ." Wait. Endlessly.

Hallinger glanced over his notes. He was a thin man with small, aching feet and a quiet voice. He was a man who took his appearance as seriously as he took his job. It was possible for him to admire Burke's casually expensive shoes while noting his nerves and anxiety.

"Mr. Logan, you had some trouble at the Bluegrass Stakes. How did your wife feel about that?"

"She was upset, naturally." Crushing out his cigar, he rose to pace.

"Upset enough to want to avoid the crowds tonight and tomorrow? Upset enough to want to escape from it, and you?"

There was a flat and dangerous look in Burke's eyes when he turned. "Erin wouldn't run from anything or anyone. The fact is I asked her to go back home until this thing was settled. She wouldn't do it. She insisted on staying and seeing it through."

"You're a fortunate man."

"I'm aware of that. Now why don't you get the hell out of here and find my wife?"

Hallinger simply made a note in his book and turned to Travis. "Mr. Grant, you're the last person we know of who spoke with Mrs. Logan this morning. What was her mood?"

"She was anxious about the race, about Burke. A little tired. She told me she intended to sleep a week when the Derby was over. The last thing on her mind was missing the race or leaving her husband. She's only been married a few weeks, and she's very much in love."

"Um-hmm," the lieutenant said again with maddening calm. "Her ring was found in the stables. You tell me she didn't go in the stables, Mr. Logan, yet she was seen walking toward them early this morning."

"To prove a point to herself, maybe, I can't be sure." His patience was stretching thinner by the second. If she'd waited for him to go with her . . . if she'd asked him to take her in, stand with her . . . He'd been the one who'd pulled away, far enough that she'd stopped asking him for anything.

"What sort of point, Mr. Logan?"

"What?"

Patience was an integral part of Hallinger's job. "You said she might have gone inside the stables to prove a point."

"She had an accident a few years ago and was afraid of horses. Over the past few weeks she's been trying to win out over it. Damn it, what difference does it make why she went in? She was there, and now she's missing."

"I work better with details."

When the phone rang, Burke jumped. His face was gray with strain when he lifted the receiver. "Yes?" With a muttered oath, he offered it to Hallinger. "It's for you."

"They're going to find her, Burke." Travis touched a hand to Burke's shoulder as he passed. "You've got to hold on to that."

"It's wrong. It's very wrong, I can feel it." It was welling up inside him; beyond the first panic, beyond the lingering fear, was a dread, a certainty. "If they don't find her soon, it's going to be too late. I've got to get out of here. Will you stay in case a call comes in?"

"Sure."

Hallinger watched Burke walk to the door and simply gestured for one of his men to follow.

* * *

She must have slept. Erin woke from the nightmare soaked with sweat and shivering with cold. She murmured for Burke and tried to reach out, but her arms wouldn't move.

It wasn't just a dream, she realized as she closed her eyes and took deep breaths to stem another wave of panic. How long? Oh, God, how long? Perhaps they were just going to leave her here to go mad or slowly starve to death.

She wouldn't go mad, because she would think of Burke. She would close her eyes and remember how it felt to lie beside him at night with the moonlight coming through the windows and his body warm against hers. She would think about the way he would kiss her in that way he had—that slow, devastating way that made her bones melt and her mind go dim. She could taste him. Even now she could taste him and feel the way his hand felt as he brushed it over her cheek and into her hair.

He had such wonderful hands, so strong and hard. They

were always so steady, always so sure. Sometimes at night she'd reach for his hand and hold it against her cheek just to have it there. She didn't think he ever knew.

If she concentrated hard enough, she could almost feel his hand against her cheek now. She could hold it there as long as she wanted.

When her eyes grew accustomed to the dark, she could see his head on the pillow beside hers. His profile was such a handsome one, with its firm jaw and the sharp planes of his cheeks. She liked it when it was shadowed just a bit with beard. Had she ever told him that? He was such a pleasure to look at.

And if she was careful, she could cuddle close, not waking him. The scent of his skin would lull her to sleep. He always smelled as she'd thought a man should, without the sweetening of colognes. So she could cuddle close, and sometimes he would shift closer, his arm stretching lazily over her waist. Those were the best times, when she could murmur that she loved him. She'd told herself that if he heard it enough times in his sleep he would begin to believe it.

So Erin kept her eyes closed and thought only of Burke. After a time, she slept again.

* * *

It was nearly three, but Burke sat in the same chair. He'd gone out for only an hour, driving to the track with some wild hope that he would find Erin waiting for him. He'd prowled the stables and badgered the stable boys and grooms with the same questions the police had already asked.

But there was no Erin, nor any sign of her.

So he'd come back, to pace the parlor, haunt the bedroom and ignore the coffee that Travis poured for him. For the past hour he'd sat unmoving, staring at the phone.

He'd told Travis to go, to get some sleep, and had been ignored. It reminded him that there had only been one other person in his life who had stuck by him. If he lost her . . . He couldn't think of that. He knew that luck could change, could turn cruel like a change in the wind. But not with Erin.

She hadn't had her chance yet, not a real one, to see everything there was. Maybe he'd been wrong to lock her in so quickly, to bind her to him. But she still had so much life, so much energy. Why was it he couldn't get past that one sick thought that whatever was happening to her now was because of him?

When the phone rang, he grabbed the receiver with both hands. "Logan." The voice in his ear was thick with liquor, but he understood. And his heart began to thud. "Where is she?"

"I don't want no trouble. Spiking the horse was one thing, but I don't want no trouble."

"Fine. Tell me where she is." He glanced up to see Travis beside him, waiting.

"I didn't want no part of it. He'll kill me if he finds out I'm talking to you."

"Just tell me where she is and I'll take care of it."

"Kept her at the track, in the van. I don't know what he's going to do. Kill her, maybe."

"What van? What van, damn it?"

"I ain't having no part in murder."

When the phone went dead, Burke simply dropped it and rose. "She's at the track. They're holding her in a van."

"I'll call the police and be right behind you."

He drove like a maniac, ignoring red lights and speed limits. *Kill her, maybe.* Those three words drummed in his head over and over so that he didn't notice the speedometer hovering at a hundred and ten. The streets were deserted. People were asleep, anticipating the race tomorrow. Some would already be camped on the infield grass.

He prayed that Erin was asleep as well. And when she woke he would be there.

Gravel spit from under the tires as he braked behind the stables. Vans were parked there for trainers, for owners who preferred to stay close to their horses, for grooms and hands who could afford a little luxury.

He only needed to find one.

He started across the lot when he heard steps behind him. Fists clenched and murder on his mind, he whirled.

"Easy, lad," Paddy told him. "Travis called me."

He nodded briefly, though in the moonlight he could see that the old man hadn't slept, either. "Durnam's van. Which is it?"

"Durnam? Travis said you didn't know which."

"Call it a hunch. Which one is Durnam's?"

"The big black one there." Paddy turned as he heard the whine of sirens. "The police are coming." But Burke was already racing to the black van.

"Erin!" The door held fast. For a moment he thought he could tear it off with his bare hands.

"Use this." Paddy handed him a crowbar. "When Travis called and filled me in, I thought we'd have use for it."

Without hesitation, Burke began to pry the door open, all the time calling to her. He wanted her to know it was him. He couldn't stand the thought of her having one more instant of fear. The metal groaned, fought back, then gave. Burke gripped the crowbar like a weapon as he jumped inside. He shoved away the plywood partition that separated the back of the van from the cab.

"Erin?" There was no answer, no sound. What if he was too late? Burke turned the crowbar in his hands, wiping sweat on metal. "Erin, it's all right. I've come to take you out of here." He cursed the lack of light and dropped to his hands and knees. He saw her then, curled in a corner in the rear.

He was with her in an instant, but he was almost afraid to touch her. His hand went to her cheek first. So cold, so still. "Erin." In a fit of rage, he tore the gag away. When her eyes fluttered open, he nearly wept with relief. "Erin, it's all right."

But when he reached for her she cringed, making small sounds in her throat.

"It's all right," he murmured. "I'm not going to let anyone hurt you. It's Burke, darling, it's okay now."

"Burke." Her eyes were still glazed with shock, but she said his name.

"That's right, and I'm going to take you out of here." He shifted her, cursing under his breath each time she whimpered. Her trembles became shudders that none of his soothing words could halt.

He found the ropes, but when he started to loosen them she cried out. "I'm sorry. I have to get them off. I don't want to hurt you. Can you stay very still?"

She simply turned her face to the wall.

The van shook as men entered, and she pressed back in the corner. "I need a knife." He looked up and saw Lieutenant Hallinger. "Give me a damn knife, then get out. She's terrified."

Hallinger reached in his pocket with one hand and signaled his men back with the other.

"Just hold on, Irish, it's all over now." He hurt her. He could feel each jerk and tremble inside his own body as he cut through the bonds. Both his skin and hers were damp before he had freed her feet as well. "I'm going to pick you up and carry you out. Just stay still."

"My arms." She bit her lip, as even the gentlest touch sent the pain throbbing.

"I know." As carefully as he could, he lifted her up. She moaned and pressed her face against his shoulder.

When they stepped outside, the lot was bright with lights. Erin squeezed her burning eyes shut. She couldn't think beyond the pain and fear, and concentrated on the sound of Burke's voice.

"You stay the hell away from her," he said very quietly, his eyes on Hallinger.

"I called an ambulance." Travis stepped between Burke and the police. "It's here now. Paddy and I will follow you."

As if in a dream, Erin felt herself laid down. The light was still too bright, so she kept her eyes closed. There were voices, too many voices, but she focused in on the only one that mattered. She jolted as she felt something cool over the raw skin of her wrist, but Burke stroked her hair and never stopped talking to her.

He didn't know what he said. Promises, vows, nonsense. But he could see the dried blood on her wrists and ankles and the bruises that ran up her arms. Each time she winced, he thought of Durnam. And how he would kill him.

"In the stables," she murmured. "I heard them in the stables, talking about drugging the horse."

"It doesn't matter." Burke kept stroking her hair.

"In the stables," she repeated in a voice that was thin and tended to float. "I couldn't get away. I tried."

"You're safe now. Just lie still."

They wouldn't let him go with her. Erin was wheeled away the moment they reached the hospital, and Burke was left helpless and hurting in the hallway.

"She's going to be all right." Travis laid a hand on his shoulder.

Burke nodded. The ambulance attendants had already assured him of that. Her wrists were the worst of her physical injuries. They would heal, just as the bruises would fade. But no one knew how badly she'd been scarred emotionally.

"Stay with her. There's something I have to do."

"Burke, you'll do her more good here. And yourself."

"Just stay with her," he repeated, then strode out through the wide glass doors.

He kept his mind carefully blank as he drove out to Durnam's farm. The rage was there, but he held it, knowing it would cloud his thinking. So he thought of nothing, and his mind stayed as cool as the early-morning air.

The thirty-minute drive took him fifteen, but still the police were faster. Burke slammed out of his car in front of Durnam's palatial stone house and faced Hallinger once again.

"Thought I'd see you here tonight." Hallinger lit one of the five cigarettes he allowed himself—which was five more than his wife knew about. "Figured a sharp man like you would have already put it together that Durnam was the one who had your horse drugged."

"Yeah, I put that together. Where is he?"

"He's my guest tonight." Hallinger blew out smoke and leaned against the hood of Burke's car. If the footbath didn't work, he was going to have to go see the damned podiatrist. "You know, sometimes cops have brains, too. We were here questioning Durnam when the call came in that you were on your way to the track to get your wife."

"Why?"

"Well, assuming that your wife's disappearance had something to do with the trouble last week, which was a big assumption, I had to figure out who had the most to gain. That would be Durnam. I take it you'd already worked that out."

"I had everything but proof."

"We've got that now, too. The man was already on the edge. Our call coming in was all it took to push him over. He'd cleaned out his bank account, what was left of it. Knew that, did you?"

"Yeah, I knew that."

"Had his bags packed. But he wasn't going to miss that race tomorrow. Today," Hallinger corrected with a glance up at the lightening sky. "He wanted that Derby win bad. Funny how people can set their minds on one thing and forget about the consequences. How's your wife?"

"She's hurt. Where are you keeping him?"

"That's police business now, Mr. Logan." He examined his cigarette thoughtfully before taking another drag. "I know how you feel."

Burke cut him off with a look. "You don't know how I feel."

Hallinger nodded slowly. "You're right. And I doubt you're in the mood for advice, but here it is. You haven't been a Boy Scout, Logan." He smiled, a little sourly, when Burke only continued to stare at him. "I make it my business to check details. You've had a few scrapes in your time. Some bad luck and some good. Right now I'd say you've got yourself a good woman and a chance to make things click. Don't blow it on something as pitiful as Charles Durnam. He lost a hell of a lot more than a horse race. Isn't that enough?"

"No." Burke pulled open the door of his car, then paused to turn back. "He gets out in a year, in twenty years—he's dead."

With some regret, Hallinger flipped the butt of his cigarette away. "I'll keep that in mind."

* * *

When Erin awoke, she opened her eyes cautiously. The hospital. The wave of relief came as it did every time she awoke to find herself safe. The light beside her bed was still burning. She'd hated to be weak, but had insisted the nurse leave it on even when the sun was coming up.

Burke hadn't been there. She'd fretted and asked for him, but they'd wheeled her to a private room and tucked her into bed, promising he'd be with her soon. She was to sleep, to relax, she wasn't to worry.

But she wanted him.

Listless, she turned her head. There were already flowers in the room. She imagined Travis or Paddy had seen to that. They'd been so kind.

But she wanted Burke.

Shifting in search of comfort, she pushed herself up in bed. And she saw him. He was standing by the window, his back to her. Everything fled but the pleasure of knowing he was there with her.

"Burke."

He turned immediately. His first thought was that she was sitting up and her cheeks were no longer pale. His second thought was that if it hadn't been for him she wouldn't be in a hospital bed with bandages on her wrists. Because she was holding out a hand, he went to her and touched it lightly.

"You're looking better," he said inadequately.

"I'm feeling better. I didn't know you were here."

"I've been around awhile. Do you want anything?"

"I could eat." She smiled and reached for his hand again, but his was in his pocket.

"I'll get the nurse."

"Burke." She stopped him as he reached the door. "It can wait. Look at you, you haven't slept."

"Busy night."

She tried another smile. "Aye, it was all of that. I'm sorry."

His eyes went hard and flat. "Don't. I'll get the nurse."

Alone, Erin lay back on the pillows. Maybe she was still confused and disoriented. He couldn't really be angry with her. With a half sigh, she closed her eyes. Of course he could. There was no telling with men, and with Burke in particular. Whether it was her fault or not, she'd put him through hell. And now she was tying him to a hospital room on the most important day of his life.

When the door opened again she made sure her smile was cheerful, and her voice, though her throat still tended to ache, mirrored it. "You should be at the track. I had no idea it was so late. Did anyone think to bring me a change of clothes? I can be ready in ten minutes."

"You're not going anywhere."

"You don't expect me to miss my first Derby? I know what the doctor said, but—"

"Then you'll know you're not getting up from that bed for twenty-four hours. Don't be stupid."

She opened her mouth, then firmly shut it again. She wouldn't argue with him. She'd been close to death, and that made a person think about how much time was wasted on pettiness. "You're right, of course. I'll just sit here and be pampered while I watch on television." Why didn't he come to her? Why didn't he hold her? Erin kept her lips curved as he turned again to stare out the window. "You'd better be on your way."

"Where?"

"To the track, of course. It's nearly noon. You've already missed the morning."

"I'm staying here."

Her heart did a quick flip, but she shook her head. "Don't be silly. You can't miss this. If I'm to be shut up here it's bad enough. At least I can have the pleasure of watching you step into the winner's circle. There's nothing for you to do here."

He thought of how helpless he'd felt through the night. Of how helpless he felt now. "No, I suppose there isn't."

"Then off with you," she told him, forcing her voice to be light.

"Yeah." He rubbed his hands over his face.

"And I don't want to see you back here until you've had some rest."

She lifted her face for a kiss, but his lips only brushed over her brow. "See you later."

"Burke." He was already out of reach. "You're going to win."

With a nod, he closed the door behind him. He leaned against the wall, almost too exhausted to stand, far too exhausted to think. He didn't give a damn about the Derby or any other race. All he could see, playing over and over in his mind, was Erin curled in the corner of that van, cringing away from him.

She'd bounced back, smiling and talking as though nothing had happened. But he could still see the white bandages on her wrists.

He was afraid to touch her, afraid she'd cringe away again. Or, if she didn't, that he'd hurt her. He was afraid to look at her too long because he'd see that glazed shock in her eyes again. He was afraid that if he didn't gather her close, keep her close, that she'd slip away from him, that he would lose her as he'd nearly lost her only hours before.

But she was urging him to go, telling him she didn't need

him beside her. All she needed was a win, a blanket of red roses and a trophy. He'd damn well give them to her.

*　*　*

She hadn't realized she would be nervous. But even watching the preliminaries, the interviews, the discussions on television, kept her pulse racing. When she saw Burke caught by the cameras as he stepped out of the stables, she laughed and hugged her pillow. Oh, if she could just be there with him, holding on. But he avoided the reporter, leaving Erin disappointed.

She'd wanted to hear him, to see his face on the screen so that they could laugh about it later.

Then it was the reporter facing the camera, recounting the story that had unfolded since the Bluegrass Stakes. It pleased her to hear that Burke's name had been cleared absolutely and that Double Bluff was considered the favorite in the Run for the Roses.

She listened, trying to be dispassionate as he talked about her kidnapping and Durnam's arrest. The groom had been picked up sleeping off a bottle in a stall. Apparently it hadn't taken much encouragement for him to spill the entire story. There were pictures of the van, with its broken door and police barriers, that she had to force herself to look at.

It almost amused her to be told that she was resting comfortably. Somehow the reporter made it all sound like a grand adventure, something out of a mystery novel—the lady in distress, the villain and the hero. She wrinkled her nose. However much she might consider Burke a hero, she didn't care to think of herself as a lady in distress.

She let it pass as she watched the horses being spotlighted as they were led from the paddock. There was Double Bluff, as big and as handsome as ever. Double Bluff, the three-year-old from Three Aces. Owners Burke and Erin Logan. She smiled at that. Though of course it was Burke's horse and the news people had made a mistake, it still gave her a good feeling to see her name flash on the screen with Burke's.

She laughed at herself again because her palms were getting sweaty. The track was just as she'd known it would be, filled to capacity. The camera panned over Dorothy Gainsfield. Erin gave herself the satisfaction of sticking out her tongue.

Then it focused on Burke, and her heart broke a little. He looked so tired. Worn to the bone. That was why he'd been so distant before. The man was exhausted. When he'd rested and had time to get his bearings, things would be right again.

"I love you, Burke," she told him, rubbing her cheek against the pillow. "Loving you is what got me through."

Then the screen flashed back to the horses. It was nearly post time.

There was the blare of the trumpet and the roar of the crowd. Again Erin found herself tempted to jump out of bed and hurry to the track. If it hadn't been for the baby, she would have ignored the doctor and done just that. Instead she forced herself to be patient.

"We'll go to our first Derby together," she murmured as she placed a hand on her stomach. "Next year, the three of us will go."

The bell sounded, and for the next two minutes she didn't take her eyes off the screen. It seemed to her that Double Bluff was running with a vengeance. And perhaps he was. Perhaps Burke had transformed some of his emotions to the horse, for the colt ran like fury.

When he broke from the pack early, Erin held her breath. It was too soon. She knew the jockey had been instructed to hold him back the first half mile. There was no holding back today. Her first concern evaporated in pure excitement as she watched him run. He was glorious, angry and unstoppable. It was as if the horse himself wanted vindication and perhaps revenge.

He clung to the rail, taking the turns hard and close. Travis's Apollo held back by a length. The Pentel colt, under a new rider, was coming up fast on the outside. And the crowd was on its feet. Erin was shouting, but was unaware of it even after the nurse came in.

As he came down the backstretch he poured on more speed, impossibly more, so that even the announcer's voice cracked with excitement. Two lengths, then three, then three and a half. He went under the wire as if he were alone on the oval.

"He never gave up the lead." Erin brushed her palms over her cheeks to dry them. "Not once."

"Congratulations, Mrs. Logan. I'd say you've just had some of the best medicine on the market."

"The very best." But her fingers curled into the sheets as she waited for the official announcement. In her mind she could picture it, the weighing in, the certification. It seemed to take forever, but then the numbers flashed on the board. "The very, very best. There's Burke." She gripped the nurse's hand. "He's worked so hard for this, waited so long. Oh, I wish I could be with him."

She watched the cameramen and reporters vie for angles as Burke and his trainer grouped in the winner's circle. Why wasn't he smiling? she wondered as she wiped another tear away. She saw him reach up and shake his jockey's hand but couldn't hear whatever it was he said.

"It's a good day for Three Aces." A reporter stuck a microphone in Burke's face. "This must make up for the disqualification last week, Mr. Logan."

"It doesn't begin to make up for it." He patted the colt's neck. "I think Double Bluff proved himself a champion here today and proved my trust in his team, but this race was run for my wife." He pulled a rose from the blanket covering his horse. "Excuse me."

"That was a lovely thing to say," the nurse murmured.

"Aye." Still, as Erin watched the jockey hold the cup over his head, she wondered why she felt so lost.

CHAPTER 12

They flew home as soon as Erin was released from the hospital, but she didn't feel like celebrating. Everything should have been right. Burke's reputation had been cleared, his prize colt had won the Derby with a track record, and she was safe. So why was it everything was wrong?

She knew Burke could be aloof, that he could be arrogant and hardheaded. Those were three ridiculous reasons to love a man, but they were reasons none the less. What she hadn't known was that he could be both withdrawn and distant. He never touched her. In fact, as the first few days passed, Erin realized he was going out of his way to avoid any opportunity to touch her. He came to bed late and rose early. He spent a great deal more time out of the house and away than he spent at home.

She tried to tell herself he was just gearing up for the Preakness—the second jewel of the Triple Crown—but she knew it wasn't true.

With too much time left to herself to think, she began to remember the words she'd heard on her wedding day. *Men are easily charmed, and just as easily bored.*

Was that it? Was he bored with her? Trying to find the answer, she took stock of herself. Her face was the same. Maybe she was a little hollow-eyed, but those things came with worry and restless nights. Her body was still firm, though she knew that would change in a matter of weeks.

And what then? she wondered. When she told him about the baby, would he turn away completely? No, she couldn't believe that of him. Burke would never turn his back on his own child. But on her? If he was tired of her now, how would he feel when she began to round and swell?

She wanted to look forward to the changes in her body, to the signs that her baby was growing and healthy. But would those same changes push Burke only farther away? How could they not, if they didn't reestablish their intimacy? Since the physical change couldn't be avoided, Erin decided she'd better do something about seducing her husband now.

She chose the wine herself. That was something she was pleased to have developed a knack for. She wouldn't do any more than play at drinking it herself, but it was the atmosphere that mattered.

And candles. She set dozens of them around the bedroom, lighting them so that their scent would be as much a part of the mood as the flames. She chose the same gown she'd worn on her wedding night, the white lace that made her feel like a bride. He'd thought her lovely once, desirable once. He would again. She picked the Chopin he'd played on their first night together and wondered if he would remember.

Tonight would be another first, another beginning. When they'd loved each other, when they'd finally come back together as they were meant to be, she would tell him about the baby. Then they would talk about the future.

* * *

He'd taken himself to the wire before he climbed the stairs. Burke found it easiest to wear himself out before he slipped into bed beside her. That way it wasn't as difficult to stop himself from pulling her against him. It wasn't as difficult to ignore the fact that she was right there next to him, soft and lovely and incredibly sweet. It wasn't as difficult to will himself to sleep and pretend he didn't want her.

But it was all a lie.

It was killing him to be with her and yet not to be with her. Still, he knew no other way to wean her away, to give her time to make a choice. She had secrets she was keeping from him. He could see them in her eyes. There were times he wanted to take her by the shoulders and shake her until she told him. Then he would remember what she had gone through because of him, and he didn't touch her at all.

She'd been the perfect wife since they'd come back. Never demanding, never questioning, never arguing. He wanted Erin back.

Then he stepped into the bedroom and his limbs went weak.

"I thought you'd never come up." She crossed to him, holding out a hand. "You're working too hard."

"There's a lot to be done."

When he didn't take her hand, she curled her fingers into her palm but made herself take the final step. "There's more to living than horses and the next race."

Involuntarily he reached up to touch her hair. "I thought you'd gone to bed."

"I've been waiting for you." She brought a hand to his cheek as she rose on her toes to kiss him. "I've missed you. Missed being alone with you. Come to bed, Burke. Make love with me."

"I haven't finished downstairs."

"It can wait." Smiling, she began to unbutton his shirt. She was sure, almost sure, that she felt his response, his need. "We haven't had an evening alone in a long time."

It only took the feel of her bandages rubbing against his skin. "I'm sorry. I only came up to see if you were all right. You should get some rest."

The rejection stung her, and she stepped back even as he did. "You don't want me anymore, do you?"

Not want her? He was nearly eaten up with wanting. "I want

you to take care of yourself, that's all. You've been through a
lot of strain."

"Aye, and you. That's why we need some time together."

He touched his fingers lightly to her cheek. "Get some sleep."

She stared at the closed door before turning away blindly
to blow out the candles.

* * *

Erin closed herself in the office and buried herself in columns
of figures. Those, at least, she could understand. With numbers, when you added two and two, you could be assured of a
logical answer. Life, she'd discovered, and Burke in particular, wasn't quite that simple.

When the call came from Travis that Dee was in labor, she
found herself not only pleased for her cousin but for herself and
the diversion. Scribbling a hasty note, she left it on her desk.
If Burke bothered to look for her, he'd find it. If he didn't . . .
then it didn't matter where she was.

She'd learned something else about marriage. Both husband
and wife should stand on their own. In the best of worlds this
was offset by an interdependence—a sharing, a love of each
other and a contentment in each other's company. In the not-so-
best, it simply meant survival. She was and always had been a
survivor.

Still, she watched the house retreat as she drove toward the
main road. Such a special place it was, the kind she'd always
dreamed of living in. The grass was green now, and the flowers were in bloom. It was hard to believe she could finally have
something so beautiful and still be unhappy. But it could be so
much more than a place to live, she thought, just as her marriage could be so much more than an agreement between two
logical adults. In time, Burke would have to decide how much
more he would permit it to be.

* * *

He was dealing with his own devils when he came into the house. All morning and half the afternoon he'd been unable to erase from his mind how lovely Erin had looked the night before, how hard it had been to walk away from her and from his own feelings. He was no longer sure he was doing her a favor, and he knew for a fact he was killing himself.

Maybe the time had come for them to talk. Plain words, plain thinking. He didn't believe himself capable of much else. It hadn't taken him long to realize he was useless without her. How that had come to be, and why, didn't seem to matter. It simply was. But nagging at him, gnawing at him, was the question of what she would be without him. He'd never given her a chance to find out.

So they'd face off. That was something he understood. Now was as good a time as any.

He glanced in her office and, finding it empty, passed it by. In the atrium, Rosa was watering geraniums. He paused there, wishing he didn't continually find himself uncomfortable when he caught her going about her household duties.

"Rosa, is Erin upstairs?"

Rosa glanced up but continued her watering. "The *señora* went out a few hours ago."

"Out?" The panic was absurd. So he told himself even as it choked him. "Where?"

"She didn't tell me."

"Did she take her car?"

"I believe so." When he swore and turned away, Rosa moved to a pot of asters. "Burke?"

"Yes?"

She smiled a little and set down her watering can. "You have little more patience now than you did when you were ten."

"I don't want her left alone."

"Yet you do so continually." She lifted her brow at his look. "It's difficult to pretend not to see what's under my nose. Your wife's unhappy. So are you."

"Erin's fine. And so am I."

"You would say the same when you came home with a black eye."

"That was a long time ago."

"It's foolish to think either of us have forgotten. To have a future, it's necessary to face the past."

"What's the point in this, Rosa?"

She did something she hadn't done since they'd been children. Crossing to him, she touched a hand to his face. "She's stronger than you think, my brother. And you, you aren't nearly as tough."

"I'm not ten anymore, Rosa."

"No, but in some ways you were easier then."

"I was never easy."

"It was the life that wasn't easy. You've changed that."

"Maybe."

"Your mother would be proud of you. She would," Rosa insisted when he started to back away.

"She never had a chance."

"No, but you do. And you gave one to me."

He made a quick gesture of dismissal. "I gave you a job."

"And the first decent home I've ever known," Rosa added. "Before you go, answer one question. Why do you let me stay? The truth, Burke."

He didn't want to answer, but she'd always had a way of looking straight and waiting for as long as it took. Maybe he owed her the truth. Maybe he owed it to himself. "Because she cared about you. And so do I."

She smiled, then went back to watering. "Your wife won't wait as long for an answer. She's impatient, like you."

"Rosa, why do you stay?"

She fluffed the leaves of a fern. "Because I love you. So does your wife. If you don't mind, I would like to pick some flowers for the sitting room."

"Yeah, sure." He left Rosa there, watering plants, and went back to Erin's office. It was the first time he'd asked himself or allowed himself to ask why he'd permitted Rosa to stay. Why he'd provided her with a job in order that she could keep her pride. She was family. It was just that simple, and just that hard to accept. She'd been right, too, when she'd said that Erin wouldn't wait so long for an answer.

He wanted Erin there, where they could sit down together. There where he could talk to her about his feelings. That would be a first, he admitted.

Restless, he began to push through the papers on her desk. She was a hell of a bookkeeper, he thought ruefully. Everything in neat little piles, all the figures in tidy rows. A man could hardly complain about having a conscientious wife. It certainly shouldn't make him want to gather up all the books and papers and dump them in the trash.

It was the doctor bill that made him frown. All medical expenses from her stay in Kentucky should have been addressed to him. Yet this one was clearly marked to her. Annoyed, he picked it up with the intention of dealing with it himself. He wanted her to have no reminders. But the doctor's address wasn't in Kentucky; it was in Maryland. And the doctor was an obstetrician.

Obstetrician? Burke lowered himself very carefully in her chair. The words "pregnancy test" seemed to jump out at him. Pregnant? Erin was pregnant? That couldn't be, because he would have known. She would have told him. Yet he had the paper in his hand. The paper stated "positive" clearly enough, and the test was dated almost a month earlier.

Erin was pregnant. And she hadn't told him. What else hadn't she told him? He sprang up again to push through the other papers as if he'd find the answers there. It was then he found her note, hastily scribbled. *Burke, I've gone to the hospital. I don't know how long it will take.*

As he stared at the note, he felt all the blood drain out of his face.

*   *   *

Oh, I don't see how Dee can be so calm and patient!"
Paddy turned a page in the magazine he was pretending to read. "You can't hurry babies into the world."

"It seems to be taking forever." Erin paced the waiting room again. "My palms are sweating, and she looked like she could take a walk in the park. It's scary."

"Having babies?" He chuckled a little and sneaked a peek at his watch while Erin wasn't looking. "Dee's an old hand at this."

Erin laid a hand on her stomach. "Was she this way when she had the first one? I mean, the first one would be the scariest. It's like taking everything on faith that nothing's going to go wrong."

"Dee's a trouper."

"Aye." She prayed she would be as well when her time came. "It must make a difference, having Travis with her through it all." She'd seen the way he'd been with Dee, standing beside the bed, holding her hand, talking, making her laugh, timing her contractions. Total support, total commitment. "I wonder, Paddy, do you think most men would do that?" Would Burke?

"I'd say when a man loves a woman the way Travis loves Dee he wouldn't be anywhere else right now. Lass, you're going to wear a rut in the floor."

"I can't sit still," she muttered. "I'm going to go downstairs and see if I can buy some flowers. Have them waiting for her."

"That's a fine idea."

"I could bring you some tea."

"You do that. Won't be long now."

He waited until she was out of sight to get up and pace himself.

Downstairs, Burke burst into the hospital like a man possessed. In seconds he had pounced on the admissions clerk. "Where's my wife?"

The clerk swiveled her chair over to her computer. "Name?"

"Logan, Erin Logan."

"When was she admitted?"

"I don't know. A couple of hours ago."

The clerk began to punch buttons. "For what purpose?"

"I—" He wasn't sure he could deal with the purpose. "She's pregnant."

"Maternity?" The clerk continued to punch. "I'm sorry, Mr. Logan. We don't have your wife."

"I know she's here, damn it. Where—" Continuing to swear, he pulled the paper out of his pocket. "Dr. Morgan. I want to see Dr. Morgan."

"Dr. Morgan's in delivery with another patient. You can check at the nurse's station on the fifth floor, but—"

She shrugged when Burke raced away. Expectant fathers, she thought. They were always crazy.

Burke jammed a fist against the elevator button. He hated hospitals. He'd lost his mother in one. Only days before, he'd watched Erin lie in one, and now . . .

"Burke, I didn't expect you."

He turned to see Erin walking toward him with a huge arrangement of rosebuds and baby's breath. Her hair was pulled back and her cheeks were glowing. The flowers nearly tipped to the floor when he grabbed her shoulders.

"What the hell are you doing?" he demanded.

"Burke, you're crushing them."

"I'll crush more than a bunch of flowers. I want you to tell me what you're doing."

"I'm taking them upstairs. If they survive. I think Dee will appreciate them more if they're not mangled."

"Dee?" He shook his head but didn't manage to clear it. "What are you talking about?"

"What are *you* talking about?" she countered. "It doesn't seem so strange to me to buy flowers for someone who's having babies."

"Dee? You came here because Dee's delivering?"

"Well, of course. Didn't you see my note?"

"I saw your note," he muttered. Taking her arm, he pulled her into the elevator. "It wasn't very clear."

"I was in a hurry. I wish they'd had more roses," she murmured. "Seems when you're having twins you should have twice as many flowers." She buried her face in them a moment, then smiled at him. "I'm glad you came. It'll mean a lot to Dee."

Struggling for calm, he stepped out when the doors opened again. "How is she?"

"She's perfect. Paddy and I are a wreck, but she's perfect."

"You shouldn't be on your feet." He took the flowers because he was abruptly afraid for her to carry anything. "You shouldn't be getting yourself worked up."

"Don't be silly." She turned into the waiting room, not to find Paddy pacing but to find him dancing.

"One of each!" he shouted to both of them. "She's gone and had one of each."

"Oh, Paddy!" Laughing, she flung herself at him and let him whirl her around. "She's all right? And the babies? Everyone's all right?"

"Everyone's fit as a fiddle, so the nurse told me. They'll be bringing them all out in a minute so we can have a peek. A fine day to you, Burke. A fine, fine day."

"Paddy. Erin, why don't you sit down?"

"Sit?" She shook her head with another laugh and hooked her arm through Paddy's. "I couldn't sit if my legs fell off. Paddy and I are going dancing, aren't we, Paddy?"

"That we are." He put his chin up and began to hum. Recognizing the tune, Erin joined in as their feet began to move.

Burke stood holding a bushel of roses and watched them. He hadn't heard her laugh like that for too long. He hadn't seen her smile just that way. He wanted to toss the flowers aside and gather her up. Snatch her away, take her home. Hold her for hours.

"Here she is!" Paddy did another quick jig as Dee was wheeled out. "Here's my little girl. Look at this." He had to pull out his handkerchief and wipe his eyes. "They're beautiful, lass. Just like you."

"What am I?" Travis wanted to know. "Chopped liver?"

"You did a fine job." Erin moved over to kiss his cheek. "A boy and a girl." She looked down at the two bundles beside her cousin. "And so tiny."

"They'll grow quick enough." Dee turned her head to the right, then the left, to nuzzle them. "The doctor said they have everything they should have. Lord, they came out squalling, both of them. Didn't they, Travis?"

"They have their mother's disposition."

"It's lucky you are I've my hands full. Burke, it's good of you to come. This is the best time to have family around."

"Are you okay?" He felt both foolish and awkward as he passed the flowers to Travis. "Is there anything you want?"

"A ham sandwich," she said with a sigh. "A huge one. But I'm afraid they'll make me wait just a little while yet."

"I'm sorry, we'll have to take Mrs. Grant now. Evening visiting hours start at seven."

"Paddy, bring the children back tonight."

"No children under twelve are allowed, Mrs. Grant," the nurse said as she began to push her away. Dee merely smiled and mouthed the request again.

"She looked wonderful, didn't she?" Erin mused.

"She's a Thoroughbred, my Dee. Always has been." Paddy stuffed his handkerchief back in his pocket. "Well, I'd better get home and think up a way to smuggle that brood in here tonight."

"Let me know if you need any help."

"That I will, lass." He kissed both her cheeks. As he walked down the hall, he jumped up and clicked his heels.

"You've been on your feet long enough," Burke said tersely. "I'll drive you home."

"I've got my car."

"Leave it." He took her arm again.

"That's silly. I'll just—"

"Leave it," he repeated, pulling her into the elevator.

"Fine." She bit the word off. "Since you're sure you can

bear to be in the same car with me." She crossed her arms and stared at the doors. Burke stuck his hands in his pockets and scowled.

Neither of them spoke again until Erin stormed into the atrium. "If it's all the same to you, I'm going upstairs. And you, you can take your foul mood out to the stables with the rest of the dumb animals."

He wondered that her neck didn't break from holding her head that high. Burke gave himself thirty seconds to calm down. When it didn't work, he strode up the stairs after her.

"Sit down." He spit out the order as he slammed the bedroom door behind him. Erin simply narrowed her eyes and crossed her arms. "I said sit down."

"And I say to hell with you."

That was all it took. Before she could evade him, he had scooped her up and plunked her down on the bed.

"All right, now I'm sitting. Don't tell me you actually want to have a conversation with me?" She tossed her hair back, then slowly crossed her legs. "I'm all aflutter." She saw his hand close into a fist and angled her chin. "Go ahead, pop me one. You've been wanting to for days."

"Don't tempt me."

"It was quite clear last night I couldn't even do that." She pulled her shoes off and tossed them aside. "If you're so fired up to talk to me, then talk."

"Yeah, I want to talk to you, and I want some straight answers." But instead of asking, he shoved his hands back into his pockets and circled the room. Where to start? he wondered. His fingers brushed over the ring he'd carried for days. Perhaps that was the best place. Burke pulled it out and held it in the palm of his hand.

"You found it." Erin's first burst of pleasure was almost blanked out by the look in his eyes. "You didn't tell me."

"You didn't ask."

"No, I didn't, because I was sick about it. Dropping it in the stables was stupid."

"Why did you?"

"Because I couldn't think of anything else. I knew I couldn't get away from them. They were already tying my hands." She was looking at her ring and didn't see him wince. "I guess I thought someone would find it and take it to you, and you'd know. Though I don't know what I expected you could do about it. Why haven't you given it back to me?"

"Because I wanted to give you time to decide if you wanted it or not." He took her hand and dropped the ring in it. "It's your choice."

"Always was," she said slowly, but she didn't put the ring on. "You're still angry with me because of what happened?"

"I was never angry with you because of what happened."

"You've been giving a champion imitation of it, then."

"It was my fault." He turned to her then, and for the first time began to let go of the rage. "Twenty hours. You lay in the dark for twenty hours because of me."

The words could still bring on a cold flash, but she was more intrigued by Burke's reaction. "I thought it was because of Durnam. You've never seemed willing to talk it through, to let me explain to you exactly what happened. If you'd—"

"You could have died." There was really nothing else but that. No explanations, no calm recounting, could change that one fact. "I sat in that damn hotel room, waiting for the phone to ring, terrified that it would and there was nothing, nothing I could do. When I found you, saw what they'd done to you . . . your wrists."

"They're healing." She stood to reach out to him, but he withdrew immediately. "Why do you do this? Why do you keep pulling away from me? Even at the hospital you weren't there. You couldn't even stay with me."

"I went to kill Durnam."

"Oh, Burke, no."

"I was too late for that." The bitterness was still there, simmering with a foul taste he'd almost grown used to. "They had him by then, where I couldn't get to him. All I could do was stand in that hospital room and watch you. And think of how close I'd come to losing you. The longer I stood there, the more I thought about the way I'd dragged you in with me right from the beginning, never giving you a choice, never letting you know what kind of man you were tied to."

"That's enough. Do you really believe I'm some weak-minded female who can't say yes or no? I had a choice and I chose you. And not for your bloody money."

It was her turn to rage around the room. "I'm sick to death of having to find ways to prove that I love you. I'll not be denying that I wanted more out of life than a few acres of dirt and someone else's dishes to wash. And I'm not ashamed of it. But hear this, Burke Logan, I'd have found a way to get it for myself."

"I never doubted it."

"You think I married you for this house?" She threw up her arms as if to encompass every room. "Well, set a match to it, then, it doesn't matter to me. You think it's for all those fine stocks and bonds? Take them all, take every last scrap of paper and put it on one spin of the wheel. Whether you win or lose makes no difference to me. And these?" She pulled open her dresser and yanked out boxes of jewelry. "These pretty shiny things? Well, take them to hell with you. I love you—God himself knows why, you thickheaded, miserable excuse for a man. Not know what kind of man I married, is it?" She tossed the jewelry aside and stormed around the room. "I know well enough who and what you are. More fool I am for not giving a damn and loving you anyway."

"You don't know anything," he said quietly. "But if you'd sit down I'll tell you."

"You won't tell me anything I don't know. Do you think I care you grew up poor without a father? Oh, you don't need to look that way. Rosa told me weeks ago. Do you think I care if you lied or cheated or stole? I know what it is to be poor, to need, but I had my family. Can't I feel sorry for the boy without thinking less of the man?"

"I don't know." She rocked him, but then it seemed she never failed to do so. "Sit down, Erin, please."

"I'm sick to death of sitting. Just like I'm sick to death of walking on eggs with you. I *did* nearly die. I thought I was going to die, and all I could think was how much time we'd wasted being at odds. I swore if we were back together there'd be no more fighting. Now for days I've held my temper, I've said nothing when you turn away from me. But no more. If you've any more questions, Burke Logan, you'd best out with them, because I've plenty more to say myself."

"Why didn't you tell me you were pregnant?"

That stopped her cold. Her mouth fell open, and for all her talk about not sitting, she lowered herself onto the bed. "How do you know?"

Burke drew out the paper he'd found and handed it to her. "You've known for a month."

"Aye."

"Didn't you intend to tell me, or were you just going to take care of it yourself?"

"I meant to tell you, but . . . What do you mean, take care of it myself? I could hardly keep it a secret when—" She stopped again as the realization hit like a wall. "That's what you thought I'd gone to the hospital for today. You thought I'd gone there to see that there would be no baby." She let the paper slip to the floor as she rose again. "You *are* a bastard, Burke Logan, that you could think that of me."

"What the hell was I supposed to think? You've had a month to tell me."

"I'd have told you the day I found out. I came to tell you. I could hardly wait to get the words out, but you started in on me about the money and the letter from my father. It always came down to the money. I put my heart on a platter for you time after time, and you keep handing it back to me. No more of that, either." She was ashamed of the tears, but more ashamed to wipe them away. "I'll go back to Ireland and have the baby there. Then neither of us will be in your way."

Before she could storm out of the room he asked, "You want the baby?"

"Damn you for a fool, of course I want the baby. It's our baby. We made it our first night together in this bed. I loved you then, with my whole heart, with everything I had. But I don't now. I detest you. I hate you for letting me love you this way and never giving it back to me. Never once taking me in your arms and telling me you loved me."

"Erin—"

"No, don't you dare touch me now. Not now that I've made as big a fool of myself as any woman could." She'd thrown up both hands to ward him off. She couldn't bear to have his pity. "I was afraid you wouldn't want the baby and me with it when you found out. That wasn't part of the bargain, was it? You wouldn't be so free and easy to come and go if there was a baby to think of."

He remembered the day she'd come to tell him about the baby, and the look in her eyes. Just as he remembered the look in her eyes when she'd left without telling him. He chose his words carefully now, knowing he'd already made enough mistakes.

"Six months ago you'd have been right. Maybe even six weeks ago, but not now. It's time we stopped moving in circles, Irish."

"And do what?"

"It's not easy for me to say what I feel. It's not easy for me to feel it." He approached her cautiously, and when she didn't back away he rested his hands on her shoulders. "I want you, and I want the baby."

She closed her fingers tightly over the ring she still had in her hand. "Why?"

"I didn't think I wanted a family. I swore when I was a kid that I'd never let anyone hurt me the way my mother had been hurt. I'd never let anyone mean so much that the life went out of me when they left. Then I went to Ireland and I met you. I'd still be there if you hadn't come back with me."

"You asked me to come here to keep your books."

"It was as good an excuse as any, for both of us. I didn't want to care about you. I didn't want to need to see you just to get through the day. But that's the way it was. I pulled you into marriage so fast because I didn't want to give you a chance to look around and find someone better."

"Seems to me I'd had chance enough."

"You'd never even been with a man before."

"Do you think I married you because you had a talent in bed?"

He had to laugh at that. "How would you know?"

"I doubt a woman has to bounce around between lovers to know when she's found the right one. Sex is as sorry an excuse to marry someone as money. Maybe we've both been fools, me for thinking you married me for the first, and you for thinking I married you for the second. I've told you why I married you, Burke. Don't you think it's time you told me?"

"I was afraid you'd get away."

She sighed and tried to make herself accept that. "All right, then, that'll do." She held her wedding ring out to him. "This belongs on my finger. You should remember which one."

He took it, and her hand. The choice had been given, to her and to him. It wasn't every day a man was given a second chance. "I love you, Erin." He saw her eyes fill and cursed himself for holding that away from both of them for so long.

"Say it again," she demanded. "Until you get used to it."

The ring slipped easily onto her finger. "I love you, Erin, and I always will." When he gathered her into his arms, he felt all the gears of his life click into place. "You mean everything to me. Everything." Their lips met and clung. It was just as sweet, just as powerful as the first time. "We're going to put down roots."

"We already have." Smiling, she took his face in her hands. "You just didn't notice."

Cautiously he laid his palm on her stomach. "How soon?"

"Seven months, a little less. There will be three of us for

Christmas." She let out a whoop when he lifted her into his arms.

"I won't let you down." He swore it as he buried his face in her hair.

"I know."

"I want you off your feet." As he started to lay her on the bed, she grabbed his shirt.

"That's fine with me, as long as you get off yours as well."

He nipped her lower lip. "I've always said, Irish, you're a woman after my heart."

From #1 *New York Times* bestselling author
NORA ROBERTS
comes a suspenseful new novel of tragedy and trauma,
love and family, and the blessings and curses of power.

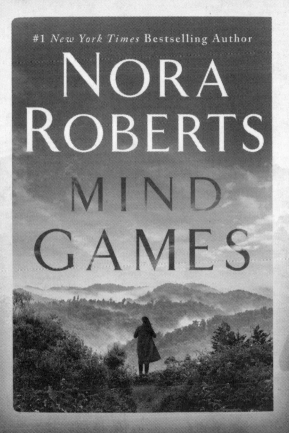

She can read minds. So can the man who killed her parents.
Who controls the gift? Who controls the game?

ST. MARTIN'S PRESS